OXFORD WORLD'S CLASSICS

THE SECRET GARDEN

FRANCES HODGSON BURNETT was born in Manchester in 1849 and emigrated to Tennessee in 1865. She took up writing to support her impoverished family and from 1868 claimed never to have had a manuscript rejected. Her first successes were realist dramas in Lancashire dialect, 'Surly Tim' (1872) and *That Lass o' Lowrie's* (1877); novels such as *A Fair Barbarian* (1881) and *Through One Administration* (1883) brought her both popular and critical acclaim. Her greatest success came with the romantic *Little Lord Fauntleroy* (1886), and her lawsuit in 1888 against a pirated dramatization of this book was instrumental in changing international copyright law. The bulk of her output was for adults, but she consolidated her reputation as a children's writer with *A Little Princess* (1905) and *The Secret Garden* (1911). Over her career, she published more than forty books and adapted several for the theatre, and crossed the Atlantic thirty-three times. She had two unsuccessful marriages, and was deeply affected by the death of her eldest son, Lionel, in 1890. After many years of living at Maytham Hall, Rolvenden, Kent, she moved to the USA where in 1905 she became an American citizen, and built a house at Plandome, Long Island, where she died in 1925.

PETER HUNT is Professor Emeritus in Children's Literature at Cardiff University and Visiting Professor, Newcastle University. He has written or edited eighteen books on children's literature, including *An Introduction to Children's Literature* (OUP 1994) and *Children's Literature: Critical Concepts in Literary and Cultural Studies* (four volumes, 2006). He has also written novels for children, including *Backtrack* (1986), and has edited *Bevis*, *Alice's Adventures in Wonderland*, *The Wind in the Willows*, and *Treasure Island* for Oxford World's Classics.

OXFORD WORLD'S CLASSICS

For over 100 years Oxford World's Classics have brought readers closer to the world's great literature. Now with over 700 titles—from the 4,000-year-old myths of Mesopotamia to the twentieth century's greatest novels—the series makes available lesser-known as well as celebrated writing.

The pocket-sized hardbacks of the early years contained introductions by Virginia Woolf, T. S. Eliot, Graham Greene, and other literary figures which enriched the experience of reading. Today the series is recognized for its fine scholarship and reliability in texts that span world literature, drama and poetry, religion, philosophy, and politics. Each edition includes perceptive commentary and essential background information to meet the changing needs of readers.

OXFORD WORLD'S CLASSICS

FRANCES HODGSON BURNETT

The Secret Garden

Edited with an Introduction and Notes by
PETER HUNT

OXFORD
UNIVERSITY PRESS

OXFORD
UNIVERSITY PRESS

Great Clarendon Street, Oxford ox2 6DP
Oxford University Press is a department of the University of Oxford.
It furthers the University's objective of excellence in research, scholarship,
and education by publishing worldwide in

Oxford New York

Auckland Cape Town Dar es Salaam Hong Kong Karachi
Kuala Lumpur Madrid Melbourne Mexico City Nairobi
New Delhi Shanghai Taipei Toronto

With offices in

Argentina Austria Brazil Chile Czech Republic France Greece
Guatemala Hungary Italy Japan Poland Portugal Singapore
South Korea Switzerland Thailand Turkey Ukraine Vietnam

Oxford is a registered trade mark of Oxford University Press
in the UK and in certain other countries

Published in the United States
by Oxford University Press Inc., New York

British Library Cataloguing in Publication Data

Data available

Library of Congress Cataloging in Publication Data
Library of Congress Control Number: 2010937003

Typeset by Glyph International, Bangalore, India
Printed in Great Britain
on acid-free paper by
Clays Ltd, St Ives plc

ISBN 978-0-19-958822-0

3

CONTENTS

INTRODUCTION

The Secret Garden has been described as the children's *Jane Eyre*; the culmination of a century of fiction for girls; a failed feminist manifesto; the first genuine twentieth-century children's book—and a book that has achieved its classic status by popular rather than critical acclaim. It is now widely recognized as a densely symbolic novel, drawing together and challenging established ideas of the Romantic child, Victorian child-rearing and cultural values, empire and religion— and of women's and children's fiction. Frances Hodgson Burnett was not the first writer to challenge these ideas, and she is perhaps an unlikely innovator, an inadvertent ironist, or simply a fortunate hack.

To an unsympathetic critic, *The Secret Garden* 'besides being made up largely of borrowings, is written in Mrs Burnett's usual careless manner. Characters are crudely drawn and predictable, and the prose style is sloppy.'[1] In 1922, *The Bookman* described her as 'the high priestess of the omnipotent cult of the second-rate',[2] and yet Burnett's considerable skills as a popular writer tapped into fundamental myths and human desires. She wrote more than forty books (only a very few of these for children) and more than a dozen plays, and had been a best-seller on both sides of the Atlantic since *That Lass o' Lowrie's* in 1877. *The Secret Garden* draws from the nineteenth-century myth kitty of the regenerative garden and its associations with sexuality, from the conventions of fairy tales such as 'Sleeping Beauty' and 'Beauty and the Beast', and the trappings of the Gothic novel. Add to this Burnett's flirtation with the quasi-mystical 'New Thought', her independence of mind, and her simultaneously sardonic and romantic Anglo-American attitude to England, and a potent mixture emerges.

Most of all, *The Secret Garden* is a book of its time. Burnett's use of the garden may be part of a long symbolic tradition, but it is also bound up with contemporary writers such as Lilias Trotter and her

---

[1] Humphrey Carpenter, *Secret Gardens: The Golden Age of Children's Literature* (London: Allen and Unwin, 1995), 189.

[2] Quoted by Beverly Lyon Clark, *Kiddie Lit: The Cultural Construction of Children's Literature in America* (Baltimore: Johns Hopkins University Press, 2003), 21–2.

mystic and artistic view of gardens, and reflects the contemporary
interest in actual gardening. Her characters may be saved by the
Romantic spirit of nature, but they also participate in the then newly
fashionable devotion to fresh air and exercise (particularly liberat-
ing for women) and the educational theories of Froebel. *The Secret
Garden* stands at the end of a long tradition of religious texts for children, but it is concerned, as many of Burnett's other books were, with
individualism, specifically with the liberation of the child from obses-
sive and repressive adult thinking. While her two earlier children's
novels, the phenomenally successful *Little Lord Fauntleroy* (1886) and
the perennial *A Little Princess* (1905), draw, like many of her adult
books, on 'Cinderella'-like traditions of security and insecurity, *The
Secret Garden* turns these traditions on their heads, almost wilfully
subverting gender and genre roles.

The combination of topicality on the one hand and radical thinking on the other may account for why the book was hardly thought
worthy of mention in Burnett's obituaries—the *New York Times* (16
November 1924) referred to it as *The Secret Orchard*.[3] But it may
also account for why, by the 1970s, *The Secret Garden* 'seems to have
become something of a cult book among high school and college
students in America . . . considering that [it] is the story of two
unhappy, sickly, overcivilised children who achieve health and happiness through a combination of communal gardening, mystical faith,
daily exercises, encounter-group-type confrontation, and a health-
food diet'. Or why a twenty-first-century popular guide to books for
teenagers can describe it thus: 'It is about a thoroughly cross and
opinionated tweenie who is a real pain in the butt, but who is trans-
formed into a decent human being through finding a secret garden
that is overgrown and needs a makeover (how modern is that?)'[4]

At first sight, *The Secret Garden* has the virtues of simplicity. A
neglected orphan girl is redeemed through contact with nature—and
(in effect) a nature spirit—and in turn redeems a neglected boy, and
eventually his morbidly Byronic father. This story is played out in

[3] Anne Lundin, 'The Critical and Commercial Reception of *The Secret Garden*', in
Gretchen Holbrook Gerzina (ed.), *The Secret Garden: A Norton Critical Edition* (New
York: Norton, 2006), 277–87 at 282.

[4] Alison Lurie, *Don't Tell the Grown-Ups: Subversive Children's Literature* (London:
Bloomsbury, 1999), 143; Cathy Hopkins in Daniel Hahn and Leonie Flynn (eds.), *The
Ultimate Teen Book Guide* (London: A and C. Black, 2006), 325.

three contrasting and linked settings: a gloomy mansion, symbolic of adult repression; a burgeoning garden—a safe place for individual growth and spiritual development; and the open moorland, representing health, freedom, and fecundity. In many ways it is the opposite of the 'girl's book' of a hundred years before, when adult influence and repression were seen as beneficial, and in which adults redeemed children through revealed religion.

An early review, by R. A. Whay in *The Bookman* (October 1911) recognized the paradox of the robust surface and the complex undercurrents. *The Secret Garden*, 'regarded purely as romance . . . is an exceedingly pretty tale,' he wrote, but it was 'more than a mere story of children; underlying it there is a deep vein of symbolism'.[5] Despite—or because of—its less-than-respectable literary origins, *The Secret Garden* has an open-minded eclecticism that, like *Treasure Island*, both synthesizes and quietly satirizes (and sometimes parodies) its origins. Just as Stevenson had fun with the language of the pirates, and unsettled the morality and the clichés of the adventure story, so Burnett finds a fresh purpose in sickbeds, noises in the night, and Pan-like nature boys. In terms of popular fiction, Burnett was the genuine article, the best-selling technician that at one stage Stevenson aspired to be, and in *The Secret Garden* her combination of efficient narrative skills and enthusiastic iconoclasm set a standard for a century of children's books for girls, just as *Treasure Island* set one for books for boys.

The Literary Background

The story for girls sprang out of the Evangelical tracts of the late eighteenth century, and in the hundred years that followed acquired a repertoire of generic characteristics common across the English-speaking world. From the Evangelicals came the pious child, redeeming fallen adults, like Maria Louisa Charlesworth's little Ruth in *Ministering Children* (1854) or Harriet Beecher Stowe's little Eva in *Uncle Tom's Cabin* (1851–2). From the Romantics came the innocent child 'trailing clouds of glory'—which, towards the end of the century

---

[5] Quoted in Gretchen Holbrook Gerzina, *Frances Hodgson Burnett: The Unexpected Life of the Author of* The Secret Garden (New Brunswick, NJ: Rutgers University Press, 2004), 269.

morphed into the cult of the 'beautiful child', producing best-sellers from Burnett's *Little Lord Fauntleroy* to A. A. Milne's *The House at Pooh Corner* (1928). From the adult novel came issues of gender, class, empire, and family; from popular literature came melodrama, transformations, confrontations, and sentimentality.

Girls' books naturally reflected the subservient and often sacrificial ideal of Victorian womanhood, of the angel of the house. This very often took the form of the sickly, dying, or dead mother (for example in Nesbit's *The Treasure Seekers*, 1899) or the injured child—at one point back injuries seem to have been almost mandatory (Charlotte Yonge's *The Daisy Chain*, 1856; Susan Coolidge's *What Katy Did*, 1872). Female self-denial was the norm, and where there was rebellion, this was resolved by the re-establishment of (usually male) authority (as in Louisa M. Alcott's *Little Women*, 1868) or marriage (*Good Wives*, 1869). As with adult novels, lachrymose deathbeds were common—although a pragmatic backlash came surprisingly early: Catherine Sinclair's central character in *Modern Accomplishments* (1836) says that she has learnt from the moral tales that it must be 'impossible for any religious child to survive, and that it would be condemning myself to death if I became truly pious'.[6]

Even if the children survived, the parents often did not, and nineteenth-century girls' books are littered with orphans. They were not merely the objects of charity—they were 'both redemptive and a threat', characterized by wild behaviour—and their lineage goes back to Jane Eyre, Becky Sharp, Magdalen and Nora in Wilkie Collins's *No Name* (1862) and characters in Dickens, George Eliot, and many others.[7] Such orphans were commonly disruptive, or ugly, or both. To take two American examples: Gerty, in Maria Susanna Cummins's *The Lamplighter* (1854)—a best-seller in England—has a darker side, a terrible temper, and when angry 'always cried aloud uttering a succession of piercing shrieks, until she sometimes quite exhausted her strength'; or Alice Hegan Rice's *Lovey Mary* (1903): ' "I wisht I was dead!" she cried passionately. "The harder I try to be good the meaner I get. Ever'body blames me, and ever'body makes fun of me. Ugly old face, and ugly old hands, and straight old rat-tail hair!

---

    [6] Quoted in J. S. Bratton, *The Impact of Victorian Children's Fiction* (London: Croom Helm, 1981), 217 n. 10.
    [7] Laura Peters, *Orphan Texts: Victorian Orphans, Culture and Empire* (Manchester: Manchester University Press, 2000), 28.

It ain't no wonder that nobody loves me. I just wisht I was dead!".'
Even the angelic Sara Crewe, Burnett's *Little Princess*, has low self-esteem: 'I have short black hair and green eyes; besides which I am a thin child and not fair in the least. I am one of the ugliest children I ever saw . . .' However, there was a difference between adults' books and children's books: 'While the orphan in women's writing for an adult market was advocating the need for social change, women writing for girls were promoting a conservative—even reactionary—message.'[8] Orphans were to be tamed, rebellious girls were to be punished and rehabilitated.

Children's books also reflected Victorian concern for the condition of the family. Increasingly fathers, once demigods of the home, become unreliable or absent, as in Ellen Montgomery's phenomenal best-seller *The Wide, Wide World* (1850). In parallel to this, female characters became more independent, as in Edith Nesbit's *The Railway Children* (1906), or became strong mystic presences in the fairy-godmother tradition, as in George MacDonald's *The Princess and Curdie* (1882) or Charles Kingsley's *The Water-Babies* (1863).

Across the nineteenth century, the child-characters' moral pilgrimages were gradually replaced by motifs taken from fairy tales and folk tales, notably riches-to-rags-to-riches transformations (epitomized by Burnett's *A Little Princess*). All of this was spiced with other characteristics of mainstream Victorian writing, such as copious sentimental tears (Martha Farquharson's notorious *Elsie Dinsmore*, 1867, and over twenty-five damp sequels), and the redemptive qualities of the country as opposed to the town. Towards the end of the century, books began to reflect the new dynamics of sexual politics, and the *fin de siècle* preoccupation with alternative forms of religion.

There was, of course, a good deal of conventional plotting and, especially, character-stereotyping. As Marghanita Laski acidly observed of an imagined gathering of the children of fiction, around the schoolroom fire:

You know them as well as I do—gentle, clear-browed Margaret, so soon to be sought by the curate; dependable Frank, aglow with muscular Christianity; hot-tempered, impetuous Jack . . . merry little Daisy; frail little Harry . . . and then . . . a little girl in a crumpled brown Holland overall, a little girl

---

[8] Kimberley Reynolds and Nicola Humble, *Victorian Heroines* (Hemel Hempstead: Harvester Wheatsheaf, 1993), 33.

with a mass of untidy dark hair, a little girl whom we might think ugly till we looked into her large grey eyes and saw that singularly sweet smile break on the rather sullen face. Yes, it is Ethel May [*The Daisy Chain*], it is Sara Crewe [*A Little Princess*], it is Rosy [in Louisa May Alcott's *Eight Cousins* (1875)], and Pixie O'Shaughnessy [in a serial in *Girl's Own Paper* by Mrs George de Horne Vaizey (1901)], it is the heroine of the Victorian children's books.[9]

The Ethel-Sara-Rosy-Pixie character rapidly developed—largely through American writers—into a series of individualistic and independent girls, such as Kate Douglas Wiggin's *Rebecca of Sunnybrook Farm* (1903), L. M. Montgomery's *Anne of Green Gables* (1908), and (a curiously pious throwback) Eleanor H. Porter's *Pollyanna* (1913). These characters (and the fairy-tale endings of many of the stories) were very popular with girls in England, where attitudes to what children could and should do were changing very slowly.[10]

Frances Hodgson Burnett, then, was the heir to all these traditions, and exploited them very successfully in *Little Lord Fauntleroy* and *A Little Princess*, but when *The Secret Garden* was written, times were changing. Despite the nostalgic setting of the book, perhaps in the 1860s (see the Note on the Date of the Story, p. 221), Burnett's is a twentieth-century voice, and part of the interest for the contemporary reader may have been the unpredictability of her use of her sources.

Mary, Orphans, and Empire

Although many critics have assumed that from its first sentence *The Secret Garden* challenges the dominant image of the fictional girl as beautiful, pious, and self-disciplined, there were plenty of precedents for Mary Lennox, 'the most disagreeable child ever seen'. Like Jane Eyre and Anne Shirley she is a disruptive orphan—but unlike her predecessors for whom home is a key symbol, Mary does not even know where hers is. She is an orphan who does not miss her parents; she is not, like her American fictional cousins, cheerfully rebellious: she simply 'knew nothing at all about authority' (p. 42).

---

[9] Marghanita Laski, *Mrs. Ewing, Mrs. Molesworth and Mrs. Hodgson Burnett* (London: Arthur Barker, 1950), 16.

[10] Gillian Avery, *Behold the Child, American Children and Their Books 1621–1922* (London: The Bodley Head, 1994), 156.

Most of all, Burnett presents a realistic picture of a psychologically damaged girl set in a distorted literary world: the first home that she encounters is not the poor-but-happy clergyman's family of the religious novels of the past hundred years, but one that is dysfunctional and cruel.

Mary is as far from being the 'prig' heroine as it is possible to be, although Burnett was not alone in challenging what she called, in 1906, 'the days when "prig" education was the child idea'.[11] Edith Nesbit had tilted at them in chapter 10 of *The Railway Children*:

'But I knew it was wrong to quarrel,' said Bobbie, in tears, 'and now you're hurt and—'

'Now look here,' said Peter, firmly, 'you just dry up. If you're not careful, you'll turn into a beastly little Sunday-school prig, so I tell you . . . it's a jolly good thing it wasn't you was hurt . . . If it had been you, you'd have been lying on the sofa looking like a suffering angel and being the light of the anxious household and all that. And I couldn't have stood it.'

Nor does Mary redeem herself through revealed religion or self-discipline: there is little of the pure and passive heroine derived from the fairy tales (which Burnett had herself exploited in *A Little Princess*). If fairy tales are referenced at all, they are inverted: *The Secret Garden* is something of an ironic version of 'Beauty and the Beast', and when Mary kisses the flowers, as her aunt had done, it is the Princess waking the sleeping beauty of the garden. Mary, the pragmatist, has little time for fairy tales:

The few books she had read and liked had been fairy-story books, and she had read of secret gardens in some of the stories. Sometimes people went to sleep in them for a hundred years, which she had thought must be rather stupid. She had no intention of going to sleep, and, in fact, she was becoming wider awake every day. (p. 66)

Something of this subversiveness seems to stem from Burnett's Anglo-American view of the world. Mary, for all her Englishness, has something of the 'new' American girl, the independent woman personified by Henry James's *Daisy Miller* (1878). As John Rowe Townsend noted, 'These are not Victorian times . . . It was no part of [the Victorian] ideal that children should be self-reliant, constructive, inner-directed. Perhaps it required someone like Mrs Hodgson

[11] Quoted in Gerzina (ed.), *The Secret Garden*, 245.

Burnett, who was no simple Christian . . . to bring forward this new, significant and potentially subversive doctrine.'[12]

Burnett was even more subversive in her treatment of the source of Mary's ills, India. In little more than a chapter, she portrays it as thoroughly corrupt and corrupting—and it is not only the cholera that is deadly. In the vignette of Mary's feckless mother talking to the 'fair boy officer' (p. 6) Burnett implies, as far as she is able in a children's novel, something of the perfervid atmosphere imagined to be characteristic of life in the Raj (possibly derived from Kipling's *Plain Tales from the Hills*, 1888). Even the soil of India does not blossom under Mary's hands. All of this is in contrast to the generally positive images of empire that appeared contemporaneously both in textbooks and periodicals for children—and, indeed in virtually all novels (Conrad's *Heart of Darkness* (1902) is a rare exception).[13] For example, the opening chapters of Juliana Horatia Ewing's *Six to Sixteen* (1875)—a favourite of Kipling's—are a detailed mirror image of Burnett's book. Margaret Vandaleur, the narrator, is brought up in India by her ayah ('I loved her very dearly . . . and . . . I spoke more Hindostanee than English'), is 'thoroughly happy'; she loves, and is loved by, her father and her mother ('the prettiest woman at the station'), and is a favourite of everyone. She is at her father's deathbed when he dies of cholera. (Later in the novel, Margaret benefits from the 'exhilarating' air of the Yorkshire moors.) Burnett's almost methodical inversion of the norm continues as the dislikeable Mary comes to Misselthwaite Manor.

Gothic and the Romantic Child

Mary's arrival (which very closely resembles Jane Eyre's arrival at Thornfield) is the first extensive example of Burnett parodying her (former) self. When the beautiful child, little Lord Fauntleroy, first approached Dorincourt Castle, Burnett devoted three pages to describing the castle as 'one of the most beautiful in all England . . . its

[12] John Rowe Townsend, *Written for Children: An Outline of English-language Children's Literature* (Harmondsworth: Penguin, 1974), 88.
  [13] See Kathryn Castle, *Britannia's Children: Reading Colonialism through Children's Books and Magazines* (Manchester: Manchester University Press, 1996), 11–62, and Patrick Brantlinger, *Rule of Darkness: British Literature and Imperialism, 1830–1914* (Ithaca, NY and London: Cornell University Press, 1988), 274.

park was one of the broadest and finest'—and the sun is shining (Chapter 5). Misselthwaite Manor, in rather stark contrast, is a self-consciously literary Gothic concoction: with its setting on the initially dismal moors, and its forbidden rooms, long corridors, mysterious sounds, and veiled picture, this is the world of the Brontës, Anne Radcliffe's *The Mysteries of Udolpho* (1794), or Edgar Allan Poe's *The Fall of the House of Usher* (1839). But, as Tess Cosslett notes, Burnett's use of the Gothic is not straightforward: 'Gothic is a literature of secrets, horrible secrets locked away in old buildings . . . Burnett reverses the movement of Gothic: the secret is renewal and growth . . . The house and its grounds are metaphors not only for Mary's psyche, with its hidden damaged child and dead mother, but also for the structure of adult civilisation, which represses what should be let out.'[14] Burnett could not, it seems, even sustain the melodramatic elements. Mrs Medlock and Dr Craven are poor descendants of Jane Eyre's Mrs Reed and Mr Brocklehurst: Mrs Medlock is a friend of the nature-mother Mrs Sowerby, and Dr Craven's role as potential villain soon peters out—'he was not an unscrupulous man' (p. 137). Even Misselthwaite Manor has sybaritic servants in the servants' hall.

If Burnett takes an anarchic approach to the pious child, and an ambivalent attitude to the Gothic, her evocation of the Romantic child is so unrestrained that it verges on parody. Probably the least subtle element of the book, Dickon, whom Mary first meets in a wood in the park, is the noble savage, the earth spirit, a benevolent, child-sized rendering of the rural Pan, trailing not only clouds of glory but a variety of animals and birds—and playing on his 'rough wooden pipe' (p. 70). In all of this, he is something of a throwback. His model might be Harry Sandford, from Thomas Day's seminal and revolutionary-minded *Sandford and Merton* (1783–9), who is contrasted with the spoilt, delicate, Tommy Merton. Harry

used to stroke the horses as they were at work, and fill his pockets with acorns for the pigs; if he walked in the fields, he was sure to gather green boughs for the sheep, who were so fond of him, that they followed him wherever he went. In the winter time, when the ground was covered with frost and snow, and the poor little birds could get at no food, he would often go supperless to bed, that he might feed the robin-redbreast; even toads,

---

[14] Tess Cosslett, 'Transformations of Pastoral and Gothic in Children's Fiction', *Signal*, 98 (2002), 91–101 at 97.

and frogs, and spiders, and such sort of disagreeable animals, which most people destroy wherever they find them, were perfectly safe with Harry; he used to say, they had a right to live as well as we, and that it was cruel and unjust to kill creatures, only because we did not like them. These sentiments made little Harry a great favourite with everybody. (chapter 1)

Dickon is not merely an exemplar of rural virtue: he has been seen as a nurturing, female element, a surrogate mother figure supplying wisdom and affection to Mary and Colin, the emotionally scarred children. He also embodies another key Romantic idea (one with a very long lineage), that of the superiority of country over city—or in this case, country over a whole repressive adult civilization. Like many other children's authors, such as Nesbit, de la Mare, and Kipling, Burnett saw this superiority as both metaphor and fact; the essentially conservative Edwardian attitude of mind yearning for the 'life-giving notion of Deep England'.[15] Her attitude was perhaps accentuated by her Anglo-American perspective: in the USA, as Gillian Avery points out, 'many plots turned on how a reverse of fortune and the resultant departure from the city brought about benefit for all. Or neurotic, pampered city children become robust and independent once they spend a few months on the farm. Very often redemption is achieved with the help of food.' Certainly the children's diet at Misselthwaite Manor becomes increasingly rich—and increasingly more American—as the book progresses—regardless of probability. The breakfasts that Mary and Colin find so hard to resist (pp. 179–80) 'betray Mrs Hodgson Burnett's American background. In reality, English children would have been given bread and milk— ham and eggs being thought too indigestible, butter and cream too rich, raspberry jam too debilitating to the character.'[16]

Dickon is also, at least for critics, the focus of certain sexual resonances. The adult Pan as portrayed in *fin de siècle* literature and Pre-Raphaelite art (and in *The Wind in the Willows*) was sexually potent, and, as Christine Wilkie notes, despite the fact that *The Secret Garden*

[15] See Paul March-Russell, 'Pagan Papers: History, Mysticism, and Edwardian Childhood', in Adrienne E. Gavin and Andrew F. Humphries (eds.), *Childhood in Edwardian Fiction: Worlds Enough and Time* (Basingstoke: Palgrave Macmillan, 2009), 23–36 at 33.

[16] Gillian Avery, 'Home and Family: English and American Ideals in the Nineteenth Century', in Dennis Butts (ed.), *Stories and Society: Children's Literature in its Social Context* (London: Macmillan, 1992), 37–49 at 47; *Behold the Child*, 158–9.

is a children's book, 'it is neither far-fetched nor prurient to find sexual connotations in the imagery and language . . . the text is littered with references to incidences of nesting and with images and the language of penetration'.[17] Certainly the proto–sexual tensions of the book were not lost on the director Agnieska Holland; in her 1993 film version, Colin asks Mary to marry him, and later, Mary exchanges significant (if not exactly smouldering) glances with Dickon. It is perhaps not surprising, then, that critics of both Burnett and of D. H. Lawrence have noted the similarities between *The Secret Garden* and *Lady Chatterley's Lover* in terms of the three central characters, their relationships, the settings, and the shared belief in an abstract life force. There are also, of course, major differences (apart from explicit sex), notably that Lawrence has a less optimistic view of class interaction, and does not believe in the restorative power of the female.

As part of the 'magic' of the garden, Dickon is also part of the fading rural dream of the Edwardians (epitomized in Kenneth Grahame's *The Wind in the Willows*), just as the garden itself is part of Burnett's fading dream of being an English Lady of the Manor.

The Garden

If the figure of Dickon seems to be overladen with symbolic meanings, the garden, the enclosed ground between the extremes of the dark, repressed, and airless manor, and the wild, beautiful-and-dangerous 'wuthering' moor, is the collision point of many more. In literature in general, and children's literature in particular, the garden has been seen since ancient times as emblematic of security, civilization, and purity—quite apart from its sexual connotations. Gardens (like schools) provide a circumscribed playground, a place where young plants, and children (and in Burnett's case, birds), can develop safely. With the spirit of Colin's dead mother, Lilias, haunting the garden (p. 198), Burnett presents a symbiotic relationship: the children nurture the garden and thus redeem the adults; the garden, containing the adult spirit, nurtures the children.

The garden was a popular motif for Pre-Raphaelite painters such as Rossetti, and for poets such as Swinburne, Tennyson, and,

---

[17] Christine Wilkie, 'Digging up *The Secret Garden*: Noble Innocents or Little Savages?', *Children's Literature in Education*, 28/2 (1997), 73–83 at 73.

of course, Stevenson in *A Child's Garden of Verses* (1885), while *Kindergarten* play was gaining popularity through the followers of Friedrich Froebel[18]—one of whom was Frances Hodgson Burnett. In 1917, she wrote an enthusiastic 'Introduction' to the first volume of *The Writings of Kate Douglas Wiggin*, praising Wiggin's 'small documentary records of kindergarten days'. For Froebel, 'the kindergarten is the free republic of childhood'—one of his books was *System of Infant Gardens* (1855).[19] One of Froebel's advocates, the Baroness Marenholtz-Bülow, wrote in *Child and Child-Nature* (1879):

To be a child who has never called a piece of ground its own, has never tilled it in the sweat of its brow, has never extended its fostering love on plants and animals, there will always be a gap in the development of the soul, and it will be difficult for that child to attain the capacity for human nurture in a comprehensive sense.[20]

On a less theoretical level, Burnett was drawing on her personal interest in gardens, particularly that at Maytham Hall, the house that she had rented in Rolvenden, Kent, and where she had established a walled rose garden. Gardens were, in any case, very much in fashion. The seasonal structure of *The Secret Garden*, moving from the dead garden of winter to lush autumn, may have been suggested by Mrs Richmond's *In My Lady's Garden* (1908), a round-the-year collection of essays by the 'late Garden editor of the "Queen"'. Roses figure very largely in this book, with advice on pruning (in the fourth week of March) and with many passages very reminiscent of *The Secret Garden*. For example, in the second week of January:

the hyacinths, tulips, and early narcissi are pushing up their green points on all sides . . . whilst the birds, gay and bright in their winter plumage, are already rehearsing their spring song of nests . . . Their courting-time is near, and though cold weather may put off their matrimonial affairs for many weeks yet, they are quite aware that the 'turn of the year' is past.[21]

[18] Peter Keating, *The Haunted Study: A Social History of the English Novel, 1875–1914* (London: Fontana, 1991), 226.

[19] Quoted by Ann Lundin, 'The Cultural Work of Kate Douglas Wiggin; Cultivating the Child's Garden', in Monika Elbert (ed.), *Enterprising Youth: Social Values and Acculturization in Nineteenth-Century American Children's Literature* (New York: Routledge, 2008), 179–94 at 188–9.

[20] Quoted in Juliet Dusinberre, *Alice to the Lighthouse: Children's Books and Radical Experiments in Art*, 2nd edn. (London: Macmillan, 1999), 198.

[21] Mrs I. L. Richmond, *In My Lady's Garden* (London: T. Fisher Unwin, 1908), 13.

Burnett may also have been familiar with Elizabeth van Arnim's very popular *Elizabeth and her German Garden* (1898) which has a feminist flavour (Arnim's adopted cousin wrote as Katherine Mansfield), and I. Lilias Trotter's lavishly illustrated *Parables of the Cross* (1890), which makes specific links between spirituality and plants. In children's books, Mrs Ewing's *Mary's Meadow* (*Aunt Judy's Magazine*, 1883–4) was part of a fashion for 'The Game of Earthly Paradise'— 'beautifying hedges and bare places' following the example of John Parkinson's *Paradisi in sole Paradisus terrestis* at Kew. The game became known as 'Mary Meadowing'.

Colin, Health, and Positive Thinking

The novel is carefully structured: the first eight chapters take Mary to the garden, and the next four are about her being in the garden; the thirteenth introduces Colin; the next eight chapters take him to the garden, and the final four are about him being in the garden. And with the introduction of Colin, the priorities of the novel shift.

In Colin, 'Burnett criticises a whole realm of fiction in which adults battened like parasites on the dying child'; he is 'a metaphor for the distortions wrought by Victorian family life', and, as we might expect from *The Secret Garden*, he is an original—he 'turns *Fauntleroy* inside-out'.[22] The invalids in children's literature had been predominantly not only females, but saintly females—Helen in *Jane Eyre*, Margaret May in *The Daisy Chain*, Cousin Helen (and then Katy) in *What Katy Did*, Beth March in *Little Women*, Clara in *Heidi*, Jill (Janey) Pecq in Louisa May Alcott's *Jack and Jill* (1880) . . . and later, Pollyanna. Very often the injuries that the girls suffered were punishments for misrule: injury was a method of repression, and a route to salvation. Burnett could not have inverted and subverted this model more thoroughly.

Colin is a parody of these long-suffering, too-good-for-this-world characters: spoiled, wilful, and male—not really suffering from a spinal problem—and the damage done to him has been done by adults.

---

[22] Dusinberre, *Alice to the Lighthouse*, 133; Fred Inglis, *The Promise of Happiness: Value and Meaning in Children's Fiction* (Cambridge: Cambridge University Press, 1981), 112; Claudia Nelson, *Boys Will be Girls: the Feminine Ethic and British Children's Fiction 1857–1917* (New Brunswick, NJ: Rutgers University Press, 1991), 26.

However, once again, Burnett takes a less than obvious course. For the suffering females (especially the Americans) in books, as Lois Keith has pointed out, 'faith rather than scientific medical intervention was at the heart of [the] cure: faith in God as the ultimate source of power and goodness, but also faith in the self. These two apparently contradictory elements, the religious and the individualistic, run side by side in such stories since they were both important lessons that progressively minded writers . . . felt children needed to learn.'[23] The point that Burnett wished to make was that individualism was compatible with a non-specific religion: indeed that conventional religion could be identified with repressive medical practices, typified by the iron back-brace which Colin is briefly forced to wear. She was also aware of psychological interpretations of behaviour that not so very long before would have been dismissed as madness—Freud's work with Joseph Breur, *Studies in Hysteria*, had been published in 1895.

But health was literally blowing in the wind, and Burnett was nothing if not open to current quasi-religious and quasi-scientific therapeutic ideas. In an interview in the *New York Times* (12 October 1913) Burnett said: 'I am not a Christian Scientist, I am not an advocate of New Thought, I am not a disciple of the Yogi teaching, I am not a Buddhist. I am not a Mohammedun. I am not a follower of Confucius. Yet I am all of those things.'[24] Nevertheless, her rather sentimental faith in positive thinking and healing is derived in part from Mary Baker Eddy's Christian Science movement. Eddy, who died in 1910, used Hamlet's observation: 'There is nothing either good or bad but thinking makes it so' (II. ii) as one of the epigraphs of her *Science and Health with Key to the Scriptures* (1875), and certainly Colin's 'affirmations' are in the tradition of self-help and autosuggestion. Yet Burnett did not accept the Christian Science theology: she wrote to her son, Vivian: 'While I could not call myself a Christian Scientist, I believe in its principle because it is the exposition of the pure Christ-spirit applied to the needs of today.'[25] While living in Boston, she dabbled in 'mind cures', part of the 'New Thought' movement, which William James in *The Varieties of Religious Experience* (1902) called 'a deliberately optimistic scheme of life'. She made an attempt to

[23] Lois Keith, *Take Up thy Bed and Walk: Death, Disability and Cure in Classic Fiction for Girls* (London: The Women's Press, 2001), 32.

[24] Quoted in Gerzina (ed.), *The Secret Garden*, 259.

[25] Quoted in Gerzina, *Frances Hodgson Burnett*, 241.

discuss religion in the dour allegory *The Dawn of a To-morrow* (1906) but her views are perhaps best and certainly most joyously expressed in the mouth of Susan Sowerby in *The Secret Garden*:

'Th' same thing as set th' seeds swellin' an' th' sun shinin' made thee a well lad an' it's th' Good Thing. It isn't like us poor fools as think it matters if us is called out of our names. Th' Big Good Thing doesn't stop to worrit, bless thee. It goes on makin' worlds by th' million—worlds like us. Never thee stop believin' in th' Big Good Thing an' knowin' th' world's full of it—an' call it what tha' likes.' (p. 196)

Mrs Sowerby, with her blue cloak and bread and milk is even more unsubtle symbolically than Dickon, being at once the holy essence of motherhood—maternal instinct was a source of power for late nineteenth-century feminists—and an earth goddess. Surprisingly, she was a second thought—originally, in the manuscript, Martha's mother was dead—but Burnett knew what she was doing. In a letter to William Heinemann (9 October 1910) she wrote that *The Secret Garden* contains 'a moorland cottage woman who is a sort of Madonna with twelve children—a warm bosomed, sane, wise, simple Mother thing. You only see her for a moment at the end of the book but she is the chief figure in it really. "Mother" baking and washing in her cottage on the Yorkshire Moor makes all things happy merely because she is.'[26]

Susan Sowerby's prescription for health (with which the less-than-villainous Mr Craven agrees (p. 87)) was part of a growing trend, and, as was often the case, Burnett was far from being a pioneer. Johanna Spyri's *Heidi* (1880–1, translated into English 1884) advocated the virtues of fresh air and exercise and was a forerunner of a widespread change in attitudes to restrictive clothing for women and the outdoor life.[27]

Good food, exercises, faith in the Big Good Thing, equality and liberation make the magic—but then, at the end of the book, something occurs which has exercised critics more than anything else. As R. A. Whay wrote in *The Bookman* (October 1911): 'Perhaps the principal reason that *The Secret Garden* is such a difficult book to review is that it is so hard to decide who is the leading character, and whose story it is.'

[26] Quoted ibid. 262.
[27] Peter Skrine, 'Johanna Spyri's *Heidi*', *Bulletin of John Rylands Library of Manchester*, 76/3 (1994), 145–64 at 162.

Are there two stories here—first Mary's and then Colin's, or is there one story—Mary's—which is ultimately a story of personal failure?

The Problem of the Ending

Mary, who has driven the action for much of the book, is, as we have seen, gradually displaced: Colin takes centre stage, and at the very end, Mary seems to fade out altogether. The most usual reading of this is that Burnett, in common with, for example, Nesbit in *The Railway Children*, or Alcott in *Little Women*, having written an essentially feminist book, allows male dominance to be reasserted: female power is only a dream.[28] Such a strategy was characteristic of 'New Thought' novels, and of the 'New Woman' fiction of the period. Is there a parallel in Mary's submission/self-immolation, with the way in which, as Kim Reynolds and Nicola Humble put it, 'rebellious women in novels surrender all obvious signs of independence when she marries?'—although many readers would not agree with their conclusion that 'the concentration of attention is on the denial and rejection of the norm: the marriages and compromises which constitute redemption at the end of these texts are therefore subservient to the bulk of the work'. Burnett's fictional children do not, despite initial appearances, grow towards independence: Mary takes her gender-subservient place, Colin takes his place in the social system. Burnett can be seen, in effect, as simply one more woman writer who exploited a certain subservient feminine image and idealized the very qualities—timidity, piety, and narcissism—that kept women powerless.[29] However, it can be argued that some traces of the radical 'New Woman' fiction of the 1890s remain, in the nostalgia for childhood and the implied protest against female repression, both features of that genre.[30]

This is not the only reading of the ending. On the positive side, Mary can be seen as an American girl, independent, but working for the good of the whole. Seen in terms of the quest story, the ending may seem to be inevitable: '*The Secret Garden* has . . . a "blocked

---

[28] See e.g. Elizabeth Lennox Keyser, '"Quite contrary": Frances Hodgson Burnett's *The Secret Garden,*' *Children's Literature*, 11 (1983), 1–13.

[29] Reynolds and Humble, *Victorian Heroines*, 23, and see Ann Douglas, *The Feminization of American Culture* (New York: Knopf, 1977).

[30] Kate Flint, *The Woman Reader, 1837–1914* (Oxford: Clarendon Press, 1993), 195.

ending" . . . Archetypal quest romances, or identity quests, or *Bildungsroman* patterns are supposed to be universal. But they are skewed or blurred in the Golden Age of children's literature, as they are in women's literature.' In short, '*The Secret Garden* illustrates the culturally prescribed differences between male and female quest.'[31] Adrian Gunther has an even more radical interpretation:

To regret that it is not Mary winning the race, holding forth berating the group and striding back into the great house, is to accept such patriarchal concepts of power on their own terms. Burnett has a much more subversive and subtle agenda . . . In terms of the quest archetype, a key state in the journey is transcendence of ego . . . [Mary's] behaviour in the last section of the book is characterised by an unselfish compassion, and a total absence of egocentric concern. Colin, however, in true masculine mode, remains intrinsically self-centred up to the very last line . . . He remains 'blocked'.[32]

The apparent shift of focus from Mary to Colin has two other effects. First, the disruption of the apparently natural progress of Mary's regeneration and dominance separates the story from its 'Sleeping Beauty' sources—which Mary has already repudiated. As U. C. Knoepflmacher observes: 'The exclusion of Mary from this final tableau at least avoids the possibility that a strong "Mistress Mary" will turn into the submissive bride of the new "master" of garden and house. Whereas several film versions suggest that Colin and Mary will marry (and others suggest that she will become Connie Chatterley to Dickon's Mellors), Burnett avoids that inference . . . she prefers to de-eroticize her narrative.'[33] In the 1993 film version, scriptwriter Caroline Thompson provides a coda in which Mr ('Lord') Craven says to Mary: 'You brought us back to life, Mary. You did something I thought no-one could do' (1:31:44), and it is Mary and Colin and Mr Craven who stride back to the Manor, hand in hand.

The second effect of this shift in focus stems from Burnett's biography, and has implications for the structure and 'voice' of the book.

---

[31] Lissa Paul, 'Enigma Variations: What Feminist Theory Knows about Children's Literature', *Signal*, 54 (1987), 186–202 at 199; Shelley O'Hearn, '*Marianne Dreams, The Secret Garden* and the Stifled Female Quest', *Papers: Explorations into Children's Literature*, 8/1 (Apr. 1998), 36–44 at 36.

[32] Adrian Gunther, '*The Secret Garden* Revisited', *Children's Literature in Education*, 25/3 (1994), 159–68 at 160.

[33] U. C. Knoepflmacher, 'Repudiating "Sleeping Beauty"', in Beverly Lyon Clark and Margaret R. Higonnet (eds.), *Girls, Boys, Books, Toys: Gender in Children's Literature and Culture* (Baltimore: Johns Hopkins University Press, 1999), 11–24 at 24.

As Colin becomes more dominant, the detached tone of voice which speaks directly to the child reader, and which epitomizes the dominant tone of twentieth-century children's literature is undermined. The initial unpleasantness of the characters allows Burnett to stand back from them, 'without setting out to coerce or delude the implied reader into the desired response as she had done herself in *A Little Princess* . . . to address a child audience without . . . the need to assert adult superiority by defining an adult presence . . . This seems an easy and obvious way of narrating for children, but it had taken generations of writers to achieve it.' However, towards the end of the novel, the adult voice asserts itself, even (in Chapter XXVII) descending to a direct lecture on Christian Science-like principles. As the balance between Mary and Colin shifts, so 'the narrator gradually loses objectivity and control'.[34] The reasons for this may be found in Burnett's personal, professional, and philosophic life.

Burnett's Biography and The Secret Garden

Frances Hodgson Burnett was one of the most successful popular novelists of her era, and her life story was worthy of one of her own books—a story of a strong (and romantic) female in a world of weak males. Born in Manchester, brought up in Tennessee, her first major success was the Lancashire dialect story 'Surly Tim' (1872). Her first international success—also heavy on dialect—was *That Lass o' Lowrie's* (1877) which was compared to the work of George Eliot; even before the phenomenal success of *Little Lord Fauntleroy* she was regarded as being in the 'front rank today in general estimation' along with William Dean Howells and Henry James: *A Fair Barbarian* (1881) was compared favourably to *Daisy Miller*. She moved in exalted circles, numbering Emerson, Louisa M. Alcott, Mark Twain, Kate Douglas Wiggin, Mary Mapes Dodge (editor of the most important nineteenth-century children's magazine, *St. Nicholas*), Oscar Wilde, Gladstone, and President Garfield among her acquaintance. She claimed that she had never had a story rejected. Marghanita Laski, somewhat waspishly, describes her as 'a facile and prolific writer. She found, she once said, a story in everything. True, it was very often the same story, but her knack of setting credible characters in

---

[34] Barbara Wall, *The Narrator's Voice: The Dilemma of Children's Fiction* (Basingstoke: Macmillan, 1991), 176.

stimulating situations made each of them, even the worst, pleasantly readable.'³⁵ Her legal challenge to an unauthorized adaptation of *Little Lord Fauntleroy* in 1888 led to a change in copyright law, and she was fêted by her fellow authors—guests at a celebratory dinner of the Society of Authors in her honour included Wilkie Collins, Jerome K. Jerome, Walter Besant, Edmund Gosse, and Rider Haggard—and Tennyson sent a welcoming telegram.

The major tragedy of her life was the death of her elder son Lionel from consumption in 1890; Burnett felt guilty for having been away from him in the year before he died, and for several years after his death wrote a journal to him. It has been said that the story of Colin is the resurrection of Lionel, which may account for the overblown portrait: 'The Athlete, the Lecturer, the Scientific Discoverer was a laughable, lovable, healthy young human thing' (p. 209). Burnett's increasing preoccupation with Colin/Lionel distorts the tone and emphasis of the whole book, and Colin's sudden appearance from the garden, dashing almost into the arms of Mr Craven, seems to many to be a moment of birth or rebirth, of ultimate wish-fulfilment.

In 1907 Burnett left Maytham Hall and the rose garden in which she had written some of her books, including expanding *Sara Crewe* into *A Little Princess*. Memories of this garden clearly inspired *The Secret Garden*, although she had already used many of the other props of the story in her ghost story *In the Closed Room* (1904): friendly birds and animals, a big empty house, a picture of a little girl, a locked room, a dead garden that is partly (if in illusion) brought back to life. There is, unusually for Burnett, little record of *The Secret Garden* being written, but she seems to have worked on it in the study at her new home in Plandome, Long Island. It was serialized in the *American Magazine*—possibly, Burnett thought, the first children's book to be serialized in a magazine for adults. She thought it necessary to explain this to her British publisher, William Heinemann (October 1910): 'Do you realize that it is not a novel, but a child's story though it is gravely beginning life as an important illustrated serial in a magazine for adults . . . Ella Hepworth Dixon said that it was a sort of children's Jane Eyre.'³⁶

³⁵ Laski, *Mrs. Ewing*, 78.
³⁶ Quoted in Gerzina, *Frances Hodgson Burnett*, 262. (Ella Hepworth Dixon was a British novelist, who edited *Woman's World* after Oscar Wilde, and was author of *The Story of a Modern Woman* (1896).)

Reviewers were well aware of its origins. The *ALA Booklist* (8 October 1911) regarded it as 'a "new-thought" story, oversentimental and dealing almost wholly with abnormal people', but the majority of reviewers praised the oversentimentality in oversentimental terms: 'no-one can make children more charming', 'will charm everyone', 'wholesome reading', 'charming illustrations', 'the characterisation is beautiful, and the sentiment delightful', 'captivating'. Some, such as the *New York Times* (3 September 1911), thought it superior to *Fauntleroy*: 'The sloppiness of sentiment, the goody-goodiness and the artificiality which characterized that highly popular story do not mar "The Secret Garden," whose underlying philosophy of the beneficent power of good thoughts and wholesome action is expressed through their influence upon the two children simply and without any trace of mawkish sentiment.' Thereafter it more or less disappeared from the critical radar, until, with the development of the serious study of children's literature, it has become a canonical text. It has been filmed three times, notably in 1949 (Fred M. Wilcox) and 1993 (Agnieska Holland), and adapted for television four times (1952, 1960, 1975, 1987); there have been two sequels (2000, 2001) and an animated version (1994).

The Secret Garden is, like *Treasure Island*, a treasure chest of sources and analogues: as we have seen, Burnett was a magpie of a writer, and the atmosphere of *Jane Eyre* and *Wuthering Heights* and the big scenes from *Six to Sixteen* and *Heidi* and others were at hand, from a common stock. Burnett had been periodically accused of plagiarism—Mark Twain gently pointed out that *Little Lord Fauntleroy* 'came from her reading "The Prince and the Pauper" '[37] and there was an embarrassing episode when she published a version of 'The Story of Prince Fairyfoot' not realizing that she had taken it from Frances Browne's *Granny's Wonderful Chair*. Even the famous (not to say notorious) velvet-and-lace costume of *Little Lord Fauntleroy* was presaged by that of the spoiled Leonard in Mrs Ewing's *The Story of a Short Life* (1885): 'A holiday dress of crimson velvet, with collar and ruffles of old lace, became him very quaintly.'

To some extent Burnett, like Arthur Ransome a generation later, played on these literary connections. When Mrs. Medlock describes Mr Craven's reclusive habits, it sounds to Mary 'like something in

---

[37] Quoted in Gerzina, *Frances Hodgson Burnett*, 110.

a book' (p. 15). This is scarcely surprising, as at that point, on their way to Misselthwaite Manor, they are already in a chapter of *Jane Eyre*—and the similarities and contrasts with that book are easy to multiply. Bessie, Jane's friendly servant, transmutes into Martha; the contrast between disease in Lowood and the freshness of spring is reflected in Misselthwaite Manor and the awakening garden; the death of Helen is echoed in Colin's illness; touring the house with Mrs Fairfax, Jane hears a strange laugh, attributed to a servant, just as Martha makes excuses for Colin's crying; Colin thinks that Mary is a dream, Mr Rochester thinks Jane is a Fairy—and Mr Craven, like Jane, hears a mystic voice calling him home. *Heidi* has some even more striking parallels: the cast includes Heidi the orphan and Peter the nature boy; Clara the disabled girl cured by goats' milk and fresh air steps out of the symbol of her dependency, the wheelchair; there is an unsympathetic housekeeper, Frau Rottenmeier, and the bitter and reclusive Alm-Uncle, who has his life changed by Heidi; Heidi brings animals into the house, Clara's father returns in time to see her walking, and there are gentians on the Tyrolean hillsides in both books. Similar analogues are not far to seek in books such as Dinah Maria Mulock Craik's *The Little Lame Prince* (1875) and *The Little Lychetts* (1855), Juliana Horatia Ewing's *The Story of a Short Life*, *Six to Sixteen*, and *Daddy Darwin's Dovecote* (1893). Ida, in *Mrs Overtheway's Remembrances* (1869), has garden yearnings:

She had been kept indoors for a long time by the weather and by a cold, and it was very pleasant to get out again, even when the only amusement was to run up and down the shingly walks and wonder how soon she might begin to garden, and whether the gardener could be induced to give her a piece of ground sufficiently extensive to grow a crop of mustard-and-cress in the form of a capital I.

(Burnett had a particular affinity with Ewing, whose books stressed independence of thought in her female characters.)

And, of course, there is *Wuthering Heights*. The relationship between the first cousins, Linton and Catherine, is echoed in *The Secret Garden* in the relationship between the first cousins Colin and Mary, and 'Mary echoes Cathy . . . both in her temper and spirit and her need to nurture and be nurtured'.[38] Then there is Émile

---

[38] Susan E. James, '*Wuthering Heights* for Children: Frances Hodgson Burnett's *The Secret Garden*', *Connotations*, 10/1 (2000/1), 59–76 at 67; Anna Krugovoy Silver,

Zola's anticlerical novel *La Faute de l'Abbé Mouret* (1875, trans. 1886, 1900, 1904), described by Ulf Boëthius as 'a provocative panegyric to procreation and sexual love that bears a striking resemblance to Burnett's classic children's book'. Boëthius argues that 'although it is masked, sexuality is nevertheless strongly present in *The Secret Garden* as a kind of imprint of the forbidden and repressed', and he points, in Zola's novel, to the nature-girl Désirée and her affinity with animals, and the way in which Albine nurses Serge back to health, with a little help from the garden:

> She laid him down in bed and shut the windows. Next morning, however, they were opened at break of day. Serge could no longer live without the sunlight. His strength was growing, he was becoming accustomed to the gusts of air which sent the alcove curtains flying . . . 'When you are able to get up,' said Albine, 'you shall sit at the window. You will see the lovely garden!' (Book 2, Chapter 3)[39]

But best-selling authors are nothing if not 'a mirror of "the mind and face" of an age', as Claude Cockburn called them[40]—and *The Secret Garden* is a masterclass in the art of the best-seller writer. Whereas Stevenson, striving to apply the tricks of the popularist writer to his material in *Treasure Island*, produced a subtle hybrid, *The Secret Garden* is popular literature at its most successfully direct. Names are if not directly symbolic, at least highly metonymic—Medlock, Misselthwaite, Mary and Martha, Sowerby, Craven, Weatherstaff; every emotional button is pressed at exactly the right moment; the pathetic fallacy rides across the moors; words are missed out in the breathless rush of the story: ' "When you see a bit of earth you want," with something like a smile, "take it, child" ' (p. 87), or ' "But he has to do his bit o' complainin' " ' with a highly entertained grin' (p. 176); accents and atmospheric effects are laid on with a spade.

As such, *The Secret Garden* demonstrates the way in which undervalued literary forms—popular and children's literature—have the potential to gather and interrogate a remarkable range of

'Domesticating Brontë's Moors: Motherhood in *The Secret Garden*', *The Lion and the Unicorn*, 21/2 (1997), 193–203 at 197.

[39] Ulf Boëthius, ' "Us is near bein' wild things ourselves": Procreation and Sexuality in *The Secret Garden*', *Children's Literature Association Quarterly*, 22/4 (1997–8), 188–95 at 188.

[40] Claude Cockburn, *Bestseller: The Books that Everyone Read 1900–1939* (Harmondsworth: Penguin, 1975), 14.

contemporary ideas. Mary both celebrates having a space of her own, and yet wishes to share its nurturing power; for a moment it seems that Mary's self-determination and Dickon's wisdom will not only overcome neglect and ill health, but class barriers as well—but, as on the enchanted island of J. M. Barrie's *The Admirable Crichton* (1902), this is an illusion. Whereas for D. H. Lawrence the gulf between the classes was central, Burnett's vision was 'truer to the Victorian tradition in suggesting the interdependence of classes . . . with the young heir to the manor restored to health and *noblesse oblige* by instruction in rural lore from a juvenile Pan among his tenants'.[41] The radical and the conservative, the assertive and the conventional, the dramatically triumphant and the intellectually ambiguous come together in a book that—possibly because it *is* a children's book—was startlingly optimistic for its time, and has managed to remain so for over a hundred years.

[41] Anthea Trodd, *A Reader's Guide to Edwardian Literature* (Hemel Hempstead: Harvester Wheatsheaf, 1991), 41, 42; see Lynne Vallone, 'Women Writing for Children', in Joanne Shattock (ed.), *Women and Literature in Britain 1800–1900* (Cambridge: Cambridge University Press, 2001), 275–300 at 295; and Mitzi Myers, 'Romancing the Moral Tale', in James Holt McGavran (ed.), *Romanticism and Children's Literature in Nineteenth Century England* (Athens, Ga.: University of Georgia Press, 1991), 96–128.

NOTE ON THE TEXT

THIS edition reproduces the text of the first British edition, published by William Heinemann in 1911, with the correction of some minor typographical errors.

Burnett wrote *The Secret Garden* in her study at Plandome, her house on Long Island, New York. The manuscript is in the New York Public Library, and consists of 360 pages of which approximately eighty are in ink; Burnett generally uses American spelling and idiosyncratic punctuation. The title on the manuscript is 'Mary Mary quite Contrary' amended to 'Mistress Mary quite Contrary'; the more significant alterations in the manuscript (such as the death of Mrs Sowerby, and Dickon's crutch) are given in the Explanatory Notes.

The Secret Garden, with twenty-two illustrations (plus decorations) by J. Scott Williams, first appeared in Frank Leslie's *American Magazine* in ten episodes between November 1910 and August 1911 (71/1–72/4). The first American edition was published in New York by Frederick A. Stokes and Company, in August 1911. The title page reads: '*The Secret Garden*, by Frances Hodgson Burnett, author of "The Shuttle," "The Making of a Marchioness," "The Methods of Lady Wanderhurst," "That Lass o' Lowrie's," "Through One Administration," "Little Lord Fauntleroy," "A Lady of Quality," etc.'

There is also a de luxe American edition (in green cloth) which was illustrated with tipped-in frontispiece and four illustrations in colour by Maria Kirk ('2nd printing'). This edition, or one very like it, seems also to have been issued by Grosset and Dunlap in 1911—quite possibly pirated by the 'kings of the reprint'. The first British edition (in green cloth) was published about a month later by William Heinemann, with illustrated title page in red and black, pictorial front endpapers, and eight full-colour plates by Charles Robinson.

There were around sixty minor changes from the *American Magazine* text to the first American edition text, which the first British edition largely follows. The most striking of these are listed below. The first American and British edition readings are given first, followed by the *American Magazine* variant.

24 tha'self." When Mary . . . black things," said Mary. The dressing process] tha'self." The dressing process

42 small self] small black-frocked self

71 curving mouth] curious mouth

84 little thing] little thing in a black frock

93 He said it as if he was so] He said it as coolly as if he was so

125 this morning] this afternoon [this is clearly a mistake in the first editions: compare pp. 118–19]

127 with her hand] with her own hand

134 There is a door into the garden. I found it. It is under the ivy on the wall] *There is a door into the garden. I found it. It is under the ivy on the wall*

143 and explored branches.] and explored branches and chirped remarks on the scenery.

177 cloak] shawl

183 reproachful dignity] reproachful rigidity

194 in a puzzled way. "Perhaps they are both: in a puzzled way.] "Perhaps that *is* the Magic," he said next, "perhaps the Magic is *that*. Perhaps they are both

197 shout out something to anything that would listen] shout out something.

198 Dickon's garden and would not come back until they were tired] Dickon's garden.

202 the black lashes rimmed so] black lashes that trimmed so

203 a few minutes later he saw that the one lying at the top of the rest was an English letter and came from] a few minutes later the one lying at the top of the rest was an English letter and he saw it came from

208 "Father," he said, "I'm Colin. You] "Father," he cried out catching his breath, "I'm Colin. You

208 shook with unbelieving joy. Colin put out his hand and laid it on his father's arm. "Aren't you glad, father?" he ended. "Aren't you glad? I'm going to live for ever and ever and ever!" Mr. Craven put his hands on both the boy's shoulders and held him still. He knew he dared not even try to speak for a moment.] shook with unbelieving joy. He put his hands on both the boy's shoulders and held him still. He knew he must not try to speak for a moment.

209 so carefully kept. The listener laughed until tears came into his eyes, and sometimes tears came into his eyes when he was not laughing.

The Athlete, the Lecturer, the Scientific Discoverer was a laughable, lovable, healthy young human thing. "Now," he said at the end of the story,] so carefully kept. "And now," Colin concluded,

There are some exceptions, where the British edition makes its own changes, notably to American usages—color, colored, armor, gray, humor, and good-by (although not 296, 'railroad').

SELECT BIBLIOGRAPHY

Editions of The Secret Garden

Gretchen Holbrook Gerzina (ed.), *The Secret Garden: A Norton Critical Edition* (New York: Norton, 2006).

Gretchen Holbrook Gerzina (ed.), *The Annotated Secret Garden* (New York: Norton, 2007).

Biography and Autobiography

Frances Hodgson Burnett, *The One I Knew the Best of All* (London: Warne, 1913).

Vivian Burnett, *The Romantick Lady: The Life Story of an Imagination* (New York: Charles Scribner's Sons, 1927).

Gretchen Holbrook Gerzina, *Frances Hodgson Burnett: The Unexpected Life of the Author of* The Secret Garden (New Brunswick, NJ: Rutgers University Press, 2004).

Marghanita Laski, *Mrs. Ewing, Mrs. Molesworth and Mrs. Hodgson Burnett* (London: Arthur Barker, 1950).

Ann Thwaite, *Waiting for the Party: The Life of Frances Hodgson Burnett, 1849–1924* (London: Secker and Warburg, 1974); reissued as *Frances Hodgson Burnett: Beyond the Secret Garden* (Stroud: Tempus, 2007).

Criticism

On Francis Hodgson Burnett

Phyllis Bixler, *Frances Hodgson Burnett* (Boston: Twayne, 1984).

Angelica Shirley Carpenter (ed.), *In the Garden: Essays in Honor of Frances Hodgson Burnett* (Lanham, Md.: Scarecrow Press, 2006).

On The Secret Garden

Gillian Adams, 'Secrets and Healing Magic in *The Secret Garden*', in Francelia Butler and Richard Rotert (eds.), *Triumphs of the Spirit in Children's Literature* (Hamden, Conn.: Library Professional Publications/ Shoe String Press, 1986), 42–54.

Barbara Almond, '*The Secret Garden*: A Therapeutic Metaphor', *Psychoanalytic Study of the Child*, 45 (1990), 477–94.

Nina Bawden, 'Returning to *The Secret Garden*', *Children's Literature in Education*, 19/3 (1988), 165–9.

Phyllis Bixler, 'Gardens, Houses, and Nurturant Power in *The Secret Garden*', in James Holt McGavran (ed.), *Romanticism and Children's*

Literature in Nineteenth-Century England (Athens, Ga.: University of Georgia Press, 1991), 208–24.

Phyllis Bixler, 'The Secret Garden "Misread": The Broadway Musical as Creative Interpretation', *Children's Literature*, 22 (1994), 101–23.

—— *The Secret Garden: Nature's Magic* (Twayne's Masterwork Studies) (New York: Twayne, 1996).

Ulf Boëthius, ' "Us is near bein' wild things ourselves": Procreation and Sexuality in *The Secret Garden*', *Children's Literature Association Quarterly*, 22/4 (1997–8), 188–95.

Jane Darcy, 'The Representation of Nature in *The Wind in the Willows* and *The Secret Garden*', *The Lion and the Unicorn*, 19/2 (1995), 211–22.

—— 'The Edwardian Child in the Garden: Childhood in the Fiction of Frances Hodgson Burnett', in Adrienne E. Gavin and Andrew F. Humphries (eds.), *Childhood in Edwardian Fiction: Worlds Enough and Time* (Basingstoke: Palgrave Macmillan, 2009), 75–88.

Gwyneth Evans, 'The Girl in the Garden: Variations on a Feminine Pastoral', *Children's Literature Association Quarterly*, 19/1 (1984), 20–4.

Shirley Foster and Judy Simons, 'Frances Hodgson Burnett and *The Secret Garden*', in *What Katy Read: Feminist Re-Readings of 'Classic' Stories for Girls* (London: Macmillan, 1995), 172–91.

Susan E. James, '*Wuthering Heights* for Children: Frances Hodgson Burnett's *The Secret Garden*', *Connotations*, 10/1 (2000/1), 59–76.

Jerry Griswold, 'Positive Thinking: *The Secret Garden*', in *Audacious Kids: Coming of Age in America's Classic Children's Books* (New York: Oxford University Press, 1992), 200–14.

Adrian Gunther, '*The Secret Garden* Revisited', *Children's Literature in Education*, 25/3 (1994), 159–68.

Elizabeth Lennox Keyser, ' "Quite contrary": Frances Hodgson Burnett's *The Secret Garden*', *Children's Literature*, 11 (1983), 1–13.

Phyllis Bixler Koppes, 'Tradition and the Individual Talent of Frances Hodgson Burnett: A Generic Analysis of *Little Lord Fauntleroy*, *A Little Princess*, and *The Secret Garden*', *Children's Literature*, 7 (1978), 191–207.

M. Daphne Kutzer, 'The Empire at Home: Burnett and Nesbit', in *Empire's Children: Empire and Imperialism in Classic British Children's Books* (New York: Garland, 2000), 47–78.

Anne Lundin, 'The Critical and Commercial Reception of *The Secret Garden*', in Gretchen Holbrook Gerzina (ed.), *The Secret Garden: A Norton Critical Edition* (New York: Norton, 2006), 277–87.

Fiona McCulloch, ' "I Shall Stop Being Queer . . . If I Go Every Day to the Garden": Edenic Childhood in *The Secret Garden*', in *The Fictional Role of Childhood in Victorian and Early Twentieth Century Children's Literature* (Lampeter: The Edwin Mellen Press, 2004), 149–73.

Roderick McGillis, ' "Secrets" and "Sequence" in Children's Stories', in Hugh T. Keenan (ed.), *Studies in the Literary Imagination*, 18/2 (1985), 35–46.

Margaret Mackey, 'Strip Mines in the Garden: Old Stories, New Formats, and the Challenge of Change', *Children's Literature in Education*, 27/1 (1996) 3–21.

Heather Murray, 'Frances Hodgson Burnett's *The Secret Garden*: The Organ(ic)ized World', in Perry Nodelman (ed.), *Touchstones: Reflections on the Best of Children's Literature* (West Lafayette, Ind.: Children's Literature Association, 1985), i. 30–43.

Shelley O'Hearn, '*Marianne Dreams*, *The Secret Garden* and the Stifled Female Quest', *Papers: Explorations into Children's Literature*, 8/1 (Apr. 1998), 36–44.

Jerry Phillips, 'The Mem Sahib, the Worthy, the Rajah and His Minions: Some Reflections on the Class Politics of *The Secret Garden*', *The Lion and the Unicorn*, 17 (1993), 168–94.

Judith Plotz, 'Secret Garden II; or, *Lady Chatterley's Lover* as Palimpsest', *Children's Literature Association Quarterly*, 19/1 (1994), 15–19.

Danielle E. Price, 'Cultivating Mary: The Victorian *Secret Garden*', *Children's Literature Association Quarterly*, 26/1 (2001), 4–14.

Gretchen V. Rector, 'Digging Up the Garden: The Manuscript of *The Secret Garden* by Frances Hodgson Burnett', in Gretchen Holbrook Gerzina (ed.), *The Secret Garden: A Norton Critical Edition* (New York: Norton, 2006), 186–99.

Stephen D. Roxburgh, 'Our First World: Form and Meaning in *The Secret Garden*', *Children's Literature in Education*, 10/3 (1979), 120–30.

Anna Krugovoy Silver, 'Domesticating Brontë's Moors: Motherhood in *The Secret Garden*', *The Lion and the Unicorn*, 21/2 (1997), 193–203.

John Stephens and Robyn McCallum, 'Ideological Re-shapings: Pruning *The Secret Garden* in 1990s Film', *Paradoxa*, 2/3–4 (1996), 357–68.

Sally Sims Stokes, 'Noel Streatfeild's Secret Gardens', *Children's Literature Association Quarterly*, 29/3 (2004), 172–206.

Rosemary Threadgold, '*The Secret Garden*: An Appreciation of Frances Hodgson Burnett as a Novelist for Children', *Children's Literature in Education*, 10/3 (1979), 120–30.

Ann Thwaite, 'Frances Hodgson Burnett, 1849–1924', in Jane M. Bingham (ed.), *Writers for Children* (New York: Charles Scribner's Sons, 1988), 103–9.

Kathleen Verduin, 'Lady Chatterley and *The Secret Garden*: Lawrence's Homage to Mrs. Hodgson Burnett', *D. H. Lawrence Review*, 17 (1984), 61–6.

Jean Webb, 'Romanticism vs. Empire in *The Secret Garden*', in Deborah Cogan Thacker and Jean Webb (eds.), *Introducing Children's Literature: From Romanticism to Postmodernism* (London: Routledge, 2002), 91–7.

Alison White, 'Tap Roots into a Rose Garden', *Children's Literature*, 1 (1972), 74–6.

Christine Wilkie, 'Digging up *The Secret Garden*: Noble Innocents or Little Savages?', *Children's Literature in Education*, 28/2 (1997), 73–83.

Further Reading in Oxford World's Classics

Charlotte Brontë, *Jane Eyre*, ed. Margaret Smith, with an introduction by Sally Shuttleworth.

Emily Brontë, *Wuthering Heights*, ed. Ian Jack, with an introduction by Helen Small.

A CHRONOLOGY OF
FRANCES HODGSON BURNETT

1849   (24 Nov.) Frances Eliza Hodgson born Cheetham Hill Road, Manchester; third child and first daughter of Edwin Hodgson (ironmonger and silversmith) and Eliza Boond.

1853   (1 Sept.) father dies of apoplexy.

1856   Charlotte Yonge, *The Daisy Chain*.

1865   The Burnetts emigrate to New Market, Tennessee, to live with Eliza Hodgson's brother, William. FHB opens 'Select Seminary for Young People'. End of American Civil War. 'Lewis Carroll', *Alice's Adventures in Wonderland*.

1868   Sells first stories 'Hearts and Diamonds' (June), and 'Miss Carruther's Engagement' (Oct.) to *Godey's Lady's Book and Magazine*. Louisa M. Alcott, *Little Women*.

1869   Moves into Knoxville. Publishing regularly in magazines.

1870   Death of Eliza Hodgson.

1871–2 George Eliot, *Middlemarch*.

1872   *Scribner's Monthly Magazine* publishes 'Surly Tim'. Meets literary editors in New York and visits England. Mrs Ewing, *Six to Sixteen*. 'Susan Coolidge', *What Katy Did*.

1873   (18 Sept.) marries local doctor, Swan Burnett. Mary Mapes Dodge becomes editor of *St. Nicholas*.

1874   (20 Sept.) first child, Lionel, born.

1875   Family move to Paris. Mary Baker Eddy, *Science and Health*. Anthony Trollope, *The Way We Live Now*.

1876   (Feb.) *That Lass o' Lowrie's* serialized in *Scribner's Monthly Magazine*. (5 Apr.) son, Vivian, born. Mark Twain, *The Adventures of Tom Sawyer*.

1877   Family moves to Washington. *That Lass o' Lowrie's* successful in book form.

1878   *That Lass o' Lowrie's* (adapted by FHB and Julian Magnus) staged on Broadway in New York. *Kathleen: a Love Story*, and other books, several in unauthorized editions.

1879 (Jan.) first children's story, 'Behind the White Brick', published in *St. Nicholas*. Henry James, *Daisy Miller*.

1881 *Esmeralda* (written with William Gillette) opens in New York.

1883 *Through One Administration*. (Oct.) *Esmeralda* (as *Young Folks' Ways*) opens in London.

1884 Johanna Spyri, *Heidi* (first English translation).

1885 (Nov.) 'Little Lord Fauntleroy' serialized in *St. Nicholas* magazine. Robert Louis Stevenson, *A Child's Garden of Verses*.

1886 Moves to Washington. *Little Lord Fauntleroy* published in book form; becomes instant international success. Mrs Ewing, *Mary's Meadow*.

1887 Visits Europe. (Dec.) *Sara Crewe* serialized in *St. Nicholas* (–Feb. 1888).

1888 Wins lawsuit against E. V. Seebohm for production of unauthorized dramatization of *Little Lord Fauntleroy*. (May) successful authorized version. (11 July) 'Lewis Carroll' attends performance. (25 July) Society of Authors dinner in honour of FHB. *Sara Crewe* and *Editha's Burglar*. (Dec.) *Little Lord Fauntleroy* on Broadway. Oscar Wilde, *The Happy Prince*. Rudyard Kipling, *Wee Willie Winkie*.

1890 (7 Dec.) Lionel dies of consumption, in Paris. I. Lilias Trotter, *Parables of the Cross*.

1891 FHB divides her time between England and the USA.

1892 Mrs Molesworth, *An Enchanted Garden*.

1893 *The One I Knew the Best of All* (autobiography).

1895 Sees Henry James frequently. Henry James's disastrous play *Guy Domville*. Kenneth Grahame, *The Golden Age*.

1896 *A Lady of Quality*.

1897 Queen Victoria's Golden Jubilee.

1898 Divorces Swan Burnett. Leases Maytham Hall, Rolvenden, Kent; spends summers there for ten years.

1899 *In Connection with the DeWilloughby Claim*. E. Nesbit, *The Story of the Treasure Seekers*.

1900 (Feb.) marries Stephen Townsend. Mrs Craik, *The Little Lame Prince*.

1901 *The Making of a Marchioness*.

1902 Separates from Townsend. *A Little Princess* opens in London. J. M. Barrie, *The Little White Bird*.

1903   Kate Douglas Wiggin, *Rebecca of Sunnybrook Farm*.

1904   *In the Closed Room*. J. M. Barrie, *Peter Pan*.

1905   *A Little Princess*. FHB becomes American citizen.

1906   *The Dawn of a To-morrow, Racketty-Packetty House*. E. Nesbit,
        The Railway Children; Rudyard Kipling, *Puck of Pook's Hill*.

1907   *The Shuttle*.

1908   Builds large house at Plandome, Long Island. Kenneth Grahame,
        The Wind in the Willows; L. M. Montgomery, *Anne of Green
        Gables*; Mrs I. Richmond, *In My Lady's Garden*.

1910   (Nov.) *The Secret Garden* serialized in *The American Magazine*.
        Death of Mary Baker Eddy.

1911   (25 Aug.) *The Secret Garden* (Stokes, New York; Heinemann,
        London).

1912   *My Robin*; first English translation of Maria Montessori's *The
        Montessori Method*.

1914   (May) makes final crossing (33rd) of the Atlantic. Film version of
        Little Lord Fauntleroy.

1915   *The Lost Prince*.

1921   Film of *Little Lord Fauntleroy*, starring Mary Pickford.

1925   (29 Oct.) dies at Plandome (colon cancer). Buried at Roslyn,
        Long Island.

THE SECRET GARDEN

CONTENTS

CHAPTER I

THERE IS NO ONE LEFT

WHEN Mary Lennox* was sent to Misselthwaite Manor to live with
her uncle everybody said she was the most disagreeable-looking child
ever seen. It was true, too. She had a little thin face and a little thin
body, thin light hair and a sour expression. Her hair was yellow, and
her face was yellow because she had been born in India and had always
been ill in one way or another. Her father had held a position under
the English Government and had always been busy and ill himself,
and her mother had been a great beauty who cared only to go to
parties and amuse herself with gay people. She had not wanted a little
girl at all, and when Mary was born she handed her over to the care of
an Ayah,* who was made to understand that if she wished to please the
Mem Sahib* she must keep the child out of sight as much as possible.
So when she was a sickly, fretful, ugly little baby she was kept out of
the way, and when she became a sickly, fretful, toddling thing she
was kept out of the way also. She never remembered seeing familiarly
anything but the dark faces of her Ayah and the other native servants,
and as they always obeyed her and gave her her own way in everything, because the Mem Sahib would be angry if she was disturbed
by her crying, by the time she was six years old she was as tyrannical
and selfish a little pig as ever lived. The young English governess who
came to teach her to read and write disliked her so much that she gave
up her place in three months, and when other governesses came to try
to fill it they always went away in a shorter time than the first one. So
if Mary had not chosen to really want to know how to read books she
would never have learned her letters at all.

One frightfully hot morning, when she was about nine years old,*
she awakened feeling very cross, and she became crosser still when
she saw that the servant who stood by her bedside was not her Ayah.

"Why did you come?" she said to the strange woman. "I will not let
you stay. Send my Ayah to me."

The woman looked frightened, but she only stammered that the
Ayah could not come and when Mary threw herself into a passion and
beat and kicked her, she looked only more frightened and repeated
that it was not possible for the Ayah to come to Missie Sahib.

There was something mysterious in the air that morning. Nothing was done in its regular order and several of the native servants seemed missing, while those whom Mary saw slunk or hurried about with ashy and scared faces. But no one would tell her anything and her Ayah did not come. She was actually left alone as the morning went on, and at last she wandered out into the garden and began to play by herself under a tree near the veranda. She pretended that she was making a flower-bed, and she stuck big scarlet hibiscus* blossoms into little heaps of earth, all the time growing more and more angry and muttering to herself the things she would say and the names she would call Saidie when she returned.

"Pig! Pig! Daughter of Pigs!" she said, because to call a native a pig is the worst insult of all.

She was grinding her teeth and saying this over and over again when she heard her mother come out on the veranda with some one. She was with a fair young man and they stood talking together in low strange voices. Mary knew the fair young man who looked like a boy. She had heard that he was a very young officer who had just come from England. The child stared at him, but she stared most at her mother. She always did this when she had a chance to see her, because the Mem Sahib—Mary used to call her that oftener than anything else—was such a tall, slim, pretty person and wore such lovely clothes. Her hair was like curly silk and she had a delicate little nose which seemed to be disdaining things, and she had large laughing eyes. All her clothes were thin and floating, and Mary said they were "full of lace." They looked fuller of lace than ever this morning, but her eyes were not laughing at all. They were large and scared and lifted imploringly to the fair boy officer's face.

"Is it so very bad? Oh, is it?" Mary heard her say.

"Awfully," the young man answered in a trembling voice. "Awfully, Mrs. Lennox. You ought to have gone to the hills* two weeks ago."

The Mem Sahib wrung her hands.

"Oh, I know I ought!" she cried. "I only stayed to go to that silly dinner party. What a fool I was!"

At that very moment such a loud sound of wailing broke out from the servants' quarters that she clutched the young man's arm, and Mary stood shivering from head to foot. The wailing grew wilder and wilder.

"What is it? What is it?" Mrs. Lennox gasped.

"Some one has died," answered the boy officer. "You did not say it had broken out among your servants."

"I did not know!" the Mem Sahib cried. "Come with me! Come with me!" and she turned and ran into the house.

After that appalling things happened, and the mysteriousness of the morning was explained to Mary. The cholera had broken out in its most fatal form and people were dying like flies. The Ayah had been taken ill in the night, and it was because she had just died that the servants had wailed in the huts. Before the next day three other servants were dead and others had run away in terror. There was panic on every side, and dying people in all the bungalows.

During the confusion and bewilderment of the second day Mary hid herself in the nursery and was forgotten by every one.* Nobody thought of her, nobody wanted her, and strange things happened of which she knew nothing. Mary alternately cried and slept through the hours. She only knew that people were ill and that she heard mysterious and frightening sounds. Once she crept into the dining-room and found it empty, though a partly finished meal was on the table and chairs and plates looked as if they had been hastily pushed back when the diners rose suddenly for some reason. The child ate some fruit and biscuits, and being thirsty she drank a glass of wine which stood nearly filled. It was sweet, and she did not know how strong it was. Very soon it made her intensely drowsy, and she went back to her nursery and shut herself in again, frightened by cries she heard in the huts and by the hurrying sound of feet. The wine made her so sleepy that she could scarcely keep her eyes open and she lay down on her bed and knew nothing more for a long time.

Many things happened during the hours in which she slept so heavily, but she was not disturbed by the wails and the sound of things being carried in and out of the bungalow.

When she awakened she lay and stared at the wall. The house was perfectly still. She had never known it to be so silent before. She heard neither voices nor footsteps, and wondered if everybody had got well of the cholera and all the trouble was over. She wondered also who would take care of her now her Ayah was dead. There would be a new Ayah, and perhaps she would know some new stories. Mary had been rather tired of the old ones. She did not cry because her nurse had died. She was not an affectionate child and had never cared much for any one. The noise and hurrying about and wailing over the cholera had frightened her, and she had been angry because no one seemed to remember that she was alive. Every one was too panic-stricken to think of a little girl no one was fond of. When people had the cholera it seemed that they remembered nothing but themselves. But if every one had got well again, surely some one would remember and come to look for her.

But no one came, and as she lay waiting the house seemed to grow more and more silent. She heard something rustling on the matting and when she looked down she saw a little snake gliding along and watching her with eyes like jewels. She was not frightened, because he was a harmless little thing who would not hurt her and he seemed in a hurry to get out of the room. He slipped under the door as she watched him.

"How queer and quiet it is," she said. "It sounds as if there was no one in the bungalow but me and the snake."

Almost the next minute she heard footsteps in the compound, and then on the veranda. They were men's footsteps, and the men entered the bungalow and talked in low voices. No one went to meet or speak to them and they seemed to open doors and look into rooms.

"What desolation!" she heard one voice say. "That pretty, pretty woman! I suppose the child, too. I heard there was a child, though no one ever saw her."

Mary was standing in the middle of the nursery when they opened the door a few minutes later. She looked an ugly, cross little thing and was frowning because she was beginning to be hungry and feel disgracefully neglected. The first man who came in was a large officer she had once seen talking to her father. He looked tired and troubled, but when he saw her he was so startled that he almost jumped back.

"Barney!" he cried out. "There is a child here! A child alone! In a place like this! Mercy on us, who is she?"

"I am Mary Lennox," the little girl said, drawing herself up stiffly. She thought the man was very rude to call her father's bungalow "A place like this!" "I fell asleep when every one had the cholera and I have only just wakened up. Why does nobody come?"

"It is the child no one ever saw!" exclaimed the man, turning to his companions. "She has actually been forgotten!"

"Why was I forgotten?" Mary said, stamping her foot. "Why does nobody come?"

The young man whose name was Barney looked at her very sadly. Mary even thought she saw him wink his eyes as if to wink tears away.

"Poor little kid!" he said. "There is nobody left to come."

It was in that strange and sudden way that Mary found out that she had neither father nor mother left; that they had died and been carried away in the night, and that the few native servants who had not died also had left the house as quickly as they could get out of it, none of them even remembering that there was a Missie Sahib. That was why the place was so quiet. It was true that there was no one in the bungalow but herself and the little rustling snake.

CHAPTER II

MARY had liked to look at her mother from a distance and she had thought her very pretty, but as she knew very little of her she could scarcely have been expected to love her or to miss her very much when she was gone. She did not miss her at all, in fact, and as she was a self-absorbed child she gave her entire thought to herself, as she had always done. If she had been older she would no doubt have been very anxious at being left alone in the world, but she was very young, and as she had always been taken care of, she supposed she always would be. What she thought was that she would like to know if she was going to nice people, who would be polite to her and give her her own way as her Ayah and the other native servants had done.

She knew that she was not going to stay at the English clergyman's house where she was taken at first. She did not want to stay. The English clergyman was poor and he had five children nearly all the same age and they wore shabby clothes and were always quarrelling and snatching toys from each other. Mary hated their untidy bungalow and was so disagreeable to them that after the first day or two nobody would play with her. By the second day they had given her a nickname which made her furious.

It was Basil who thought of it first.* Basil was a little boy with impudent blue eyes and a turned-up nose and Mary hated him. She was playing by herself under a tree, just as she had been playing the day the cholera broke out. She was making heaps of earth and paths for a garden and Basil came and stood near to watch her. Presently he got rather interested and suddenly made a suggestion.

"Why don't you put a heap of stones there and pretend it is a rockery?" he said. "There in the middle," and he leaned over her to point.

"Go away!" cried Mary. "I don't want boys. Go away!"

For a moment Basil looked angry, and then he began to tease. He was always teasing his sisters. He danced round and round her and made faces and sang and laughed.

> "Mistress Mary, quite contrary,
> How does your garden grow?

> With silver bells, and cockle shells,
> And marigolds all in a row."*

He sang it until the other children heard and laughed, too; and the crosser Mary got, the more they sang "Mistress Mary Quite Contrary"; and after that as long as she stayed with them they called her "Mistress Mary Quite Contrary" when they spoke of her to each other, and often when they spoke to her.

"You are going to be sent home," Basil said to her, "at the end of the week. And we're glad of it."

"I am glad of it, too," answered Mary. "Where is home?"

"She doesn't know where home is*!" said Basil, with seven-year-old scorn. "It's England, of course. Our grandmama lives there and our sister Mabel was sent to her last year.* You are not going to your grandmama. You have none. You are going to your uncle. His name is Mr. Archibald Craven."*

"I don't know anything about him," snapped Mary.

"I know you don't," Basil answered. "You don't know anything. Girls never do. I heard father and mother talking about him. He lives in a great, big, desolate old house in the country and no one goes near him. He's so cross he won't let them, and they wouldn't come if he would let them. He's a hunchback, and he's horrid."

"I don't believe you," said Mary; and she turned her back and stuck her fingers in her ears, because she would not listen any more.

But she thought over it a great deal afterward; and when Mrs. Crawford told her that night that she was going to sail away to England in a few days and going to her uncle, Mr. Archibald Craven, who lived at Misselthwaite Manor,* she looked so stony and stubbornly uninterested that they did not know what to think about her. They tried to be kind to her, but she only turned her face away when Mrs. Crawford attempted to kiss her, and held herself stiffly when Mr. Crawford patted her shoulder.

"She is such a plain child," Mrs. Crawford said pityingly, afterward. "And her mother was such a pretty creature. She had a very pretty manner, too, and Mary has the most unattractive ways I ever saw in a child. The children call her 'Mistress Mary Quite Contrary,' and though it's naughty of them, one can't help understanding it."

"Perhaps if her mother had carried her pretty face and her pretty manners oftener into the nursery Mary might have learned some pretty ways too. It is very sad, now the poor beautiful thing is gone, to remember that many people never even knew that she had a child at all."

"I believe she scarcely ever looked at her," sighed Mrs. Crawford. "When her Ayah was dead there was no one to give a thought to the little thing. Think of the servants running away and leaving her all alone in that deserted bungalow. Colonel McGrew said he nearly jumped out of his skin when he opened the door and found her standing by herself in the middle of the room."

Mary made the long voyage to England under the care of an officer's wife, who was taking her children to leave them in a boarding-school.* She was very much absorbed in her own little boy and girl, and was rather glad to hand the child over to the woman Mr. Archibald Craven sent to meet her, in London. The woman was his housekeeper at Misselthwaite Manor, and her name was Mrs. Medlock.* She was a stout woman, with very red cheeks and sharp black eyes. She wore a very purple dress, a black silk mantle* with jet fringe on it and a black bonnet with purple velvet flowers* which stuck up and trembled when she moved her head. Mary did not like her at all, but as she very seldom liked people there was nothing remarkable in that; besides which it was very evident Mrs. Medlock did not think much of her.

"My word! she's a plain little piece of goods!" she said. "And we'd heard that her mother was a beauty. She hasn't handed much of it down, has she, ma'am?"

"Perhaps she will improve as she grows older," the officer's wife said good-naturedly. "If she were not so sallow and had a nicer expression, her features are rather good. Children alter so much."

"She'll have to alter a good deal," answered Mrs. Medlock. "And there's nothing likely to improve children at Misselthwaite—if you ask me!"

They thought Mary was not listening because she was standing a little apart from them at the window of the private hotel they had gone to. She was watching the passing buses and cabs, and people, but she heard quite well and was made very curious about her uncle and the place he lived in. What sort of a place was it, and what would he be like? What was a hunchback? She had never seen one. Perhaps there were none in India.

Since she had been living in other people's houses and had had no Ayah, she had begun to feel lonely and to think queer thoughts which were new to her. She had begun to wonder why she had never seemed to belong to any one even when her father and mother had been alive. Other children seemed to belong to their fathers and mothers, but she had never seemed to really be any one's little girl. She had had servants, and food and clothes, but no one had taken any notice of her. She did not know that this was because she was a disagreeable child; but then, of course, she did not know she was disagreeable. She often thought that other people were, but she did not know that she was so herself.

She thought Mrs. Medlock the most disagreeable person she had ever seen, with her common, highly coloured face and her common fine bonnet. When the next day they set out on their journey to Yorkshire, she walked through the station to the railway carriage with her head up and trying to keep as far away from her as she could, because she did not want to seem to belong to her. It would have made her very angry to think people imagined she was her little girl.

But Mrs. Medlock was not in the least disturbed by her and her thoughts. She was the kind of woman who would "stand no nonsense from young ones." At least, that is what she would have said if she had been asked. She had not wanted to go to London just when her sister Maria's daughter was going to be married, but she had a comfortable, well paid place as housekeeper at Misselthwaite Manor and the only way in which she could keep it was to do at once what Mr. Archibald Craven told her to do. She never dared even to ask a question.

"Captain Lennox and his wife died of the cholera," Mr. Craven had said in his short, cold way. "Captain Lennox was my wife's brother and I am their daughter's guardian. The child is to be brought here. You must go to London and bring her yourself."

So she packed her small trunk and made the journey.

Mary sat in her corner of the railway carriage and looked plain and fretful. She had nothing to read or to look at, and she had folded her thin little black-gloved hands in her lap. Her black dress made her look yellower than ever, and her limp light hair straggled from under her black crêpe hat.*

"A more marred-looking young one I never saw in my life," Mrs. Medlock thought. (Marred is a Yorkshire word and means spoiled and pettish.) She had never seen a child who sat so still without doing anything; and at last she got tired of watching her and began to talk in a brisk, hard voice.

"I suppose I may as well tell you something about where you are going to," she said. "Do you know anything about your uncle?"

"No," said Mary.

"Never heard your father and mother talk about him?"

"No," said Mary frowning. She frowned because she remembered that her father and mother had never talked to her about anything in particular. Certainly they had never told her things.

"Humph," muttered Mrs. Medlock, staring at her queer, unresponsive little face. She did not say any more for a few moments and then she began again.

"I suppose you might as well be told something—to prepare you. You are going to a queer place."

Mary said nothing at all, and Mrs. Medlock looked rather discomfited by her apparent indifference, but, after taking a breath, she went on.

"Not but that it's a grand big place in a gloomy way, and Mr. Craven's proud of it in his way—and that's gloomy enough, too. The house is six hundred years old, and it's on the edge of the moor, and there's near a hundred rooms in it, though most of them's shut up and locked. And there's pictures and fine old furniture and things that's been there for ages, and there's a big park round it and gardens and trees with branches trailing to the ground—some of them." She paused and took another breath. "But there's nothing else," she ended suddenly.

Mary had begun to listen in spite of herself. It all sounded so unlike India, and anything new rather attracted her. But she did not intend to look as if she were interested. That was one of her unhappy, disagreeable ways. So she sat still.

"Well," said Mrs. Medlock. "What do you think of it?"

"Nothing," she answered. "I know nothing about such places."

That made Mrs. Medlock laugh a short sort of laugh.

"Eh!" she said, "but you are like an old woman. Don't you care?"

"It doesn't matter," said Mary, "whether I care or not."

"You are right enough there," said Mrs. Medlock. "It doesn't. What you're to be kept at Misselthwaite Manor for I don't know, unless because it's the easiest way. *He's* not going to trouble himself about you, that's sure and certain. He never troubles himself about no one."

She stopped herself as if she had just remembered something in time.

"He's got a crooked back," she said. "That set him wrong. He was a sour young man and got no good of all his money and big place till he was married."

Mary's eyes turned towards her in spite of her intention not to seem to care. She had never thought of the hunchback's being married and she was a trifle surprised. Mrs. Medlock saw this, and as she was a talkative woman she continued with more interest. This was one way of passing some of the time at any rate.

"She was a sweet, pretty thing and he'd have walked the world over to get her a blade o' grass she wanted. Nobody thought she'd marry him, but she did, and people said she married him for his money. But she didn't—she didn't," positively. "When she died—"

Mary gave a little involuntary jump.

"Oh! did she die?" she exclaimed, quite without meaning to. She had just remembered a French fairy story she had once read called "Riquet à la Houppe."* It had been about a poor hunchback and a beautiful princess and it had made her suddenly sorry for Mr. Archibald Craven.

"Yes, she died," Mrs. Medlock answered. "And it made him queerer than ever. He cares about nobody. He won't see people. Most of the time he goes away, and when he is at Misselthwaite he shuts himself up in the West Wing and won't let any one but Pitcher see him. Pitcher's an old fellow, but he took care of him when he was a child and he knows his ways."

It sounded like something in a book and it did not make Mary feel cheerful. A house with a hundred rooms, nearly all shut up and with their doors locked—a house on the edge of a moor—whatsoever a moor was—sounded dreary. A man with a crooked back who shut himself up also! She stared out of the window with her lips pinched together, and it seemed quite natural that the rain should have begun to pour down in grey slanting lines and splash and stream down the window-panes. If the pretty wife had been alive she might have made things cheerful by being something like her own mother and by running in and out and going to parties as she had done in frocks "full of lace." But she was not there any more.

"You needn't expect to see him, because ten to one you won't," said Mrs. Medlock. "And you mustn't expect that there will be people to talk to you. You'll have to play about and look after yourself. You'll be told what rooms you can go into and what rooms you're to keep out of. There's gardens enough. But when you're in the house don't go wandering and poking about. Mr. Craven won't have it."

"I shall not want to go poking about," said sour little Mary; and just as suddenly as she had begun to be rather sorry for Mr. Archibald Craven she began to cease to be sorry and to think he was unpleasant enough to deserve all that had happened to him.

And she turned her face toward the streaming panes of the window of the railway carriage and gazed out at the grey rain-storm which looked as if it would go on forever and ever. She watched it so long and steadily that the greyness grew heavier and heavier before her eyes and she fell asleep.

CHAPTER III

ACROSS THE MOOR

SHE slept a long time, and when she awakened Mrs. Medlock had bought a lunch-basket at one of the stations and they had some chicken and cold beef and bread-and-butter and some hot tea. The rain seemed to be streaming down more heavily than ever, and everybody in the station wore wet and glistening waterproofs. The guard lighted the lamps in the carriage, and Mrs. Medlock cheered up very much over her tea and chicken and beef. She ate a great deal and afterward fell asleep herself, and Mary sat and stared at her and watched her fine bonnet slip on one side until she herself fell asleep once more in the corner of the carriage, lulled by the splashing of the rain against the windows. It was quite dark when she awakened again. The train had stopped at a station and Mrs. Medlock was shaking her.*

"You have had a sleep!" she said. "It's time to open your eyes! We're at Thwaite Station,* and we've got a long drive before us."

Mary stood up and tried to keep her eyes open while Mrs. Medlock collected her parcels. The little girl did not offer to help her, because in India native servants always picked up or carried things, and it seemed quite proper that other people should wait on one.

The station was a small one and nobody but themselves seemed to be getting out of the train. The station-master spoke to Mrs. Medlock in a rough good-natured way, pronouncing his words in a queer broad fashion which Mary found out afterward was Yorkshire.

"I see tha's got back," he said. "An' tha's browt th' young 'un with thee."

"Aye, that's her," answered Mrs. Medlock, speaking with a Yorkshire accent herself and jerking her head over her shoulder toward Mary. "How's thy missus?"

"Well enow. Th' carriage is waitin' outside for thee."

A brougham* stood on the road before the little outside platform.* Mary saw that it was a smart carriage and that it was a smart foot-man* who helped her in. His long waterproof coat and the waterproof covering of his hat were shining and dripping with rain as everything was, the burly station-master included.

When he shut the door, mounted the box with the coachman, and they drove off, the little girl found herself seated in a comfortably cushioned corner, but she was not inclined to go to sleep again. She sat and looked out of the window, curious to see something of the road over which she was being driven to the queer place Mrs. Medlock had spoken of. She was not at all a timid child and she was not exactly frightened, but she felt that there was no knowing what might happen in a house with a hundred rooms nearly all shut up—a house standing on the edge of a moor.

"What is a moor?" she said suddenly to Mrs. Medlock.

"Look out of the window in about ten minutes and you'll see," the woman answered. "We've got to drive five miles across Missel Moor before we get to the Manor. You won't see much because it's a dark night, but you can see something."

Mary asked no more questions, but waited in the darkness of her corner, keeping her eyes on the window. The carriage lamps cast rays of light a little distance ahead of them and she caught glimpses of the things they passed. After they had left the station they had driven through a tiny village and she had seen whitewashed cottages and the lights of a public-house. Then they had passed a church and a vicarage and a little shop-window or so in a cottage with toys and sweets and odd things set out for sale. Then they were on the high road and she saw hedges and trees. After that there seemed nothing different for a long time—or at least it seemed a long time to her.

At last the horses began to go more slowly, as if they were climbing up-hill, and presently there seemed to be no more hedges and no more trees. She could see nothing, in fact, but a dense darkness on either side. She leaned forward and pressed her face against the window just as the carriage gave a big jolt.

"Eh! We're on the moor now sure enough," said Mrs. Medlock.

The carriage lamps shed a yellow light on a rough-looking road which seemed to be cut through bushes and low growing things which ended in the great expanse of dark apparently spread out before and around them. A wind was rising and making a singular, wild, low, rushing sound.

"It's—it's not the sea, is it?" said Mary, looking round at her companion.

"No, not it," answered Mrs. Medlock. "Nor it isn't fields nor mountains, it's just miles and miles and miles of wild land that nothing grows on but heather and gorse and broom, and nothing lives on but wild ponies and sheep."

"I feel as if it might be the sea, if there were water on it," said Mary. "It sounds like the sea just now."

"That's the wind blowing through the bushes," Mrs. Medlock said. "It's a wild, dreary enough place to my mind, though there's plenty that likes it—particularly when the heather's in bloom."

On and on they drove through the darkness, and though the rain stopped, the wind rushed by and whistled and made strange sounds. The road went up and down, and several times the carriage passed over a little bridge beneath which water rushed very fast with a great deal of noise. Mary felt as if the drive would never come to an end, and that the wide, bleak moor was a wide expanse of black ocean through which she was passing on a strip of dry land.

"I don't like it," she said to herself. "I don't like it," and she pinched her thin lips more tightly together.

The horses were climbing up a hilly piece of road when she first caught sight of a light. Mrs. Medlock saw it as soon as she did and drew a long sigh of relief.

"Eh, I am glad to see that bit o' light twinkling," she exclaimed. "It's the light in the lodge window. We shall get a good cup of tea after a bit, at all events."

It was "after a bit," as she said, for when the carriage passed through the park gates there was still two miles of avenue to drive through, and the trees (which nearly met overhead) made it seem as if they were driving through a long dark vault.

They drove out of the vault into a clear space and stopped before an immensely long but low-built house which seemed to ramble round a stone court. At first Mary thought that there were no lights at all in the windows, but as she got out of the carriage she saw that one room in a corner upstairs showed a dull glow.

The entrance door was a huge one made of massive, curiously shaped panels of oak studded with big iron nails and bound with great iron bars. It opened into an enormous hall, which was so dimly lighted that the faces in the portraits on the walls and the figures in the suits of armour made Mary feel that she did not want to look at them. As she stood on the stone floor she looked a very small, odd little black figure, and she felt as small and lost and odd as she looked.

A neat, thin old man stood near the manservant who opened the door for them.*

"You are to take her to her room," he said in a husky voice. "He doesn't want to see her. He's going to London in the morning."

"Very well, Mr. Pitcher," Mrs. Medlock answered. "So long as I know what's expected of me, I can manage."

"What's expected of you, Mrs. Medlock," Mr. Pitcher said, "is that you make sure that he's not disturbed and that he doesn't see what he doesn't want to see."

And then Mary Lennox was led up a broad staircase and down a long corridor and up a short flight of steps and through another corridor and another, until a door opened in a wall and she found herself in a room with a fire in it and a supper on a table.

Mrs. Medlock said unceremoniously:

"Well, here you are! This room and the next are where you'll live*—and you must keep to them. Don't you forget that!"

It was in this way Mistress Mary arrived at Misselthwaite Manor, and she had perhaps never felt quite so contrary in all her life.

CHAPTER IV

MARTHA

WHEN she opened her eyes in the morning it was because a young housemaid* had come into her room to light the fire and was kneeling on the hearth-rug raking out the cinders noisily. Mary lay and watched her for a few moments and then began to look about the room. She had never seen a room at all like it, and thought it curious and gloomy. The walls were covered with tapestry with a forest scene embroidered on it.* There were fantastically dressed people under the trees, and in the distance there was a glimpse of the turrets of a castle. There were hunters and horses and dogs and ladies. Mary felt as if she were in the forest with them. Out of a deep window she could see a great climbing stretch of land which seemed to have no trees on it, and to look rather like an endless, dull, purplish sea.

"What is that?" she said, pointing out of the window.

Martha,* the young housemaid, who had just risen to her feet, looked and pointed also.

"That there?" she said.

"Yes."

"That's th' moor," with a good-natured grin. "Does tha' like it?"

"No," answered Mary. "I hate it."

"That's because tha'rt not used to it," Martha said, going back to her hearth. "Tha' thinks it's too big an' bare now. But tha' will like it."

"Do you?" inquired Mary.

"Aye, that I do," answered Martha, cheerfully polishing away at the grate. "I just love it. It's none bare. It's covered wi' growin' things as smells sweet. It's fair lovely in spring an' summer when th' gorse an' broom an' heather's in flower. It smells o' honey an' there's such a lot o' fresh air—an' th' sky looks so high an' th' bees an' skylarks makes such a nice noise hummin' an' singin'. Eh! I wouldn't live away from th' moor for anythin'."

Mary listened to her with a grave, puzzled expression. The native servants she had been used to in India were not in the least like this. They were obsequious and servile and did not presume to talk to their masters as if they were their equals. They made salaams* and called them "protector of the poor" and names of that sort. Indian servants were commanded to do things, not asked. It was not the custom to say "please" and "thank you," and Mary had always slapped her Ayah in the face when she was angry. She wondered a little what this girl would do if one slapped her in the face. She was a round, rosy, good-natured looking creature, but she had a sturdy way which made Mistress Mary wonder if she might not even slap back—if the person who slapped her was only a little girl.

"You are a strange servant," she said from her pillows, rather haughtily.

Martha sat up on her heels, with her blacking-brush* in her hand, and laughed, without seeming the least out of temper.

"Eh! I know that," she said. "If there was a grand missus at Misselthwaite I should never have been even one of th' under house-maids. I might have been let to be scullery-maid, but I'd never have been let up-stairs. I'm too common an' I talk too much Yorkshire. But this is a funny house for all it's so grand. Seems like there's neither master nor mistress except Mr. Pitcher and Mrs. Medlock. Mr. Craven, he won't be troubled about anythin' when he's here, an' he's nearly always away. Mrs. Medlock gave me th' place out o' kindness.* She told me she could never have done it if Misselthwaite had been like other big houses."

"Are you going to be my servant?" Mary asked, still in her imperious little Indian way.

Martha began to rub her grate again.

"I'm Mrs. Medlock's servant," she said stoutly. "An' she's Mr. Craven's—but I'm to do the housemaid's work up here an' wait on you a bit. But you won't need much waitin' on."

"Who is going to dress me?" demanded Mary.

Martha sat up on her heels again and stared. She spoke in broad Yorkshire in her amazement.

"Canna' tha' dress thysen!" she said.

"What do you mean? I don't understand your language," said Mary.

"Eh! I forgot," Martha said. "Mrs. Medlock told me I'd have to be careful or you wouldn't know what I was sayin'. I mean can't you put on your own clothes?"

"No," answered Mary, quite indignantly. "I never did in my life. My Ayah dressed me, of course."

"Well," said Martha, evidently not in the least aware that she was impudent, "it's time tha' should learn. Tha' cannot begin younger. It'll do thee good to wait on thysen a bit. My mother always said she couldn't see why grand people's children didn't turn out fair fools— what with nurses an' bein' washed an' dressed an' took out to walk as if they was puppies!"

"It is different in India," said Mistress Mary disdainfully. She could scarcely stand this.

But Martha was not at all crushed.

"Eh! I can see it's different," she answered almost sympathetically. "I dare say it's because there's such a lot o' blacks there instead o' respectable white people. When I heard you was comin' from India I thought you was a black too."

Mary sat up in bed furious.

"What!" she said. "What! You thought I was a native. You—you daughter of a pig!"

Martha stared and looked hot.

"Who are you callin' names?" she said. "You needn't be so vexed. That's not th' way for a young lady to talk. I've nothin' against th' blacks. When you read about 'em in tracts they're always very religious. You always read as a black's a man an' a brother.* I've never seen a black, an' I was fair pleased to think I was goin' to see one close. When I come in to light your fire this mornin' I crep' up to your bed an' pulled th' cover back careful to look at you. An' there you was," disappointedly, "no more black than me—for all you're so yeller."

Mary did not even try to control her rage and humiliation.

"You thought I was a native! You dared! You don't know anything about natives! They are not people—they're servants who must salaam to you. You know nothing about India. You know nothing about anything!"

She was in such a rage and felt so helpless before the girl's simple stare, and somehow she suddenly felt so horribly lonely and far away from everything she understood and which understood her, that she threw herself face downward on the pillows and burst into passionate sobbing. She sobbed so unrestrainedly that good-natured Yorkshire Martha was a little frightened and quite sorry for her. She went to the bed and bent over her.

"Eh! you mustn't cry like that there!" she begged. "You mustn't for sure. I didn't know you'd be vexed. I don't know anythin' about anythin'—just like you said. I beg your pardon, miss. Do stop cryin'."

There was something comforting and really friendly in her queer Yorkshire speech and sturdy way which had a good effect on Mary. She gradually ceased crying and became quiet. Martha looked relieved.

"It's time for thee to get up now," she said. "Mrs. Medlock said I was to carry tha' breakfast an' tea an' dinner into th' room next to this. It's been made into a nursery for thee. I'll help thee on with thy clothes if tha'll get out o' bed. If th' buttons are at th' back tha' cannot button them up tha'self."

When Mary at last decided to get up, the clothes Martha took from the wardrobe were not the ones she had worn when she arrived the night before with Mrs. Medlock.

"Those are not mine," she said. "Mine are black."

She looked the thick white wool coat and dress over, and added with cool approval:

"Those are nicer than mine."

"These are th' ones tha' must put on," Martha answered. "Mr. Craven ordered Mrs. Medlock to get 'em in London. He said 'I won't have a child dressed in black wanderin' about like a lost soul,' he said. 'It'd make the place sadder than it is. Put colour on her.' Mother she said she knew what he meant. Mother always knows what a body means. She doesn't hold with black hersel'."

"I hate black things," said Mary.

The dressing process was one which taught them both something. Martha had "buttoned up" her little sisters and brothers, but she had never seen a child who stood still and waited for another person to do things for her as if she had neither hands nor feet of her own.

"Why doesn't tha' put on tha' own shoes?" she said when Mary quietly held out her foot.

"My Ayah did it," answered Mary, staring. "It was the custom."

She said that very often—"It was the custom." The native servants were always saying it. If one told them to do a thing their ancestors had not done for a thousand years they gazed at one mildly and said, "It is not the custom" and one knew that was the end of the matter.

It had not been the custom that Mistress Mary should do anything but stand and allow herself to be dressed like a doll, but before she was ready for breakfast she began to suspect that her life at Misselthwaite Manor would end by teaching her a number of things quite new to her*—things such as putting on her own shoes and stockings, and picking up things she let fall. If Martha had been a well-trained fine young lady's-maid she would have been more subservient and respectful and would have known that it was her business to brush hair, and button boots, and pick things up and lay them away. She was, however, only an untrained Yorkshire rustic who had been brought up in a moorland cottage with a swarm of little brothers and sisters who had never dreamed of doing anything but waiting on themselves and on the younger ones who were either babies in arms or just learning to totter about and tumble over things.

If Mary Lennox had been a child who was ready to be amused she would perhaps have laughed at Martha's readiness to talk, but Mary only listened to her coldly and wondered at her freedom of manner. At first she was not at all interested, but gradually, as the girl rattled on in her good-tempered, homely way, Mary began to notice what she was saying.

"Eh! you should see 'em all," she said. "There's twelve of us an' my father only gets sixteen shilling a week.* I can tell you my mother's put to it to get porridge for 'em all. They tumble about on th' moor an' play there all day, an' mother says th' air of th' moor fattens 'em. She says she believes they eat th' grass same as th' wild ponies do. Our Dickon,* he's twelve years old and he's got a young pony he calls his own."

"Where did he get it?" asked Mary.

"He found it on th' moor with its mother when it was a little one, an' he began to make friends with it an' give it bits o' bread an' pluck young grass for it. And it got to like him so it follows him about an' it lets him get on its back. Dickon's a kind lad an' animals likes him."

Mary had never possessed an animal pet of her own and had always thought she should like one. So she began to feel a slight interest in Dickon, and as she had never before been interested in any one but herself, it was the dawning of a healthy sentiment. When she went into the room which had been made into a nursery for her, she found that it was rather like the one she had slept in. It was not a child's room, but a grown-up person's room, with gloomy old pictures on the walls and heavy old oak chairs. A table in the centre was set with a good substantial breakfast. But she had always had a very small appetite, and she looked with something more than indifference at the first plate Martha set before her.

"I don't want it," she said.

"Tha' doesn't want thy porridge!" Martha exclaimed incredulously.

"No."

"Tha' doesn't know how good it is. Put a bit o' treacle on it or a bit o' sugar."

"I don't want it," repeated Mary.

"Eh!" said Martha. "I can't abide to see good victuals go to waste. If our children was at this table they'd clean it bare in five minutes."

"Why?" said Mary coldly.

"Why!" echoed Martha. "Because they scarce ever had their stomachs full in their lives. They're as hungry as young hawks an' foxes."

"I don't know what it is to be hungry," said Mary, with the indifference of ignorance.

Martha looked indignant.

"Well, it would do thee good to try it. I can see that plain enough," she said outspokenly. "I've no patience with folk as sits an' just stares at good bread an' meat. My word! don't I wish Dickon and Phil an' Jane an' th' rest of 'em had what's here under their pinafores."

"Why don't you take it to them?" suggested Mary.

"It's not mine," answered Martha stoutly. "An' this isn't my day out. I get my day out once a month same as th' rest. Then I go home an' clean up for mother an' give her a day's rest."

Mary drank some tea and ate a little toast and some marmalade.

"You wrap up warm an' run out an' play you," said Martha. "It'll do you good and give you some stomach for your meat."

Mary went to the window. There were gardens and paths and big trees, but everything looked dull and wintry.

"Out? Why should I go out on a day like this?"

"Well, if tha' doesn't go out tha'lt have to stay in, an' what has tha' got to do?"

Mary glanced about her. There was nothing to do. When Mrs. Medlock had prepared the nursery she had not thought of amusement. Perhaps it would be better to go and see what the gardens were like.

"Who will go with me?" she inquired.

Martha stared.

"You'll go by yourself," she answered. "You'll have to learn to play like other children does when they haven't got sisters and brothers.

Our Dickon goes off on th' moor by himself an' plays for hours. That's
how he made friends with th' pony. He's got sheep on th' moor that
knows him, an' birds as comes an' eats out of his hand. However little
there is to eat, he always saves a bit o' his bread to coax his pets."

It was really this mention of Dickon which made Mary decide to
go out, though she was not aware of it. There would be birds outside,
though there would not be ponies or sheep. They would be different
from the birds in India, and it might amuse her to look at them.

Martha found her coat and hat for her and a pair of stout little
boots and she showed her her way down-stairs.

"If tha' goes round that way tha'll come to th' gardens," she said,
pointing to a gate in a wall of shrubbery. "There's lots o' flowers in
summer-time, but there's nothin' bloomin' now." She seemed to hesi-
tate a second before she added, "One of th' gardens is locked up. No
one has been in it for ten years."

"Why?" asked Mary in spite of herself. Here was another locked
door added to the hundred in the strange house.

"Mr. Craven had it shut when his wife died so sudden. He won't
let no one go inside. It was her garden. He locked th' door an' dug
a hole and buried th' key.* There's Mrs. Medlock's bell ringing—
I must run."

After she was gone Mary turned down the walk which led to the
door in the shrubbery. She could not help thinking about the garden
which no one had been into for ten years. She wondered what it would
look like and whether there were any flowers still alive in it. When she
had passed through the shrubbery gate she found herself in great gardens, with wide lawns and winding walks with clipped borders. There
were trees, and flower-beds, and evergreens clipped into strange
shapes, and a large pool with an old grey fountain in its midst. But
the flower-beds were bare and wintry and the fountain was not playing.* This was not the garden which was shut up. How could a garden
be shut up? You could always walk into a garden.

She was just thinking this when she saw that, at the end of the path
she was following, there seemed to be a long wall, with ivy growing
over it. She was not familiar enough with England to know that she
was coming upon the kitchen-gardens where the vegetables and fruit
were growing. She went toward the wall and found that there was a
green door in the ivy, and that it stood open. This was not the closed
garden, evidently, and she could go into it.

She went through the door and found that it was a garden with walls all around it and that it was only one of several walled gardens which seemed to open into one another. She saw another open green door, revealing bushes and pathways between beds containing winter vegetables. Fruit-trees were trained flat against the wall, and over some of the beds there were glass frames. The place was bare and ugly enough, Mary thought, as she stood and stared about her. It might be nicer in summer when things were green, but there was nothing pretty about it now.

Presently an old man with a spade over his shoulder walked through the door leading from the second garden. He looked startled when he saw Mary, and then touched his cap. He had a surly old face, and did not seem at all pleased to see her—but then she was displeased with his garden and wore her "quite contrary" expression, and certainly did not seem at all pleased to see him.

"What is this place?" she asked.

"One o' th' kitchen-gardens," he answered.

"What is that?" said Mary, pointing through the other green door.

"Another of 'em," shortly. "There's another on t'other side o' th' wall an' there's th' orchard t'other side o' that."

"Can I go in them?" asked Mary.

"If tha' likes. But there's nowt to see."

Mary made no response. She went down the path and through the second green door. There she found more walls and winter vegetables and glass frames, but in the second wall there was another green door and it was not open. Perhaps it led into the garden which no one had seen for ten years. As she was not at all a timid child and always did what she wanted to do, Mary went to the green door and turned the handle. She hoped the door would not open because she wanted to be sure she had found the mysterious garden—but it did open quite easily and she walked through it and found herself in an orchard. There were walls all around it also and trees trained against them, and there were bare fruit-trees growing in the winter-browned grass— but there was no green door to be seen anywhere. Mary looked for it, and yet when she had entered the upper end of the garden she had noticed that the wall did not seem to end with the orchard, but to extend beyond it as if it enclosed a place at the other side. She could see the tops of trees above the wall, and when she stood still she saw a bird with a bright red breast sitting on the topmost branch of one of them, and suddenly he burst into his winter song*—almost as if he had caught sight of her and was calling to her.

She stopped and listened to him, and somehow his cheerful, friendly little whistle gave her a pleased feeling—even a disagreeable little girl may be lonely, and the big closed house and big bare moor and big bare gardens had made this one feel as if there was no one left in the world but herself. If she had been an affectionate child, who had been used to being loved, she would have broken her heart, but even though she was "Mistress Mary Quite Contrary" she was desolate, and the bright-breasted little bird brought a look into her sour little face which was almost a smile. She listened to him until he flew away. He was not like an Indian bird, and she liked him and wondered if she should ever see him again. Perhaps he lived in the mysterious garden and knew all about it.

Perhaps it was because she had nothing whatever to do that she thought so much of the deserted garden. She was curious about it, and wanted to see what it was like. Why had Mr. Archibald Craven buried the key? If he had liked his wife so much why did he hate her garden? She wondered if she should ever see him, but she knew that if she did she should not like him, and he would not like her, and that she should only stand and stare at him and say nothing, though she should be wanting dreadfully to ask him why he had done such a queer thing.

"People never like me and I never like people," she thought. "And I never can talk as the Crawford children could. They were always talking and laughing and making noises."

She thought of the robin and of the way he seemed to sing his song at her, and as she remembered the tree-top he perched on she stopped rather suddenly on the path.

"I believe that tree was in the secret garden—I feel sure it was," she said. "There was a wall round the place and there was no door."

She walked back into the first kitchen-garden she had entered and found the old man digging there. She went and stood beside him and watched him a few moments in her cold little way. He took no notice of her, and so at last she spoke to him.

"I have been into the other gardens," she said.

"There was nothin' to prevent thee," he answered crustily.

"I went into the orchard."

"There was no dog at th' door to bite thee," he answered.

"There was no door there into the other garden," said Mary.

"What garden?" he said in a rough voice, stopping his digging for a moment.

"The one on the other side of the wall," answered Mistress Mary. "There are trees there—I saw the tops of them. A bird with a red breast was sitting on one of them, and he sang."

To her surprise the surly old weather-beaten face actually changed its expression. A slow smile spread over it and the gardener looked quite different. It made her think that it was curious how much nicer a person looked when he smiled. She had not thought of it before.

He turned about to the orchard side of his garden and began to whistle—a low soft whistle. She could not understand how such a surly man could make such a coaxing sound.

Almost the next moment a wonderful thing happened. She heard a soft little rushing flight through the air—and it was the bird with the red breast flying to them, and he actually alighted on the big clod of earth quite near to the gardener's foot.

"Here he is," chuckled the old man, and then he spoke to the bird as if he were speaking to a child.

"Where has tha' been, tha' cheeky little beggar?" he said. "I've not seen thee before to-day. Has tha' begun tha' courtin' this early in th' season? Tha'rt too forrad."*

The bird put his tiny head on one side and looked up at him with his soft bright eye which was like a black dewdrop. He seemed quite familiar and not the least afraid. He hopped about and pecked the earth briskly, looking for seeds and insects. It actually gave Mary a queer feeling in her heart, because he was so pretty and cheerful and seemed so like a person. He had a tiny plump body and a delicate beak, and slender delicate legs.

"Will he always come when you call him?" she asked almost in a whisper.

"Aye, that he will. I've knowed him ever since he was a fledgling. He come out of th' nest in th' other garden, an' when first he flew over th' wall he was too weak to fly back for a few days an' we got friendly. When he went over th' wall again th' rest of th' brood was gone an' he was lonely an' he come back to me."

"What kind of a bird is he?" Mary asked.

"Doesn't tha' know? He's a robin redbreast, an' they're th' friend-liest, curiousest birds alive. They're almost as friendly as dogs—if you know how to get on with 'em. Watch him peckin' about there an' lookin' round at us now an' again. He knows we're talkin' about him."

It was the queerest thing in the world to see the old fellow. He looked at the plump little scarlet-waistcoated bird as if he were both proud and fond of him.

"He's a conceited one," he chuckled. "He likes to hear folk talk about him. An' curious—bless me, there never was his like for curiosity an' meddlin'. He's always comin' to see what I'm plantin'. He knows all th' things Mester Craven never troubles hissel' to find out. He's th' head gardener,* he is."

The robin hopped about busily pecking the soil, and now and then stopped and looked at them a little. Mary thought his black dewdrop eyes gazed at her with great curiosity. It really seemed as if he were finding out all about her. The queer feeling in her heart increased.

"Where did the rest of the brood fly to?" she asked.

"There's no knowin'. The old ones turn 'em out o' their nest an' make 'em fly, an' they're scattered before you know it. This one was a knowin' one an' he knew he was lonely."

Mistress Mary went a step nearer to the robin and looked at him very hard.

"I'm lonely," she said.

She had not known before that this was one of the things which made her feel sour and cross. She seemed to find it out when the robin looked at her and she looked at the robin.

The old gardener pushed his cap back on his bald head and stared at her a minute.

"Art tha' th' little wench from India?" he asked.

Mary nodded.

"Then no wonder tha'rt lonely. Tha'lt be lonelier before tha's done," he said.

He began to dig again, driving his spade deep into the rich black garden soil while the robin hopped about very busily employed.

"What is your name?" Mary inquired.

He stood up to answer her.

"Ben Weatherstaff,"* he answered, and then he added with a surly chuckle, "I'm lonely mysel' except when he's with me," and he jerked his thumb toward the robin. "He's th' only friend I've got."

"I have no friends at all," said Mary. "I never had. My Ayah didn't like me, and I never played with any one."

It is a Yorkshire habit to say what you think with blunt frankness, and old Ben Weatherstaff was a Yorkshire moor man.

"Tha' an' me are a good bit alike," he said. "We was wove out of th' same cloth. We're neither of us good-lookin' an' we're both of us as sour as we look. We've got the same nasty tempers, both of us, I'll warrant."

This was plain speaking, and Mary Lennox had never heard the truth about herself in her life. Native servants always salaamed and submitted to you, whatever you did. She had never thought much about her looks, but she wondered if she was as unattractive as Ben Weatherstaff, and she also wondered if she looked as sour as he had looked before the robin came. She actually began to wonder also if she was "nasty-tempered." She felt uncomfortable.

Suddenly a clear rippling little sound broke out near her and she turned round. She was standing a few feet from a young apple-tree, and the robin had flown on to one of its branches and had burst out into a scrap of a song. Ben Weatherstaff laughed outright.

"What did he do that for?" asked Mary.

"He's made up his mind to make friends with thee," replied Ben. "Dang me* if he hasn't took a fancy to thee."

"To me?" said Mary, and she moved toward the little tree softly and looked up.

"Would you make friends with me?" she said to the robin just as if she were speaking to a person. "Would you?" And she did not say it either in her hard little voice or in her imperious Indian voice, but in a tone so soft and eager and coaxing that Ben Weatherstaff was as surprised as she had been when she heard him whistle.

"Why," he cried out, "tha' said that as nice an' human as if tha' was a real child instead of a sharp old woman. Tha' said it almost like Dickon talks to his wild things on th' moor."

"Do you know Dickon?" Mary asked, turning round rather in a hurry.

"Everybody knows him. Dickon's wanderin' about everywhere. Th' very blackberries an' heather-bells knows him. I warrant th' foxes shows him where their cubs lies an' th' skylarks doesn't hide their nests from him."*

Mary would have liked to ask some more questions. She was almost as curious about Dickon as she was about the deserted garden.

But just that moment the robin, who had ended his song, gave a little shake of his wings, spread them and flew away. He had made his visit and had other things to do.

"He has flown over the wall!" Mary cried out, watching him. "He has flown into the orchard—he has flown across the other wall—into the garden where there is no door!"

"He lives there," said old Ben. "He came out o' th' egg there. If he's courtin', he's makin' up to some young madam of a robin that lives among th' old rose-trees there."

"Rose-trees," said Mary. "Are there rose-trees?"

Ben Weatherstaff took up his spade again and began to dig.

"There was ten year' ago," he mumbled.

"I should like to see them," said Mary. "Where is the green door?* There must be a door somewhere."

Ben drove his spade deep and looked as uncompanionable as he had looked when she first saw him.

"There was ten year' ago, but there isn't now," he said.

"No door!" cried Mary. "There must be."

"None as any one can find, an' none as is any one's business. Don't you be a meddlesome wench an' poke your nose where it's no cause to go. Here, I must go on with my work. Get you gone an' play you. I've no more time."

And he actually stopped digging, threw his spade over his shoulder and walked off, without even glancing at her or saying good-bye.

CHAPTER V

THE CRY IN THE CORRIDOR

AT first each day which passed by for Mary Lennox was exactly like the others. Every morning she awoke in her tapestried room and found Martha kneeling upon the hearth building her fire; every morning she ate her breakfast in the nursery which had nothing amusing in it; and after each breakfast she gazed out of the window across to the huge moor which seemed to spread out on all sides and climb up to the sky, and after she had stared for a while she realised that if she did not go out she would have to stay in and do nothing—and so she went out. She did not know that this was the best thing she could have done, and she did not know that, when she began to walk quickly or even run along the paths and down the avenue, she was stirring her slow blood and making herself stronger by fighting with the wind which swept down from the moor. She ran only to make herself warm, and she hated the wind which rushed at her face and roared and held her back as if it were some giant she could not see. But the big breaths of rough fresh air blown over the heather filled her lungs with something which was good for her whole thin body and whipped some red colour into her cheeks and brightened her dull eyes when she did not know anything about it.

But after a few days spent almost entirely out of doors she wakened one morning knowing what it was to be hungry, and when she sat down to her breakfast she did not glance disdainfully at her porridge and push it away, but took up her spoon and began to eat it and went on eating it until her bowl was empty.

"Tha' got on well enough with that this mornin', didn't tha'?" said Martha.

"It tastes nice to-day," said Mary, feeling a little surprised herself.

"It's th' air of th' moor that's givin' thee stomach for tha' victuals," answered Martha. "It's lucky for thee that tha's got victuals as well as an appetite. There's been twelve in our cottage as had th' stomach an' nothin' to put in it. You go on playin' you out o' doors every day an' you'll get some flesh on your bones an' you won't be so yeller."

"I don't play," said Mary. "I have nothing to play with."

"Nothin' to play with!" exclaimed Martha. "Our children plays with sticks and stones. They just runs about an' shouts an' looks at things."

Mary did not shout, but she looked at things. There was nothing else to do. She walked round and round the gardens and wandered about the paths in the park. Sometimes she looked for Ben Weatherstaff, but though several times she saw him at work he was too busy to look at her or was too surly. Once when she was walking toward him he picked up his spade and turned away as if he did it on purpose.

One place she went to oftener than to any other. It was the long walk outside the gardens with the walls round them. There were bare flower-beds on either side of it and against the walls ivy grew thickly. There was one part of the wall where the creeping dark green leaves were more bushy than elsewhere. It seemed as if for a long time that part had been neglected. The rest of it had been clipped and made to look neat, but at this lower end of the walk it had not been trimmed at all.

A few days after she had talked to Ben Weatherstaff Mary stopped to notice this and wondered why it was so. She had just paused and was looking up at a long spray of ivy swinging in the wind when she saw a gleam of scarlet and heard a brilliant chirp, and there, on the top of the wall, perched Ben Weatherstaff's robin redbreast, tilting forward to look at her with his small head on one side.

"Oh!" she cried out, "is it you—is it you?" And it did not seem at all queer to her that she spoke to him as if she was sure that he would understand and answer her.

He did answer. He twittered and chirped and hopped along the wall as if he were telling her all sorts of things. It seemed to Mistress Mary as if she understood him, too, though he was not speaking in words. It was as if he said:

"Good morning! Isn't the wind nice? Isn't the sun nice? Isn't everything nice? Let us both chirp and hop and twitter. Come on! Come on!"

Mary began to laugh, and as he hopped and took little flights along the wall she ran after him. Poor little thin, sallow, ugly Mary—she actually looked almost pretty for a moment.

"I like you! I like you!" she cried out, pattering down the walk; and she chirped and tried to whistle, which last she did not know how to do in the least. But the robin seemed to be quite satisfied and chirped and whistled back at her. At last he spread his wings and made a darting flight to the top of a tree, where he perched and sang loudly.

That reminded Mary of the first time she had seen him. He had been swinging on a tree-top then and she had been standing in the orchard. Now she was on the other side of the orchard and standing in the path outside a wall—much lower down—and there was the same tree inside.

"It's in the garden no one can go into," she said to herself. "It's the garden without a door. He lives in there. How I wish I could see what it is like!"

She ran up the walk to the green door she had entered the first morning. Then she ran down the path through the other door and then into the orchard, and when she stood and looked up there was the tree on the other side of the wall, and there was the robin just finishing his song and beginning to preen his feathers with his beak.

"It is the garden," she said. "I am sure it is."

She walked round and looked closely at that side of the orchard wall, but she only found what she had found before—that there was no door in it. Then she ran through the kitchen-gardens again and out into the walk outside the long ivy-covered wall, and she walked to the end of it and looked at it, but there was no door; and then she walked to the other end, looking again, but there was no door.

"It's very queer," she said. "Ben Weatherstaff said there was no door and there is no door. But there must have been one ten years ago, because Mr. Craven buried the key."

This gave her so much to think of that she began to be quite interested and feel that she was not sorry that she had come to Misselthwaite Manor. In India she had always felt hot and too languid to care much about anything. The fact was that the fresh wind from the moor had begun to blow the cobwebs out of her young brain and to waken her up a little.

She stayed out of doors nearly all day, and when she sat down to her supper at night she felt hungry and drowsy and comfortable. She did not feel cross when Martha chattered away. She felt as if she rather liked to hear her, and at last she thought she would ask her a question. She asked it after she had finished her supper and had sat down on the hearth-rug before the fire.

"Why did Mr. Craven hate the garden?" she said.

She had made Martha stay with her and Martha had not objected at all. She was very young, and used to a crowded cottage full of brothers and sisters, and she found it dull in the great servants' hall* down-stairs where the footman and upper-housemaids made fun of her Yorkshire speech and looked upon her as a common little thing, and sat and whispered among themselves. Martha liked to talk, and the strange child who had lived in India, and been waited upon by "blacks," was novelty enough to attract her.

She sat down on the hearth herself without waiting to be asked.

"Art tha' thinkin' about that garden yet?" she said. "I knew tha' would. That was just the way with me when I first heard about it."

"Why did he hate it?" Mary persisted.

Martha tucked her feet under her and made herself quite comfortable.

"Listen to th' wind wutherin' round the house," she said. "You could bare stand up on the moor if you was out on it to-night."

Mary did not know what "wutherin'" meant until she listened, and then she understood. It must mean that hollow shuddering sort of roar which rushed round and round the house as if the giant no one could see were buffeting it and beating at the walls and windows to try to break in. But one knew he could not get in, and somehow it made one feel very safe and warm inside a room with a red coal fire.

"But why did he hate it so?" she asked, after she had listened. She intended to know if Martha did.

Then Martha gave up her store of knowledge.

"Mind," she said, "Mrs. Medlock said it's not to be talked about. There's lots o' things in this place that's not to be talked over. That's Mr. Craven's orders. His troubles are none servants' business, he says. But for th' garden he wouldn't be like he is. It was Mrs. Craven's garden that she had made when first they were married an' she just loved it, an' they used to 'tend the flowers themselves. An' none o' th' gardeners was ever let to go in. Him an' her used to go in an' shut th' door an' stay there hours an' hours, readin' an' talkin'. An' she was just a bit of a girl an' there was an old tree with a branch bent like a seat on it. An' she made roses grow over it an' she used to sit there. But one day when she was sittin' there th' branch broke an' she fell on th' ground an' was hurt so bad that next day she died. Th' doctors thought he'd go out o' his mind an' die, too. That's why he

hates it. No one's never gone in since, an' he won't let any one talk
about it."

Mary did not ask any more questions. She looked at the red fire
and listened to the wind "wutherin'." It seemed to be "wutherin'"
louder than ever.

At that moment a very good thing was happening to her. Four good
things had happened to her, in fact, since she came to Misselthwaite
Manor. She had felt as if she had understood a robin and that he had
understood her; she had run in the wind until her blood had grown
warm; she had been healthily hungry for the first time in her life;
and she had found out what it was to be sorry for some one. She was
getting on.

But as she was listening to the wind she began to listen to something else. She did not know what it was, because at first she could
scarcely distinguish it from the wind itself. It was a curious sound—it
seemed almost as if a child were crying somewhere. Sometimes the
wind sounded rather like a child crying, but presently Mistress Mary
felt quite sure that this sound was inside the house, not outside it.
It was far away, but it was inside. She turned round and looked at
Martha.

"Do you hear any one crying?" she said.

Martha suddenly looked confused.

"No," she answered. "It's th' wind. Sometimes it sounds like
as if some one was lost on th' moor an' wailin'. It's got all sorts o'
sounds."

"But listen," said Mary. "It's in the house—down one of those
long corridors."

And at that very moment a door must have been opened somewhere
down-stairs; for a great rushing draught blew along the passage and
the door of the room they sat in was blown open with a crash, and as
they both jumped to their feet the light was blown out and the crying
sound was swept down the far corridor so that it was to be heard more
plainly than ever.

"There!" said Mary. "I told you so! It is some one crying—and it
isn't a grown-up person."

Martha ran and shut the door and turned the key, but before she
did it they both heard the sound of a door in some far passage shutting with a bang, and then everything was quiet, for even the wind
ceased "wutherin'" for a few moments.

"It was th' wind," said Martha stubbornly. "An' if it wasn't, it was little Betty Butterworth, th' scullery-maid. She's had th' toothache all day."*

But something troubled and awkward in her manner made Mistress Mary stare very hard at her. She did not believe she was speaking the truth.

CHAPTER VI

"THERE WAS SOME ONE CRYING—THERE WAS!"

THE next day the rain poured down in torrents again, and when Mary looked out of her window the moor was almost hidden by grey mist and cloud. There could be no going out to-day.

"What do you do in your cottage when it rains like this?" she asked Martha.

"Try to keep from under each other's feet mostly," Martha answered. "Eh! there does seem a lot of us then. Mother's a good-tempered woman but she gets fair moithered.* The biggest ones goes out in th' cow-shed and plays there. Dickon he doesn't mind th' wet. He goes out just th' same as if th' sun was shinin'. He says he sees things on rainy days as doesn't show when it's fair weather. He once found a little fox cub half drowned in its hole and he brought it home in th' bosom of his shirt to keep it warm. Its mother had been killed nearby an' th' hole was swum out* an' th' rest o' th' litter was dead. He's got it at home now. He found a half-drowned young crow another time an' he brought it home, too, an' tamed it. It's named Soot because it's so black an' it hops an' flies about with him everywhere."

The time had come when Mary had forgotten to resent Martha's familiar talk. She had even begun to find it interesting and to be sorry when she stopped or went away. The stories she had been told by her Ayah when she lived in India had been quite unlike those Martha had to tell about the moorland cottage which held fourteen people who lived in four little rooms and never had quite enough to eat. The children seemed to tumble about and amuse themselves like a litter of rough, good-natured collie puppies. Mary was most attracted by the mother and Dickon. When Martha told stories of what "mother" said or did they always sounded comfortable.

"If I had a raven or a fox cub I could play with it," said Mary. "But I have nothing."

Martha looked perplexed.

"Can tha' knit?" she asked.

"No," answered Mary.

"Can tha' sew?"

"No."

"Can tha' read?"

"Yes."

"Then why doesn't tha' read somethin', or learn a bit o' spellin'? Tha'st old enough to be learnin' thy book a good bit now."

"I haven't any books," said Mary. "Those I had were left in India."

"That's a pity," said Martha. "If Mrs. Medlock'd let thee go into th' library, there's thousands o' books there."

Mary did not ask where the library was, because she was suddenly inspired by a new idea. She made up her mind to go and find it herself. She was not troubled about Mrs. Medlock. Mrs. Medlock seemed always to be in her comfortable housekeeper's sitting-room down-stairs. In this queer place one scarcely ever saw any one at all. In fact, there was no one to see but the servants, and when their master was away they lived a luxurious life below stairs, where there was a huge kitchen hung about with shining brass and pewter, and a large servants' hall where there were four or five abundant meals eaten every day, and where a great deal of lively romping went on when Mrs. Medlock was out of the way.

Mary's meals were served regularly, and Martha waited on her, but no one troubled themselves about her in the least. Mrs. Medlock came and looked at her every day or two, but no one inquired what she did or told her what to do. She supposed that perhaps this was the English way of treating children. In India she had always been attended by her Ayah, who had followed her about and waited on her, hand and foot. She had often been tired of her company. Now she was followed by nobody and was learning to dress herself because Martha looked as though she thought she was silly and stupid when she wanted to have things handed to her and put on.

"Hasn't tha' got good sense?" she said once, when Mary had stood waiting for her to put on her gloves for her. "Our Susan Ann is twice as sharp as thee an' she's only four year' old. Sometimes tha' looks fair soft in th' head."

Mary had worn her contrary scowl for an hour after that, but it made her think several entirely new things.

She stood at the window for about ten minutes this morning after Martha had swept up the hearth for the last time and gone downstairs. She was thinking over the new idea which had come to her when she heard of the library. She did not care very much about the library itself, because she had read very few books; but to hear of it brought back to her mind the hundred rooms with closed doors. She wondered if they were all really locked and what she would find if she could get into any of them. Were there a hundred really? Why shouldn't she go and see how many doors she could count? It would be something to do on this morning when she could not go out. She had never been taught to ask permission to do things, and she knew nothing at all about authority, so she would not have thought it necessary to ask Mrs. Medlock if she might walk about the house, even if she had seen her.

She opened the door of the room and went into the corridor, and then she began her wanderings. It was a long corridor and it branched into other corridors and it led her up short flights of steps which mounted to others again. There were doors and doors, and there were pictures on the walls. Sometimes they were pictures of dark, curious landscapes, but oftenest they were portraits of men and women in queer, grand costumes made of satin and velvet. She found herself in one long gallery whose walls were covered with these portraits. She had never thought there could be so many in any house. She walked slowly down this place and stared at the faces which also seemed to stare at her. She felt as if they were wondering what a little girl from India was doing in their house. Some were pictures of children—little girls in thick satin frocks which reached to their feet and stood out about them, and boys with puffed sleeves and lace collars and long hair, or with big ruffs around their necks. She always stopped to look at the children, and wonder what their names were, and where they had gone, and why they wore such odd clothes. There was a stiff, plain little girl rather like herself. She wore a green brocade* dress and held a green parrot on her finger. Her eyes had a sharp, curious look.*

"Where do you live now?" said Mary aloud to her. "I wish you were here."

Surely no other little girl ever spent such a queer morning. It seemed as if there was no one in all the huge rambling house but her own small self, wandering about upstairs and down, through narrow passages and wide ones, where it seemed to her that no one but herself had ever walked. Since so many rooms had been built, people must have lived in them, but it all seemed so empty that she could not quite believe it true.*

It was not until she climbed to the second floor that she thought of turning the handle of a door. All the doors were shut, as Mrs. Medlock had said they were, but at last she put her hand on the handle of one of them and turned it. She was almost frightened for a moment when she felt that it turned without difficulty and that when she pushed upon the door itself it slowly and heavily opened. It was a massive door and opened into a big bedroom. There were embroidered hangings on the wall, and inlaid furniture such as she had seen in India stood about the room. A broad window with leaded panes looked out upon the moor; and over the mantel was another portrait of the stiff, plain little girl who seemed to stare at her more curiously than ever.

"Perhaps she slept here once," said Mary. "She stares at me so that she makes me feel queer."

After that she opened more doors and more. She saw so many rooms that she became quite tired and began to think that there must be a hundred, though she had not counted them. In all of them there were old pictures or old tapestries with strange scenes worked on them. There were curious pieces of furniture and curious ornaments in nearly all of them.

In one room, which looked like a lady's sitting-room, the hangings were all embroidered velvet, and in a cabinet were about a hundred little elephants made of ivory. They were of different sizes, and some had their mahouts or palanquins* on their backs. Some were much bigger than the others and some were so tiny that they seemed only babies. Mary had seen carved ivory in India and she knew all about elephants. She opened the door of the cabinet and stood on a footstool and played with these for quite a long time. When she got tired she set the elephants in order and shut the door of the cabinet.

In all her wanderings through the long corridors and the empty rooms she had seen nothing alive; but in this room she saw something. Just after she had closed the cabinet door she heard a tiny rustling sound. It made her jump and look around at the sofa by the fireplace, from which it seemed to come. In the corner of the sofa there was a cushion, and in the velvet which covered it there was a hole, and out of the hole peeped a tiny head with a pair of frightened eyes in it.

Mary crept softly across the room to look. The bright eyes belonged to a little grey mouse, and the mouse had eaten a hole into the cushion and made a comfortable nest there. Six baby mice were cuddled up asleep near her. If there was no one else alive in the hundred rooms there were seven mice who did not look lonely at all.

"If they wouldn't be so frightened I would take them back with me," said Mary.

She had wandered about long enough to feel too tired to wander any farther, and she turned back. Two or three times she lost her way by turning down the wrong corridor and was obliged to ramble up and down until she found the right one; but at last she reached her own floor again, though she was some distance from her own room and did not know exactly where she was.

"I believe I have taken a wrong turning again," she said, standing still at what seemed the end of a short passage with tapestry on the wall. "I don't know which way to go. How still everything is!"

It was while she was standing here and just after she had said this that the stillness was broken by a sound. It was another cry, but not quite like the one she had heard last night; it was only a short one, a fretful, childish whine muffled by passing through walls.

"It's nearer than it was," said Mary, her heart beating rather faster. "And it *is* crying."

She put her hand accidentally upon the tapestry near her, and then sprang back, feeling quite startled. The tapestry was the covering of a door which fell open and showed her that there was another part of the corridor behind it, and Mrs. Medlock was coming up it with her bunch of keys in her hand and a very cross look on her face.

"What are you doing here?" she said, and she took Mary by the arm and pulled her away. "What did I tell you?"

"I turned round the wrong corner," explained Mary. "I didn't know which way to go and I heard some one crying."

She quite hated Mrs. Medlock at the moment, but she hated her more the next.

"You didn't hear anything of the sort," said the housekeeper. "You come along back to your own nursery or I'll box your ears."

And she took her by the arm and half pushed, half pulled her up one passage and down another until she pushed her in at the door of her own room.

"Now," she said, "you stay where you're told to stay or you'll find yourself locked up. The master had better get you a governess, same as he said he would. You're one that needs some one to look sharp after you. I've got enough to do."

She went out of the room and slammed the door after her, and

Mary went and sat on the hearth-rug, pale with rage. She did not cry, but ground her teeth.

"There *was* some one crying—there *was*—there *was*!" she said to herself.

She had heard it twice now, and sometime she would find out. She had found out a great deal this morning. She felt as if she had been on a long journey, and at any rate she had had something to amuse her all the time, and she had played with the ivory elephants and had seen the grey mouse and its babies in their nest in the velvet cushion.

CHAPTER VII

THE KEY OF THE GARDEN

Two days after this, when Mary opened her eyes she sat upright in bed immediately, and called to Martha.

"Look at the moor! Look at the moor!"

The rain-storm had ended and the grey mist and clouds had been swept away in the night by the wind. The wind itself had ceased and a brilliant, deep blue sky arched high over the moorland. Never, never had Mary dreamed of a sky so blue. In India skies were hot and blazing; this was of a deep cool blue which almost seemed to sparkle like the waters of some lovely bottomless lake, and here and there, high, high in the arched blueness floated small clouds of snow-white fleece. The far-reaching world of the moor itself looked softly blue instead of gloomy purple-black or awful dreary grey.

"Aye," said Martha with a cheerful grin. "Th' storm's over for a bit. It does like this at this time o' th' year. It goes off in a night like it was pretendin' it had never been here an' never meant to come again. That's because th' spring-time's on its way. It's a long way off yet, but it's comin'."

"I thought perhaps it always rained or looked dark in England," Mary said.

"Eh! no!" said Martha, sitting up on her heels among her black lead brushes. "Nowt o' th' soart!"

"What does that mean?" asked Mary seriously. In India the natives spoke different dialects which only a few people understood, so she was not surprised when Martha used words she did not know.

Martha laughed as she had done the first morning.

"There now," she said. "I've talked broad Yorkshire again like Mrs. Medlock said I mustn't. 'Nowt o' th' soart' means 'nothin'-of-the-sort,'" slowly and carefully, "but it takes so long to say it. Yorkshire's th' sunniest place on earth when it is sunny. I told thee tha'd like th' moor after a bit. Just you wait till you see th' gold-coloured gorse blossoms an' th' blossoms o' th' broom, an' th' heather flowerin', all purple bells, an' hundreds o' butterflies flutterin' an' bees hummin' an' skylarks soarin' up an' singin'. You'll want to get out on it at sunrise an' live out on it all day like Dickon does."

"Could I ever get there?" asked Mary wistfully, looking through her window at the far-off blue. It was so new and big and wonderful and such a heavenly colour.

"I don't know," answered Martha. "Tha's never used tha' legs since tha' was born, it seems to me. Tha' couldn't walk five mile. It's five mile to our cottage."

"I should like to see your cottage."

Martha stared at her a moment curiously before she took up her polishing brush and began to rub the grate again. She was thinking that the small plain face did not look quite as sour at this moment as it had done the first morning she saw it. It looked just a trifle like little Susan Ann's when she wanted something very much.

"I'll ask my mother about it," she said. "She's one o' them that nearly always sees a way to do things. It's my day out to-day an' I'm goin' home. Eh! I am glad. Mrs. Medlock thinks a lot o' mother. Perhaps she could talk to her."

"I like your mother," said Mary.

"I should think tha' did," agreed Martha, polishing away.

"I've never seen her," said Mary.

"No, tha' hasn't," replied Martha.

She sat up on her heels again and rubbed the end of her nose with the back of her hand as if puzzled for a moment, but she ended quite positively.

"Well, she's that sensible an' hard workin' an' good-natured an' clean that no one could help likin' her whether they'd seen her or not. When I'm goin' home to her on my day out I just jump for joy when I'm crossin' th' moor."

"I like Dickon," added Mary. "And I've never seen him."

"Well," said Martha stoutly, "I've told thee that th' very birds likes him an' th' rabbits an' wild sheep an' ponies, an' th' foxes themselves. I wonder," staring at her reflectively, "what Dickon would think of thee?"

"He wouldn't like me," said Mary in her stiff, cold little way. "No one does."

Martha looked reflective again.

"How does tha' like thysel'?" she inquired, really quite as if she were curious to know.

Mary hesitated a moment and thought it over.

"Not at all—really," she answered. "But I never thought of that before."

Martha grinned a little as if at some homely recollection.

"Mother said that to me once," she said. "She was at her wash-tub an' I was in a bad temper an' talkin' ill of folk, an' she turns round on me an' says: 'Tha' young vixon, tha'! There tha' stands sayin' tha' doesn't like this one an' tha' doesn't like that one. How does tha' like thysel'?' It made me laugh an' it brought me to my senses in a minute."

She went away in high spirits as soon as she had given Mary her breakfast. She was going to walk five miles across the moor to the cottage, and she was going to help her mother with the washing and do the week's baking and enjoy herself thoroughly.

Mary felt lonelier than ever when she knew she was no longer in the house. She went out into the garden as quickly as possible, and the first thing she did was to run round and round the fountain flower garden ten times. She counted the times carefully and when she had finished she felt in better spirits. The sunshine made the whole place look different. The high, deep, blue sky arched over Misselthwaite as well as over the moor, and she kept lifting her face and looking up into it, trying to imagine what it would be like to lie down on one of the little snow-white clouds and float about. She went into the first kitchen-garden and found Ben Weatherstaff working there with two other gardeners. The change in the weather seemed to have done him good. He spoke to her of his own accord.

"Springtime's comin'," he said. "Cannot tha' smell it?"

Mary sniffed and thought she could.

"I smell something nice and fresh and damp," she said.

"That's th' good rich earth," he answered, digging away. "It's in a good humour makin' ready to grow things. It's glad when plantin' time comes. It's dull in th' winter when it's got nowt to do. In th' flower gardens out there things will be stirrin' down below in th' dark. Th' sun's warmin' 'em. You'll see bits o' green spikes stickin' out o' th' black earth after a bit."

"What will they be?" asked Mary.

"Crocuses an' snowdrops an' daffydowndillys.* Has tha' never seen them?"

"No. Everything is hot, and wet, and green after the rains in India," said Mary. "And I think things grow up in a night."

"These won't grow up in a night," said Weatherstaff. "Tha'll have to wait for 'em. They'll poke up a bit higher here, an' push out a spike more there, an' uncurl a leaf this day an' another that. You watch 'em."

"I am going to," answered Mary.

Very soon she heard the soft rustling flight of wings again and she knew at once that the robin had come again. He was very pert and lively, and hopped about so close to her feet, and put his head on one side and looked at her so slyly that she asked Ben Weatherstaff a question.

"Do you think he remembers me?" she said.

"Remembers thee!" said Weatherstaff indignantly. "He knows every cabbage stump in th' gardens, let alone th' people. He's never seen a little wench here before, an' he's bent on findin' out all about thee. Tha's no need to try to hide anything from *him*."

"Are things stirring down below in the dark in that garden where he lives?" Mary inquired.

"What garden?" grunted Weatherstaff, becoming surly again.

"The one where the old rose-trees are." She could not help asking, because she wanted so much to know. "Are all the flowers dead, or do some of them come again in the summer? Are there ever any roses?"

"Ask him," said Ben Weatherstaff, hunching his shoulders toward the robin. "He's the only one as knows. No one else has seen inside it for ten year'."

Ten years was a long time, Mary thought. She had been born ten years ago.

She walked away, slowly thinking. She had begun to like the garden just as she had begun to like the robin and Dickon and Martha's mother. She was beginning to like Martha, too. That seemed a good many people to like—when you were not used to liking. She thought of the robin as one of the people. She went to her walk outside the long, ivy-covered wall over which she could see the tree-tops; and the second time she walked up and down the most interesting and exciting thing happened to her, and it was all through Ben Weatherstaff's robin.

She heard a chirp and a twitter, and when she looked at the bare flower-bed at her left side there he was hopping about and pretending to peck things out of the earth to persuade her that he had not followed her. But she knew he had followed her, and the surprise so filled her with delight that she almost trembled a little.

"You do remember me!" she cried out. "You do! You are prettier than anything else in the world!"

She chirped, and talked, and coaxed and he hopped and flirted his tail and twittered. It was as if he were talking. His red waistcoat was like satin and he puffed his tiny breast out and was so fine and so grand and so pretty that it was really as if he were showing her how important and like a human person a robin could be. Mistress Mary forgot that she had ever been contrary in her life when he allowed her to draw closer and closer to him, and bend down and talk and try to make something like robin sounds.

Oh! to think that he should actually let her come as near to him as that! He knew nothing in the world would make her put out her hand toward him or startle him in the least tiniest way. He knew it because he was a real person—only nicer than any other person in the world. She was so happy that she scarcely dared to breathe.

The flower-bed was not quite bare. It was bare of flowers because the perennial plants had been cut down for their winter rest, but there were tall shrubs and low ones which grew together at the back of the bed, and as the robin hopped about under them she saw him hop over a small pile of freshly turned up earth. He stopped on it to look for a worm. The earth had been turned up because a dog had been trying to dig up a mole and he had scratched quite a deep hole.

Mary looked at it, not really knowing why the hole was there, and as she looked she saw something almost buried in the newly-turned soil. It was something like a ring of rusty iron or brass, and when the robin flew up into a tree near by she put out her hand and picked the ring up. It was more than a ring, however; it was an old key* which looked as if it had been buried a long time.

Mistress Mary stood up and looked at it with an almost frightened face as it hung from her finger.

"Perhaps it has been buried for ten years," she said in a whisper. "Perhaps it is the key to the garden!"

CHAPTER VIII

THE ROBIN WHO SHOWED THE WAY

SHE looked at the key quite a long time. She turned it over and over, and thought about it. As I have said before, she was not a child who had been trained to ask permission or consult her elders about things. All she thought about the key was that if it was the key to the closed garden, and she could find out where the door was, she could perhaps open it and see what was inside the walls, and what had happened to the old rose-trees. It was because it had been shut up so long that she wanted to see it. It seemed as if it must be different from other places and that something strange must have happened to it during ten years. Besides that, if she liked it she could go into it every day and shut the door behind her, and she could make up some play of her own and play it quite alone, because nobody would ever know where she was, but would think the door was still locked and the key buried in the earth. The thought of that pleased her very much.

Living as it were, all by herself in a house with a hundred mysteriously closed rooms and having nothing whatever to do to amuse herself, had set her inactive brain to working and was actually awakening her imagination. There is no doubt that the fresh, strong, pure air from the moor had a great deal to do with it. Just as it had given her an appetite, and fighting with the wind had stirred her blood, so the same things had stirred her mind. In India she had always been too hot and languid and weak to care much about anything, but in this place she was beginning to care and to want to do new things. Already she felt less "contrary," though she did not know why.

She put the key in her pocket and walked up and down her walk. No one but herself ever seemed to come there, so she could walk slowly and look at the wall, or, rather, at the ivy growing on it. The ivy was the baffling thing. Howsoever carefully she looked she could see nothing but thickly-growing, glossy, dark green leaves. She was very much disappointed. Something of her contrariness came back to her as she paced the wall and looked over it at the tree-tops inside. It seemed so silly, she said to herself, to be near it and not be able to get in. She took the key* in her pocket when she went back to the house, and she made up her mind that she would always carry it with her when she went out, so that if she ever should find the hidden door she would be ready.

Mrs. Medlock had allowed Martha to sleep all night at the cottage, but she was back at her work in the morning with cheeks redder than ever and in the best of spirits.

"I got up at four o'clock," she said. "Eh! it was pretty on th' moor with th' birds gettin' up an' th' rabbits scamperin' about an' th' sun risin'. I didn't walk all th' way. A man gave me a ride in his cart an' I can tell you I did enjoy myself."

She was full of stories of the delights of her day out. Her mother had been glad to see her and they had got the baking and washing all out of the way. She had even made each of the children a dough-cake* with a bit of brown sugar in it.

"I had 'em all pipin' hot when they came in from playin' on th' moor. An' th' cottage all smelt o' nice, clean hot bakin' an' there was a good fire, an' they just shouted for joy. Our Dickon he said our cottage was good enough for a king to live in."

In the evening they had all sat round the fire, and Martha and her mother had sewed patches on torn clothes and mended stockings and Martha had told them about the little girl who had come from India and who had been waited on all her life by what Martha called "blacks" until she didn't know how to put on her own stockings.

"Eh! they did like to hear about you," said Martha. "They wanted to know all about th' blacks an' about th' ship you came in. I couldn't tell 'em enough."

Mary reflected a little.

"I'll tell you a great deal more before your next day out," she said, "so that you will have more to talk about. I daresay they would like to hear about riding on elephants and camels, and about the officers going to hunt tigers."

"My word!" cried delighted Martha. "It would set 'em clean off their heads. Would tha' really do that, Miss? It would be same as a wild beast show like we heard they had in York once."*

"India is quite different from Yorkshire," Mary said slowly, as she thought the matter over. "I never thought of that. Did Dickon and your mother like to hear you talk about me?"

"Why, our Dickon's eyes nearly started out o' his head, they got that round," answered Martha. "But mother, she was put out about your seemin' to be all by yourself like. She said, 'Hasn't Mr. Craven got no governess for her, nor no nurse?' and I said, 'No, he hasn't, though Mrs. Medlock says he will when he thinks of it, but she says he mayn't think of it for two or three years.' "

"I don't want a governess," said Mary sharply.

"But mother says you ought to be learnin' your book by this time an' you ought to have a woman to look after you, an' she says: 'Now, Martha, you just think how you'd feel yourself, in a big place like that, wanderin' about all alone, an' no mother. You do your best to cheer her up,' she says, an' I said I would."

Mary gave her a long, steady look.

"You do cheer me up," she said. "I like to hear you talk."

Presently Martha went out of the room and came back with something held in her hands under her apron.

"What does tha' think," she said, with a cheerful grin. "I've brought thee a present."

"A present!" exclaimed Mistress Mary. How could a cottage full of fourteen hungry people give any one a present!

"A man was drivin' across the moor peddlin',"* Martha explained. "An' he stopped his cart at our door. He had pots an' pans an' odds an' ends, but mother had no money to buy anythin'. Just as he was goin' away our 'Lizabeth Ellen called out, 'Mother, he's got skippin'-ropes with red an' blue handles.' An' mother she calls out quite sudden, 'Here, stop, mister! How much are they?' An' he says 'Tuppence,' an' mother she began fumblin' in her pocket an' she says to me, 'Martha, tha's brought thee thy wages like a good lass, an' I've got four places to put every penny, but I'm just goin' to take tuppence out of it to buy that child a skippin'-rope,' an' she bought one an' here it is."

She brought it out from under her apron and exhibited it quite proudly. It was a strong, slender rope with a striped red and blue handle at each end, but Mary Lennox had never seen a skipping-rope before. She gazed at it with a mystified expression.

"What is it for?" she asked curiously.

"For!" cried out Martha. "Does tha' mean that they've not got skippin'-ropes in India, for all they've got elephants and tigers and camels! No wonder most of 'em's black. This is what it's for; just watch me."

And she ran into the middle of the room and, taking a handle in each hand, began to skip, and skip, and skip, while Mary turned in her chair to stare at her, and the queer faces in the old portraits seemed to stare at her, too, and wonder what on earth this common little cottager had the impudence to be doing under their very noses. But Martha did not even see them. The interest and curiosity in Mistress Mary's face delighted her, and she went on skipping and counted as she skipped until she had reached a hundred.

"I could skip longer than that," she said when she stopped. "I've skipped as much as five hundred when I was twelve, but I wasn't as fat then as I am now, an' I was in practice."

Mary got up from her chair beginning to feel excited herself.

"It looks nice," she said. "Your mother is a kind woman. Do you think I could ever skip like that?"

"You just try it," urged Martha, handing her the skipping-rope. "You can't skip a hundred at first, but if you practice you'll mount up. That's what mother said. She says, 'Nothin' will do her more good than skippin' rope. It's th' sensiblest toy a child can have. Let her play out in th' fresh air skippin' an' it'll stretch her legs an' arms an' give her some strength in 'em.'"

It was plain that there was not a great deal of strength in Mistress Mary's arms and legs when she first began to skip. She was not very clever at it, but she liked it so much that she did not want to stop.

"Put on tha' things and run an' skip out o' doors," said Martha. "Mother said I must tell you to keep out o' doors as much as you could, even when it rains a bit, so as tha' wrap up warm."

Mary put on her coat and hat and took her skipping-rope over her arm. She opened the door to go out, and then suddenly thought of something and turned back rather slowly.

"Martha," she said, "they were your wages. It was your twopence really. Thank you." She said it stiffly because she was not used to thanking people or noticing that they did things for her. "Thank you," she said, and held out her hand because she did not know what else to do.

Martha gave her hand a clumsy little shake, as if she was not accustomed to this sort of thing either. Then she laughed.

"Eh! tha' art a queer, old-womanish thing," she said. "If tha'd been our 'Lizabeth Ellen tha'd have give me a kiss."

Mary looked stiffer than ever.

"Do you want me to kiss you?"*

Martha laughed again.

"Nay, not me," she answered. "If tha' was different, p'raps tha'd want to thysel'. But tha' isn't. Run off outside an' play with thy rope."

Mistress Mary felt a little awkward as she went out of the room. Yorkshire people seemed strange, and Martha was always rather a puzzle to her. At first she had disliked her very much, but now she did not.

The skipping-rope was a wonderful thing. She counted and skipped, and skipped and counted, until her cheeks were quite red, and she was more interested than she had ever been since she was born. The sun was shining and a little wind was blowing—not a rough wind, but one which came in delightful little gusts and brought a fresh scent of newly-turned earth with it. She skipped round the fountain garden, and up one walk and down another. She skipped at last into the kitchen-garden and saw Ben Weatherstaff digging and talking to his robin, which was hopping about him. She skipped down the walk toward him and he lifted his head and looked at her with a curious expression. She had wondered if he would notice her. She really wanted him to see her skip.

"Well!" he exclaimed. "Upon my word! P'raps tha' art a young 'un, after all, an' p'raps tha's got child's blood in thy veins instead of sour buttermilk. Tha's skipped red into thy cheeks* as sure as my name's Ben Weatherstaff. I wouldn't have believed tha' could do it."

"I never skipped before," Mary said. "I'm just beginning. I can only go up to twenty."

"Tha' keep on," said Ben. "Tha' shapes well enough at it for a young 'un that's lived with heathen. Just see how he's watchin' thee," jerking his head toward the robin. "He followed after thee yesterday. He'll be at it again to-day. He'll be bound to find out what th' skippin'-rope is. He's never seen one. Eh!" shaking his head at the bird, "tha' curiosity will be th' death of thee sometime if tha' doesn't look sharp."

Mary skipped round all the gardens and round the orchard, resting every few minutes. At length she went to her own special walk and made up her mind to try if she could skip the whole length of it. It was a good long skip and she began slowly, but before she had gone half-way down the path she was so hot and breathless that she was obliged to stop. She did not mind much, because she had already counted up to thirty. She stopped with a little laugh of pleasure, and there, lo and behold, was the robin swaying on a long branch of ivy. He had followed her and he greeted her with a chirp. As Mary had skipped toward him she felt something heavy in her pocket strike against her at each jump, and when she saw the robin she laughed again.

"You showed me where the key was yesterday," she said. "You ought to show me the door to-day; but I don't believe you know!"

The robin flew from his swinging spray of ivy on to the top of the wall and he opened his beak and sang a loud, lovely trill, merely to show off. Nothing in the world is quite as adorably lovely as a robin when he shows off—and they are nearly always doing it.

Mary Lennox had heard a great deal about Magic in her Ayah's stories, and she always said that what happened almost at that moment was Magic.

One of the nice little gusts of wind rushed down the walk, and it was a stronger one than the rest. It was strong enough to wave the branches of the trees, and it was more than strong enough to sway the trailing sprays of untrimmed ivy hanging from the wall. Mary had stepped close to the robin, and suddenly the gust of wind swung aside some loose ivy trails, and more suddenly still she jumped toward it and caught it in her hand. This she did because she had seen something under it—a round knob which had been covered by the leaves hanging over it. It was the knob of a door.

She put her hands under the leaves and began to pull and push them aside. Thick as the ivy hung, it nearly all was a loose and swinging curtain, though some had crept over wood and iron. Mary's heart began to thump and her hands to shake a little in her delight and excitement. The robin kept singing and twittering away and tilting his head on one side, as if he were as excited as she was.* What was this under her hands which was square and made of iron and which her fingers found a hole in?

It was the lock of the door which had been closed ten years and she put her hand in her pocket, drew out the key and found it fitted the keyhole. She put the key in and turned it. It took two hands to do it, but it did turn.

And then she took a long breath and looked behind her up the long walk to see if anyone was coming. No one was coming. No one ever did come, it seemed, and she took another long breath, because she could not help it, and she held back the swinging curtain of ivy and pushed back the door which opened slowly—slowly.

Then she slipped through it, and shut it behind her, and stood with her back against it, looking about her and breathing quite fast with excitement, and wonder, and delight.

She was standing *inside** the secret garden.

CHAPTER IX

THE STRANGEST HOUSE ANY ONE EVER LIVED IN

IT was the sweetest, most mysterious-looking place any one could imagine. The high walls which shut it in were covered with the leafless stems of climbing roses, which were so thick that they were matted together. Mary Lennox knew they were roses because she had seen a great many roses in India. All the ground was covered with grass of a wintry brown, and out of it grew clumps of bushes which were surely rose-bushes if they were alive. There were numbers of standard roses* which had so spread their branches that they were like little trees. There were other trees in the garden, and one of the things which made the place look strangest and loveliest was that climbing roses had run all over them and swung down long tendrils which made light swaying curtains, and here and there they had caught at each other or at a far-reaching branch and had crept from one tree to another and made lovely bridges of themselves. There were neither leaves nor roses on them now, and Mary did not know whether they were dead or alive, but their thin grey or brown branches and sprays looked like a sort of hazy mantle spreading over everything, walls, and trees, and even brown grass, where they had fallen from their fastenings and run along the ground. It was this hazy tangle from tree to tree which made it all look so mysterious. Mary had thought it must be different from other gardens which had not been left all by themselves so long; and indeed it was different from any other place she had ever seen in her life.*

"How still it is!" she whispered. "How still!"

Then she waited a moment and listened at the stillness. The robin, who had flown to his tree-top, was still as all the rest. He did not even flutter his wings; he sat without stirring, and looked at Mary.

"No wonder it is still," she whispered again. "I am the first person who has spoken in here for ten years."

She moved away from the door, stepping as softly as if she were afraid of awakening some one. She was glad that there was grass under her feet and that her steps made no sounds. She walked under one of the fairy-like grey arches between the trees and looked up at the sprays and tendrils which formed them.

"I wonder if they are all quite dead," she said. "Is it all a quite dead garden? I wish it wasn't."*

If she had been Ben Weatherstaff she could have told whether the wood was alive by looking at it, but she could only see that there were only grey or brown sprays and branches and none showed any signs of even a tiny leaf-bud anywhere.

But she was *inside* the wonderful garden and she could come through the door under the ivy any time, and she felt as if she had found a world all her own.

The sun was shining inside the four walls and the high arch of blue sky over this particular piece of Misselthwaite seemed even more brilliant and soft than it was over the moor. The robin flew down from his tree-top and hopped about or flew after her from one bush to another. He chirped a good deal and had a very busy air, as if he were showing her things. Everything was strange and silent and she seemed to be hundreds of miles away from any one, but somehow she did not feel lonely at all. All that troubled her was her wish that she knew whether all the roses were dead, or if perhaps some of them had lived and might put out leaves and buds as the weather got warmer. She did not want it to be a quite dead garden. If it were a quite alive garden, how wonderful it would be, and what thousands of roses would grow on every side!

Her skipping-rope had hung over her arm when she came in, and after she had walked about for a while she thought she would skip round the whole garden, stopping when she wanted to look at things. There seemed to have been grass paths here and there, and in one or two corners there were alcoves of evergreen with stone seats or tall moss-covered flower urns in them.

As she came near the second of these alcoves she stopped skipping. There had once been a flower-bed in it, and she thought she saw something sticking out of the black earth—some sharp little pale green points. She remembered what Ben Weatherstaff had said and she knelt down to look at them.

"Yes, they are tiny growing things and they *might* be crocuses or snowdrops or daffodils," she whispered.

She bent very close to them and sniffed the fresh scent of the damp earth. She liked it very much.

"Perhaps there are some other ones coming up in other places," she said. "I will go all over the garden and look."

She did not skip, but walked. She went slowly and kept her eyes on the ground. She looked in the old border beds and among the grass, and after she had gone round, trying to miss nothing, she had found ever so many more sharp, pale green points, and she had become quite excited again.

"It isn't a quite dead garden," she cried out softly to herself. "Even if the roses are dead, there are other things alive."

She did not know anything about gardening, but the grass seemed so thick in some of the places where the green points were pushing their way through that she thought they did not seem to have room enough to grow. She searched about until she found a rather sharp piece of wood and knelt down and dug and weeded out the weeds and grass until she made nice little clear places around them.

"Now they look as if they could breathe," she said, after she had finished with the first ones. "I am going to do ever so many more. I'll do all I can see. If I haven't time to-day I can come to-morrow."

She went from place to place, and dug and weeded, and enjoyed herself so immensely that she was led on from bed to bed and into the grass under the trees. The exercise made her so warm that she first threw her coat off, and then her hat, and without knowing it she was smiling down on to the grass and the pale green points all the time.

The robin was tremendously busy. He was very much pleased to see gardening begun on his own estate. He had often wondered at Ben Weatherstaff. Where gardening is done all sorts of delightful things to eat are turned up with the soil. Now here was this new kind of creature who was not half Ben's size and yet had had the sense to come into his garden and begin at once.

Mistress Mary worked in her garden until it was time to go to her midday dinner. In fact, she was rather late in remembering, and when she put on her coat and hat, and picked up her skipping-rope, she could not believe that she had been working two or three hours. She had been actually happy all the time; and dozens and dozens of the tiny, pale green points were to be seen in cleared places, looking twice as cheerful as they had looked before when the grass and weeds had been smothering them.

"I shall come back this afternoon," she said, looking all round at her new kingdom, and speaking to the trees and the rose-bushes as if they heard her.

Then she ran lightly across the grass, pushed open the slow old door and slipped through it under the ivy. She had such red cheeks and such bright eyes and ate such a dinner that Martha was delighted.

"Two pieces o' meat an' two helps o' rice puddin'!" she said. "Eh! mother will be pleased when I tell her what th' skippin'-rope's done for thee."

In the course of her digging with her pointed stick Mistress Mary had found herself digging up a sort of white root rather like an onion. She had put it back in its place and patted the earth carefully down on it, and just now she wondered if Martha could tell her what it was.

"Martha," she said, "what are those white roots that look like onions?"

"They're bulbs," answered Martha. "Lots o' spring flowers grow from 'em. Th' very little ones are snowdrops an' crocuses an' th' big ones are narcissusis* an' jonquils an' daffydowndillys. Th' biggest of all is lilies an' purple flags.* Eh! they are nice. Dickon's got a whole lot of 'em planted in our bit o' garden."

"Does Dickon know all about them?" asked Mary, a new idea taking possession of her.

"Our Dickon can make a flower grow out of a brick walk. Mother says he just whispers things out o' th' ground."

"Do bulbs live a long time? Would they live years and years if no one helped them?" inquired Mary anxiously.

"They're things as helps themselves," said Martha. "That's why poor folk can afford to have 'em. If you don't trouble 'em, most of 'em'll work away underground for a lifetime an' spread out an' have little 'uns. There's a place in th' park woods here where there's snowdrops by thousands. They're the prettiest sight in Yorkshire when th' spring comes. No one knows when they was first planted."

"I wish the spring was here now," said Mary. "I want to see all the things that grow in England."

She had finished her dinner and gone to her favourite seat on the hearth-rug.

"I wish—I wish I had a little spade," she said.

"Whatever does tha' want a spade for?" asked Martha, laughing. "Art tha' goin' to take to diggin'? I must tell mother that, too."

Mary looked at the fire and pondered a little. She must be careful if she meant to keep her secret kingdom. She wasn't doing any harm, but if Mr. Craven found out about the open door he would be fearfully angry and get a new key and lock it up forevermore. She really could not bear that.

"This is such a big lonely place," she said slowly, as if she were turning matters over in her mind. "The house is lonely, and the park is lonely, and the gardens are lonely. So many places seem shut up. I never did many things in India, but there were more people to look at—natives and soldiers marching by—and sometimes bands playing, and my Ayah told me stories. There is no one to talk to here except you and Ben Weatherstaff. And you have to do your work and Ben Weatherstaff won't speak to me often. I thought if I had a little spade I could dig somewhere as he does, and I might make a little garden if he would give me some seeds."

Martha's face quite lighted up.

"There now!" she exclaimed, "if that wasn't one of th' things mother said. She says, 'There's such a lot o' room in that big place, why don't they give her a bit for herself, even if she doesn't plant nothin' but parsley an' radishes? She'd dig an' rake away an' be right down happy over it.' Them was the very words she said."

"Were they?" said Mary. "How many things she knows, doesn't she?"

"Eh!" said Martha. "It's like she says: 'A woman as brings up twelve children learns something besides her A B C.* Children's as good as 'rithmetic to set you findin' out things.'"

"How much would a spade cost—a little one?" Mary asked.

"Well," was Martha's reflective answer, "at Thwaite village there's a shop or so an' I saw little garden sets with a spade an' a rake an' a fork all tied together for two shillings. An' they was stout enough to work with, too."

"I've got more than that in my purse," said Mary. "Mrs. Morrison gave me five shillings, and Mrs. Medlock gave me some money from Mr. Craven."

"Did he remember thee that much?" exclaimed Martha.

"Mrs. Medlock said I was to have a shilling a week to spend. She gives me one every Saturday. I didn't know what to spend it on."

"My word! that's riches," said Martha. "Tha' can buy anything in th' world tha' wants. The rent of our cottage is only one an' three-pence an' it's like pulling eye-teeth to get it. Now I've just thought of somethin'," putting her hands on her hips.

"What?" said Mary eagerly.

"In the shop at Thwaite they sell packages o' flower-seeds for a penny each, and our Dickon he knows which is th' prettiest ones an' how to make 'em grow. He walks over to Thwaite many a day just for th' fun of it. Does tha' know how to print letters?" suddenly.

"I know how to write," Mary answered.

Martha shook her head.

"Our Dickon can only read printin'. If tha' could print we could write a letter to him an' ask him to go an' buy th' garden tools an' th' seeds at th' same time."

"Oh! you're a good girl!" Mary cried. "You are, really. I didn't know you were so nice. I know I can print letters if I try. Let's ask Mrs. Medlock for a pen and ink and some paper."

"I've got some of my own," said Martha. "I bought 'em so I could print a bit of a letter to mother of a Sunday. I'll go and get it."

She ran out of the room, and Mary stood by the fire and twisted her thin little hands together with sheer pleasure.

"If I have a spade," she whispered, "I can make the earth nice and soft and dig up weeds. If I have seeds and can make flowers grow the garden won't be dead at all—it will come alive."

She did not go out again that afternoon because when Martha returned with her pen and ink and paper she was obliged to clear the table and carry the plates and dishes downstairs, and when she got into the kitchen Mrs. Medlock was there and told her to do something, so Mary waited for what seemed to her a long time before she came back. Then it was a serious piece of work to write to Dickon. Mary had been taught very little because her governesses had disliked her too much to stay with her. She could not spell particularly well, but she found that she could print letters when she tried. This was the letter Martha dictated to her:

"My dear Dickon:

"This comes hoping to find you well as it leaves me at present. Miss Mary has plenty of money and will you go to Thwaite and buy her some flower seeds and a set of garden tools to make a flower-bed. Pick the prettiest ones and easy to grow because she has never done it before and lived in India which is different. Give my love to mother and every one of you. Miss Mary is going to tell me a lot more so that on my next day out you can hear about elephants and camels and gentlemen going hunting lions and tigers.

"Your loving sister,

"MARTHA PHŒBE SOWERBY."*

"We'll put the money in th' envelope an' I'll get th' butcher's boy to take it in his cart. He's a great friend o' Dickon's," said Martha.

"How shall I get the things when Dickon buys them?" asked Mary.

"He'll bring 'em to you himself. He'll like to walk over this way."

"Oh!" exclaimed Mary, "then I shall see him! I never thought I should see Dickon."

"Does tha' want to see him?" asked Martha suddenly, she had looked so pleased.

"Yes, I do. I never saw a boy foxes and crows loved. I want to see him very much."

Martha gave a little start, as if she suddenly remembered something.

"Now to think," she broke out, "to think o' me forgettin' that there; an' I thought I was goin' to tell you first thing this mornin'. I asked mother—and she said she'd ask Mrs. Medlock her own self."

"Do you mean—" Mary began.

"What I said Tuesday. Ask her if you might be driven over to our cottage some day and have a bit o' mother's hot oat cake, an' butter, an' a glass o' milk."

It seemed as if all the interesting things were happening in one day. To think of going over the moor in the daylight and when the sky was blue! To think of going into the cottage which held twelve children!

"Does she think Mrs. Medlock would let me go?" she asked, quite anxiously.

"Aye, she thinks she would. She knows what a tidy woman mother is and how clean she keeps the cottage."

"If I went I should see your mother as well as Dickon," said Mary, thinking it over and liking the idea very much. "She doesn't seem to be like the mothers in India."

Her work in the garden and the excitement of the afternoon ended by making her feel quiet and thoughtful. Martha stayed with her until tea-time, but they sat in comfortable quiet and talked very little. But just before Martha went downstairs for the tea-tray, Mary asked a question.

"Martha," she said, "has the scullery-maid had the toothache again to-day?"

Martha certainly started slightly.

"What makes thee ask that?" she said.

"Because when I waited so long for you to come back I opened the door and walked down the corridor to see if you were coming. And I heard that far-off crying again, just as we heard it the other night. There isn't a wind to-day, so you see it couldn't have been the wind."

"Eh!" said Martha restlessly. "Tha' mustn't go walkin' about in corridors an' listenin'. Mr. Craven would be that there angry there's no knowin' what he'd do."

"I wasn't listening," said Mary. "I was just waiting for you—and I heard it. That's three times."

"My word! There's Mrs. Medlock's bell," said Martha, and she almost ran out of the room.

"It's the strangest house any one ever lived in," said Mary drowsily, as she dropped her head on the cushioned seat of the armchair near her. Fresh air, and digging, and skipping-rope had made her feel so comfortably tired that she fell asleep.

CHAPTER X

DICKON

THE sun shone down for nearly a week on the secret garden. The Secret Garden was what Mary called it when she was thinking of it. She liked the name, and she liked still more the feeling that when its beautiful old walls shut her in no one knew where she was. It seemed almost like being shut out of the world in some fairy place. The few books she had read and liked had been fairy-story books, and she had read of secret gardens in some of the stories. Sometimes people went to sleep in them for a hundred years, which she had thought must be rather stupid. She had no intention of going to sleep, and, in fact, she was becoming wider awake every day which passed at Misselthwaite. She was beginning to like to be out of doors; she no longer hated the wind, but enjoyed it. She could run faster, and longer, and she could skip up to a hundred. The bulbs in the secret garden must have been much astonished. Such nice clear places were made round them that they had all the breathing space they wanted, and really, if Mistress Mary had known it, they began to cheer up under the dark earth and work tremendously. The sun could get at them and warm them, and when the rain came down it could reach them at once, so they began to feel very much alive.

Mary was an odd, determined little person, and, now she had something interesting to be determined about, she was very much absorbed indeed. She worked and dug and pulled up weeds steadily, only becoming more pleased with her work every hour instead of tiring of it. It seemed to her like a fascinating sort of play. She found many more of the sprouting pale green points than she had ever hoped to find. They seemed to be starting up everywhere and each day she was sure she found tiny new ones, some so tiny that they barely peeped above the earth. There were so many that she remembered what Martha had said about the "snowdrops by the thousands," and about bulbs spreading and making new ones. These had been left to themselves for ten years and perhaps they had spread, like the snowdrops, into thousands. She wondered how long it would be before they showed that they were flowers. Sometimes she stopped digging to look at the garden and try to imagine what it would be like when it was covered with thousands of lovely things in bloom.

During that week of sunshine, she became more intimate with Ben Weatherstaff. She surprised him several times by seeming to start up beside him as if she sprang out of the earth. The truth was that she was afraid that he would pick up his tools and go away if he saw her coming, so she always walked toward him as silently as possible. But, in fact, he did not object to her as strongly as he had at first. Perhaps he was secretly rather flattered by her evident desire for his elderly company. Then, also, she was more civil than she had been. He did not know that when she first saw him she spoke to him as she would have spoken to a native, and had not known that a cross, sturdy old Yorkshireman was not accustomed to salaam to his masters, and be merely commanded by them to do things.

"Tha'rt like th' robin," he said to her one morning when he lifted his head and saw her standing by him. "I never knows when I shall see thee or which side tha'll come from."

"He's friends with me now," said Mary.

"That's like him," snapped Ben Weatherstaff. "Makin' up to th' women folk just for vanity an' flightiness. There's nothin' he wouldn't do for th' sake o' showin' off an' flirtin' his tail-feathers. He's as full o' pride as an egg's full o' meat."

He very seldom talked much and sometimes did not even answer Mary's questions except by a grunt, but this morning he said more than usual. He stood up and rested one hobnailed boot on the top of his spade while he looked her over.

"How long has tha' been here?" he jerked out.

"I think it's about a month," she answered.

"Tha's beginnin' to do Misselthwaite credit," he said. "Tha's a bit fatter than tha' was an' tha's not quite so yeller. Tha' looked like a young plucked crow when tha' first came into this garden. Thinks I to myself I never set eyes on an uglier, sourer faced young 'un."

Mary was not vain and as she had never thought much of her looks she was not greatly disturbed.

"I know I'm fatter," she said. "My stockings are getting tighter. They used to make wrinkles. There's the robin, Ben Weatherstaff."

There, indeed, was the robin, and she thought he looked nicer than ever. His red waistcoat was as glossy as satin and he flirted his wings and tail and tilted his head and hopped about with all sorts of lively graces. He seemed determined to make Ben Weatherstaff admire him. But Ben was sarcastic.

"Aye, there tha' art!" he said. "Tha' can put up with me for a bit sometimes when tha's got no one better. Tha's been reddinin' up thy waistcoat an' polishin' thy feathers this two weeks. I know what tha's up to. Tha's courtin' some bold young madam somewhere, tellin' thy lies to her about bein' th' finest cock robin on Missel Moor an' ready to fight all th' rest of 'em."

"Oh! look at him!" exclaimed Mary.

The robin was evidently in a fascinating, bold mood. He hopped closer and closer and looked at Ben Weatherstaff more and more engagingly. He flew on to the nearest currant bush and tilted his head and sang a little song right at him.

"Tha' thinks tha'll get over me by doin' that," said Ben, wrinkling his face up in such a way that Mary felt sure he was trying not to look pleased. "Tha' thinks no one can stand out against thee—that's what tha' thinks."

The robin spread his wings—Mary could scarcely believe her eyes. He flew right up to the handle of Ben Weatherstaff's spade and alighted on the top of it. Then the old man's face wrinkled itself slowly into a new expression. He stood still as if he were afraid to breathe—as if he would not have stirred for the world, lest his robin should start away. He spoke quite in a whisper.

"Well, I'm danged!" he said as softly as if he were saying something quite different. "Tha' does know how to get at a chap—tha' does! Tha's fair unearthly, tha's so knowin'."

And he stood without stirring—almost without drawing his breath—until the robin gave another flirt to his wings and flew away. Then he stood looking at the handle of the spade as if there might be Magic in it, and then he began to dig again and said nothing for several minutes.

But because he kept breaking into a slow grin now and then, Mary was not afraid to talk to him.

"Have you a garden of your own?" she asked.

"No. I'm bachelder* an' lodge with Martin at th' gate."

"If you had one," said Mary, "what would you plant?"

"Cabbages an' 'taters an' onions."

"But if you wanted to make a flower garden," persisted Mary, "what would you plant?"

"Bulbs an' sweet-smellin' things—but mostly roses."

Mary's face lighted up.

"Do you like roses?" she said.

Ben Weatherstaff rooted up a weed and threw it aside before he answered.

"Well, yes, I do. I was learned that by a young lady I was gardener to. She had a lot in a place she was fond of, an' she loved 'em like they was children—or robins. I've seen her bend over an' kiss 'em." He dragged out another weed and scowled at it. "That were as much as ten year' ago."

"Where is she now?" asked Mary, much interested.

"Heaven," he answered, and drove his spade deep into the soil, "'cording to what parson says."

"What happened to the roses?" Mary asked again, more interested than ever.

"They was left to themselves."

Mary was becoming quite excited.

"Did they quite die? Do roses quite die when they are left to themselves?" she ventured.

"Well, I'd got to like 'em—an' I liked her—an' she liked 'em," Ben Weatherstaff admitted reluctantly. "Once or twice a year I'd go an' work at 'em a bit—prune 'em an' dig about th' roots. They run wild, but they was in rich soil, so some of 'em lived."

"When they have no leaves and look grey and brown and dry, how can you tell whether they are dead or alive?" inquired Mary.

"Wait till th' spring gets at 'em—wait till th' sun shines on th' rain an' th' rain falls on th' sunshine an' then tha'll find out."

"How—how?" cried Mary, forgetting to be careful.

"Look along th' twigs an' branches an' if tha' sees a bit of a brown lump swelling here an' there, watch it after th' warm rain an' see what happens." He stopped suddenly and looked curiously at her eager face. "Why does tha' care so much about roses an' such, all of a sudden?" he demanded.

Mistress Mary felt her face grow red. She was almost afraid to answer.

"I—I want to play that—that I have a garden of my own," she stammered. "I—there is nothing for me to do. I have nothing—and no one."

"Well," said Ben Weatherstaff slowly, as he watched her, "that's true. Tha' hasn't."

He said it in such an odd way that Mary wondered if he was actually a little sorry for her. She had never felt sorry for herself; she had only felt tired and cross, because she disliked people and things so much. But now the world seemed to be changing and getting nicer. If no one found out about the secret garden, she should enjoy herself always.

She stayed with him for ten or fifteen minutes longer and asked him as many questions as she dared. He answered every one of them in his queer grunting way and he did not seem really cross and did not pick up his spade and leave her. He said something about roses just as she was going away and it reminded her of the ones he had said he had been fond of.

"Do you go and see those other roses now?" she asked.

"Not been this year. My rheumatics has made me too stiff in th' joints."

He said it in his grumbling voice, and then quite suddenly he seemed to get angry with her, though she did not see why he should.

"Now look here!" he said sharply. "Don't tha' ask so many questions. Tha'rt th' worst wench for askin' questions I've ever come across. Get thee gone an' play thee. I've done talkin' for to-day."

And he said it so crossly that she knew there was not the least use in staying another minute. She went skipping slowly down the outside walk, thinking him over and saying to herself that, queer as it was, here was another person whom she liked in spite of his crossness. She liked old Ben Weatherstaff. Yes, she did like him. She always wanted to try to make him talk to her. Also she began to believe that he knew everything in the world about flowers.

There was a laurel-hedged walk which curved round the secret garden and ended at a gate which opened into a wood, in the park. She thought she would skip round this walk and look into the wood and see if there were any rabbits hopping about. She enjoyed the skipping very much and when she reached the little gate she opened it and went through because she heard a low, peculiar whistling sound and wanted to find out what it was.

It was a very strange thing indeed. She quite caught her breath as she stopped to look at it. A boy was sitting under a tree, with his back against it, playing on a rough wooden pipe. He was a funny looking boy about twelve. He looked very clean and his nose turned up and his cheeks were as red as poppies and never had Mistress Mary seen such round and such blue eyes in any boy's face. And on the trunk of the tree he leaned against, a brown squirrel was clinging and watching him, and from behind a bush near by a cock pheasant was delicately stretching his neck to peep out, and quite near him were two rabbits sitting up and sniffing with tremulous noses—and actually it appeared as if they were all drawing near to watch him and listen to the strange low little call his pipe seemed to make.

When he saw Mary he held up his hand and spoke to her in a voice almost as low as and rather like his piping.

"Don't tha' move," he said. "It'd flight 'em."*

Mary remained motionless. He stopped playing his pipe and began to rise from the ground. He moved so slowly that it scarcely seemed as though he were moving at all, but at last he stood on his feet and then the squirrel scampered back up into the branches of his tree, the pheasant withdrew his head and the rabbits dropped on all fours and began to hop away, though not at all as if they were frightened.

"I'm Dickon,"* the boy said. "I know tha'rt Miss Mary."

Then Mary realised that somehow she had known at first that he was Dickon. Who else could have been charming rabbits and pheasants as the natives charm snakes in India? He had a wide, red, curving mouth and his smile spread all over his face.

"I got up slow," he explained, "because if tha' makes a quick move it startles 'em. A body 'as to move gentle an' speak low when wild things is about."

He did not speak to her as if they had never seen each other before but as if he knew her quite well. Mary knew nothing about boys and she spoke to him a little stiffly because she felt rather shy.

"Did you get Martha's letter?" she asked.

He nodded his curly, rust-coloured head.

"That's why I come."

He stooped to pick up something which had been lying on the ground beside him when he piped.

"I've got th' garden tools. There's a little spade an' rake an' a fork an' hoe. Eh! they are good 'uns. There's a trowel, too. An' th' woman in th' shop threw in a packet o' white poppy an' one o' blue larkspur when I bought th' other seeds."

"Will you show the seeds to me?" Mary said.

She wished she could talk as he did. His speech was so quick and easy. It sounded as if he liked her and was not the least afraid she would not like him, though he was only a common moor boy, in patched clothes and with a funny face and a rough, rusty-red head. As she came closer to him she noticed that there was a clean fresh scent of heather and grass and leaves about him, almost as if he were made of them. She liked it very much and when she looked into his funny face with the red cheeks and round blue eyes she forgot that she had felt shy.

"Let us sit down on this log and look at them," she said.

They sat down and he took a clumsy little brown paper package out of his coat pocket. He untied the string and inside there were ever so many neater and smaller packages with a picture of a flower on each one.

"There's a lot o' mignonette an' poppies," he said "Mignonette's* th' sweetest smellin' thing as grows an' it'll grow wherever you cast it, same as poppies will. Them as'll come up an' bloom if you just whistle to 'em, them's th' nicest of all."

He stopped and turned his head quickly, his poppy-cheeked face lighting up.

"Where's that robin as is callin' us?" he said.

The chirp came from a thick holly bush, bright with scarlet berries, and Mary thought she knew whose it was.

"Is it really calling us?" she asked.

"Aye," said Dickon, as if it was the most natural thing in the world, "he's callin' some one he's friends with. That's same as sayin' 'Here I am. Look at me. I wants a bit of a chat.' There he is in the bush. Whose is he?"

"He's Ben Weatherstaff's, but I think he knows me a little," answered Mary.

"Aye, he knows thee," said Dickon in his low voice again. "An' he likes thee. He's took thee on. He'll tell me all about thee in a minute."

He moved quite close to the bush with the slow movement Mary had noticed before, and then he made a sound almost like the robin's own twitter. The robin listened a few seconds, intently, and then answered quite as if he were replying to a question.

"Aye, he's a friend o' yours," chuckled Dickon.

"Do you think he is?" cried Mary, eagerly. She did so want to know. "Do you think he really likes me?"

"He wouldn't come near thee if he didn't," answered Dickon. "Birds is rare choosers an' a robin can flout a body worse than a man. See, he's making up to thee now. 'Cannot tha' see a chap?' he's sayin'."

And it really seemed as if it must be true. He so sidled and twittered and tilted as he hopped on his bush.

"Do you understand everything birds say?" said Mary.

Dickon's grin spread until he seemed all wide, red, curving mouth, and he rubbed his rough head.

"I think I do, and they think I do," he said. "I've lived on th' moor with 'em so long. I've watched 'em break shell an' come out an' fledge an' learn to fly an' begin to sing, till I think I'm one of 'em. Sometimes I think p'raps I'm a bird, or a fox, or a rabbit, or a squirrel, or even a beetle, an' I don't know it."

He laughed and came back to the log and began to talk about the flower seeds again. He told her what they looked like when they were flowers; he told her how to plant them, and watch them, and feed and water them.

"See here," he said suddenly, turning round to look at her. "I'll plant them for thee myself. Where is tha' garden?"

Mary's thin hands clutched each other as they lay on her lap. She did not know what to say, so for a whole minute she said nothing. She had never thought of this. She felt miserable. And she felt as if she went red and then pale.

"Tha's got a bit o' garden, hasn't tha'?" Dickon said.

It was true that she had turned red and then pale. Dickon saw her do it, and as she still said nothing, he began to be puzzled.

"Wouldn't they give thee a bit?" he asked. "Hasn't tha' got any yet?"

She held her hands even tighter and turned her eyes toward him.

"I don't know anything about boys," she said slowly. "Could you keep a secret, if I told you one? It's a great secret. I don't know what I should do if any one found it out. I believe I should die!" She said the last sentence quite fiercely.

Dickon looked more puzzled than ever and even rubbed his hand over his rough head again, but he answered quite good-humouredly.

"I'm keepin' secrets all th' time," he said. "If I couldn't keep secrets from th' other lads, secrets about foxes' cubs, an' birds' nests, an' wild things' holes, there'd be naught safe on th' moor. Aye, I can keep secrets."

Mistress Mary did not mean to put out her hand and clutch his sleeve, but she did it.

"I've stolen a garden," she said very fast. "It isn't mine. It isn't anybody's. Nobody wants it, nobody cares for it, nobody ever goes into it. Perhaps everything is dead in it already; I don't know."

She began to feel hot and as contrary as she had ever felt in her life.

"I don't care, I don't care! Nobody has any right to take it from me when I care about it and they don't. They're letting it die, all shut in by itself," she ended passionately, and she threw her arms over her face and burst out crying—poor little Mistress Mary.

Dickon's curious blue eyes grew rounder and rounder.

"Eh-h-h!" he said, drawing his exclamation out slowly, and the way he did it meant both wonder and sympathy.

"I've nothing to do," said Mary. "Nothing belongs to me. I found it myself and I got into it myself. I was only just like the robin, and they wouldn't take it from the robin."

"Where is it?" asked Dickon in a dropped voice.

Mistress Mary got up from the log at once. She knew she felt contrary again, and obstinate, and she did not care at all. She was imperious and Indian, and at the same time hot and sorrowful.

"Come with me and I'll show you," she said.

She led him round the laurel path and to the walk where the ivy grew so thickly. Dickon followed her with a queer, almost pitying, look on his face. He felt as if he were being led to look at some strange bird's nest and must move softly. When she stepped to the wall and lifted the hanging ivy he started. There was a door and Mary pushed it slowly open and they passed in together, and then Mary stood and waved her hand round defiantly.

"It's this," she said. "It's a secret garden, and I'm the only one in the world who wants it to be alive."

Dickon looked round and round about it, and round and round again.

"Eh!" he almost whispered, "it is a queer, pretty place! It's like as if a body was in a dream."

CHAPTER XI

THE NEST OF THE MISSEL THRUSH*

FOR two or three minutes he stood looking round him, while Mary watched him, and then he began to walk about softly, even more lightly than Mary had walked the first time she had found herself inside the four walls. His eyes seemed to be taking in everything—the grey trees with the grey creepers climbing over them and hanging from their branches, the tangle on the walls and among the grass, the evergreen alcoves with the stone seats and tall flower urns standing in them.

"I never thought I'd see this place," he said at last in a whisper.

"Did you know about it?" asked Mary.

She had spoken aloud and he made a sign to her.

"We must talk low," he said, "or some one'll hear us an' wonder what's to do in here."

"Oh! I forgot!" said Mary, feeling frightened and putting her hand quickly against her mouth. "Did you know about the garden?" she asked again when she had recovered herself.

Dickon nodded.

"Martha told me there was one as no one ever went inside," he answered. "Us used to wonder what it was like."

He stopped and looked round at the lovely grey tangle about him, and his round eyes looked queerly happy.

"Eh! the nests as'll be here come springtime," he said. "It'd be th' safest nestin' place in England. No one never comin' near an' tangles o' trees an' roses to build in. I wonder all th' birds on th' moor don't build here."

Mistress Mary put her hand on his arm again without knowing it.

"Will there be roses?" she whispered. "Can you tell? I thought perhaps they were all dead."

"Eh! No! Not them—not all of 'em!" he answered. "Look here!"

He stepped over to the nearest tree—an old, old one with grey lichen all over its bark, but upholding a curtain of tangled sprays and branches. He took a thick knife out of his pocket and opened one of its blades.

"There's lots o' dead wood as ought to be cut out,"* he said. "An' there's a lot o' old wood, but it made some new last year. This here's a new bit," and he touched a shoot which looked brownish-green instead of hard, dry grey.

Mary touched it herself in an eager, reverent way.

"That one?" she said. "Is that one quite alive—quite?"

Dickon curved his wide smiling mouth.

"It's as wick as you or me," he said; and Mary remembered that Martha had told her that "wick" meant "alive" or "lively."

"I'm glad it's wick!" she cried out in her whisper. "I want them all to be wick. Let us go round the garden and count how many wick ones there are."

She quite panted with eagerness, and Dickon was as eager as she was. They went from tree to tree and from bush to bush. Dickon carried his knife in his hand and showed her things which she thought wonderful.

"They've run wild," he said, "but th' strongest ones has fair thrived on it. The delicatest ones has died out, but th' others has growed an' growed, an' spread and spread, till they's a wonder. See here!" and he pulled down a thick grey, dry-looking branch. "A body might think this was dead wood, but I don't believe it is—down to th' root. I'll cut it low down an' see."

He knelt and with his knife cut the lifeless-looking branch through, not far above the earth.

"There!" he said exultantly. "I told thee so. There's green in that wood yet. Look at it."

Mary was down on her knees before he spoke, gazing with all her might.

"When it looks a bit greenish an' juicy like that, it's wick," he explained. "When th' inside is dry an' breaks easy, like this here piece I've cut off, it's done for. There's a big root here as all this live wood sprung out of, an' if th' old wood's cut off an' it's dug round, an' took care of there'll be—" he stopped and lifted his face to look up at the climbing and hanging sprays above him—"there'll be a fountain o' roses here this summer."

They went from bush to bush and from tree to tree. He was very strong and clever with his knife and knew how to cut the dry and dead wood away, and could tell when an unpromising bough or twig had still green life in it. In the course of half an hour Mary thought she could tell too, and when he cut through a lifeless-looking branch she would cry out joyfully under her breath when she caught sight of the least shade of moist green. The spade, and hoe, and fork were very useful. He showed her how to use the fork while he dug about roots with the spade and stirred the earth and let the air in.

They were working industriously round one of the biggest standard roses when he caught sight of something which made him utter an exclamation of surprise.

"Why!" he cried, pointing to the grass a few feet away. "Who did that there?"

It was one of Mary's own little clearings round the pale green points.

"I did it," said Mary.

"Why, I thought tha' didn't know nothin' about gardenin'," he exclaimed.

"I don't," she answered, "but they were so little, and the grass was so thick and strong, and they looked as if they had no room to breathe. So I made a place for them. I don't even know what they are."

Dickon went and knelt down by them, smiling his wide smile.

"Tha' was right," he said. "A gardener couldn't have told thee better. They'll grow now like Jack's bean-stalk. They're crocuses an' snowdrops, an' these here is narcissuses," turning to another patch, "an' here's daffydowndillys. Eh! they will be a sight."

He ran from one clearing to another.

"Tha' has done a lot o' work for such a little wench," he said, looking her over.

"I'm growing fatter," said Mary, "and I'm growing stronger. I used always to be tired. When I dig I'm not tired at all. I like to smell the earth when it's turned up."

"It's rare good for thee," he said, nodding his head wisely. "There's naught as nice as th' smell o' good clean earth, except th' smell o' fresh growin' things when th' rain falls on 'em. I get out on th' moor many a day when it's rainin' an' I lie under a bush an' listen to th' soft swish o' drops on th' heather an' I just sniff an' sniff. My nose end fair quivers like a rabbit's, mother says."

"Do you never catch cold?" inquired Mary, gazing at him wonderingly. She had never seen such a funny boy, or such a nice one.

"Not me," he said, grinning. "I never ketched cold since I was born. I wasn't brought up nesh* enough. I've chased about th' moor in all weathers same as th' rabbits does. Mother says I've sniffed up too much fresh air for twelve year' to ever get to sniffin' with cold. I'm as tough as a white-thorn knobstick."*

He was working all the time he was talking and Mary was following him and helping him with her fork or the trowel.

"There's a lot of work to do here!" he said once, looking about quite exultantly.

"Will you come again and help me to do it?" Mary begged. "I'm sure I can help, too. I can dig and pull up weeds, and do whatever you tell me. Oh! do come, Dickon!"

"I'll come every day if tha' wants me, rain or shine," he answered stoutly. "It's th' best fun I ever had in my life—shut in here an' wakenin' up a garden."

"If you will come," said Mary, "if you will help me to make it alive I'll—I don't know what I'll do," she ended helplessly. What could you do for a boy like that?

"I'll tell thee what tha'll do," said Dickon, with his happy grin. "Tha'll get fat an' tha'll get as hungry as a young fox an' tha'll learn how to talk to th' robin same as I do. Eh! we'll have a lot o' fun."

He began to walk about, looking up in the trees and at the walls and bushes with a thoughtful expression.

"I wouldn't want to make it look like a gardener's garden, all clipped an' spick an' span, would you?" he said. "It's nicer like this with things runnin' wild, an' swingin' an' catchin' hold of each other."

"Don't let us make it tidy," said Mary anxiously. "It wouldn't seem like a secret garden if it was tidy."

Dickon stood rubbing his rusty-red head with a rather puzzled look.

"It's a secret garden sure enough," he said, "but seems like some one besides th' robin must have been in it since it was shut up ten year' ago."

"But the door was locked and the key was buried," said Mary. "No one could get in."

"That's true," he answered. "It's a queer place. Seems to me as if there'd been a bit o' prunin' done here an' there, later than ten year' ago."

"But how could it have been done?" said Mary.

He was examining a branch of a standard rose and he shook his head.

"Aye! how could it!" he murmured. "With th' door locked an' th' key buried."

Mistress Mary always felt that however many years she lived she should never forget that first morning when her garden began to grow. Of course, it did seem to begin to grow for her that morning. When Dickon began to clear places to plant seeds, she remembered what Basil had sung at her when he wanted to tease her.

"Are there any flowers that look like bells?" she inquired.

"Lilies o' th' valley does," he answered, digging away with the trowel, "an' there's Canterbury bells, an' campanulas."*

"Let us plant some," said Mary.

"There's lilies o' th' valley here already; I saw 'em. They'll have growed too close an' we'll have to separate 'em, but there's plenty. Th' other ones take two years to bloom from seed, but I can bring you some bits o' plants from our cottage garden. Why does tha' want 'em?"

Then Mary told him about Basil and his brothers and sisters in India and of how she had hated them and of their calling her "Mistress Mary Quite Contrary."

"They used to dance round and sing at me. They sang—

> 'Mistress Mary, quite contrary,
>   How does your garden grow?
> With silver bells and cockle shells,
>   And marigolds all in a row.'

I just remembered it and it made me wonder if there were really flowers like silver bells."

She frowned a little and gave her trowel a rather spiteful dig into the earth.

"I wasn't as contrary as they were."

But Dickon laughed.

"Eh!" he said, and as he crumbled the rich black soil she saw he was sniffing up the scent of it, "there doesn't seem to be no need for no one to be contrary when there's flowers an' such like, an' such lots o' friendly wild things runnin' about makin' homes for themselves, or buildin' nests an' singin' an' whistlin', does there?"

Mary, kneeling by him holding the seeds, looked at him and stopped frowning.

"Dickon," she said. "You are as nice as Martha said you were. I like you, and you make the fifth person. I never thought I should like five people."

Dickon sat up on his heels as Martha did when she was polishing the grate. He did look funny and delightful, Mary thought, with his round blue eyes and red cheeks and happy looking turned-up nose.

"Only five folk as tha' likes?" he said. "Who is th' other four?"

"Your mother and Martha," Mary checked them off on her fingers, "and the robin and Ben Weatherstaff."

Dickon laughed so that he was obliged to stifle the sound by putting his arm over his mouth.

"I know tha' thinks I'm a queer lad," he said, "but I think tha' art th' queerest little lass I ever saw."

Then Mary did a strange thing. She leaned forward and asked him a question she had never dreamed of asking any one before. And she tried to ask it in Yorkshire because that was his language, and in India a native was always pleased if you knew his speech.

"Does tha' like me?" she said.

"Eh!" he answered heartily, "that I does. I likes thee wonderful, an' so does th' robin, I do believe!"

"That's two, then," said Mary. "That's two for me."

And then they began to work harder than ever and more joyfully. Mary was startled and sorry when she heard the big clock in the courtyard strike the hour of her midday dinner.

"I shall have to go," she said mournfully. "And you will have to go too, won't you?"

Dickon grinned.

"My dinner's easy to carry about with me," he said. "Mother always lets me put a bit o' somethin' in my pocket."

He picked up his coat from the grass and brought out of a pocket a lumpy little bundle tied up in a quite clean, coarse, blue and white handkerchief. It held two thick pieces of bread with a slice of something laid between them.

"It's oftenest naught but bread," he said, "but I've got a fine slice o' fat bacon with it to-day."

Mary thought it looked a queer dinner, but he seemed ready to enjoy it.

"Run on an' get thy victuals," he said. "I'll be done with mine first. I'll get some more work done before I start back home."

He sat down with his back against a tree.

"I'll call th' robin up," he said, "and give him th' rind o' th' bacon to peck at. They likes a bit o' fat wonderful."

Mary could scarcely bear to leave him. Suddenly it seemed as if he might be a sort of wood fairy who might be gone when she came into the garden again. He seemed too good to be true. She went slowly half-way to the door in the wall and then she stopped and went back.

"Whatever happens, you—you never would tell?" she said.

His poppy-coloured cheeks were distended with his first big bite of bread and bacon, but he managed to smile encouragingly.

"If tha' was a missel thrush an' showed me where thy nest was, does tha' think I'd tell any one? Not me," he said. "Tha' art as safe as a missel thrush."

And she was quite sure she was.

CHAPTER XII

"MIGHT I HAVE A BIT OF EARTH?"

MARY ran so fast that she was rather out of breath when she reached her room. Her hair was ruffled on her forehead and her cheeks were bright pink. Her dinner was waiting on the table, and Martha was waiting near it.

"Tha's a bit late," she said. "Where has tha' been?"

"I've seen Dickon!" said Mary. "I've seen Dickon!"

"I knew he'd come," said Martha exultantly. "How does tha' like him?"

"I think—I think he's beautiful!" said Mary in a determined voice.

Martha looked rather taken aback, but she looked pleased, too.

"Well," she said, "he's th' best lad as ever was born, but us never thought he was handsome. His nose turns up too much."

"I like it to turn up," said Mary.

"An' his eyes is so round," said Martha, a trifle doubtful. "Though they're a nice colour."

"I like them round," said Mary. "And they are exactly the colour of the sky over the moor."

Martha beamed with satisfaction.

"Mother says he made 'em that colour with always lookin' up at th' birds an' th' clouds. But he has got a big mouth, hasn't he, now?"

"I love his big mouth," said Mary obstinately. "I wish mine were just like it."

Martha chuckled delightedly.

"It'd look rare an' funny in thy bit of a face," she said. "But I knowed it would be that way when tha' saw him. How did tha' like th' seeds an' th' garden tools?"

"How did you know he brought them?" asked Mary.

"Eh! I never thought of him not bringin' 'em. He'd be sure to bring 'em if they was in Yorkshire. He's such a trusty lad."

Mary was afraid that she might begin to ask difficult questions, but she did not. She was very much interested in the seeds and gardening tools, and there was only one moment when Mary was frightened. This was when she began to ask where the flowers were to be planted.

"Who did tha' ask about it?" she inquired.

"I haven't asked anybody yet," said Mary, hesitating.

"Well, I wouldn't ask th' head gardener. He's too grand, Mr. Roach is."

"I've never seen him," said Mary. "I've only seen under-gardeners and Ben Weatherstaff."

"If I was you, I'd ask Ben Weatherstaff," advised Martha. "He's not half as bad as he looks, for all he's so crabbed. Mr. Craven lets him do what he likes because he was here when Mrs. Craven was alive, an' he used to make her laugh. She liked him. Perhaps he'd find you a corner somewhere out o' the way."

"If it was out of the way and no one wanted it, no one *could* mind my having it, could they?" Mary said anxiously.

"There wouldn't be no reason," answered Martha. "You wouldn't do no harm."

Mary ate her dinner as quickly as she could, and when she rose from the table she was going to run to her room to put on her hat again, but Martha stopped her.

"I've got somethin' to tell you," she said. "I thought I'd let you eat your dinner first. Mr. Craven came back this mornin' and I think he wants to see you."

Mary turned quite pale.

"Oh!" she said. "Why! Why! He didn't want to see me when I came. I heard Pitcher say he didn't."

"Well," explained Martha, "Mrs. Medlock says it's because o' mother. She was walkin' to Thwaite village an' she met him. She'd never spoke to him before, but Mrs. Craven had been to our cottage two or three times. He'd forgot, but mother hadn't, an' she made bold to stop him. I don't know what she said to him about you, but she said somethin' as put him in th' mind to see you before he goes away again, to-morrow."

"Oh!" cried Mary, "is he going away to-morrow? I'm so glad!"

"He's goin' for a long time. He mayn't come back till autumn or winter. He's goin' to travel in foreign places. He's always doin' it."

"Oh! I'm so glad—so glad!" said Mary thankfully.

If he did not come back until winter, or even autumn, there would be time to watch the secret garden come alive. Even if he found out then and took it away from her she would have had that much at least.

"When do you think he will want to see—"

She did not finish the sentence, because the door opened, and Mrs. Medlock walked in. She had on her best black dress and cap, and her collar was fastened with a large brooch with a picture of a man's face on it. It was a coloured photograph* of Mr. Medlock, who had died years ago, and she always wore it when she was dressed up. She looked nervous and excited.

"Your hair's rough," she said quickly. "Go and brush it. Martha, help her to slip on her best dress. Mr. Craven sent me to bring her to him in his study."

All the pink left Mary's cheeks. Her heart began to thump and she felt herself changing into a stiff, plain, silent child again. She did not even answer Mrs. Medlock, but turned and walked into her bedroom, followed by Martha. She said nothing while her dress was changed, and her hair brushed, and after she was quite tidy she followed Mrs. Medlock down the corridors, in silence. What was there for her to say? She was obliged to go and see Mr. Craven, and he would not like her, and she would not like him. She knew what he would think of her.

She was taken to a part of the house she had not been into before. At last Mrs. Medlock knocked at a door, and when some one said, "Come in," they entered the room together. A man was sitting in an armchair before the fire, and Mrs. Medlock spoke to him.

"This is Miss Mary, sir," she said.

"You can go and leave her here. I will ring for you when I want you to take her away," said Mr. Craven.

When she went out and closed the door, Mary could only stand waiting, a plain little thing, twisting her thin hands together. She could see that the man in the chair was not so much a hunchback as a man with high, rather crooked shoulders, and he had black hair streaked with white. He turned his head over his high shoulders and spoke to her.

"Come here!" he said.

Mary went to him.

He was not ugly. His face would have been handsome if it had not been so miserable. He looked as if the sight of her worried and fretted him and as if he did not know what in the world to do with her.

"Are you well?" he asked.

"Yes," answered Mary.

"Do they take good care of you?"

"Yes."

He rubbed his forehead fretfully as he looked her over.

"You are very thin," he said.

"I am getting fatter," Mary answered in what she knew was her stiffest way.

What an unhappy face he had! His black eyes seemed as if they scarcely saw her, as if they were seeing something else, and he could hardly keep his thoughts upon her.

"I forgot you," he said. "How could I remember you? I intended to send you a governess or a nurse or some one of that sort, but I forgot."

"Please," began Mary. "Please—" and then the lump in her throat choked her.

"What do you want to say?" he inquired.

"I am—I am too big for a nurse," said Mary. "And please—please don't make me have a governess yet."

He rubbed his forehead again and stared at her.

"That was what the Sowerby woman said," he muttered absent-mindedly.

Then Mary gathered a scrap of courage.

"Is she—is she Martha's mother?" she stammered.

"Yes, I think so," he replied.

"She knows about children," said Mary. "She has twelve. She knows."

He seemed to rouse himself.

"What do you want to do?"

"I want to play out of doors," Mary answered, hoping that her voice did not tremble. "I never liked it in India. It makes me hungry here, and I am getting fatter."

He was watching her.

"Mrs. Sowerby said it would do you good. Perhaps it will," he said. "She thought you had better get stronger before you had a governess."

"It makes me feel strong when I play and the wind comes over the moor," argued Mary.

"Where do you play?" he asked next.

"Everywhere," gasped Mary. "Martha's mother sent me a skipping-rope. I skip and run—and I look about to see if things are beginning to stick up out of the earth. I don't do any harm."

"Don't look so frightened," he said in a worried voice. "You could not do any harm, a child like you! You may do what you like."

Mary put her hand up to her throat because she was afraid he might see the excited lump which she felt jump into it. She came a step nearer to him.

"May I?" she said tremulously.

Her anxious little face seemed to worry him more than ever.

"Don't look so frightened," he exclaimed. "Of course you may. I am your guardian, though I am a poor one for any child. I cannot give you time or attention. I am too ill, and wretched and distracted; but I wish you to be happy and comfortable. I don't know anything about children, but Mrs. Medlock is to see that you have all you need. I sent for you to-day because Mrs. Sowerby said I ought to see you. Her daughter had talked about you. She thought you needed fresh air and freedom and running about."

"She knows all about children," Mary said again in spite of herself.

"She ought to," said Mr. Craven. "I thought her rather bold to stop me on the moor, but she said—Mrs. Craven had been kind to her." It seemed hard for him to speak his dead wife's name. "She is a respectable woman. Now I have seen you I think she said sensible things. Play out of doors as much as you like. It's a big place, and you may go where you like and amuse yourself as you like. Is there anything you want?" as if a sudden thought had struck him. "Do you want toys, books, dolls?"

"Might I," quavered Mary, "might I have a bit of earth?"

In her eagerness she did not realise how queer the words would sound and that they were not the ones she had meant to say. Mr. Craven looked quite startled.

"Earth!" he repeated. "What do you mean?"

"To plant seeds in—to make things grow—to see them come alive," Mary faltered.

He gazed at her a moment and then passed his hand quickly over his eyes.

"Do you—care about gardens so much?" he said slowly.

"I didn't know about them in India," said Mary. "I was always ill and tired, and it was too hot. I sometimes made little beds in the sand and stuck flowers in them. But here it is different."

Mr. Craven got up and began to walk slowly across the room.

"A bit of earth," he said to himself, and Mary thought that some-how she must have reminded him of something. When he stopped and spoke to her his dark eyes looked almost soft and kind.

"You can have as much earth as you want," he said. "You remind me of some one else who loved the earth and things that grow. When you see a bit of earth you want," with something like a smile, "take it, child, and make it come alive."

"May I take it from anywhere—if it's not wanted?"

"Anywhere," he answered. "There! You must go now, I am tired." He touched the bell to call Mrs. Medlock. "Good-bye. I shall be away all summer."

Mrs. Medlock came so quickly that Mary thought she must have been waiting in the corridor.

"Mrs. Medlock," Mr. Craven said to her, "now I have seen the child I understand what Mrs. Sowerby meant. She must be less deli-cate before she begins lessons. Give her simple, healthy food. Let her run wild in the garden. Don't look after her too much. She needs liberty and fresh air and romping about. Mrs. Sowerby is to come and see her now and then, and she may sometimes go to the cottage."

Mrs. Medlock looked pleased. She was relieved to hear that she need not "look after" Mary too much. She had felt her a tiresome charge, and had, indeed, seen as little of her as she dared. In addition to this she was fond of Martha's mother.

"Thank you, sir," she said. "Susan Sowerby and me went to school together, and she's as sensible and good-hearted a woman as you'd find in a day's walk. I never had any children myself and she's had twelve, and there never was healthier or better ones. Miss Mary can get no harm from them. I'd always take Susan Sowerby's advice about children myself. She's what you might call healthy-minded—if you understand me."

"I understand," Mr. Craven answered. "Take Miss Mary away now and send Pitcher to me."

When Mrs. Medlock left her at the end of her own corridor Mary flew back to her room. She found Martha waiting there. Martha had, in fact, hurried back after she had removed the dinner service.

"I can have my garden!" cried Mary. "I may have it where I like! I am not going to have a governess for a long time! Your mother is coming to see me and I may go to your cottage! He says a little girl like me could not do any harm and I may do what I like—anywhere!"

"Eh!" said Martha delightedly, "that was nice of him, wasn't it?"

"Martha," said Mary solemnly, "he is really a nice man, only his face is so miserable and his forehead is all drawn together."

She ran as quickly as she could to the garden. She had been away so much longer than she had thought she should, and she knew Dickon would have to set out early on his five-mile walk. When she slipped through the door under the ivy, she saw he was not working where she had left him. The gardening tools were laid together under a tree. She ran to them, looking all round the place, but there was no Dickon to be seen. He had gone away and the secret garden was empty—except for the robin, who had just flown across the wall and sat on a standard rose-bush watching her.

"He's gone," she said wofully. "Oh! was he—was he—was he only a wood fairy?"

Something white fastened to the standard rose-bush caught her eye. It was a piece of paper—in fact, it was a piece of the letter she had printed for Martha to send to Dickon. It was fastened on the bush with a long thorn, and in a minute she knew Dickon had left it there. There were some roughly printed letters on it and a sort of picture. At first she could not tell what it was. Then she saw it was meant for a nest with a bird sitting on it. Underneath were the printed letters, and they said:

"I will cum bak."

CHAPTER XIII

"I AM COLIN"

MARY took the picture back to the house when she went to her supper and she showed it to Martha.

"Eh!" said Martha with great pride. "I never knew our Dickon was as clever as that. That there's a picture of a missel thrush on her nest, as large as life an' twice as natural."

Then Mary knew Dickon had meant the picture to be a message. He had meant that she might be sure he would keep her secret. Her garden was her nest and she was like a missel thrush. Oh, how she did like that queer, common boy!

She hoped he would come back the very next day and she fell asleep looking forward to the morning.

But you never know what the weather will do in Yorkshire, particularly in the springtime. She was awakened in the night by the sound of rain beating with heavy drops against her window. It was pouring down in torrents and the wind was "wuthering" round the corners and in the chimneys of the huge old house. Mary sat up in bed and felt miserable and angry.

"The rain is as contrary as I ever was," she said. "It came because it knew I did not want it."

She threw herself back on her pillow and buried her face. She did not cry, but she lay and hated the sound of the heavily beating rain, she hated the wind and its "wuthering." She could not go to sleep again. The mournful sound kept her awake because she felt mournful herself. If she had felt happy it would probably have lulled her to sleep. How it "wuthered" and how the big rain-drops poured down and beat against the pane!

"It sounds just like a person lost on the moor and wandering on and on crying,"* she said.

She had been lying awake turning from side to side for about an hour, when suddenly something made her sit up in bed and turn her head toward the door listening. She listened and she listened.

"It isn't the wind now," she said in a loud whisper. "That isn't the wind. It is different. It is that crying I heard before."

The door of her room was ajar and the sound came down the corridor, a far-off faint sound of fretful crying. She listened for a few minutes and each minute she became more and more sure. She felt as if she must find out what it was. It seemed even stranger than the secret garden and the buried key. Perhaps the fact that she was in a rebellious mood made her bold. She put her foot out of bed and stood on the floor.

"I am going to find out what it is," she said. "Everybody is in bed and I don't care about Mrs. Medlock—I don't care!"

There was a candle by her bedside and she took it up and went softly out of the room. The corridor looked very long and dark, but she was too excited to mind that. She thought she remembered the corners she must turn to find the short corridor with the door covered with tapestry—the one Mrs. Medlock had come through the day she lost herself. The sound had come up that passage. So she went on with her dim light, almost feeling her way, her heart beating so loud that she fancied she could hear it. The far-off faint crying went on and led her. Sometimes it stopped for a moment or so and then began again. Was this the right corner to turn? She stopped and thought. Yes, it was. Down this passage and then to the left, and then up two broad steps, and then to the right again. Yes, there was the tapestry door.

She pushed it open very gently and closed it behind her, and she stood in the corridor and could hear the crying quite plainly, though it was not loud. It was on the other side of the wall at her left and a few yards farther on there was a door. She could see a glimmer of light coming from beneath it. The Someone was crying in that room, and it was quite a young Someone.

So she walked to the door and pushed it open, and there she was standing in the room!

It was a big room with ancient, handsome furniture in it. There was a low fire glowing faintly on the hearth and a night light burning by the side of a carved four-posted bed hung with brocade, and on the bed was lying a boy, crying fretfully.

Mary wondered if she was in a real place or if she had fallen asleep again and was dreaming without knowing it.

The boy had a sharp, delicate face the colour of ivory and he seemed to have eyes too big for it. He had also a lot of hair which tumbled over his forehead in heavy locks and made his thin face seem smaller. He looked like a boy who had been ill, but he was crying more as if he were tired and cross than as if he were in pain.

Mary stood near the door with her candle in her hand, holding her breath. Then she crept across the room, and as she drew nearer the light attracted the boy's attention and he turned his head on his pillow and stared at her, his grey eyes opening so wide that they seemed immense.

"Who are you?" he said at last in a half-frightened whisper. "Are you a ghost?"

"No, I am not," Mary answered, her own whisper sounding half frightened. "Are you one?"

He stared and stared and stared. Mary could not help noticing what strange eyes he had. They were agate grey and they looked too big for his face because they had black lashes all round them.

"No," he replied after waiting a moment or so. "I am Colin."

"Who is Colin?" she faltered.

"I am Colin Craven. Who are you?"

"I am Mary Lennox. Mr. Craven is my uncle."

"He is my father," said the boy.

"Your father!" gasped Mary. "No one ever told me he had a boy! Why didn't they?"

"Come here," he said, still keeping his strange eyes fixed on her with an anxious expression.

She came close to the bed and he put out his hand and touched her.

"You are real, aren't you?" he said. "I have such real dreams very often. You might be one of them."

Mary had slipped on a woollen wrapper before she left her room and she put a piece of it between his fingers.

"Rub that and see how thick and warm it is," she said. "I will pinch you a little if you like, to show you how real I am. For a minute I thought you might be a dream, too."

"Where did you come from?" he asked.

"From my own room. The wind wuthered so I couldn't go to sleep and I heard some one crying and wanted to find out who it was. What were you crying for?"

"Because I couldn't go to sleep either and my head ached. Tell me your name again."

"Mary Lennox. Did no one ever tell you I had come to live here?"

He was still fingering the fold of her wrapper, but he began to look a little more as if he believed in her reality.

"No," he answered. "They daren't."

"Why?" asked Mary.

"Because I should have been afraid you would see me. I won't let people see me and talk me over."

"Why?" Mary asked again, feeling more mystified every moment.

"Because I am like this always, ill and having to lie down. My father won't let people talk me over either. The servants are not allowed to speak about me. If I live I may be a hunchback, but I shan't live. My father hates to think I may be like him."

"Oh, what a queer house this is!" Mary said. "What a queer house! Everything is a kind of secret. Rooms are locked up and gardens are locked up—and you! Have you been locked up?"

"No. I stay in this room because I don't want to be moved out of it. It tires me too much."

"Does your father come and see you?" Mary ventured.

"Sometimes. Generally when I am asleep. He doesn't want to see me."*

"Why?" Mary could not help asking again.

A sort of angry shadow passed over the boy's face.

"My mother died when I was born and it makes him wretched to look at me. He thinks I don't know, but I've heard people talking. He almost hates me."

"He hates the garden, because she died," said Mary half speaking to herself.

"What garden?" the boy asked.

"Oh! just—just a garden she used to like," Mary stammered. "Have you been here always?"

"Nearly always. Sometimes I have been taken to places at the seaside, but I won't stay because people stare at me. I used to wear an iron thing to keep my back straight, but a grand doctor came from London to see me and said it was stupid. He told them to take it off and keep me out in the fresh air.* I hate fresh air and I don't want to go out."

"I didn't when first I came here," said Mary. "Why do you keep looking at me like that?"

"Because of the dreams that are so real," he answered rather fretfully. "Sometimes when I open my eyes I don't believe I'm awake."

"We're both awake," said Mary. She glanced round the room with its high ceiling and shadowy corners and dim firelight. "It looks quite like a dream, and it's the middle of the night, and everybody in the house is asleep—everybody but us. We are wide awake."

"I don't want it to be a dream," the boy said restlessly.

Mary thought of something all at once.

"If you don't like people to see you," she began, "do you want me to go away?"

He still held the fold of her wrapper and he gave it a little pull.

"No," he said. "I should be sure you were a dream if you went. If you are real, sit down on that big footstool and talk. I want to hear about you."

Mary put down her candle on the table near the bed and sat down on the cushioned stool. She did not want to go away at all. She wanted to stay in the mysterious hidden-away room and talk to the mysterious boy.

"What do you want me to tell you?" she said.

He wanted to know how long she had been at Misselthwaite; he wanted to know which corridor her room was on; he wanted to know what she had been doing; if she disliked the moor as he disliked it; where she had lived before she came to Yorkshire. She answered all these questions and many more and he lay back on his pillow and listened. He made her tell him a great deal about India and about her voyage across the ocean. She found out that because he had been an invalid he had not learned things as other children had. One of his nurses had taught him to read when he was quite little and he was always reading and looking at pictures in splendid books.

Though his father rarely saw him when he was awake, he was given all sorts of wonderful things to amuse himself with. He never seemed to have been amused, however. He could have anything he asked for and was never made to do anything he did not like to do.

"Everyone is obliged to do what pleases me," he said indifferently. "It makes me ill to be angry. No one believes I shall live to grow up."

He said it as if he was so accustomed to the idea that it had ceased to matter to him at all. He seemed to like the sound of Mary's voice. As she went on talking he listened in a drowsy interested way. Once or twice she wondered if he were not gradually falling into a doze. But at last he asked a question which opened up a new subject.

"How old are you?" he asked.

"I am ten," answered Mary, forgetting herself for the moment, "and so are you."

"How do you know that?" he demanded in a surprised voice.

"Because when you were born the garden door was locked and the key was buried. And it has been locked for ten years."

Colin half sat up, turning toward her, leaning on his elbows.

"What garden door was locked? Who did it? Where was the key buried?" he exclaimed as if he were suddenly very much interested.

"It—it was the garden Mr. Craven hates," said Mary nervously. "He locked the door. No one—no one knew where he buried the key."

"What sort of a garden is it?" Colin persisted eagerly.

"No one has been allowed to go into it for ten years," was Mary's careful answer.

But it was too late to be careful. He was too much like herself. He too had had nothing to think about and the idea of a hidden garden attracted him as it had attracted her. He asked question after question. Where was it? Had she never looked for the door? Had she never asked the gardeners?"

"They won't talk about it," said Mary. "I think they have been told not to answer questions."

"I would make them," said Colin.

"Could you?" Mary faltered, beginning to feel frightened. If he could make people answer questions, who knew what might happen!

"Every one is obliged to please me. I told you that," he said. "If I were to live, this place would some time belong to me. They all know that. I would make them tell me."

Mary had not known that she herself had been spoiled, but she could see quite plainly that this mysterious boy had been. He thought that the whole world belonged to him. How peculiar he was and how coolly he spoke of not living.

"Do you think you won't live?" she asked, partly because she was curious and partly in hope of making him forget the garden.

"I don't suppose I shall," he answered as indifferently as he had spoken before. "Ever since I remember anything I have heard people say I shan't. At first they thought I was too little to understand and now they think I don't hear. But I do. My doctor is my father's cousin. He is quite poor and if I die he will have all Misselthwaite when my father is dead. I should think he wouldn't want me to live."

"Do you want to live?" inquired Mary.

"No," he answered, in a cross, tired fashion. "But I don't want to die. When I feel ill I lie here and think about it until I cry and cry."

"I have heard you crying three times," Mary said, "but I did not know who it was. Were you crying about that?" She did so want him to forget the garden.

"I dare say," he answered. "Let us talk about something else. Talk about that garden. Don't you want to see it?"

"Yes," answered Mary in quite a low voice.

"I do," he went on persistently. "I don't think I ever really wanted to see anything before, but I want to see that garden. I want the key dug up. I want the door unlocked. I would let them take me there in my chair. That would be getting fresh air. I am going to make them open the door."

He had become quite excited and his strange eyes began to shine like stars and looked more immense than ever.

"They have to please me," he said. "I will make them take me there and I will let you go, too."

Mary's hands clutched each other. Everything would be spoiled—everything! Dickon would never come back. She would never again feel like a missel thrush with a safe-hidden nest.

"Oh, don't—don't—don't—don't do that!" she cried out.

He stared as if he thought she had gone crazy!

"Why?" he exclaimed. "You said you wanted to see it."

"I do," she answered almost with a sob in her throat, "but if you make them open the door and take you in like that it will never be a secret again."

He leaned still farther forward.

"A secret," he said. "What do you mean? Tell me."

Mary's words almost tumbled over one another.

"You see—you see," she panted, "if no one knows but ourselves—if there was a door, hidden somewhere under the ivy—if there was—and we could find it; and if we could slip through it together and shut it behind us, and no one knew any one was inside and we called it our garden and pretended that—that we were missel thrushes and it was our nest, and if we played there almost every day and dug and planted seeds and made it all come alive—"

"Is it dead?" he interrupted her.

"It soon will be if no one cares for it," she went on. "The bulbs will live but the roses—"

He stopped her again as excited as she was herself.

"What are bulbs?" he put in quickly.

"They are daffodils and lilies and snowdrops. They are working in the earth now—pushing up pale green points because the spring is coming."

"Is the spring coming?" he said. "What is it like? You don't see it in rooms if you are ill."

"It is the sun shining on the rain and the rain falling on the sunshine, and things pushing up and working under the earth," said Mary. "If the garden was a secret and we could get into it we could watch the things grow bigger every day, and see how many roses are alive. Don't you see? Oh, don't you see how much nicer it would be if it was a secret?"

He dropped back on his pillow and lay there with an odd expression on his face.

"I never had a secret," he said, "except that one about not living to grow up. They don't know I know that, so it is a sort of secret. But I like this kind better."

"If you won't make them take you to the garden," pleaded Mary, "perhaps—I feel almost sure I can find out how to get in sometime. And then—if the doctor wants you to go out in your chair, and if you can always do what you want to do, perhaps—perhaps we might find some boy who would push you, and we could go alone and it would always be a secret garden."

"I should—like—that," he said very slowly, his eyes looking dreamy. "I should like that. I should not mind fresh air in a secret garden."

Mary began to recover her breath and feel safer because the idea of keeping the secret seemed to please him. She felt almost sure that if she kept on talking and could make him see the garden in his mind as she had seen it he would like it so much that he could not bear to think that everybody might tramp into it when they chose.

"I'll tell you what I *think* it would be like, if we could go into it," she said. "It has been shut up so long things have grown into a tangle perhaps."

He lay quite still and listened while she went on talking about the roses which *might* have clambered from tree to tree and hung down—about the many birds which *might* have built their nests there because it was so safe. And then she told him about the robin and Ben Weatherstaff, and there was so much to tell about the robin and it was so easy and safe to talk about it that she ceased to feel afraid. The robin pleased him so much that he smiled until he looked almost beautiful, and at first Mary had thought that he was even plainer than herself, with his big eyes and heavy locks of hair.

"I did not know birds could be like that," he said. "But if you stay in a room you never see things. What a lot of things you know. I feel as if you had been inside that garden."

She did not know what to say, so she did not say anything. He evidently did not expect an answer and the next moment he gave her a surprise.

"I am going to let you look at something," he said. "Do you see that rose-coloured silk curtain hanging on the wall over the mantelpiece?"

Mary had not noticed it before, but she looked up and saw it. It was a curtain of soft silk hanging over what seemed to be some picture.

"Yes," she answered.

"There is a cord hanging from it," said Colin. "Go and pull it."

Mary got up, much mystified, and found the cord. When she pulled it the silk curtain ran back on rings and when it ran back it uncovered a picture. It was the picture of a girl with a laughing face. She had bright hair tied up with a blue ribbon and her gay, lovely eyes were exactly like Colin's unhappy ones, agate grey and looking twice as big as they really were because of the black lashes all round them.

"She is my mother," said Colin complainingly. "I don't see why she died. Sometimes I hate her for doing it."

"How queer!" said Mary.

"If she had lived I believe I should not have been ill always," he grumbled. "I dare say I should have lived, too. And my father would not have hated to look at me. I dare say I should have had a strong back. Draw the curtain again."

Mary did as she was told and returned to her foot-stool.

"She is much prettier than you," she said, "but her eyes are just like yours—at least they are the same shape and colour. Why is the curtain drawn over her?"

He moved uncomfortably.

"I made them do it," he said. "Sometimes I don't like to see her looking at me. She smiles too much when I am ill and miserable. Besides, she is mine and I don't want every one to see her."

There were a few moments of silence and then Mary spoke.

"What would Mrs. Medlock do if she found out that I had been here?" she inquired.

"She would do as I told her to do," he answered. "And I should tell her that I wanted you to come here and talk to me every day. I am glad you came."

"So am I," said Mary. "I will come as often as I can, but"—she hesitated—"I shall have to look every day for the garden door."

"Yes, you must," said Colin, "and you can tell me about it afterward."

He lay thinking a few minutes, as he had done before, and then he spoke again.

"I think you shall be a secret, too," he said. "I will not tell them until they find out. I can always send the nurse out of the room and say that I want to be by myself. Do you know Martha?"

"Yes, I know her very well," said Mary. "She waits on me."

He nodded his head toward the outer corridor.

"She is the one who is asleep in the other room. The nurse went away yesterday to stay all night with her sister and she always makes Martha attend to me when she wants to go out. Martha shall tell you when to come here."

Then Mary understood Martha's troubled look when she had asked questions about the crying.

"Martha knew about you all the time?" she said.

"Yes; she often attends to me. The nurse likes to get away from me and then Martha comes."

"I have been here a long time," said Mary. "Shall I go away now? Your eyes look sleepy."

"I wish I could go to sleep before you leave me," he said rather shyly.

"Shut your eyes," said Mary, drawing her footstool closer, "and I will do what my Ayah used to do in India. I will pat your hand and stroke it and sing something quite low."

"I should like that perhaps," he said drowsily.

Somehow she was sorry for him and did not want him to lie awake, so she leaned against the bed and began to stroke and pat his hand and sing a very low little chanting song in Hindustani.*

"That is nice," he said more drowsily still, and she went on chanting and stroking, but when she looked at him again his black lashes were lying close against his cheeks, for his eyes were shut and he was fast asleep. So she got up softly, took her candle and crept away without making a sound.

CHAPTER XIV

A YOUNG RAJAH*

THE moor was hidden in mist when the morning came and the rain had not stopped pouring down. There could be no going out of doors. Martha was so busy that Mary had no opportunity of talking to her, but in the afternoon she asked her to come and sit with her in the nursery. She came bringing the stocking she was always knitting when she was doing nothing else.

"What's the matter with thee?" she asked as soon as they sat down. "Tha' looks as if tha'd somethin' to say."

"I have. I have found out what the crying was," said Mary.

Martha let her knitting drop on her knee and gazed at her with startled eyes.

"Tha' hasn't!" she exclaimed. "Never!"

"I heard it in the night," Mary went on. "And I got up and went to see where it came from. It was Colin. I found him."

Martha's face became red with fright.

"Eh! Miss Mary!" she said half crying. "Tha' shouldn't have done it—tha' shouldn't! Tha'll get me in trouble. I never told thee nothin' about him—but tha'll get me in trouble. I shall lose my place and what'll mother do!"

"You won't lose your place," said Mary. "He was glad I came. We talked and talked and he said he was glad I came."

"Was he?" cried Martha. "Art tha' sure? Tha' doesn't know what he's like when anything vexes him. He's a big lad to cry like a baby, but when he's in a passion he'll fair scream just to frighten us. He knows us daren't call our souls our own."

"He wasn't vexed," said Mary. "I asked him if I should go away and he made me stay. He asked me questions and I sat on a big footstool and talked to him about India and about the robin and gardens. He wouldn't let me go. He let me see his mother's picture. Before I left him I sang him to sleep."

Martha fairly gasped with amazement.

"I can scarcely believe thee!" she protested. "It's as if tha'd walked straight into a lion's den. If he'd been like he is most times he'd have throwed himself into one of his tantrums and roused th' house. He won't let strangers look at him."

"He let me look at him. I looked at him all the time and he looked at me. We stared!" said Mary.

"I don't know what to do!" cried agitated Martha. "If Mrs. Medlock finds out, she'll think I broke orders and told thee and I shall be packed back to mother."

"He is not going to tell Mrs. Medlock anything about it yet. It's to be a sort of secret just at first," said Mary firmly. "And he says everybody is obliged to do as he pleases."

"Aye, that's true enough—th' bad lad!" sighed Martha, wiping her forehead with her apron.

"He says Mrs. Medlock must. And he wants me to come and talk to him every day. And you are to tell me when he wants me."

"Me!" said Martha; "I shall lose my place—I shall for sure!"

"You can't if you are doing what he wants you to do and everybody is ordered to obey him," Mary argued.

"Does tha' mean to say," cried Martha with wide open eyes, "that he was nice to thee!"

"I think he almost liked me," Mary answered.

"Then tha' must have bewitched him!" decided Martha, drawing a long breath.

"Do you mean Magic?" inquired Mary. "I've heard about Magic in India, but I can't make it. I just went into his room and I was so surprised to see him I stood and stared. And then he turned round and stared at me. And he thought I was a ghost or a dream and I thought perhaps he was. And it was so queer being there alone together in the middle of the night and not knowing about each other. And we began to ask each other questions. And when I asked him if I must go away he said I must not."

"Th' world's comin' to a end!" gasped Martha.

"What is the matter with him?" asked Mary.

"Nobody knows for sure and certain," said Martha. "Mr. Craven went off his head like when he was born. Th' doctors thought he'd have to be put in a 'sylum. It was because Mrs. Craven died like I told you. He wouldn't set eyes on th' baby. He just raved and said it'd be another hunchback like him and it'd better die."

"Is Colin a hunchback?" Mary asked. "He didn't look like one."

"He isn't yet," said Martha. "But he began all wrong. Mother said that there was enough trouble and raging in th' house to set any child wrong. They was afraid his back was weak an' they've always been takin' care of it—keepin' him lyin' down and not lettin' him walk. Once they made him wear a brace, but he fretted so he was downright ill. Then a big doctor came to see him an' made them take it off. He talk'd to th' other doctor quite rough—in a polite way. He said there'd been too much medicine and too much lettin' him have his own way."

"I think he's a very spoiled boy," said Mary.

"He's th' worst young nowt* as ever was!" said Martha. "I won't say as he hasn't been ill a good bit. He's had coughs an' colds that's nearly killed him two or three times. Once he had rheumatic fever an' once he had typhoid. Eh! Mrs. Medlock did get a fright then. He'd been out of his head an' she was talkin' to th' nurse, thinkin' he didn't know nothin', an' she said, 'He'll die this time sure enough, an' best thing for him an' for everybody.' An' she looked at him an' there he was with his big eyes open, starin' at her as sensible as she was herself. She didn't know what'd happen but he just stared at her an' says, 'You give me some water an' stop talkin'.'"

"Do you think he will die?" asked Mary.

"Mother says there's no reason why any child should live that gets no fresh air an' doesn't do nothin' but lie on his back an' read picture-books an' take medicine. He's weak and hates th' trouble o' bein' taken out o' doors, an' he gets cold so easy he says it makes him ill."

Mary sat and looked at the fire.

"I wonder," she said slowly, "if it would not do him good to go out into a garden and watch things growing. It did me good."

"One of th' worst fits he ever had," said Martha, "was one time they took him out where the roses is by the fountain. He'd been readin' in a paper about people gettin' somethin' he called 'rose cold'* an' he began to sneeze an' said he'd got it an' then a new gardener as didn't know th' rules passed by an' looked at him curious. He threw himself into a passion an' he said he'd looked at him because he was going to be a hunchback. He cried himself into a fever an' was ill all night."

"If he ever gets angry at me, I'll never go and see him again," said Mary.

"He'll have thee if he wants thee," said Martha. "Tha' may as well know that at th' start."

Very soon afterward a bell rang and she rolled up her knitting.

"I dare say th' nurse wants me to stay with him a bit," she said. "I hope he's in a good temper."

She was out of the room about ten minutes and then she came back with a puzzled expression.

"Well, tha' has bewitched him," she said. "He's up on his sofa with his picture-books. He's told the nurse to stay away until six o'clock. I'm to wait in the next room. Th' minute she was gone he called me to him an' says, 'I want Mary Lennox to come and talk to me, and remember you're not to tell any one.' You'd better go as quick as you can."

Mary was quite willing to go quickly. She did not want to see Colin as much as she wanted to see Dickon, but she wanted to see him very much.

There was a bright fire on the hearth when she entered his room, and in the daylight she saw it was a very beautiful room indeed. There were rich colours in the rugs and hangings and pictures and books on the walls, which made it look glowing and comfortable even in spite of the grey sky and falling rain. Colin looked rather like a picture himself. He was wrapped in a velvet dressing-gown and sat against a big brocaded cushion. He had a red spot on each cheek.

"Come in," he said. "I've been thinking about you all the morning."

"I've been thinking about you, too," answered Mary. "You don't know how frightened Martha is. She says Mrs. Medlock will think she told me about you and then she will be sent away."

He frowned.

"Go and tell her to come here," he said. "She is in the next room."

Mary went and brought her back. Poor Martha was shaking in her shoes. Colin was still frowning.

"Have you to do what I please or have you not?" he demanded.

"I have to do what you please, sir," Martha faltered, turning quite red.

"Has Medlock to do what I please?"

"Everybody has, sir," said Martha.

"Well, then, if I order you to bring Miss Mary to me, how can Medlock send you away if she finds it out?"

"Please don't let her, sir," pleaded Martha.

"I'll send *her* away if she dares to say a word about such a thing," said Master Craven grandly. "She wouldn't like that, I can tell you."

"Thank you, sir," bobbing a curtsey. "I want to do my duty, sir."

"What I want is your duty," said Colin more grandly still. "I'll take care of you. Now go away."

When the door closed behind Martha, Colin found Mistress Mary gazing at him as if he had set her wondering.

"Why do you look at me like that?" he asked her. "What are you thinking about?"

"I am thinking about two things."

"What are they? Sit down and tell me."

"This is the first one," said Mary, seating herself on the big stool. "Once in India I saw a boy who was a Rajah. He had rubies and emeralds and diamonds stuck all over him. He spoke to his people just as you spoke to Martha. Everybody had to do everything he told them—in a minute. I think they would have been killed if they hadn't."

"I shall make you tell me about Rajahs presently," he said, "but first tell me what the second thing was."

"I was thinking," said Mary, "how different you are from Dickon."

"Who is Dickon?" he said. "What a queer name!"

She might as well tell him, she thought. She could talk about Dickon without mentioning the secret garden. She had liked to hear Martha talk about him. Besides, she longed to talk about him. It would seem to bring him nearer.

"He is Martha's brother. He is twelve years old," she explained. "He is not like any one else in the world. He can charm foxes and squirrels and birds just as the natives in India charm snakes. He plays a very soft tune on a pipe and they come and listen."

There were some big books on a table at his side, and he dragged one suddenly toward him.

"There is a picture of a snake-charmer in this," he exclaimed. "Come and look at it."

The book was a beautiful one with superb coloured illustrations, and he turned to one of them.

"Can he do that?" he asked eagerly.

"He played on his pipe and they listened," Mary explained. "But he doesn't call it Magic. He says it's because he lives on the moor so much and he knows their ways. He says he feels sometimes as if he was a bird or a rabbit himself, he likes them so. I think he asked the robin questions. It seemed as if they talked to each other in soft chirps."

Colin lay back on his cushion and his eyes grew larger and larger and the spots on his cheeks burned.

"Tell me some more about him," he said.

"He knows all about eggs and nests," Mary went on. "And he knows where foxes and badgers and otters live. He keeps them secret so that other boys won't find their holes and frighten them. He knows about everything that grows or lives on the moor."

"Does he like the moor?" said Colin. "How can he when it's such a great, bare, dreary place?"

"It's the most beautiful place," protested Mary. "Thousands of lovely things grow on it, and there are thousands of little creatures all busy building nests and making holes and burrows and chippering or singing or squeaking to each other. They are so busy and having such fun under the earth or in the trees or heather. It's their world."

"How do you know all that!" said Colin, turning on his elbow to look at her.

"I have never been there once, really," said Mary suddenly remembering. "I only drove over it in the dark. I thought it was hideous. Martha told me about it first, and then Dickon. When Dickon talks about it you feel as if you saw things and heard them, and as if you were standing in the heather with the sun shining and the gorse smelling like honey—and all full of bees and butterflies."

"You never see anything if you are ill," said Colin restlessly. He looked like a person listening to a new sound in the distance and wondering what it was.

"You can't if you stay in a room," said Mary.

"I couldn't go on the moor," he said in a resentful tone.

Mary was silent for a minute and then she said something bold.

"You might—sometime."

He moved as if he were startled.

"Go on the moor! How could I? I am going to die."

"How do you know?" said Mary unsympathetically. She didn't like the way he had of talking about dying. She did not feel very sympathetic. She felt rather as if he almost boasted about it.

"Oh, I've heard it ever since I remember," he answered crossly. "They are always whispering about it and thinking I don't notice. They wish I would, too."

Mistress Mary felt quite contrary. She pinched her lips together.

"If they wished I would," she said, "I wouldn't. Who wishes you would?"

"The servants—and of course Dr. Craven because he would get Misselthwaite and be rich instead of poor. He daren't say so, but he always looks cheerful when I am worse. When I had typhoid fever his face got quite fat. I think my father wishes it, too."

"I don't believe he does," said Mary quite obstinately.

That made Colin turn and look at her again.

"Don't you?" he said.

And then he lay back on his cushion and was still, as if he were thinking. And there was quite a long silence. Perhaps they were both of them thinking strange things children do not usually think of.

"I like the grand doctor from London, because he made them take the iron thing off," said Mary at last. "Did he say you were going to die?"

"No."

"What did he say?"

"He didn't whisper," Colin answered. "Perhaps he knew I hated whispering. I heard him say one thing quite aloud. He said, 'The lad might live if he would make up his mind to it. Put him in the humour.' It sounded as if he was in a temper."

"I'll tell you who would put you in the humour, perhaps," said Mary reflecting. She felt as if she would like this thing to be settled one way or the other. "I believe Dickon would. He's always talking about live things. He never talks about dead things or things that are ill. He's always looking up in the sky to watch birds flying—or looking down at the earth to see something growing. He has such round blue eyes and they are so wide open with looking about. And he laughs such a big laugh with his wide mouth—and his cheeks are as red—as red as cherries."

She pulled her stool nearer to the sofa and her expression quite changed at the remembrance of the wide curving mouth and wide open eyes.

"See here," she said. "Don't let us talk about dying; I don't like it. Let us talk about living. Let us talk and talk about Dickon. And then we will look at your pictures."

It was the best thing she could have said. To talk about Dickon meant to talk about the moor and about the cottage and the four-teen people who lived in it on sixteen shillings a week—and the children who got fat on the moor grass like the wild ponies. And about Dickon's mother—and the skipping-rope—and the moor with the sun on it—and about pale green points sticking up out of the black sod. And it was all so alive that Mary talked more than she had ever talked before—and Colin both talked and listened as he had never done either before. And they both began to laugh over nothings as children will when they are happy together. And they laughed so that in the end they were making as much noise as if they had been two ordinary healthy natural ten-year-old creatures—instead of a hard, little, unloving girl and a sickly boy who believed that he was going to die.

They enjoyed themselves so much that they forgot the pictures and they forgot about the time. They had been laughing quite loudly over Ben Weatherstaff and his robin, and Colin was actually sitting up as if he had forgotten about his weak back when he suddenly remembered something.

"Do you know there is one thing we have never once thought of?" he said. "We are cousins."

It seemed so queer that they had talked so much and never remembered this simple thing that they laughed more than ever, because they had got into the humour to laugh at anything. And in the midst of the fun the door opened and in walked Dr. Craven and Mrs. Medlock.

Dr. Craven started in actual alarm and Mrs. Medlock almost fell back because he had accidentally bumped against her.

"Good Lord!" exclaimed poor Mrs. Medlock, with her eyes almost starting out of her head. "Good Lord!"

"What is this?" said Dr. Craven, coming forward. "What does it mean?"

Then Mary was reminded of the boy Rajah again. Colin answered as if neither the doctor's alarm nor Mrs. Medlock's terror were of the slightest consequence. He was as little disturbed or frightened as if an elderly cat and dog had walked into the room.

"This is my cousin, Mary Lennox," he said. "I asked her to come and talk to me. I like her. She must come and talk to me whenever I send for her."

Dr. Craven turned reproachfully to Mrs. Medlock.

"Oh, sir," she panted. "I don't know how it's happened. There's not a servant on the place that'd dare to talk—they all have their orders."

"Nobody told her anything," said Colin. "She heard me crying and found me herself. I am glad she came. Don't be silly, Medlock."

Mary saw that Dr. Craven did not look pleased, but it was quite plain that he dare not oppose his patient. He sat down by Colin and felt his pulse.

"I am afraid there has been too much excitement. Excitement is not good for you, my boy," he said.

"I should be excited if she kept away," answered Colin, his eyes beginning to look dangerously sparkling. "I am better. She makes me better. The nurse must bring up her tea with mine. We will have tea together."

Mrs. Medlock and Dr. Craven looked at each other in a troubled way, but there was evidently nothing to be done.

"He does look rather better, sir," ventured Mrs. Medlock. "But"—thinking the matter over—"he looked better this morning before she came into the room."

"She came into the room last night. She stayed with me a long time. She sang a Hindustani song to me and it made me go to sleep," said Colin. "I was better when I wakened up. I wanted my breakfast. I want my tea now. Tell nurse, Medlock."

Dr. Craven did not stay very long. He talked to the nurse for a few minutes when she came into the room and said a few words of warning to Colin. He must not talk too much; he must not forget that he was ill; he must not forget that he was very easily tired. Mary thought that there seemed to be a number of uncomfortable things he was not to forget.

Colin looked fretful and kept his strange black-lashed eyes fixed on Dr. Craven's face.

"I *want* to forget it," he said at last. "She makes me forget it. That is why I want her."

Dr. Craven did not look happy when he left the room. He gave a puzzled glance at the little girl sitting on the large stool. She had become a stiff, silent child again as soon as he entered and he could not see what the attraction was. The boy actually did look brighter, however—and he sighed rather heavily as he went down the corridor.

"They are always wanting me to eat things when I don't want to," said Colin, as the nurse brought in the tea and put it on the table by the sofa. "Now, if you'll eat I will. Those muffins look so nice and hot. Tell me about Rajahs."

CHAPTER XV

NEST BUILDING

AFTER another week of rain the high arch of blue sky appeared again and the sun which poured down was quite hot. Though there had been no chance to see either the secret garden or Dickon, Mistress Mary had enjoyed herself very much. The week had not seemed long. She had spent hours of every day with Colin in his room, talking about Rajahs or gardens or Dickon and the cottage on the moor. They had looked at the splendid books and pictures and sometimes Mary had read things to Colin, and sometimes he had read a little to her. When he was amused and interested she thought he scarcely looked like an invalid at all, except that his face was so colourless and he was always on the sofa.

"You are a sly young one to listen and get out of your bed to go following things up like you did that night," Mrs. Medlock said once. "But there's no saying it's not been a sort of blessing to the lot of us. He's not had a tantrum or a whining fit since you made friends. The nurse was just going to give up the case because she was so sick of him, but she says she doesn't mind staying now you've gone on duty with her," laughing a little.

In her talks with Colin, Mary had tried to be very cautious about the secret garden. There were certain things she wanted to find out from him, but she felt that she must find them out without asking him direct questions. In the first place, as she began to like to be with him, she wanted to discover whether he was the kind of boy you could tell a secret to. He was not in the least like Dickon, but he was evidently so pleased with the idea of a garden no one knew anything about that she thought perhaps he could be trusted. But she had not known him long enough to be sure. The second thing she wanted to find out was this: If he could be trusted—if he really could—wouldn't it be possible to take him to the garden without having any one find it out? The grand doctor had said that he must have fresh air and Colin had said that he would not mind fresh air in a secret garden. Perhaps if he had a great deal of fresh air and knew Dickon and the robin and saw things growing he might not think so much about dying. Mary had seen herself in the glass sometimes lately when she had realised

that she looked quite a different creature from the child she had seen
when she arrived from India. This child looked nicer. Even Martha
had seen a change in her.

"Th' air from th' moor has done thee good already," she had said.
"Tha'rt not nigh so yeller and tha'rt not nigh so scrawny. Even tha'
hair doesn't slamp* down on tha' head so flat. It's got some life in it
so as it sticks out a bit."

"It's like me," said Mary. "It's growing stronger and fatter. I'm
sure there's more of it."

"It looks it, for sure," said Martha, ruffling it up a little round her
face. "Tha'rt not half so ugly when it's that way an' there's a bit o' red
in tha' cheeks."

If gardens and fresh air had been good for her perhaps they would
be good for Colin. But then, if he hated people to look at him, perhaps
he would not like to see Dickon.

"Why does it make you angry when you are looked at?" she inquired
one day.

"I always hated it," he answered, "even when I was very little.
Then when they took me to the seaside and I used to lie in my carriage everybody used to stare and ladies would stop and talk to my
nurse and then they would begin to whisper and I knew then they
were saying I shouldn't live to grow up. Then sometimes the ladies
would pat my cheeks and say 'Poor child!' Once when a lady did that
I screamed out loud and bit her hand. She was so frightened she ran
away."

"She thought you had gone mad like a dog," said Mary, not at all
admiringly.

"I don't care what she thought," said Colin frowning.

"I wonder why you didn't scream and bite me when I came into
your room?" said Mary. Then she began to smile slowly.

"I thought you were a ghost or a dream," he said. "You can't bite a
ghost or a dream, and if you scream they don't care."

"Would you hate it if—if a boy looked at you?" Mary asked
uncertainly.

He lay back on his cushion and paused thoughtfully.

"There's one boy," he said quite slowly, as if he were thinking over
every word, "there's one boy I believe I shouldn't mind. It's that boy
who knows where the foxes live—Dickon."

"I'm sure you wouldn't mind him," said Mary.

"The birds don't and other animals," he said, still thinking it over, "perhaps that's why I shouldn't. He's a sort of animal charmer and I am a boy animal."

Then he laughed and she laughed too; in fact it ended in their both laughing a great deal and finding the idea of a boy animal hiding in his hole very funny indeed.

What Mary felt afterward was that she need not fear about Dickon.

On that first morning when the sky was blue again Mary wakened very early. The sun was pouring in slanting rays through the blinds and there was something so joyous in the sight of it that she jumped out of bed and ran to the window. She drew up the blinds and opened the window itself and a great waft of fresh, scented air blew in upon her. The moor was blue and the whole world looked as if something Magic had happened to it. There were tender little fluting sounds here and there and everywhere, as if scores of birds were beginning to tune up for a concert. Mary put her hand out of the window and held it in the sun.

"It's warm—warm!" she said. "It will make the green points push up and up and up, and it will make the bulbs and roots work and struggle with all their might under the earth."

She kneeled down and leaned out of the window as far as she could, breathing big breaths and sniffing the air until she laughed because she remembered what Dickon's mother had said about the end of his nose quivering like a rabbit's.

"It must be very early," she said. "The little clouds are all pink and I've never seen the sky look like this. No one is up. I don't even hear the stable boys."

A sudden thought made her scramble to her feet.

"I can't wait! I am going to see the garden!"

She had learnt to dress herself by this time and she put on her clothes in five minutes. She knew a small side door which she could unbolt herself and she flew down-stairs in her stocking feet and put on her shoes in the hall. She unchained and unbolted and unlocked and when the door was open she sprang across the step with one bound, and there she was standing on the grass, which seemed to have turned green, and with the sun pouring down on her and warm sweet wafts about her and the fluting and twittering and singing coming from every bush and tree. She clasped her hands for pure joy and looked up in the sky and it was so blue and pink and pearly and white and flooded with springtime light that she felt as if she must flute* and sing aloud herself and knew that thrushes and robins and sky-larks could not possibly help it. She ran around the shrubs and paths towards the secret garden.

"It is all different already," she said. "The grass is greener and things are sticking up everywhere and things are uncurling and green buds of leaves are showing. This afternoon I am sure Dickon will come."

The long warm rain had done strange things to the herbaceous beds which bordered the walk by the lower wall. There were things sprouting and pushing out from the roots of clumps of plants and there were actually here and there glimpses of royal purple and yellow unfurling among the stems of crocuses. Six months before Mistress Mary would not have seen how the world was waking up, but now she missed nothing.

When she had reached the place where the door hid itself under the ivy, she was startled by a curious loud sound. It was the caw—caw of a crow and it came from the top of the wall, and when she looked up, there sat a big glossy-plumaged blue-black bird, looking down at her very wisely indeed. She had never seen a crow so close before and he made her a little nervous, but the next moment he spread his wings and flapped away across the garden. She hoped he was not going to stay inside and she pushed the door open wondering if he would. When she got fairly into the garden she saw that he probably did intend to stay because he had alighted on a dwarf apple-tree, and under the apple-tree was lying a little reddish animal with a bushy tail, and both of them were watching the stooping body and rust-red head of Dickon, who was kneeling on the grass working hard.

Mary flew across the grass to him.

"Oh, Dickon! Dickon!" she cried out. "How could you get here so early! How could you! The sun has only just got up!"

He got up himself, laughing and glowing, and tousled; his eyes like a bit of the sky.

"Eh!" he said. "I was up long before him. How could I have stayed abed! Th' world's all fair begun again this mornin', it has. An' it's workin' an' hummin' an' scratchin' an' pipin' an' nest-buildin' an' breathin' out scents, till you've got to be out on it 'stead o' lyin' on

your back. When th' sun did jump up, th' moor went mad for joy, an'
I was in the midst of th' heather, an' I run like mad myself, shoutin'
an' singin'. An' I come straight here. I couldn't have stayed away.
Why, th' garden was lyin' here waitin'!"

Mary put her hands on her chest, panting, as if she had been running herself.

"Oh, Dickon! Dickon!" she said. "I'm so happy I can scarcely
breathe!"

Seeing him talking to a stranger, the little bushy-tailed animal rose
from its place under the tree and came to him, and the rook, cawing
once, flew down from its branch and settled quietly on his shoulder.

"This is th' little fox cub," he said, rubbing the little reddish animal's head. "It's named Captain. An' this here's Soot. Soot he flew
across th' moor with me an' Captain he run same as if th' hounds had
been after him. They both felt same as I did."

Neither of the creatures looked as if he were the least afraid of
Mary. When Dickon began to walk about, Soot stayed on his shoulder
and Captain trotted quietly close to his side.

"See here!" said Dickon. "See how these has pushed up, an' these
an' these! An' Eh! look at these here."

He threw himself upon his knees and Mary went down beside him.
They had come upon a whole clump of crocuses burst into purple
and orange and gold. Mary bent her face down and kissed and kissed
them.

"You never kiss a person in that way," she said when she lifted her
head. "Flowers are so different."

He looked puzzled but smiled.

"Eh!" he said, "I've kissed mother many a time that way when I
come in from th' moor after a day's roamin' an' she stood there at th'
door in th' sun, lookin' so glad an' comfortable."

They ran from one part of the garden to another and found so
many wonders that they were obliged to remind themselves that they
must whisper or speak low. He showed her swelling leaf-buds on rose
branches which had seemed dead. He showed her ten thousand new
green points pushing through the mould. They put their eager young
noses close to the earth and sniffed its warmed springtime breathing; they dug and pulled and laughed low with rapture until Mistress
Mary's hair was as tumbled as Dickon's and her cheeks were almost
as poppy red as his.

There was every joy on earth in the secret garden that morning, and in the midst of them came a delight more delightful than all, because it was more wonderful. Swiftly something flew across the wall and darted through the trees to a close grown corner, a little flare of red-breasted bird with something hanging from its beak. Dickon stood quite still and put his hand on Mary almost as if they had suddenly found themselves laughing in a church.

"We munnot* stir," he whispered in broad Yorkshire. "We munnot scarce breathe. I knowed he was mate-huntin' when I seed him last. It's Ben Weatherstaff's robin. He's buildin' his nest. He'll stay here if us don't flight him."

They settled down softly upon the grass and sat there without moving.

"Us mustn't seem as if us was watchin' him too close," said Dickon. "He'd be out with us for good if he got th' notion us was interferin' now. He'll be a good bit different till all this is over. He's settin' up housekeepin'. He'll be shyer an' readier to take things ill. He's got no time for visitin' an' gossipin'. Us must keep still a bit an' try to look as if us was grass an' trees an' bushes. Then when he's got used to seein' us I'll chirp a bit an' he'll know us'll not be in his way."

Mistress Mary was not at all sure that she knew, as Dickon seemed to, how to try to look like grass and trees and bushes. But he had said the queer thing as if it were the simplest and most natural thing in the world, and she felt it must be quite easy to him, and indeed she watched him for a few minutes carefully, wondering if it was possible for him to quietly turn green and put out branches and leaves. But he only sat wonderfully still, and when he spoke dropped his voice to such a softness that it was curious that she could hear him, but she could.

"It's part o' th' springtime, this nest-buildin' is," he said. "I warrant it's been goin' on in th' same way every year since th' world was begun. They've got their way o' thinkin' and doin' things an' a body had better not meddle. You can lose a friend in springtime easier than any other season if you're too curious."

"If we talk about him I can't help looking at him," Mary said as softly as possible. "We must talk of something else. There is something I want to tell you."

"He'll like it better if us talks o' somethin' else," said Dickon. "What is it tha's got to tell me?"

"Well—do you know about Colin?" she whispered.

He turned his head to look at her.

"What does tha' know about him?" he asked.

"I've seen him. I have been to talk to him every day this week. He wants me to come. He says I'm making him forget about being ill and dying," answered Mary.

Dickon looked actually relieved as soon as the surprise died away from his round face.

"I am glad o' that," he exclaimed. "I'm right down glad. It makes me easier. I knowed I must say nothin' about him an' I don't like havin' to hide things."

"Don't you like hiding the garden?" said Mary.

"I'll never tell about it," he answered. "But I says to mother, 'Mother,' I says, 'I got a secret to keep. It's not a bad 'un, tha' knows that. It's no worse than hidin' where a bird's nest is. Tha' doesn't mind it, does tha'?'"

Mary always wanted to hear about mother.

"What did she say?" she asked, not at all afraid to hear.

Dickon grinned sweet-temperedly.

"It was just like her, what she said," he answered. "She give my head a bit of a rub an' laughed an' she says, 'Eh, lad, tha' can have all th' secrets tha' likes I've knowed thee twelve year'.'"

"How did you know about Colin?" asked Mary.

"Everybody as knowed about Mester Craven knowed there was a little lad as was like to be a cripple, an' they knowed Mester Craven didn't like him to be talked about. Folks is sorry for Mester Craven because Mrs. Craven was such a pretty young lady an' they was so fond of each other. Mrs. Medlock stops in our cottage whenever she goes to Thwaite an' she doesn't mind talkin' to mother before us children, because she knows us has been brought up to be trusty. How did tha' find out about him? Martha was in fine trouble th' last time she came home. She said tha'd heard him frettin' an' tha' was askin' questions an' she didn't know what to say."

Mary told him her story about the midnight wuthering of the wind which had wakened her and about the faint far-off sounds of the complaining voice which had led her down the dark corridors with her candle and had ended with her opening of the door of the dimly lighted room with the carven four-posted bed in the corner. When she described the small ivory-white face and the strange black-rimmed eyes Dickon shook his head.

"Them's just like his mother's eyes, only hers was always laughin', they say," he said. "They say as Mr. Craven can't bear to see him when he's awake an' it's because his eyes is so like his mother's an' yet looks so different in his miserable bit of a face."

"Do you think he wants him to die?" whispered Mary.

"No, but he wishes he'd never been born. Mother she says that's th' worst thing on earth for a child. Them as is not wanted scarce ever thrives.* Mester Craven he'd buy anythin' as money could buy for th' poor lad but he'd like to forget as he's on earth. For one thing, he's afraid he'll look at him some day and find he's growed hunchback."

"Colin's so afraid of it himself that he won't sit up," said Mary. "He says he's always thinking that if he should feel a lump coming he should go crazy and scream himself to death."

"Eh! he oughtn't to lie there thinkin' things like that," said Dickon. "No lad could get well as thought them sort o' things."

The fox was lying on the grass close by him looking up to ask for a pat now and then, and Dickon bent down and rubbed his neck softly and thought a few minutes in silence. Presently he lifted his head and looked round the garden.

"When first we got in here," he said, "it seemed like everything was grey. Look round now and tell me if tha' doesn't see a difference."

Mary looked and caught her breath a little.

"Why!" she cried, "the grey wall is changing. It is as if a green mist were creeping over it. It's almost like a green gauze veil."

"Aye," said Dickon. "An' it'll be greener and greener till th' grey's all gone. Can tha' guess what I was thinkin'?"

"I know it was something nice," said Mary eagerly. "I believe it was something about Colin."

"I was thinkin' that if he was out here he wouldn't be watchin' for lumps to grow on his back; he'd be watchin' for buds to break on th' rose-bushes, an' he'd likely be healthier," explained Dickon. "I was wonderin' if us could ever get him in th' humour to come out here an' lie under th' trees in his carriage."

"I've been wondering that myself. I've thought of it almost every time I've talked to him," said Mary. "I've wondered if he could keep a secret and I've wondered if we could bring him here without anyone seeing us. I thought perhaps you could push his carriage. The doctor said he must have fresh air and if he wants us to take him out no one dare disobey him. He won't go out for other people and perhaps they will be glad if he will go out with us. He could order the gardeners to keep away so they wouldn't find out."

Dickon was thinking very hard as he scratched Captain's back.

"It'd be good for him, I'll warrant," he said. "Us'd not be thinkin' he'd better never been born. Us'd be just two children watchin' a garden grow, an' he'd be another. Two lads an' a little lass just lookin' on at th' springtime. I warrant it'd be better than doctor's stuff."

"He's been lying in his room so long and he's always been so afraid of his back that it has made him queer," said Mary. "He knows a good many things out of books but he doesn't know anything else. He says he has been too ill to notice things and he hates going out of doors and hates gardens and gardeners. But he likes to hear about this garden because it is a secret. I daren't tell him much but he said he wanted to see it."

"Us'll have him out here sometime for sure," said Dickon. "I could push his carriage well enough. Has tha' noticed how th' robin an' his mate has been workin' while we've been sittin' here? Look at him perched on that branch wonderin' where it'd be best to put that twig he's got in his beak."

He made one of his low whistling calls and the robin turned his head and looked at him inquiringly, still holding his twig. Dickon spoke to him as Ben Weatherstaff did, but Dickon's tone was one of friendly advice.

"Wheres'ever tha' puts it," he said, "it'll be all right. Tha' knew how to build tha' nest before tha' came out o' th' egg. Get on with thee, lad. Tha'st got no time to lose."

"Oh, I do like to hear you talk to him!" Mary said, laughing delightedly. "Ben Weatherstaff scolds him and makes fun of him, and he hops about and looks as if he understood every word, and I know he likes it. Ben Weatherstaff says he is so conceited he would rather have stones thrown at him than not be noticed."

Dickon laughed too and went on talking.

"Tha' knows us won't trouble thee," he said to the robin. "Us is near bein' wild things ourselves. Us is nest-buildin' too, bless thee. Look out tha' doesn't tell on us."

And though the robin did not answer, because his beak was occupied, Mary knew that when he flew away with his twig to his own corner of the garden the darkness of his dew-bright eye meant that he would not tell their secret for the world.

THEY found a great deal to do that morning, and Mary was late in returning to the house and was also in such a hurry to get back to her work that she quite forgot Colin until the last moment.

"Tell Colin that I can't come and see him yet," she said to Martha. "I'm very busy in the garden."

Martha looked rather frightened.

"Eh! Miss Mary," she said, "it may put him all out of humour when I tell him that."

But Mary was not as afraid of him as other people were, and she was not a self-sacrificing person.

"I can't stay," she answered. "Dickon's waiting for me;" and she ran away.

The afternoon was even lovelier and busier than the morning had been. Already nearly all the weeds were cleared out of the garden and most of the roses and trees had been pruned or dug about. Dickon had brought a spade of his own and he had taught Mary to use all her tools, so that by this time it was plain that though the lovely wild place was not likely to become a "gardener's garden," it would be a wilderness of growing things before the springtime was over.

"There'll be apple blossoms an' cherry blossoms overhead," Dickon said, working away with all his might. "An' there'll be peach an' plum trees in bloom against th' walls, an' th' grass'll be a carpet o' flowers."

The little fox and the rook were as happy and busy as they were, and the robin and his mate flew backward and forward like tiny streaks of lightning. Sometimes the rook flapped his black wings and soared away over the tree-tops in the park. Each time he came back and perched near Dickon and cawed several times as if he were relating his adventures, and Dickon talked to him just as he had talked to the robin. Once when Dickon was so busy that he did not answer him at first, Soot flew on to his shoulder and gently tweaked his ear with his large beak. When Mary wanted to rest a little Dickon sat down with her under a tree, and once he took his pipe out of his pocket and played the soft strange little notes and two squirrels appeared on the wall and looked and listened.

"Tha's a good bit stronger than tha' was," Dickon said, looking at her as she was digging. "Tha's beginnin' to look different, for sure."

Mary was glowing with exercise and good spirits.

"I'm getting fatter and fatter every day," she said quite exultantly. "Mrs. Medlock will have to get me some bigger dresses. Martha says my hair is growing thicker. It isn't so flat and stringy."

The sun was beginning to set and sending deep gold-coloured rays slanting under the trees when they parted.

"It'll be fine to-morrow," said Dickon. "I'll be at work by sunrise."

"So will I," said Mary.

She ran back to the house as quickly as her feet would carry her. She wanted to tell Colin about Dickon's fox cub and the rook and about what the springtime had been doing. She felt sure he would like to hear. So it was not very pleasant when she opened the door of her room, to see Martha standing waiting for her with a doleful face.

"What is the matter?" she asked. "What did Colin say when you told him I couldn't come?"

"Eh!" said Martha, "I wish tha'd gone. He was nigh goin' into one o' his tantrums. There's been a nice to do all afternoon to keep him quiet. He would watch the clock all th' time."

Mary's lips pinched themselves together. She was no more used to considering other people than Colin was and she saw no reason why an ill-tempered boy should interfere with the thing she liked best. She knew nothing about the pitifulness of people who had been ill and nervous and who did not know that they could control their tempers and need not make other people ill and nervous too. When she had had a headache in India she had done her best to see that everybody else also had a headache or something quite as bad. And she felt she was quite right; but of course now she felt that Colin was quite wrong.

He was not on his sofa when she went into his room. He was lying flat on his back in bed and he did not turn his head toward her as she came in. This was a bad beginning and Mary marched up to him with her stiff manner.

"Why didn't you get up?" she said.

"I did get up this morning when I thought you were coming," he answered, without looking at her. "I made them put me back in bed this afternoon. My back ached and my head ached and I was tired. Why didn't you come?"

"I was working in the garden with Dickon," said Mary.

Colin frowned and condescended to look at her.

"I won't let that boy come here if you go and stay with him instead of coming to talk to me," he said.

Mary flew into a fine passion. She could fly into a passion without making a noise. She just grew sour and obstinate and did not care what happened.

"If you send Dickon away, I'll never come into this room again!" she retorted.

"You'll have to if I want you," said Colin.

"I won't!" said Mary.

"I'll make you," said Colin. "They shall drag you in."

"Shall they, Mr. Rajah!" said Mary fiercely. "They may drag me in but they can't make me talk when they get me here. I'll sit and clench my teeth and never tell you one thing. I won't even look at you. I'll stare at the floor!"

They were a nice agreeable pair as they glared at each other. If they had been two little street boys they would have sprung at each other and had a rough-and-tumble fight. As it was, they did the next thing to it.

"You are a selfish thing!" cried Colin.

"What are you?" said Mary. "Selfish people always say that. Any one is selfish who doesn't do what they want. You're more selfish than I am. You're the most selfish boy I ever saw."

"I'm not!" snapped Colin. "I'm not as selfish as your fine Dickon is! He keeps you playing in the dirt when he knows I am all by myself. He's selfish, if you like!"

Mary's eyes flashed fire.

"He's nicer than any other boy that ever lived!" she said. "He's—he's like an angel!" It might sound rather silly to say that but she did not care.

"A nice angel!" Colin sneered ferociously. "He's a common cottage boy off the moor!"

"He's better than a common Rajah!" retorted Mary. "He's a thousand times better!"

Because she was the stronger of the two she was beginning to get the better of him. The truth was that he had never had a fight with anyone like himself in his life and, upon the whole, it was rather good for him, though neither he nor Mary knew anything about that. He turned his head on his pillow and shut his eyes and a big tear was squeezed out and ran down his cheek. He was beginning to feel pathetic and sorry for himself—not for any one else.

"I'm not as selfish as you, because I'm always ill, and I'm sure there is a lump coming on my back," he said. "And I am going to die besides."

"You're not!" contradicted Mary unsympathetically.

He opened his eyes quite wide with indignation He had never heard such a thing said before. He was at once furious and slightly pleased, if a person could be both at the same time.

"I'm not?" he cried. "I am! You know I am! Everybody says so."

"I don't believe it!" said Mary sourly. "You just say that to make people sorry. I believe you're proud of it. I don't believe it! If you were a nice boy it might be true—but you're too nasty!"

In spite of his invalid back Colin sat up in bed in quite a healthy rage.

"Get out of the room!" he shouted and he caught hold of his pillow and threw it at her. He was not strong enough to throw it far and it only fell at her feet, but Mary's face looked as pinched as a nutcracker.

"I'm going," she said. "And I won't come back!"

She walked to the door and when she reached it she turned round and spoke again.

"I was going to tell you all sorts of nice things," she said. "Dickon brought his fox and his rook and I was going to tell you all about them. Now I won't tell you a single thing!"

She marched out of the door and closed it behind her, and there to her great astonishment she found the trained nurse standing as if she had been listening and, more amazing still—she was laughing. She was a big handsome young woman who ought not to have been a trained nurse at all, as she could not bear invalids and she was always making excuses to leave Colin to Martha or any one else who would take her place. Mary had never liked her, and she simply stood and gazed up at her as she stood giggling into her handkerchief.

"What are you laughing at?" she asked her.

"At you two young ones," said the nurse. "It's the best thing that could happen to the sickly pampered thing to have some one to stand up to him that's as spoiled as himself"; and she laughed into her handkerchief again. "If he'd had a young vixen of a sister to fight with it would have been the saving of him."

"Is he going to die?"

"I don't know and I don't care," said the nurse. "Hysterics and temper are half what ails him."

"What are hysterics?" asked Mary.

"You'll find out if you work him into a tantrum after this—but at any rate you've given him something to have hysterics about, and I am glad of it."

Mary went back to her room not feeling at all as she had felt when she had come in from the garden. She was cross and disappointed but not at all sorry for Colin. She had looked forward to telling him a great many things and she had meant to try to make up her mind whether it would be safe to trust him with the great secret. She had been beginning to think it would be, but now she had changed her mind entirely. She would never tell him and he could stay in his room and never get any fresh air and die if he liked! It would serve him right! She felt so sour and unrelenting that for a few minutes she almost forgot about Dickon and the green veil creeping over the world and the soft wind blowing down from the moor.

Martha was waiting for her and the trouble in her face had been temporarily replaced by interest and curiosity. There was a wooden box on the table and its cover had been removed and revealed that it was full of neat packages.

"Mr. Craven sent it to you," said Martha. "It looks as if it had picture-books in it."

Mary remembered what he had asked her the day she had gone to his room. "Do you want anything—dolls—toys—books?" She opened the package wondering if he had sent a doll, and also wondering what she should do with it if he had. But he had not sent one. There were several beautiful books such as Colin had, and two of them were about gardens and were full of pictures. There were two or three games and there was a beautiful little writing-case with a gold monogram on it and a gold pen and inkstand.

Everything was so nice that her pleasure began to crowd her anger out of her mind. She had not expected him to remember her at all and her hard little heart grew quite warm.

"I can write better than I can print," she said, "and the first thing I shall write with that pen will be a letter to tell him I am much obliged."

If she had been friends with Colin she would have run to show him her presents at once, and they would have looked at the pictures and read some of the gardening books and perhaps tried playing the games, and he would have enjoyed himself so much he would never once have thought he was going to die or have put his hand on his spine to see if there was a lump coming. He had a way of doing that which she could not bear. It gave her an uncomfortable frightened feeling because he always looked so frightened himself. He said that if he felt even quite a little lump some day he should know his hunch had begun to grow. Something he had heard Mrs. Medlock whispering to the nurse had given him the idea and he had thought over it in secret until it was quite firmly fixed in his mind. Mrs. Medlock had said his father's back had begun to show its crookedness in that way when he was a child. He had never told any one but Mary that most of his "tantrums" as they called them grew out of his hysterical hidden fear. Mary had been sorry for him when he had told her.

"He always began to think about it when he was cross or tired," she said to herself. "And he has been cross to-day. Perhaps—perhaps he has been thinking about it all the afternoon."

She stood still, looking down at the carpet and thinking.

"I said I would never go back again—" she hesitated, knitting her brows—"but perhaps, just perhaps, I will go and see—if he wants me—in the morning. Perhaps he'll try to throw his pillow at me again, but—I think—I'll go."

CHAPTER XVII

A TANTRUM

SHE had got up very early in the morning and had worked hard in the garden and she was tired and sleepy, so as soon as Martha had brought her supper and she had eaten it, she was glad to go to bed. As she laid her head on the pillow she murmured to herself:

"I'll go out before breakfast and work with Dickon and then afterward—I believe—I'll go to see him."

She thought it was the middle of the night when she was wakened by such dreadful sounds that she jumped out of bed in an instant. What was it—what was it? The next minute she felt quite sure she knew. Doors were opened and shut and there were hurrying feet in the corridors and some one was crying and screaming at the same time, screaming and crying in a horrible way.

"It's Colin," she said. "He's having one of those tantrums the nurse calls hysterics. How awful it sounds."

As she listened to the sobbing screams she did not wonder that people were so frightened that they gave him his own way in everything rather than hear them. She put her hands over her ears and felt sick and shivering.

"I don't know what to do. I don't know what to do," she kept saying. "I can't bear it."

Once she wondered if he would stop if she dared go to him and then she remembered how he had driven her out of the room and thought that perhaps the sight of her might make him worse. Even when she pressed her hands more tightly over her ears she could not keep the awful sounds out. She hated them so and was so terrified by them that suddenly they began to make her angry and she felt as if she should like to fly into a tantrum herself and frighten him as he was frightening her. She was not used to any one's tempers but her own. She took her hands from her ears and sprang up and stamped her foot.

"He ought to be stopped! Somebody ought to make him stop! Somebody ought to beat him!" she cried out.

Just then she heard feet almost running down the corridor and her door opened and the nurse came in. She was not laughing now by any means. She even looked rather pale.

"He's worked himself into hysterics," she said in a great hurry. "He'll do himself harm. No one can do anything with him. You come and try, like a good child. He likes you."

"He turned me out of the room this morning," said Mary, stamping her foot in excitement.

The stamp rather pleased the nurse. The truth was that she had been afraid she might find Mary crying and hiding her head under the bedclothes.

"That's right," she said. "You're in the right humour. You go and scold him. Give him something new to think of. Do go, child, as quick as ever you can."

It was not until afterward that Mary realised that the thing had been funny as well as dreadful—that it was funny that all the grown-up people were so frightened that they came to a little girl just because they guessed she was almost as bad as Colin himself.

She flew along the corridor and the nearer she got to the screams the higher her temper mounted. She felt quite wicked by the time she reached the door. She slapped it open with her hand and ran across the room to the four-posted bed.*

"You stop!" she almost shouted. "You stop! I hate you! Everybody hates you! I wish everybody would run out of the house and let you scream yourself to death! You *will* scream yourself to death in a minute, and I wish you would!"

A nice sympathetic child could neither have thought nor said such things, but it just happened that the shock of hearing them was the best possible thing for this hysterical boy whom no one had ever dared to restrain or contradict.

He had been lying on his face beating his pillow with his hands and he actually almost jumped around, he turned so quickly at the sound of the furious little voice. His face looked dreadful, white and red, and swollen, and he was gasping and choking; but savage little Mary did not care an atom.

"If you scream another scream," she said, "I'll scream too—and I can scream louder than you can, and I'll frighten you, I'll frighten you!"

He actually had stopped screaming because she had startled him so. The scream which had been coming almost choked him. The tears were streaming down his face and he shook all over.

"I can't stop!" he gasped and sobbed. "I can't—I can't!"

"You can!" shouted Mary. "Half that ails you is hysterics and temper—just hysterics—hysterics—hysterics!" and she stamped each time she said it.

"I felt the lump—I felt it," choked out Colin. "I knew I should. I shall have a hunch on my back and then I shall die," and he began to writhe again and turned on his face and sobbed and wailed, but he didn't scream.

"You didn't feel a lump!" contradicted Mary fiercely. "If you did it was only a hysterical lump. Hysterics makes lumps. There's nothing the matter with your horrid back—nothing but hysterics! Turn over and let me look at it!"

She liked the word "hysterics" and felt somehow as if it had an effect on him. He was probably like herself and had never heard it before.

"Nurse," she commanded, "come here and show me his back this minute!"

The nurse, Mrs. Medlock and Martha had been standing huddled together near the door staring at her, their mouths half open. All three had gasped with fright more than once. The nurse came forward as if she were half afraid. Colin was heaving with great breathless sobs.

"Perhaps he—he won't let me," she hesitated, in a low voice.

Colin heard her, however, and he gasped out between two sobs: "Sh-show her! She-she'll see then!"

It was a poor thin back to look at when it was bared. Every rib could be counted and every joint of the spine, though Mistress Mary did not count them as she bent over and examined them with a solemn savage little face. She looked so sour and old-fashioned that the nurse turned her head aside to hide the twitching of her mouth. There was just a minute's silence, for even Colin tried to hold his breath while Mary looked up and down his spine, and down and up, as intently as if she had been the great doctor from London.

"There's not a single lump there!" she said at last. "There's not a lump as big as a pin—except backbone lumps, and you can only feel them because you're thin. I've got backbone lumps myself, and they used to stick out as much as yours do, until I began to get fatter, and I am not fat enough yet to hide them. There's not a lump as big as a pin! If you ever say there is again, I shall laugh!"

No one but Colin himself knew what effect those crossly spoken childish words had on him. If he had ever had any one to talk to

about his secret terrors—if he had ever dared to let himself ask
questions—if he had had childish companions and had not lain on
his back in the huge closed house, breathing an atmosphere heavy
with the fears of people who were most of them ignorant and tired of
him, he would have found out that most of his fright and illness was
created by himself.* But he had lain and thought of himself and his
aches and weariness for hours and days and months and years. And
now that an angry unsympathetic little girl insisted obstinately that
he was not as ill as he thought he was, he actually felt as if she might
be speaking the truth.

"I didn't know," ventured the nurse, "that he thought he had a
lump on his spine. His back is weak because he won't try to sit up. I
could have told him there was no lump there."

Colin gulped and turned his face a little to look at her.

"C–could you?" he said pathetically.

"Yes, sir."

"There!" said Mary, and she gulped too.

Colin turned on his face again and but for his long-drawn broken
breaths, which were the dying down of his storm of sobbing, he lay
still for a minute, though great tears streamed down his face and
wet the pillow. Actually the tears meant that a curious great relief
had come to him. Presently he turned and looked at the nurse again,
and strangely enough he was not like a Rajah at all as he spoke
to her.

"Do you think—I could—live to grow up?" he said.

The nurse was neither clever nor soft-hearted, but she could repeat
some of the London doctor's words.

"You probably will if you will do what you are told to do, and not
give way to your temper, and stay out a great deal in the fresh air."

Colin's tantrum had passed and he was weak and worn out with
crying and this perhaps made him feel gentle. He put out his hand a
little toward Mary, and I am glad to say that, her own tantrum having
passed, she was softened too and met him half-way with her hand, so
that it was a sort of making up.

"I'll—I'll go out with you, Mary," he said. "I shan't hate fresh air
if we can find—" He remembered just in time to stop himself from
saying "if we can find the secret garden" and he ended, "I shall like to
go out with you if Dickon will come and push my chair. I do so want
to see Dickon and the fox and the crow."

The nurse remade the tumbled bed and shook and straightened the pillows. Then she made Colin a cup of beef tea and gave a cup to Mary, who really was very glad to get it after her excitement. Mrs. Medlock and Martha gladly slipped away, and after everything was neat and calm and in order the nurse looked as if she would very gladly slip away also. She was a healthy young woman who resented being robbed of her sleep and she yawned quite openly as she looked at Mary, who had pushed her big footstool close to the four-posted bed and was holding Colin's hand.

"You must go back and get your sleep out," she said. "He'll drop off after a while—if he's not too upset. Then I'll lie down myself in the next room."

"Would you like me to sing you that song I learned from my Ayah?" Mary whispered to Colin.

His hand pulled hers gently and he turned his tired eyes on her appealingly.

"Oh, yes!" he answered. "It's such a soft song. I shall go to sleep in a minute."

"I will put him to sleep," Mary said to the yawning nurse. "You can go if you like."

"Well," said the nurse, with an attempt at reluctance. "If he doesn't go to sleep in half an hour you must call me."

"Very well," answered Mary.

The nurse was out of the room in a minute and as soon as she was gone Colin pulled Mary's hand again.

"I almost told," he said; "but I stopped myself in time. I won't talk and I'll go to sleep, but you said you had a whole lot of nice things to tell me. Have you—do you think you have found out anything at all about the way into the secret garden?"

Mary looked at his poor little tired face and swollen eyes and her heart relented.

"Ye-es," she answered, "I think I have. And if you will go to sleep I will tell you to-morrow."

His hand quite trembled.

"Oh, Mary!" he said. "Oh, Mary! If I could get into it I think I should live to grow up! Do you suppose that instead of singing the Ayah song—you could just tell me softly as you did that first day what you imagine it looks like inside? I am sure it will make me go to sleep."

"Yes," answered Mary. "Shut your eyes."

He closed his eyes and lay quite still and she held his hand and began to speak very slowly and in a very low voice.

"I think it has been left alone so long—that it has grown all into a lovely tangle. I think the roses have climbed and climbed and climbed until they hang from the branches and walls and creep over the ground—almost like a strange grey mist. Some of them have died but many—are alive and when the summer comes there will be curtains and fountains of roses. I think the ground is full of daffodils and snowdrops and lilies and iris working their way out of the dark. Now the spring has begun—perhaps—perhaps—"

The soft drone of her voice was making him stiller and stiller and she saw it and went on.

"Perhaps they are coming up through the grass—perhaps there are clusters of purple crocuses and gold ones—even now. Perhaps the leaves are beginning to break out and uncurl—and perhaps—the grey is changing and a green gauze veil is creeping—and creeping over—everything. And the birds are coming to look at it—because it is—so safe and still. And perhaps—perhaps—perhaps—" very softly and slowly indeed, "the robin has found a mate—and is building a nest."

And Colin was asleep.

CHAPTER XVIII

"THA' MUNNOT WASTE NO TIME"

OF course Mary did not waken early the next morning. She slept late because she was tired, and when Martha brought her breakfast she told her that though Colin was quite quiet he was ill and feverish as he always was after he had worn himself out with a fit of crying. Mary ate her breakfast slowly as she listened.

"He says he wishes tha' would please go and see him as soon as tha' can," Martha said. "It's queer what a fancy he's took to thee. Tha' did give it him last night for sure—didn't tha'? Nobody else would have dared to do it. Eh! poor lad! He's been spoiled till salt won't save him. Mother says as th' two worst things as can happen to a child is never to have his own way—or always to have it. She doesn't know which is th' worst. Tha' was in a fine temper tha'self, too. But he says to me when I went into his room, 'Please ask Miss Mary if she'll please come an' talk to me?' Think o' him saying please! Will you go, Miss?"

"I'll run and see Dickon first," said Mary. "No, I'll go and see Colin first and tell him—I know what I'll tell him," with a sudden inspiration.

She had her hat on when she appeared in Colin's room and for a second he looked disappointed. He was in bed and his face was pitifully white and there were dark circles round his eyes.

"I'm glad you came," he said. "My head aches and I ache all over because I'm so tired. Are you going somewhere?"

Mary went and leaned against his bed.

"I won't be long," she said. "I'm going to Dickon, but I'll come back. Colin, it's—it's something about the secret garden."

His whole face brightened and a little colour came into it.

"Oh! is it!" he cried out. "I dreamed about it all night. I heard you say something about grey changing into green, and I dreamed I was standing in a place all filled with trembling little green leaves—and there were birds on nests everywhere and they looked so soft and still. I'll lie and think about it until you come back."

In five minutes Mary was with Dickon in their garden. The fox and the crow were with him again and this time he had brought two tame squirrels.

"I came over on the pony this mornin'," he said. "Eh! he is a good little chap—Jump is! I brought these two in my pockets. This here one he's called Nut an' this here other one's called Shell."

When he said "Nut" one squirrel leaped on to his right shoulder and when he said "Shell" the other one leaped on to his left shoulder.

When they sat down on the grass with Captain curled at their feet, Soot solemnly listening on a tree and Nut and Shell nosing about close to them, it seemed to Mary that it would be scarcely bearable to leave such delightfulness, but when she began to tell her story somehow the look in Dickon's funny face gradually changed her mind. She could see he felt sorrier for Colin than she did. He looked up at the sky and all about him.

"Just listen to them birds—th' world seems full of 'em—all whistlin' an' pipin'," he said. "Look at 'em dartin' about, an' hearken at 'em callin' to each other. Come springtime seems like as if all th' world's callin'. The leaves is uncurlin' so you can see 'em—an', my word, th' nice smells there is about!" sniffing with his happy turned-up nose. "An' that poor lad lyin' shut up an' seein' so little that he gets to thinkin' o' things as sets him screamin'. Eh! my! we mun get him out here—we mun get him watchin' an' listenin' an' sniffin' up th' air an' get him just soaked through wi' sunshine. An' we munnot lose no time about it."

When he was very much interested he often spoke quite broad Yorkshire though at other times he tried to modify his dialect so that Mary could better understand. But she loved his broad Yorkshire and had in fact been trying to learn to speak it herself. So she spoke a little now.

"Aye, that we mun," she said (which meant "Yes, indeed, we must"). "I'll tell thee what us'll do first," she proceeded, and Dickon grinned, because when the little wench tried to twist her tongue into speaking Yorkshire it amused him very much. "He's took a graidely* fancy to thee. He wants to see thee and he wants to see Soot an' Captain. When I go back to the house to talk to him I'll ax him if tha' canna come an' see him to-morrow mornin'—an' bring tha' creatures wi' thee—an' then—in a bit, when there's more leaves out, an' happen a bud or two, we'll get him to come out an' tha' shall push him in his chair an' we'll bring him here an' show him everything."

When she stopped she was quite proud of herself. She had never made a long speech in Yorkshire before and she had remembered very well.

"Tha' mun talk a bit o' Yorkshire like that to Mester Colin," Dickon chuckled. "Tha'll make him laugh an' there's nowt as good for ill folk as laughin' is. Mother says she believes as half a hour's good laugh every mornin' 'ud cure a chap as was making ready for typhus fever."

"I'm going to talk Yorkshire to him this very day," said Mary, chuckling herself.

The garden had reached the time when every day and every night it seemed as if Magicians were passing through it drawing loveliness out of the earth and the boughs with wands. It was hard to go away and leave it all, particularly as Nut had actually crept on to her dress and Shell had scrambled down the trunk of the apple-tree they sat under and stayed there looking at her with inquiring eyes. But she went back to the house and when she sat down close to Colin's bed he began to sniff as Dickon did, though not in such an experienced way.

"You smell like flowers and—and fresh things," he cried out quite joyously. "What is it you smell of? It's cool and warm and sweet all at the same time."

"It's th' wind from th' moor," said Mary. "It comes o' sittin' on th' grass under a tree wi' Dickon an' wi' Captain an' Soot an' Nut an' Shell. It's th' spring-time an' out o' doors an' sunshine as smells so graidely."

She said it as broadly as she could, and you do not know how broadly Yorkshire sounds until you have heard some one speak it. Colin began to laugh.

"What are you doing?" he said. "I never heard you talk like that before. How funny it sounds."

"I'm givin' thee a bit o' Yorkshire," answered Mary triumphantly. "I canna talk as graidely as Dickon an' Martha can but tha' sees I can shape* a bit. Doesn't tha' understand a bit o' Yorkshire when tha' hears it? An' tha' a Yorkshire lad thysel' bred an' born! Eh! I wonder tha'rt not ashamed o' thy face."

And then she began to laugh too and they both laughed until they could not stop themselves and they laughed until the room echoed and Mrs. Medlock opening the door to come in drew back into the corridor and stood listening amazed.

"Well, upon my word!" she said, speaking rather broad Yorkshire herself because there was no one to hear her and she was so astonished. "Whoever heard th' like! Whoever on earth would ha' thought it!"

There was so much to talk about. It seemed as if Colin could never hear enough of Dickon and Captain and Soot and Nut and Shell and the pony whose name was Jump. Mary had run round into the wood with Dickon to see Jump. He was a tiny little shaggy moor pony with thick locks hanging over his eyes and with a pretty face and a nuzzling velvet nose. He was rather thin with living on moor grass but he was as tough and wiry as if the muscle in his little legs had been made of steel springs. He had lifted his head and whinnied softly the moment he saw Dickon and he had trotted up to him and put his head across his shoulder and then Dickon had talked into his ear and Jump had talked back in odd little whinnies and puffs and snorts. Dickon had made him give Mary his small front hoof and kiss her on her cheek with his velvet muzzle.

"Does he really understand everything Dickon says?" Colin asked.

"It seems as if he does," answered Mary. "Dickon says anything will understand if you're friends with it for sure, but you have to be friends for sure."

Colin lay quiet a little while and his strange grey eyes seemed to be staring at the wall, but Mary saw he was thinking.

"I wish I was friends with things," he said at last, "but I'm not. I never had anything to be friends with, and I can't bear people."

"Can't you bear me?" asked Mary.

"Yes, I can," he answered. "It's very funny, but I even like you."

"Ben Weatherstaff said I was like him," said Mary. "He said he'd warrant we'd both got the same nasty tempers. I think you are like him too. We are all three alike—you and I and Ben Weatherstaff. He said we were neither of us much to look at and we were as sour as we looked. But I don't feel as sour as I used to before I knew the robin and Dickon."

"Did you feel as if you hated people?"

"Yes," answered Mary without any affectation. "I should have detested you if I had seen you before I saw the robin and Dickon."

Colin put out his thin hand and touched her.

"Mary," he said, "I wish I hadn't said what I did about sending Dickon away. I hated you when you said he was like an angel and I laughed at you but—but perhaps he is."

"Well, it was rather funny to say it," she admitted frankly, "because his nose does turn up and he has a big mouth and his clothes have patches all over them and he talks broad Yorkshire, but—but if an angel did come to Yorkshire and live on the moor—if there was a Yorkshire angel—I believe he'd understand the green things and know how to make them grow and he would know how to talk to the wild creatures as Dickon does and they'd know he was friends for sure."

"I shouldn't mind Dickon looking at me," said Colin; "I want to see him."

"I'm glad you said that," answered Mary, "because—because—"

Quite suddenly it came into her mind that this was the minute to tell him. Colin knew something new was coming.

"Because what?" he cried eagerly.

Mary was so anxious that she got up from her stool and came to him and caught hold of both his hands.

"Can I trust you? I trusted Dickon because birds trusted him. Can I trust you—for sure—*for sure*?" she implored.

Her face was so solemn that he almost whispered his answer.

"Yes—yes!"

"Well, Dickon will come to see you to-morrow morning, and he'll bring his creatures with him."

"Oh! Oh!" Colin cried out in delight.

"But that's not all," Mary went on almost pale with solemn excitement. "The rest is better. There is a door into the garden. I found it. It is under the ivy on the wall."

If he had been a strong healthy boy Colin would probably have shouted "Hooray! Hooray! Hooray!" but he was weak and rather hysterical; his eyes grew bigger and bigger and he gasped for breath.

"Oh! Mary!" he cried out with a half sob. "Shall I see it? Shall I get into it? Shall I *live* to get into it?" and he clutched her hands and dragged her toward him.

"Of course you'll see it!" snapped Mary indignantly. "Of course you'll live to get into it! Don't be silly!"

And she was so un-hysterical and natural and childish that she brought him to his senses and he began to laugh at himself and a few minutes afterward she was sitting on her stool again telling him not what she imagined the secret garden to be like but what it really was, and Colin's aches and tiredness were forgotten and he was listening enraptured.

"It is just what you thought it would be," he said at last. "It sounds just as if you had really seen it. You know I said that when you told me first."

Mary hesitated about two minutes and then boldly spoke the truth.

"I had seen it—and I had been in," she said. "I found the key and got in weeks ago. But I daren't tell you—I daren't because I was so afraid I couldn't trust you—*for sure!*"

CHAPTER XIX

"IT HAS COME!"

OF course Dr. Craven had been sent for the morning after Colin had had his tantrum. He was always sent for at once when such a thing occurred and he always found, when he arrived, a white shaken boy lying on his bed, sulky and still so hysterical that he was ready to break into fresh sobbing at the least word. In fact, Dr. Craven dreaded and detested the difficulties of these visits. On this occasion he was away from Misselthwaite Manor until afternoon.

"How is he?" he asked Mrs. Medlock rather irritably when he arrived. "He will break a blood-vessel in one of those fits some day. The boy is half insane with hysteria and self-indulgence."

"Well, sir," answered Mrs. Medlock, "you'll scarcely believe your eyes when you see him. That plain sour-faced child that's almost as bad as himself has just bewitched him. How she's done it there's no telling. The Lord knows she's nothing to look at and you scarcely ever hear her speak, but she did what none of us dare do. She just flew at him like a little cat last night, and stamped her feet and ordered him to stop screaming, and somehow she startled him so that he actually did stop, and this afternoon—well just come up and see, sir. It's past crediting."

The scene which Dr. Craven beheld when he entered his patient's room was indeed rather astonishing to him. As Mrs. Medlock opened the door he heard laughing and chattering. Colin was on his sofa in his dressing-gown and he was sitting up quite straight looking at a picture in one of the garden books and talking to the plain child who at that moment could scarcely be called plain at all because her face was so glowing with enjoyment.

"Those long spires of blue ones—we'll have a lot of those," Colin was announcing. "They're called Del-phin-iums."

"Dickon says they're larkspurs made big and grand," cried Mistress Mary. "There are clumps there already."

Then they saw Dr. Craven and stopped. Mary became quite still and Colin looked fretful.

"I am sorry to hear you were ill last night, my boy," Dr. Craven said a trifle nervously. He was rather a nervous man.

"I'm better now—much better," Colin answered, rather like a Rajah. "I'm going out in my chair in a day or two if it is fine. I want some fresh air."

Dr. Craven sat down by him and felt his pulse and looked at him curiously.

"It must be a very fine day," he said, "and you must be very careful not to tire yourself."

"Fresh air won't tire me," said the young Rajah.

As there had been occasions when this same young gentleman had shrieked aloud with rage and had insisted that fresh air would give him cold and kill him, it is not to be wondered at that his doctor felt somewhat startled.

"I thought you did not like fresh air," he said.

"I don't when I am by myself," replied the Rajah; "but my cousin is going out with me."

"And the nurse, of course?" suggested Dr. Craven.

"No, I will not have the nurse," so magnificently that Mary could not help remembering how the young native Prince had looked with his diamonds and emeralds and pearls stuck all over him and the great rubies on the small dark hand he had waved to command his servants to approach with salaams and receive his orders.

"My cousin knows how to take care of me. I am always better when she is with me. She made me better last night. A very strong boy I know will push my carriage."

Dr. Craven felt rather alarmed. If this tiresome hysterical boy should chance to get well he himself would lose all chance of inheriting Misselthwaite; but he was not an unscrupulous man, though he was a weak one, and he did not intend to let him run into actual danger.

"He must be a strong boy and a steady boy," he said. "And I must know something about him. Who is he? What is his name?"

"It's Dickon," Mary spoke up suddenly. She felt somehow that everybody who knew the moor must know Dickon. And she was right, too. She saw that in a moment Dr. Craven's serious face relaxed into a relieved smile.

"Oh, Dickon," he said. "If it is Dickon you will be safe enough. He's as strong as a moor pony, is Dickon."

"And he's trusty," said Mary. "He's th' trustiest lad i' Yorkshire."
She had been talking Yorkshire to Colin and she forgot herself.

"Did Dickon teach you that?" asked Dr. Craven laughing outright.

"I'm learning it as if it was French," said Mary rather coldly. "It's like a native dialect in India. Very clever people try to learn them. I like it and so does Colin."

"Well, well," he said. "If it amuses you perhaps it won't do you any harm. Did you take your bromide* last night, Colin?"

"No," Colin answered. "I wouldn't take it at first, and after Mary made me quiet she talked me to sleep—in a low voice—about the spring creeping into a garden."

"That sounds soothing," said Dr. Craven, more perplexed than ever and glancing sideways at Mistress Mary sitting on her stool and looking down silently at the carpet. "You are evidently better, but you must remember—"

"I don't want to remember," interrupted the Rajah, appearing again. "When I lie by myself and remember I begin to have pains everywhere, and I think of things that make me begin to scream because I hate them so. If there was a doctor anywhere who could make you forget you were ill instead of remembering it, I would have him brought here." And he waved a thin hand which ought really to have been covered with royal signet rings made of rubies. "It is because my cousin makes me forget that she makes me better."

Dr. Craven had never made such a short stay after a "tantrum"; usually he was obliged to remain a very long time and do a great many things. This afternoon he did not give any medicine or leave any new orders, and he was spared any disagreeable scenes. When he went downstairs he looked very thoughtful, and when he talked to Mrs. Medlock in the library she felt that he was a much puzzled man.

"Well, sir," she ventured, "could you have believed it?"

"It is certainly a new state of affairs," said the doctor. "And there's no denying it is better than the old one."

"I believe Susan Sowerby's right—I do that," said Mrs. Medlock. "I stopped in her cottage on my way to Thwaite yesterday, and had a bit of talk with her. And she says to me, 'Well, Sarah Ann, she mayn't be a good child, an' she mayn't be a pretty one, but she's a child, an' children needs children.' We went to school together, Susan Sowerby and me."

"She's the best sick nurse I know," said Dr. Craven. "When I find her in a cottage I know the chances are that I shall save my patient."

Mrs. Medlock smiled. She was fond of Susan Sowerby.

"She's got a way with her, has Susan," she went on quite volubly. "I've been thinking all morning of one thing she said yesterday. She says, 'Once when I was givin' th' children a bit of a preach after they'd been fightin' I ses to 'em all, "When I was at school my jography told as th' world was shaped like a orange an' I found out before I was ten that th' whole orange doesn't belong to nobody. No one owns more than his bit of a quarter an' there's times it seems like there's not enow quarters to go round. But don't you—none o' you—think as you own th' whole orange or you'll find out you're mistaken, an' you won't find it out without hard knocks." What children learns from children,' she says, 'is that there's no sense in grabbin' at th' whole orange—peel an' all. If you do you'll likely not get even th' pips, an' them's too bitter to eat.'"

"She's a shrewd woman," said Dr. Craven, putting on his coat.

"Well, she's got a way of saying things," ended Mrs. Medlock, much pleased. "Sometimes I've said to her, 'Eh! Susan, if you was a different woman an' didn't talk such broad Yorkshire I've seen the times when I should have said you was clever.'"

That night Colin slept without once awakening, and when he opened his eyes in the morning he lay still and smiled without knowing it—smiled because he felt so curiously comfortable. It was actually nice to be awake, and he turned over and stretched his limbs luxuriously. He felt as if tight strings which had held him had loosened themselves and let him go. He did not know that Dr. Craven would have said that his nerves had relaxed and rested themselves. Instead of lying and staring at the wall and wishing he had not awakened, his mind was full of the plans he and Mary had made yesterday, of pictures of the garden and of Dickon and his wild creatures. It was so nice to have things to think about. And he had not been awake more than ten minutes when he heard feet running along the corridor and Mary was at the door. The next minute she was in the room and had run across to his bed, bringing with her a waft of fresh air full of the scent of the morning.

"You've been out! You've been out! There's that nice smell of leaves!" he cried.

She had been running and her hair was loose and blown, and she was bright with the air and pink-cheeked, though he could not see it.

"It's so beautiful!" she said, a little breathless with her speed. "You never saw anything so beautiful! It has *come!* I thought it had come that other morning, but it was only coming. It is here now! It has come, the Spring! Dickon says so!"

"Has it?" cried Colin, and though he really knew nothing about it he felt his heart beat. He actually sat up in bed.

"Open the window!" he added, laughing half with joyful excitement and half at his own fancy. "Perhaps we may hear golden trumpets!"

And though he laughed, Mary was at the window in a moment and in a moment more it was opened wide and freshness and softness and scents and birds' songs were pouring through.

"That's fresh air," she said. "Lie on your back and draw in long breaths of it. That's what Dickon does when he's lying on the moor. He says he feels it in his veins and it makes him strong and he feels as if he could live for ever and ever. Breathe it and breathe it."

She was only repeating what Dickon had told her, but she caught Colin's fancy.

"'For ever and ever'! Does it make him feel like that?" he said, and he did as she told him, drawing in long deep breaths over and over again until he felt that something quite new and delightful was happening to him.

Mary was at his bedside again.

"Things are crowding up out of the earth," she ran on in a hurry. "And there are flowers uncurling and buds on everything and the green veil has covered nearly all the grey and the birds are in such a hurry about their nests for fear they may be too late that some of them are even fighting for places in the secret garden. And the rose-bushes look as wick as wick can be, and there are primroses in the lanes and woods, and the seeds we planted are up, and Dickon has brought the fox and the crow and the squirrels and a new-born lamb."

And then she paused for breath. The new-born lamb Dickon had found three days before lying by its dead mother among the gorse bushes on the moor. It was not the first motherless lamb he had found and he knew what to do with it. He had taken it to the cottage wrapped in his jacket and he had let it lie near the fire and had fed it with warm milk. It was a soft thing with a darling silly baby face and legs rather long for its body. Dickon had carried it over the moor in his arms and its feeding bottle was in his pocket with a squirrel, and when Mary had sat under a tree with its limp warmness huddled on her lap she had felt as if she were too full of strange joy to speak. A lamb—a lamb! A living lamb who lay on your lap like a baby!

She was describing it with great joy and Colin was listening and drawing in long breaths of air when the nurse entered. She started a little at the sight of the open window. She had sat stifling in the room many a warm day because her patient was sure that open windows gave people cold.

"Are you sure you are not chilly, Master Colin?" she inquired.

"No," was the answer. "I am breathing long breaths of fresh air. It makes you strong. I am going to get up to the sofa for breakfast and my cousin will have breakfast with me."

The nurse went away, concealing a smile, to give the order for two breakfasts. She found the servants' hall a more amusing place than the invalid's chamber and just now everybody wanted to hear the news from upstairs. There was a great deal of joking about the unpopular young recluse who, as the cook said, "had found his master, and good for him." The servants' hall had been very tired of the tantrums, and the butler, who was a man with a family, had more than once expressed his opinion that the invalid would be all the better "for a good hiding."

When Colin was on his sofa and the breakfast for two was put upon the table he made an announcement to the nurse in his most Rajah-like manner.

"A boy, and a fox, and a crow, and two squirrels, and a new-born lamb, are coming to see me this morning. I want them brought upstairs as soon as they come," he said. "You are not to begin playing with the animals in the servants' hall and keep them there. I want them here."

The nurse gave a slight gasp and tried to conceal it with a cough.

"Yes, sir," she answered.

"I'll tell you what you can do," added Colin, waving his hand. "You can tell Martha to bring them here. The boy is Martha's brother. His name is Dickon and he is an animal charmer."

"I hope the animals won't bite, Master Colin," said the nurse.

"I told you he was a charmer," said Colin austerely. "Charmers' animals never bite."

"There are snake-charmers in India," said Mary; "and they can put their snakes' heads in their mouths."

"Goodness!" shuddered the nurse.

They ate their breakfast with the morning air pouring in upon them. Colin's breakfast was a very good one and Mary watched him with serious interest.

"You will begin to get fatter just as I did," she said. "I never wanted my breakfast when I was in India and now I always want it."

"I wanted mine this morning," said Colin. "Perhaps it was the fresh air. When do you think Dickon will come?"

He was not long in coming. In about ten minutes Mary held up her hand.

"Listen!" she said. "Did you hear a caw?"

Colin listened and heard it, the oddest sound in the world to hear inside a house, a hoarse "caw-caw."

"Yes," he answered.

"That's Soot," said Mary. "Listen again! Do you hear a bleat—a tiny one?"

"Oh, yes!" cried Colin, quite flushing.

"That's the new-born lamb," said Mary. "He's coming."

Dickon's moorland boots were thick and clumsy and though he tried to walk quietly they made a clumping sound as he walked through the long corridors. Mary and Colin heard him marching—marching, until he passed through the tapestry door on to the soft carpet of Colin's own passage.

"If you please, sir," announced Martha, opening the door, "if you please, sir, here's Dickon an' his creatures."

Dickon came in smiling his nicest wide smile. The new-born lamb was in his arms and the little red fox trotted by his side. Nut sat on his left shoulder and Soot on his right and Shell's head and paws peeped out of his coat pocket.

Colin slowly sat up and stared and stared—as he had stared when he first saw Mary; but this was a stare of wonder and delight. The truth was that in spite of all he had heard he had not in the least understood what this boy would be like and that his fox and his crow and his squirrels and his lamb were so near to him and his friendliness that they seemed almost to be part of himself. Colin had never talked to a boy in his life and he was so overwhelmed by his own pleasure and curiosity that he did not even think of speaking.

But Dickon did not feel the least shy or awkward. He had not felt embarrassed because the crow had not known his language and had only stared and had not spoken to him the first time they met.

Creatures were always like that until they found out about you. He walked over to Colin's sofa and put the new-born lamb quietly on his lap, and immediately the little creature turned to the warm velvet dressing-gown and began to nuzzle and nuzzle into its folds and butt its tight-curled head with soft impatience against his side. Of course no boy could have helped speaking then.

"What is it doing?" cried Colin. "What does it want?"

"It wants its mother," said Dickon, smiling more and more. "I brought it to thee a bit hungry because I knowed tha'd like to see it feed."

He knelt down by the sofa and took a feeding-bottle from his pocket.

"Come on, little 'un," he said, turning the small woolly white head with a gentle brown hand. "This is what tha's after. Tha'll get more out o' this than tha' will out o' silk velvet coats. There now," and he pushed the rubber tip of the bottle into the nuzzling mouth and the lamb began to suck it with ravenous ecstasy.

After that there was no wondering what to say. By the time the lamb fell asleep questions poured forth and Dickon answered them all. He told them how he had found the lamb just as the sun was rising three mornings ago. He had been standing on the moor listening to a skylark and watching him swing higher and higher into the sky until he was only a speck in the heights of blue.

"I'd almost lost him but for his song an' I was wonderin' how a chap could hear it when it seemed as if he'd get out o' th' world in a minute—an' just then I heard somethin' else far off among th' gorse bushes. It was a weak bleatin' an' I knowed it was a new lamb as was hungry an' I knowed it wouldn't be hungry if it hadn't lost its mother somehow, so I set off searchin'. Eh! I did have a look for it. I went in an' out among th' gorse bushes an' round an' round an' I always seemed to take th' wrong turnin'. But at last I seed a bit o' white by a rock on top o' th' moor an' I climbed up an' found th' little 'un half dead wi' cold an' clemmin'."*

While he talked, Soot flew solemnly in and out of the open window and cawed remarks about the scenery, while Nut and Shell made excursions into the big trees outside and ran up and down trunks and explored branches. Captain curled up near Dickon, who sat on the hearth-rug from preference.

They looked at the pictures in the gardening books and Dickon

knew all the flowers by their country names and knew exactly which
ones were already growing in the secret garden.

"I couldna' say that there name," he said, pointing to one under
which was written "Aquilegia," "but us calls that a columbine, an'
that there one it's a snapdragon and they both grow wild in hedges,
but these is garden ones an' they're bigger and grander. There's some
big clumps o' columbine in th' garden. They'll look like a bed o' blue
an' white butterflies flutterin' when they're out."

"I'm going to see them," cried Colin. "I am going to see them!"

"Aye, that tha' mun," said Mary quite seriously. "An tha' munnot
lose no time about it."

CHAPTER XX

"I SHALL LIVE FOREVER—AND EVER—AND EVER!"

BUT they were obliged to wait more than a week, because first there came some very windy days and then Colin was threatened with a cold, which two things happening one after the other would no doubt have thrown him into a rage but that there was so much careful and mysterious planning to do and almost every day Dickon came in, if only for a few minutes, to talk about what was happening on the moor and in the lanes and hedges and on the borders of streams. The things he had to tell about otters' and badgers' and water-rats' houses,* not to mention birds' nests and field-mice and their burrows, were enough to make you almost tremble with excitement when you heard all the intimate details from an animal charmer and realised with what thrilling eagerness and anxiety the whole busy underworld was working.

"They're same as us," said Dickon, "only they have to build their homes every year. An' it keeps 'em so busy they fair scuffle to get 'em done."

The most absorbing thing, however, was the preparations to be made before Colin could be transported with sufficient secrecy to the garden. No one must see the chair-carriage and Dickon and Mary after they turned a certain corner of the shrubbery and entered upon the walk outside the ivied walls. As each day passed, Colin had become more and more fixed in his feeling that the mystery surrounding the garden was one of its greatest charms. Nothing must spoil that. No one must ever suspect that they had a secret. People must think that he was simply going out with Mary and Dickon because he liked them and did not object to their looking at him. They had long and quite delightful talks about their route. They would go up this path and down that one and cross the other and go round among the fountain flower-beds as if they were looking at the "bedding-out plants"* the head gardener, Mr. Roach, had been having arranged. That would seem such a rational thing to do that no one would think it at all mysterious. They would turn into the shrubbery walks and lose themselves until they came to the long walls. It was almost as serious and elaborately thought out as the plans of march made by great generals in time of war.

Rumours of the new and curious things which were occurring in the invalid's apartments had of course filtered through the servants' hall into the stable yards and out among the gardeners, but notwithstanding this, Mr. Roach was startled one day when he received orders from Master Colin's room to the effect that he must report himself in the apartment no outsider had ever seen, as the invalid himself desired to speak to him.

"Well, well," he said to himself as he hurriedly changed his coat, "what's to do now? His Royal Highness that wasn't to be looked at calling up a man he's never set eyes on."

Mr. Roach was not without curiosity. He had never caught even a glimpse of the boy and had heard a dozen exaggerated stories about his uncanny looks and ways and his insane tempers. The thing he had heard oftenest was that he might die at any moment and there had been numerous fanciful descriptions of a humped back and helpless limbs, given by people who had never seen him.

"Things are changing in this house, Mr. Roach," said Mrs. Medlock, as she led him up the back staircase to the corridor on to which opened the hitherto mysterious chamber.

"Let's hope they're changing for the better, Mrs. Medlock," he answered.

"They couldn't well change for the worse," she continued; "and queer as it all is there's them as finds their duties made a lot easier to stand up under. Don't you be surprised, Mr. Roach, if you find yourself in the middle of a menagerie and Martha Sowerby's Dickon more at home than you or me could ever be."

There really was a sort of Magic about Dickon as Mary always privately believed. When Mr. Roach heard his name he smiled quite leniently.

"He'd be at home in Buckingham Palace or at the bottom of a coal mine," he said. "And yet it's not impudence, either. He's just fine, is that lad."

It was perhaps well he had been prepared or he might have been startled. When the bedroom door was opened a large crow, which seemed quite at home perched on the high back of a carven chair, announced the entrance of a visitor by saying "Caw—Caw" quite loudly. In spite of Mrs. Medlock's warning, Mr. Roach only just escaped being sufficiently undignified to jump backward.

The young Rajah was neither in bed nor on his sofa. He was sitting in an armchair and a young lamb was standing by him shaking its tail in feeding-lamb fashion as Dickon knelt giving it milk from its bottle. A squirrel was perched on Dickon's bent back attentively nibbling a nut. The little girl from India was sitting on a big footstool looking on.

"Here is Mr. Roach, Master Colin," said Mrs. Medlock.

The young Rajah turned and looked his servitor over—at least that was what the head gardener felt happened.

"Oh, you are Roach, are you?" he said. "I sent for you to give you some very important orders."

"Very good, sir," answered Roach, wondering if he was to receive instructions to fell all the oaks in the park or to transform the orchards into water-gardens.

"I am going out in my chair this afternoon," said Colin. "If the fresh air agrees with me I may go out every day. When I go, none of the gardeners are to be anywhere near the Long Walk by the garden walls. No one is to be there. I shall go out about two o'clock and every one must keep away until I send word that they may go back to their work."

"Very good, sir," replied Mr. Roach, much relieved to hear that the oaks might remain and that the orchards were safe.

"Mary," said Colin, turning to her, "what is that thing you say in India when you have finished talking and want people to go?"

"You say, 'You have my permission to go,' " answered Mary.

The Rajah waved his hand.

"You have my permission to go, Roach," he said. "But, remember, this is very important."

"Caw—Caw!" remarked the crow hoarsely but not impolitely.

"Very good, sir. Thank you, sir," said Mr. Roach, and Mrs. Medlock took him out of the room.

Outside in the corridor, being a rather good-natured man, he smiled until he almost laughed.

"My word!" he said, "he's got a fine lordly way with him, hasn't he? You'd think he was a whole Royal Family rolled into one—Prince Consort* and all."

"Eh!" protested Mrs. Medlock, "we've had to let him trample all over every one of us ever since he had feet and he thinks that's what folks was born for."

"Perhaps he'll grow out of it, if he lives," suggested Mr. Roach.

"Well, there's one thing pretty sure," said Mrs. Medlock. "If he does live and that Indian child stays here I'll warrant she teaches him that the whole orange does not belong to him, as Susan Sowerby says. And he'll be likely to find out the size of his own quarter."

Inside the room Colin was leaning back on his cushions.

"It's all safe now," he said. "And this afternoon I shall see it—this afternoon I shall be in it!"

Dickon went back to the garden with his creatures and Mary stayed with Colin. She did not think he looked tired, but he was very quiet before their lunch came, and he was quiet while they were eating it. She wondered why and asked him about it.

"What big eyes you've got, Colin," she said. "When you are think-ing they get as big as saucers. What are you thinking about now?"

"I can't help thinking about what it will look like," he answered.

"The garden?" asked Mary.

"The springtime," he said. "I was thinking that I've really never seen it before. I scarcely ever went out and when I did go I never looked at it. I didn't even think about it."

"I never saw it in India because there wasn't any," said Mary.

Shut in and morbid as his life had been, Colin had more imagin-ation than she had and at least he had spent a good deal of time looking at wonderful books and pictures.

"That morning when you ran in and said 'It's come! It's come!' you made me feel quite queer. It sounded as if things were coming with a great procession and big bursts and wafts of music. I've a picture like it in one of my books—crowds of lovely people and children with garlands and branches with blossoms on them, every one laughing and dancing and crowding and playing on pipes. That was why I said, 'Perhaps we shall hear golden trumpets' and told you to throw open the window."

"How funny!" said Mary. "That's really just what it feels like. And if all the flowers and leaves and green things and birds, and wild creatures danced past at once, what a crowd it would be! I'm sure they'd dance and sing and flute and that would be the wafts of music."

They both laughed but it was not because the idea was laughable, but because they both so liked it.

A little later the nurse made Colin ready. She noticed that instead of lying like a log while his clothes were put on he sat up and made some efforts to help himself, and he talked and laughed with Mary all the time.

"This is one of his good days, sir," she said to Dr. Craven, who dropped in to inspect him. "He's in such good spirits that it makes him stronger."

"I'll call in again later in the afternoon, after he has come in," said Dr. Craven. "I must see how the going out agrees with him. I wish," in a very low voice, "that he would let you go with him."

"I'd rather give up the case this moment, sir, than even stay here while it's suggested," answered the nurse with sudden firmness.

"I hadn't really decided to suggest it," said the doctor, with his slight nervousness. "We'll try the experiment. Dickon's a lad I'd trust with a new-born child."

The strongest footman in the house carried Colin down-stairs and put him in his wheeled chair near which Dickon waited outside. After the manservant had arranged his rugs and cushions the Rajah waved his hand to him and to the nurse.

"You have my permission to go," he said, and they both disappeared quickly and it must be confessed giggled when they were safely inside the house.

Dickon began to push the wheeled chair slowly and steadily. Mistress Mary walked beside it and Colin leaned back and lifted his face to the sky. The arch of it looked very high and the small snowy clouds seemed like white birds floating on outspread wings below its crystal blueness. The wind swept in soft big breaths down from the moor and was strange with a wild clear scented sweetness. Colin kept lifting his thin chest to draw it in, and his big eyes looked as if it were they which were listening—listening, instead of his ears.

"There are so many sounds of singing and humming and calling out," he said. "What is that scent the puffs of wind bring?"

"It's gorse on th' moor that's openin' out," answered Dickon. "Eh! th' bees are at it wonderful to-day."

Not a human creature was to be caught sight of in the paths they took. In fact every gardener or gardener's lad had been witched away. But they wound in and out among the shrubbery and out and round the fountain beds, following their carefully planned route for the mere mysterious pleasure of it. But when at last they turned into the Long Walk by the ivied walls the excited sense of an approaching thrill made them, for some curious reason they could not have explained, begin to speak in whispers.

"This is it," breathed Mary. "This is where I used to walk up and down and wonder and wonder."

"Is it?" cried Colin, and his eyes began to search the ivy with eager curiousness. "But I can see nothing," he whispered. "There is no door."

"That's what I thought," said Mary.

Then there was a lovely breathless silence and the chair wheeled on.

"That is the garden where Ben Weatherstaff works," said Mary.

"Is it?" said Colin.

A few yards more and Mary whispered again.

"This is where the robin flew over the wall," she said.

"Is it?" cried Colin. "Oh! I wish he'd come again!"

"And that," said Mary with solemn delight pointing under a big lilac bush, "is where he perched on the little heap of earth and showed me the key."

Then Colin sat up.

"Where? Where? There?" he cried, and his eyes were as big as the wolf's in Red Riding-Hood, when Red Riding-Hood felt called upon to remark on them. Dickon stood still and the wheeled chair stopped.

"And this," said Mary, stepping on to the bed close to the ivy, "is where I went to talk to him when he chirped at me from the top of the wall. And this is the ivy the wind blew back," and she took hold of the hanging green curtain.

"Oh! is it—is it!" gasped Colin.

"And here is the handle, and here is the door. Dickon, push him in—push him in quickly!"

And Dickon did it with one strong, steady, splendid push.

But Colin had actually dropped back against his cushions, even though he gasped with delight, and he had covered his eyes with his hands and held them there shutting out everything until they were inside and the chair stopped as if by magic and the door was closed. Not till then did he take them away and look round and round and round as Dickon and Mary had done. And over walls and earth and trees and swinging sprays and tendrils the fair green veil of tender little leaves had crept, and in the grass under the trees and the grey urns in the alcoves and here and there everywhere were touches or splashes of gold and purple and white and the trees were showing pink and snow above his head and there were fluttering of wings and faint sweet pipes and humming and scents and scents.* And the sun fell warm upon his face like a hand with a lovely touch. And in wonder Mary and Dickon stood and stared at him. He looked so strange and different because a pink glow of colour had actually crept all over him—ivory face and neck and hands and all.

"I shall get well! I shall get well!" he cried out. "Mary! Dickon! I shall get well! And I shall live forever and ever and ever!"

CHAPTER XXI

BEN WEATHERSTAFF

ONE of the strange things about living in the world is that it is only now and then one is quite sure one is going to live forever and ever and ever. One knows it sometimes when one gets up at the tender solemn dawn-time and goes out and stands alone and throws one's head far back and looks up and up and watches the pale sky slowly changing and flushing and marvellous unknown things happening until the East almost makes one cry out and one's heart stands still at the strange unchanging majesty of the rising of the sun—which has been happening every morning for thousands and thousands and thousands of years. One knows it then for a moment or so. And one knows it sometimes when one stands by oneself in a wood at sunset and the mysterious deep gold stillness slanting through and under the branches seems to be saying slowly again and again something one cannot quite hear, however much one tries. Then sometimes the immense quiet of the dark blue at night with millions of stars waiting and watching makes one sure; and sometimes a sound of far-off music makes it true; and sometimes a look in some one's eyes.

And it was like that with Colin when he first saw and heard and felt the Springtime inside the four high walls of a hidden garden. That afternoon the whole world seemed to devote itself to being perfect and radiantly beautiful and kind to one boy. Perhaps out of pure heavenly goodness the spring came and crowded everything it possibly could into that one place. More than once Dickon paused in what he was doing and stood still with a sort of growing wonder in his eyes, shaking his head softly.

"Eh! it is graidely," he said. "I'm twelve goin' on thirteen an' there's a lot o' afternoons in thirteen years, but seems to me like I never seed one as graidely as this 'ere."

"Aye, it is a graidely one," said Mary, and she sighed for mere joy. "I'll warrant it's th' graidelest one as ever was in this world."

"Does tha' think," said Colin with dreamy carefulness, "as happen it was made loike this 'ere all o' purpose for me?"

"My word!" cried Mary admiringly, "that there is a bit o' good Yorkshire. Tha'rt shapin' first-rate—that—tha' art."

And delight reigned.

They drew the chair under the plum-tree, which was snow-white with blossoms and musical with bees. It was like a king's canopy, a fairy king's. There were flowering cherry-trees near and apple-trees whose buds were pink and white, and here and there one had burst open wide. Between the blossoming branches of the canopy bits of blue sky looked down like wonderful eyes.

Mary and Dickon worked a little here and there and Colin watched them. They brought him things to look at—buds which were opening, buds which were tight closed, bits of twig whose leaves were just showing green, the feather of a woodpecker which had dropped on the grass, the empty shell of some bird early hatched. Dickon pushed the chair slowly round and round the garden, stopping every other moment to let him look at wonders springing out of the earth or trailing down from trees. It was like being taken in state round the country of a magic king and queen and shown all the mysterious riches it contained.

"I wonder if we shall see the robin?" said Colin.

"Tha'll see him often enow after a bit," answered Dickon. "When th' eggs hatches out th' little chap he'll be kep' so busy it'll make his head swim. Tha'll see him flyin' backward an' for'ard carryin' worms nigh as big as himsel' an' that much noise goin' on in th' nest when he gets there as fair flusters him so as he scarce knows which big mouth to drop th' first piece in. An' gapin' beaks an' squawks on every side. Mother says as when she sees th' work a robin has to keep them gapin' beaks filled, she feels like she was a lady with nothin' to do. She says she's seen th' little chaps when it seemed like th' sweat must be droppin' off 'em, though folk can't see it."

This made them giggle so delightedly that they were obliged to cover their mouths with their hands, remembering that they must not be heard. Colin had been instructed as to the law of whispers and low voices several days before. He liked the mysteriousness of it and did his best, but in the midst of excited enjoyment it is rather difficult never to laugh above a whisper.

Every moment of the afternoon was full of new things and every hour the sunshine grew more golden. The wheeled chair had been drawn back under the canopy and Dickon had sat down on the grass and had just drawn out his pipe when Colin saw something he had not had time to notice before.

"That's a very old tree over there, isn't it?" he said.

Dickon looked across the grass at the tree and Mary looked and there was a brief moment of stillness.

"Yes," answered Dickon, after it, and his low voice had a very gentle sound.

Mary gazed at the tree and thought.

"The branches are quite grey and there's not a single leaf any-where," Colin went on. "It's quite dead, isn't it?"

"Aye," admitted Dickon. "But them roses as has climbed all over it will near hide every bit o' th' dead wood when they're full o' leaves an' flowers. It won't look dead then. It'll be th' prettiest of all."

Mary still gazed at the tree and thought.

"It looks as if a big branch had been broken off," said Colin. "I wonder how it was done."

"It's been done many a year," answered Dickon. "Eh!" with a sudden relieved start and laying his hand on Colin. "Look at that robin! There he is! He's been foragin' for his mate."

Colin was almost too late but he just caught sight of him, the flash of red-breasted bird with something in his beak. He darted through the greenness and into the close-grown corner and was out of sight. Colin leaned back on his cushion again, laughing a little.

"He's taking her tea to her. Perhaps it's five o'clock. I think I'd like some tea myself."

And so they were safe.

"It was Magic which sent the robin," said Mary secretly to Dickon afterward. "I know it was Magic." For both she and Dickon had been afraid Colin might ask something about the tree whose branch had broken off ten years ago, and they had talked it over together and Dickon had stood and rubbed his head in a troubled way.

"We mun look as if it wasn't no different from th' other trees," he had said. "We couldn't never tell him how it broke, poor lad. If he says anything about it we mun—we mun try to look cheerful."

"Aye, that we mun," had answered Mary.

But she had not felt as if she looked cheerful when she gazed at the tree. She wondered and wondered in those few moments if there was any reality in that other thing Dickon had said. He had gone on rub-bing his rust-red hair in a puzzled way, but a nice comforted look had begun to grow in his blue eyes.

"Mrs. Craven was a very lovely young lady," he had gone on rather hesitatingly. "An' mother she thinks maybe she's about Misselthwaite many a time lookin' after Mester Colin, same as all mothers do when they're took out o' th' world. They have to come back, tha' sees. Happen* she's been in the garden an' happen it was her set us to work, an' told us to bring him here."

Mary had thought he meant something about Magic. She was a great believer in Magic. Secretly she quite believed that Dickon worked Magic, of course good Magic, on everything near him and that was why people liked him so much and wild creatures knew he was their friend. She wondered, indeed, if it were not possible that his gift had brought the robin just at the right moment when Colin asked that dangerous question. She felt that his Magic was working all the afternoon and making Colin look like an entirely different boy. It did not seem possible that he could be the crazy creature who had screamed and beaten and bitten his pillow. Even his ivory whiteness seemed to change. The faint glow of colour which had shown on his face and neck and hands when he first got inside the garden really never quite died away. He looked as if he were made of flesh instead of ivory or wax.

They saw the robin carry food to his mate two or three times, and it was so suggestive of afternoon tea that Colin felt they must have some.

"Go and make one of the men servants bring some in a basket to the rhododendron walk," he said. "And then you and Dickon can bring it here."

It was an agreeable idea; easily carried out, and when the white cloth was spread upon the grass, with hot tea and buttered toast and crumpets, a delightfully hungry meal was eaten, and several birds on domestic errands paused to inquire what was going on and were led into investigating crumbs with great activity. Nut and Shell whisked up trees with pieces of cake and Soot took the entire half of a buttered crumpet into a corner and pecked at and examined and turned it over and made hoarse remarks about it until he decided to swallow it all joyfully in one gulp.

The afternoon was dragging toward its mellow hour. The sun was deepening the gold of its lances, the bees were going home and the birds were flying past less often. Dickon and Mary were sitting on the grass, the tea-basket was repacked ready to be taken back to the house, and Colin was lying against his cushions with his heavy locks pushed back from his forehead and his face looking quite a natural colour.

"I don't want this afternoon to go," he said; "but I shall come back to-morrow, and the day after, and the day after, and the day after."

"You'll get plenty of fresh air, won't you?" said Mary.

"I'm going to get nothing else," he answered. "I've seen the spring now and I'm going to see the summer. I'm going to see everything grow here. I'm going to grow here myself."

"That tha' will," said Dickon. "Us'll have thee walkin' about here an' diggin' same as other folk afore long."

Colin flushed tremendously.

"Walk!" he said. "Dig! Shall I?"

Dickon's glance at him was delicately cautious. Neither he nor Mary had ever asked if anything was the matter with his legs.

"For sure tha' will," he said stoutly. "Tha'—tha's got legs o' thine own, same as other folks!"

Mary was rather frightened until she heard Colin's answer.

"Nothing really ails them," he said, "but they are so thin and weak. They shake so that I'm afraid to try to stand on them."

Both Mary and Dickon drew a relieved breath.

"When tha' stops bein' afraid tha'lt stand on 'em," Dickon said with renewed cheer. "An' tha'lt stop bein' afraid in a bit."

"I shall?" said Colin, and he lay still as if he were wondering about things.

They were really very quiet for a little while. The sun was dropping lower. It was that hour when everything stills itself, and they really had had a busy and exciting afternoon. Colin looked as if he were resting luxuriously. Even the creatures had ceased moving about and had drawn together and were resting near them. Soot had perched on a low branch and drawn up one leg and dropped the grey film* drowsily over his eyes. Mary privately thought he looked as if he might snore in a minute.

In the midst of this stillness it was rather startling when Colin half lifted his head and exclaimed in a loud, suddenly alarmed whisper:

"Who is that man?"

Dickon and Mary scrambled to their feet.

"Man?" they both cried in low quick voices.

Colin pointed to the high wall.

"Look!" he whispered excitedly. "Just look!"

Mary and Dickon wheeled about and looked. There was Ben Weatherstaff's indignant face glaring at them over the wall from the top of a ladder! He actually shook his fist at Mary.

"If I wasn't a bachelder, an' tha' was a wench o' mine," he cried, "I'd give thee a hidin'!"

He mounted another step threateningly as if it were his energetic intention to jump down and deal with her; but as she came toward him he evidently thought better of it and stood on the top step of his ladder shaking his fist down at her.

"I never thowt much o' thee!" he harangued. "I couldna' abide thee th' first time I set eyes on thee. A scrawny buttermilk-faced young besom,* allus askin' questions an' pokin' tha' nose where it wasna' wanted. I never knowed how tha' got so thick wi' me. If it hadna' been for th' robin—Drat him—"

"Ben Weatherstaff," called out Mary, finding her breath. She stood below him and called up to him with a sort of gasp. "Ben Weatherstaff, it was the robin who showed me the way!"

Then it did seem as if Ben really would scramble down on her side of the wall, he was so outraged.

"Tha' young bad 'un!" he called down at her. "Layin' tha' badness on a robin,—not but what he's impidint enow for anythin'. Him showin' thee th' way! Him! Eh! tha' young nowt,"—she could see his next words burst out because he was overpowered by curiosity— "however i' this world did tha' get in?"

"It was the robin who showed me the way," she protested obstinately. "He didn't know he was doing it but he did. And I can't tell you from here while you're shaking your fist at me."

He stopped shaking his fist very suddenly at that very moment and his jaw actually dropped as he stared over her head at something he saw coming over the grass toward him.

At the first sound of his torrent of words Colin had been so surprised that he had only sat up and listened as if he were spellbound. But in the midst of it he had recovered himself and beckoned imperiously to Dickon.

"Wheel me over there!" he commanded. "Wheel me quite close and stop right in front of him!"

And this, if you please, this is what Ben Weatherstaff beheld and which made his jaw drop. A wheeled chair with luxurious cushions and robes which came toward him looking rather like some sort of

State Coach because a young Rajah leaned back in it with royal command in his great black-rimmed eyes and a thin white hand extended haughtily toward him. And it stopped right under Ben Weatherstaff's nose. It was really no wonder his mouth dropped open.

"Do you know who I am?" demanded the Rajah.

How Ben Weatherstaff stared! His red old eyes fixed themselves on what was before him as if he were seeing a ghost. He gazed and gazed and gulped a lump down his throat and did not say a word.

"Do you know who I am?" demanded Colin still more imperiously. "Answer!"

Ben Weatherstaff put his gnarled hand up and passed it over his eyes and over his forehead and then he did answer in a queer shaky voice.

"Who tha' art?" he said. "Aye, that I do—wi' tha' mother's eyes starin' at me out o' tha' face. Lord knows how tha' come here. But tha'rt th' poor cripple."

Colin forgot that he had ever had a back. His face flushed scarlet and he sat bolt upright.

"I'm not a cripple!" he cried out furiously. "I'm not!"

"He's not!" cried Mary, almost shouting up the wall in her fierce indignation. "He's not got a lump as big as a pin! I looked and there was none there—not one!"

Ben Weatherstaff passed his hand over his forehead again and gazed as if he could never gaze enough. His hand shook and his mouth shook and his voice shook. He was an ignorant old man and a tactless old man and he could only remember the things he had heard.

"Tha'—tha' hasn't got a crooked back?" he said hoarsely.

"No!" shouted Colin.

"Tha'—tha' hasn't got crooked legs?" quavered Ben more hoarsely yet.

It was too much. The strength which Colin usually threw into his tantrums rushed through him now in a new way. Never yet had he been accused of crooked legs—even in whispers—and the perfectly simple belief in their existence which was revealed by Ben Weatherstaff's voice was more than Rajah flesh and blood could endure. His anger and insulted pride made him forget everything but this one moment and filled him with a power he had never known before, an almost unnatural strength.*

"Come here!" he shouted to Dickon, and he actually began to tear the coverings off his lower limbs and disentangle himself. "Come here! Come here! This minute!"

Dickon was by his side in a second. Mary caught her breath in a short gasp and felt herself turn pale.

"He can do it! He can do it! He can do it! He can!" she gabbled over to herself under her breath as fast as ever she could.

There was a brief fierce scramble, the rugs were tossed on to the ground, Dickon held Colin's arm, the thin legs were out, the thin feet were on the grass. Colin was standing upright—upright—as straight as an arrow and looking strangely tall—his head thrown back and his strange eyes flashing lightning.

"Look at me!" he flung up at Ben Weatherstaff. "Just look at me—you! Just look at me!"

"He's as straight as I am!" cried Dickon. "He's as straight as any lad i' Yorkshire!"

What Ben Weatherstaff did Mary thought queer beyond measure. He choked and gulped and suddenly tears ran down his weather-wrinkled cheeks as he struck his old hands together.

"Eh!" he burst forth, "th' lies folk tells! Tha'rt as thin as a lath an' as white as a wraith, but there's not a knob on thee. Tha'lt make a mon yet. God bless thee!"

Dickon held Colin's arm strongly but the boy had not begun to falter. He stood straighter and straighter and looked Ben Weatherstaff in the face.

"I'm your master," he said, "when my father is away. And you are to obey me. This is my garden. Don't dare to say a word about it! You get down from that ladder and go out to the Long Walk and Miss Mary will meet you and bring you here. I want to talk to you. We did not want you, but now you will have to be in the secret. Be quick!"

Ben Weatherstaff's crabbed old face was still wet with that one queer rush of tears. It seemed as if he could not take his eyes from thin straight Colin standing on his feet with his head thrown back.

"Eh! lad," he almost whispered. "Eh! my lad!" And then remembering himself he suddenly touched his hat gardener fashion and said, "Yes, sir! Yes, sir!" and obediently disappeared as he descended the ladder.

WHEN his head was out of sight Colin turned to Mary.

"Go and meet him," he said; and Mary flew across the grass to the door under the ivy.

Dickon was watching him with sharp eyes. There were scarlet spots on his cheeks and he looked amazing, but he showed no signs of falling.

"I can stand," he said, and his head was still held up and he said it quite grandly.

"I told thee tha' could as soon as tha' stopped bein' afraid," answered Dickon. "An' tha's stopped."

"Yes, I've stopped," said Colin.

Then suddenly he remembered something Mary had said.

"Are you making Magic?"* he asked sharply.

Dickon's curly mouth spread in a cheerful grin.

"Tha's doin' Magic thysel'," he said. "It's same Magic as made these 'ere work out o' th' earth," and he touched with his thick boot a clump of crocuses in the grass.

Colin look down at them.

"Aye," he said slowly, "there couldna' be bigger Magic then that there—there couldna' be."

He drew himself up straighter than ever.

"I'm going to walk to that tree," he said, pointing to one a few feet away from him. "I'm going to be standing when Weatherstaff comes here. I can rest against the tree if I like. When I want to sit down I will sit down, but not before. Bring a rug from the chair."

He walked to the tree and though Dickon held his arm he was wonderfully steady. When he stood against the tree trunk it was not too plain that he supported himself against it, and he still held himself so straight that he looked tall.

When Ben Weatherstaff came through the door in the wall he saw him standing there and he heard Mary muttering something under her breath.

"What art sayin'?" he asked rather testily because he did not want his attention distracted from the long thin straight boy figure and proud face.

But she did not tell him. What she was saying was this:

"You can do it! You can do it! I told you you could! You can do it! You can do it! You *can!*"*

She was saying it to Colin because she wanted to make Magic and keep him on his feet looking like that. She could not bear that he should give in before Ben Weatherstaff. He did not give in. She was uplifted by a sudden feeling that he looked quite beautiful in spite of his thinness. He fixed his eyes on Ben Weatherstaff in his funny imperious way.

"Look at me!" he commanded. "Look at me all over! Am I a hunchback? Have I got crooked legs?"

Ben Weatherstaff had not quite got over his emotion, but he had recovered a little and answered almost in his usual way.

"Not tha'," he said. "Nowt o' th' sort. What's tha' been doin' with thysel'—hidin' out o' sight an' lettin' folk think tha' was cripple an' half-witted?"

"Half-witted!" said Colin angrily. "Who thought that?"

"Lots o' fools," said Ben. "Th' world's full o' jackasses brayin' an' they never bray nowt but lies. What did tha' shut thysel' up for?"

"Every one thought I was going to die," said Colin shortly. "I'm not!"

And he said it with such decision Ben Weatherstaff looked him over, up and down, down and up.

"Tha' die!" he said with dry exultation. "Nowt o' th' sort! Tha's got too much pluck in thee. When I seed thee put tha' legs on th' ground in such a hurry I knowed tha' was all right. Sit thee down on th' rug a bit young Mester an' give me thy orders."

There was a queer mixture of crabbed tenderness and shrewd understanding in his manner. Mary had poured out speech as rapidly as she could as they had come down the Long Walk. The chief thing to be remembered, she had told him, was that Colin was getting well—getting well. The garden was doing it. No one must let him remember about having humps and dying.

The Rajah condescended to seat himself on a rug under the tree.

"What work do you do in the gardens, Weatherstaff?" he inquired.

"Anythin' I'm told to do," answered old Ben. "I'm kep' on by favour—because she liked me."

"She?" said Colin.

"Tha' mother," answered Ben Weatherstaff.

"My mother?" said Colin, and he looked about him quietly. "This was her garden, wasn't it?"

"Aye, it was that!" and Ben Weatherstaff looked about him too. "She were main fond of it."

"It is my garden now. I am fond of it. I shall come here every day," announced Colin. "But it is to be a secret. My orders are that no one is to know that we come here. Dickon and my cousin have worked and made it come alive. I shall send for you sometimes to help—but you must come when no one can see you."

Ben Weatherstaff's face twisted itself in a dry old smile.

"I've come here before when no one saw me," he said.

"What!" exclaimed Colin. "When?"

"Th' last time I was here," rubbing his chin and looking round, "was about two year' ago."

"But no one has been in it for ten years!" cried Colin. "There was no door!"

"I'm no one," said old Ben dryly. "An' I didn't come through th' door. I come over th' wall. Th' rheumatics held me back th' last two year'."

"Tha' come an' did a bit o' prunin'!" cried Dickon. "I couldn't make out how it had been done."

"She was so fond of it—she was!" said Ben Weatherstaff slowly. "An' she was such a pretty young thing. She says to me once, 'Ben,' says she laughin', 'if ever I'm ill or if I go away you must take care of my roses.' When she did go away th' orders was no one was ever to come nigh. But I come," with grumpy obstinacy. "Over th' wall I come—until th' rheumatics stopped me—an' I did a bit o' work once a year. She'd gave her order first."

"It wouldn't have been as wick as it is if tha' hadn't done it," said Dickon. "I did wonder."

"I'm glad you did it, Weatherstaff," said Colin. "You'll know how to keep the secret."

"Aye, I'll know, sir," answered Ben. "An' it'll be easier for a man wi' rheumatics to come in at th' door."

On the grass near the tree Mary had dropped her trowel. Colin stretched out his hand and took it up. An odd expression came into his face and he began to scratch at the earth. His thin hand was weak enough but presently as they watched him—Mary with quite breathless interest—he drove the end of the trowel into the soil and turned some over.

"You can do it! You can do it!" said Mary to herself. "I tell you, you can!"

Dickon's round eyes were full of eager curiousness but he said not a word. Ben Weatherstaff looked on with interested face.

Colin persevered. After he had turned a few trowelfuls of soil he spoke exultantly to Dickon in his best Yorkshire.

"Tha' said as tha'd have me walkin' about here same as other folk—an' tha' said tha'd have me diggin'. I thowt tha' was just leein' to please me. This is only th' first day an' I've walked—an' here I am diggin'."

Ben Weatherstaff's mouth fell open again when he heard him, but he ended by chuckling.

"Eh!" he said, "that sounds as if tha'd got wits enow. Tha'rt a Yorkshire lad for sure. An' tha'rt diggin', too. How'd tha' like to plant a bit o' somethin'? I can get thee a rose in a pot."

"Go and get it!" said Colin, digging excitedly. "Quick! Quick!"

It was done quickly enough indeed. Ben Weatherstaff went his way forgetting rheumatics. Dickon took his spade and dug the hole deeper and wider than a new digger with thin white hands could make it. Mary slipped out to run and bring back a watering-can. When Dickon had deepened the hole Colin went on turning the soft earth over and over. He looked up at the sky, flushed and glowing with the strangely new exercise, slight as it was.

"I want to do it before the sun goes quite—quite down," he said.

Mary thought that perhaps the sun held back a few minutes just on purpose. Ben Weatherstaff brought the rose in its pot from the greenhouse. He hobbled over the grass as fast as he could. He had begun to be excited, too. He knelt down by the hole and broke the pot from the mould.

"Here, lad," he said, handing the plant to Colin. "Set it in the earth thysel' same as th' king does when he goes to a new place."

The thin white hands shook a little and Colin's flush grew deeper as he set the rose in the mould and held it while old Ben made firm the earth. It was filled in and pressed down and made steady. Mary was leaning forward on her hands and knees. Soot had flown down and marched forward to see what was being done. Nut and Shell chattered about it from a cherry-tree.

"It's planted!" said Colin at last. "And the sun is only slipping over the edge. Help me up, Dickon. I want to be standing when it goes. That's part of the Magic."

And Dickon helped him, and the Magic—or whatever it was—so gave him strength that when the sun did slip over the edge and end the strange lovely afternoon for them there he actually stood on his two feet—laughing.

CHAPTER XXIII

MAGIC

DR. CRAVEN had been waiting some time at the house when they returned to it. He had indeed begun to wonder if it might not be wise to send some one out to explore the garden paths. When Colin was brought back to his room the poor man looked him over seriously.

"You should not have stayed so long," he said. "You must not over exert yourself."

"I am not tired at all," said Colin. "It has made me well. To-morrow I am going out in the morning as well as in the afternoon."

"I am not sure that I can allow it," answered Dr. Craven. "I am afraid it would not be wise."

"It would not be wise to try to stop me," said Colin quite seriously. "I am going."

Even Mary had found out that one of Colin's chief peculiarities was that he did not know in the least what a rude little brute he was with his way of ordering people about. He had lived on a sort of desert island all his life and as he had been the king of it he had made his own manners and had had no one to compare himself with. Mary had indeed been rather like him herself and since she had been at Misselthwaite had gradually discovered that her own manners had not been of the kind which is usual or popular. Having made this discovery she naturally thought it of enough interest to communicate to Colin. So she sat and looked at him curiously for a few minutes after Dr. Craven had gone. She wanted to make him ask her why she was doing it and of course she did.

"What are you looking at me for?" he said.

"I'm thinking that I am rather sorry for Dr. Craven."

"So am I," said Colin calmly, but not without an air of some satisfaction. "He won't get Misselthwaite at all now I'm not going to die."

"I'm sorry for him because of that, of course," said Mary, "but I was thinking just then that it must have been very horrid to have had to be polite for ten years to a boy who was always rude. I would never have done it."

"Am I rude?" Colin inquired undisturbedly.

"If you had been his own boy and he had been a slapping sort of man," said Mary, "he would have slapped you."

"But he daren't," said Colin.

"No, he daren't," answered Mistress Mary, thinking the thing out quite without prejudice. "Nobody ever dared to do anything you didn't like—because you were going to die and things like that. You were such a poor thing."

"But," announced Colin stubbornly, "I am not going to be a poor thing. I won't let people think I'm one. I stood on my feet this afternoon."

"It is always having your own way that has made you so queer," Mary went on, thinking aloud.

Colin turned his head, frowning.

"Am I queer?" he demanded.

"Yes," answered Mary, "very. But you needn't be cross," she added impartially, "because so am I queer—and so is Ben Weatherstaff. But I am not as queer as I was before I began to like people and before I found the garden."

"I don't want to be queer," said Colin. "I am not going to be," and he frowned again with determination.

He was a very proud boy. He lay thinking for a while and then Mary saw his beautiful smile begin and gradually change his whole face.

"I shall stop being queer," he said, "if I go every day to the garden. There is Magic in there—good Magic, you know, Mary. I am sure there is."

"So am I," said Mary.

"Even if it isn't real Magic," Colin said, "we can pretend it is. *Something* is there—*something!*"

"It's Magic," said Mary, "but not black. It's as white as snow."

They always called it Magic and indeed it seemed like it in the months that followed—the wonderful months—the radiant months—the amazing ones. Oh! the things which happened in that garden! If you have never had a garden, you cannot understand, and if you have had a garden you will know that it would take a whole book to describe all that came to pass there. At first it seemed that green things would never cease pushing their way through the earth, in the grass, in the beds, even in the crevices of the walls. Then the green things began to show buds, and the buds began to unfurl and show colour, every shade of blue, every shade of purple, every tint and hue of crimson. In its happy days flowers had been tucked away into every inch and hole and corner. Ben Weatherstaff had seen it done and had himself scraped out mortar from between the bricks of the wall and made pockets of earth for lovely clinging things to grow on. Iris and white lilies rose out of the grass in sheaves, and the green alcoves filled themselves with amazing armies of the blue and white flower lances of tall delphiniums or columbines or campanulas.

"She was main fond o' them—she was," Ben Weatherstaff said. "She liked them things as was allus pointin' up to th' blue sky, she used to tell. Not as she was one o' them as looked down on th' earth—not her. She just loved it but she said as th' blue sky allus looked so joyful."

The seeds Dickon and Mary had planted grew as if fairies had tended them. Satiny poppies of all tints danced in the breeze by the score, gaily defying flowers which had lived in the garden for years, and which it might be confessed seemed rather to wonder how such new people had got there. And the roses—the roses! Rising out of the grass, tangled round the sun-dial, wreathing the tree trunks, and hanging from their branches, climbing up the walls and spreading over them with long garlands falling in cascades—they came alive day by day, hour by hour. Fair fresh leaves, and buds—and buds—tiny at first but swelling and working Magic until they burst and uncurled into cups of scent delicately spilling themselves over their brims and filling the garden air.

Colin saw it all, watching each change as it took place. Every morning he was brought out and every hour of each day, when it didn't rain he spent in the garden. Even grey days pleased him. He would lie on the grass "watching things growing," he said. If you watched long enough, he declared, you could see buds unsheath themselves. Also you could make the acquaintance of strange busy insect things running about on various unknown but evidently serious errands, sometimes carrying tiny scraps of straw or feather or food, or climbing blades of grass as if they were trees from whose tops one could look out to explore the country. A mole throwing up its mound at the end of its burrow and making its way out at last with the long-nailed paws which looked so like elfish hands, had absorbed him one whole morning. Ants' ways, beetles' ways, bees' ways, frogs' ways, birds' ways, plants' ways, gave him a new world to explore, and when Dickon revealed them all and added foxes' ways, otters' ways, ferrets' ways, squirrels' ways, and trouts' and water-rats' and badgers' ways, there was no end to the things to talk about and think over.

And this was not the half of the Magic. The fact that he had really once stood on his feet had set Colin thinking tremendously and when Mary told him of the spell she had worked he was excited and approved of it greatly. He talked of it constantly.

"Of course there must be lots of Magic in the world," he said wisely one day, "but people don't know what it is like or how to make it. Perhaps the beginning is just to say nice things are going to happen until you make them happen. I am going to try and experiment."

The next morning when they went to the secret garden he sent at once for Ben Weatherstaff. Ben came as quickly as he could and found the Rajah standing on his feet under a tree and looking very grand but also very beautifully smiling.

"Good morning, Ben Weatherstaff," he said. "I want you and Dickon and Miss Mary to stand in a row and listen to me because I am going to tell you something very important."

"Aye, aye, sir!" answered Ben Weatherstaff, touching his forehead. (One of the long concealed charms of Ben Weatherstaff was that in his boyhood he had once run away to sea and had made voyages. So he could reply like a sailor.)

"I am going to try a scientific experiment," explained the Rajah. "When I grow up I am going to make great scientific discoveries and I am going to begin now with this experiment."

"Aye, aye, sir!" said Ben Weatherstaff promptly, though this was the first time he had heard of great scientific discoveries.

It was the first time Mary had heard of them, either, but even at this stage she had begun to realise that, queer as he was, Colin had read about a great many singular things and was somehow a very convincing sort of boy. When he held up his head and fixed his strange eyes on you it seemed as if you believed him almost in spite of yourself, though he was only ten years old—going on eleven. At this moment he was especially convincing because he suddenly felt the fascination of actually making a sort of speech like a grown-up person.

"The great scientific discoveries I am going to make," he went on, "will be about Magic. Magic is a great thing and scarcely any one knows anything about it except a few people in old books—and Mary a little, because she was born in India where there are fakirs.* I believe Dickon knows some Magic, but perhaps he doesn't know he knows it. He charms animals and people. I would never have let him come to see me if he had not been an animal charmer—which is a boy charmer, too, because a boy is an animal. I am sure there is Magic in everything, only we have not sense enough to get hold of it and make it do things for us—like electricity and horses and steam."

This sounded so imposing that Ben Weatherstaff became quite excited and really could not keep still.

"Aye, aye, sir," he said and he began to stand up quite straight.

"When Mary found this garden it looked quite dead," the orator proceeded. "Then something began pushing things up out of the soil and making things out of nothing. One day things weren't there and another they were. I had never watched things before and it made me feel very curious. Scientific people are always curious and I am going to be scientific. I keep saying to myself, 'What is it? What is it?' It's something. It can't be nothing! I don't know its name so I call it Magic. I have never seen the sun rise but Mary and Dickon have and from what they tell me I am sure that is Magic too. Something pushes it up and draws it. Sometimes since I've been in the garden I've looked up through the trees at the sky and I have had a strange feeling of being happy as if something were pushing and drawing in my chest and making me breathe fast. Magic is always pushing and drawing and making things out of nothing. Everything is made out of Magic, leaves and trees, flowers and birds, badgers and foxes and squirrels and people. So it must be all around us. In this garden—in all the places. The Magic in this garden has made me stand up and know I am going to live to be a man. I am going to make the scientific experiment of trying to get some and put it in myself and make it push and draw me and make me strong. I don't know how to do it but I think that if you keep thinking about it and calling it perhaps it will come. Perhaps that is the first baby way to get it. When I was going to try to stand that first time Mary kept saying to herself as fast as she could, 'You can do it! You can do it!' and I did. I had to try myself at the same time, of course, but her Magic helped me—and so did Dickon's. Every morning and evening and as often in the daytime as I can remember I am going to say, 'Magic is in me! Magic is making me well! I am going to be as strong as Dickon, as strong as Dickon!'* And you must all do it, too. That is my experiment. Will you help, Ben Weatherstaff?"

"Aye, aye, sir!" said Ben Weatherstaff. "Aye, aye!"

"If you keep doing it every day as regularly as soldiers go through drill we shall see what will happen and find out if the experiment succeeds. You learn things by saying them over and over and thinking about them until they stay in your mind forever and I think it will be the same with Magic. If you keep calling it to come to you and help you it will get to be part of you and it will stay and do things."

"I once heard an officer in India tell my mother that there were fakirs who said words over and over thousands of times," said Mary.

"I've heard Jem Fettleworth's wife say th' same thing over thousands o' times—callin' Jem a drunken brute," said Ben Weatherstaff dryly. "Summat allus come o' that, sure enough. He gave her a good hidin' an' went to th' 'Blue Lion' an' got as drunk as a lord."

Colin drew his brows together and thought a few minutes. Then he cheered up.

"Well," he said, "you see something did come of it. She used the wrong Magic until she made him beat her. If she'd used the right Magic and had said something nice perhaps he wouldn't have got as drunk as a lord and perhaps—perhaps he might have bought her a new bonnet."

Ben Weatherstaff chuckled and there was shrewd admiration in his little old eyes.

"Tha'rt a clever lad as well as a straight-legged one, Mester Colin," he said. "Next time I see Bess Fettleworth I'll give her a bit of a hint o' what Magic will do for her. She'd be rare an' pleased if th' sinetifik 'speriment worked—an' so 'ud Jem."

Dickon had stood listening to the lecture, his round eyes shining with curious delight. Nut and Shell were on his shoulders and he held a long-eared white rabbit in his arm and stroked and stroked it softly while it laid its ears along its back and enjoyed itself.

"Do you think the experiment will work?" Colin asked him, wondering what he was thinking. He so often wondered what Dickon was thinking when he saw him looking at him or at one of his "creatures" with his happy wide smile.

He smiled now and his smile was wider than usual.

"Aye," he answered, "that I do. It'll work same as th' seeds do when th' sun shines on 'em. It'll work for sure. Shall us begin it now?"

Colin was delighted and so was Mary. Fired by recollections of fakirs and devotees in illustrations Colin suggested that they should all sit cross-legged under the tree, which made a canopy.

"It will be like sitting in a sort of temple," said Colin. "I'm rather tired and I want to sit down."

"Eh!" said Dickon, "tha' mustn't begin by sayin' tha'rt tired. Tha' might spoil th' Magic."

Colin turned and looked at him—into his innocent round eyes.

"That's true," he said slowly. "I must only think of the Magic."

It all seemed most majestic and mysterious when they sat down in their circle. Ben Weatherstaff felt as if he had somehow been led into appearing at a prayer-meeting. Ordinarily he was very fixed in being what he called "agen' prayer-meetin's" but this being the Rajah's affair he did not resent it and was indeed inclined to be gratified at being called upon to assist. Mistress Mary felt solemnly enraptured. Dickon held his rabbit in his arm, and perhaps he made some charmer's signal no one heard, for when he sat down, cross-legged like the rest, the crow, the fox, the squirrels and the lamb slowly drew near and made part of the circle, settling each into a place of rest as if of their own desire.

"The 'creatures' have come," said Colin gravely. "They want to help us."

Colin really looked quite beautiful, Mary thought. He held his head high as if he felt like a sort of priest and his strange eyes had a wonderful look in them. The light shone on him through the tree canopy.

"Now we will begin," he said. "Shall we sway backward and forward, Mary, as if we were dervishes?"*

"I canna' do no swayin' back'ard and for'ard," said Ben Weatherstaff. "I've got th' rheumatics."

"The Magic will take them away," said Colin in a High Priest tone, "but we won't sway until it has done it. We will only chant."

"I canna' do no chantin'," said Ben Weatherstaff a trifle testily. "They turned me out o' th' church choir th' only time I ever tried it."

No one smiled. They were all too much in earnest. Colin's face was not even crossed by a shadow. He was thinking only of the Magic.

"Then I will chant," he said. And he began, looking like a strange boy spirit. "The sun is shining—the sun is shining. That is the Magic. The flowers are growing—the roots are stirring. That is the Magic. Being alive is the Magic—being strong is the Magic. The Magic is in me—the Magic is in me. It is in me—it is in me. It's in every one of us. It's in Ben Weatherstaff's back. Magic! Magic! Come and help!"

He said it a great many times—not a thousand times but quite a goodly number. Mary listened entranced. She felt as if it were at once queer and beautiful and she wanted him to go on and on. Ben Weatherstaff began to feel soothed into a sort of dream which was quite agreeable. The humming of the bees in the blossoms mingled with the chanting voice and drowsily melted into a doze. Dickon sat cross-legged with his rabbit asleep on his arm and a hand resting on the lamb's back. Soot had pushed away a squirrel and huddled close to him on his shoulder, the grey film dropped over his eyes. At last Colin stopped.

"Now I am going to walk round the garden," he announced.

Ben Weatherstaff's head had just dropped forward and he lifted it with a jerk.

"You have been asleep," said Colin.

"Nowt o' th' sort," mumbled Ben. "Th' sermon was good enow—but I'm bound to get out afore th' collection."

He was not quite awake yet.

"You're not in church," said Colin.

"Not me," said Ben, straightening himself. "Who said I were? I heard every bit of it. You said th' Magic was in my back. Th' doctor calls it rheumatics."

The Rajah waved his hand.

"That was the wrong Magic," he said. "You will get better. You have my permission to go to your work. But come back to-morrow."

"I'd like to see thee walk round the garden," grunted Ben.

It was not an unfriendly grunt, but it was a grunt. In fact, being a stubborn old party and not having entire faith in Magic he had made up his mind that if he were sent away he would climb his ladder and look over the wall so that he might be ready to hobble back if there were any stumbling.

The Rajah did not object to his staying and so the procession was formed. It really did look like a procession. Colin was at its head with Dickon on one side and Mary on the other. Ben Weatherstaff walked behind, and the "creatures" trailed after them, the lamb and the fox cub keeping close to Dickon, the white rabbit hopping along or stopping to nibble and Soot following with the solemnity of a person who felt himself in charge.

It was a procession which moved slowly but with dignity. Every few yards it stopped to rest. Colin leaned on Dickon's arm and privately Ben Weatherstaff kept a sharp lookout, but now and then Colin took his hand from its support and walked a few steps alone. His head was held up all the time and he looked very grand.

"The Magic is in me!" he kept saying. "The Magic is making me strong! I can feel it! I can feel it!"

It seemed very certain that something was upholding and uplifting him. He sat on the seats in the alcoves, and once or twice he sat down on the grass and several times he paused in the path and leaned on Dickon, but he would not give up until he had gone all round the garden. When he returned to the canopy tree his cheeks were flushed and he looked triumphant.

"I did it! The Magic worked!" he cried. "That is my first scientific discovery."

"What will Dr. Craven say?" broke out Mary.

"He won't say anything," Colin answered, "because he will not be told. This is to be the biggest secret of all. No one is to know anything about it until I have grown so strong that I can walk and run like any other boy. I shall come here every day in my chair and I shall be taken back in it. I won't have people whispering and asking questions and I won't let my father hear about it until the experiment has quite succeeded. Then sometime when he comes back to Misselthwaite I shall just walk into his study and say 'Here I am; I am like any other boy. I am quite well and I shall live to be a man. It has been done by a scientific experiment.'"

"He will think he is in a dream," cried Mary. "He won't believe his eyes."

Colin flushed triumphantly. He had made himself believe that he was going to get well, which was really more than half the battle, if he had been aware of it. And the thought which stimulated him more than any other was this imagining what his father would look like when he saw that he had a son who was as straight and strong as other fathers' sons. One of his darkest miseries in the unhealthy morbid past days had been his hatred of being a sickly weak-backed boy whose father was afraid to look at him.

"He'll be obliged to believe them," he said. "One of the things I am going to do, after the Magic works and before I begin to make scientific discoveries, is to be an athlete."

"We shall have thee takin' to boxin' in a week or so," said Ben Weatherstaff. "Tha'lt end wi' winnin' th' Belt an' bein' champion prize-fighter* of all England."

Colin fixed his eyes on him sternly.

"Weatherstaff," he said, "that is disrespectful. You must not take liberties because you are in the secret. However much the Magic works I shall not be a prize-fighter. I shall be a Scientific Discoverer."

"Ax pardon—ax pardon, sir," answered Ben, touching his forehead in salute. "I ought to have seed it wasn't a jokin' matter," but his eyes twinkled and secretly he was immensely pleased. He really did not mind being snubbed since the snubbing meant that the lad was gaining strength and spirit.

CHAPTER XXIV

"LET THEM LAUGH"

THE secret garden was not the only one Dickon worked in. Round the cottage on the moor there was a piece of ground enclosed by a low wall of rough stones. Early in the morning and late in the fading twilight and on all the days Colin and Mary did not see him, Dickon worked there planting or tending potatoes and cabbages, turnips and carrots and herbs for his mother. In the company of his "creatures" he did wonders there and was never tired of doing them, it seemed. While he dug or weeded he whistled or sang bits of Yorkshire moor songs or talked to Soot or Captain or the brothers and sisters he had taught to help him.

"We'd never get on as comfortable as we do," Mrs. Sowerby said, "if it wasn't for Dickon's garden. Anything'll grow for him. His 'taters and cabbages is twice th' size of any one else's an' they've got a flavour with 'em as nobody's has."

When she found a moment to spare she liked to go out and talk to him. After supper there was still a long clear twilight to work in and that was her quiet time. She could sit upon the low rough wall and look on and hear stories of the day. She loved this time. There were not only vegetables in this garden, Dickon had bought penny packages of flower seeds now and then and sown bright sweet-scented things among gooseberry bushes and even cabbages and he grew borders of mignonette and pinks and pansies and things whose seeds he could save year after year or whose roots would bloom each spring and spread in time into fine clumps. The low wall was one of the prettiest things in Yorkshire because he had tucked moorland foxglove and ferns and rockcress* and hedgerow flowers into every crevice until only here and there glimpses of the stones were to be seen.

"All a chap's got to do to make 'em thrive, mother," he would say, "is to be friends with 'em for sure. They're just like th' 'creatures.' If they're thirsty give 'em a drink, and if they're hungry give 'em a bit o' food. They want to live same as we do. If they died I should feel as if I'd been a bad lad and somehow treated them heartless."

It was in these twilight hours that Mrs. Sowerby heard of all that happened at Misselthwaite Manor. At first she was only told that

"Mester Colin" had taken a fancy to going out into the grounds with Miss Mary and that it was doing him good. But it was not long before it was agreed between the two children that Dickon's mother might "come into the secret." Somehow it was not doubted that she was "safe for sure."

So one beautiful still evening Dickon told the whole story, with all the thrilling details of the buried key and the robin and the grey haze which had seemed like deadness and the secret Mistress Mary had planned never to reveal. The coming of Dickon and how it had been told to him, the doubt of Mester Colin and the final drama of his introduction to the hidden domain, combined with the incident of Ben Weatherstaff's angry face peering over the wall and Mester Colin's sudden indignant strength, made Mrs. Sowerby's nice-looking face quite change colour several times.

"My word!" she said. "It was a good thing that little lass came to th' Manor.* It's been th' makin' o' her an' th' savin' o' him. Standin' on his feet! An' us all thinkin' he was a poor half-witted lad with not a straight bone in him."

She asked a great many questions and her blue eyes were full of deep thinking.

"What do they make of it at th' Manor—him being so well an' cheerful an' never complainin'?" she inquired.

"They don't know what to make of it," answered Dickon. "Every day as comes round his face looks different. It's fillin' out and doesn't look so sharp an' th' waxy colour is goin'. But he has to do his bit o' complainin'," with a highly entertained grin.

"What for, i' Mercy's name?" asked Mrs. Sowerby.

Dickon chuckled.

"He does it to keep them from guessin' what's happened. If the doctor knew he'd found out he could stand on his feet he'd likely write and tell Mester Craven. Mester Colin's savin' th' secret to tell himself. He's goin' to practise his Magic on his legs every day till his father comes back an' then he's goin' to march into his room an' show him he's as straight as other lads. But him an' Miss Mary thinks it's best plan to do a bit o' groanin' an' frettin' now an' then to throw folk off th' scent."

Mrs. Sowerby was laughing a low comfortable laugh long before he had finished his last sentence.

"Eh!" she said, "that pair's enjoyin' theirselves, I'll warrant. They'll get a good bit o' play actin' out of it, an' there's nothin' children likes as much as play actin'. Let's hear what they do, Dickon, lad."

Dickon stopped weeding and sat up on his heels to tell her. His eyes were twinkling with fun.

"Mester Colin is carried down to his chair every time he goes out," he explained. "An' he flies out at John, th' footman, for not carryin' him careful enough. He makes himself as helpless lookin' as he can an' never lifts his head until we're out o' sight o' th' house. An' he grunts an' frets a good bit when he's bein' settled into his chair. Him an' Miss Mary's both got to enjoyin' it an' when he groans an' complains she'll say, 'Poor Colin! Does it hurt you so much? Are you so weak as that, poor Colin?'—but th' trouble is that sometimes they can scarce keep from burstin' out laughin'. When we get safe into the garden they laugh till they've no breath left to laugh with. An' they have to stuff their faces into Mester Colin's cushions to keep the gardeners from hearin', if any of 'em's about."

"Th' more they laugh th' better for 'em!" said Mrs. Sowerby, still laughing herself. "Good healthy child laughin's better than pills any day o' th' year. That pair'll plump up for sure."

"They are plumpin' up," said Dickon. "They're that hungry they don't know how to get enough to eat without makin' talk. Mester Colin says if he keeps sendin' for more food they won't believe he's an invalid at all. Miss Mary says she'll let him eat her share, but he says that if she goes hungry she'll get thin an' they mun both get fat at once."

Mrs. Sowerby laughed so heartily at the revelation of this difficulty, that she quite rocked backward and forward in her blue cloak,* and Dickon laughed with her.

"I'll tell thee what, lad," Mrs. Sowerby said when she could speak. "I've thought of a way to help 'em. When tha' goes to 'em in th' mornin's tha' shall take a pail o' good new milk an' I'll bake 'em a crusty cottage loaf or some buns wi' currants in 'em, same as you children like. Nothin's so good as fresh milk an' bread.* Then they could take off th' edge o' their hunger while they were in their garden an' th' fine food they get indoors 'ud polish off th' corners."

"Eh! mother!" said Dickon admiringly, "what a wonder tha' art! Tha' always sees a way out o' things. They was quite in a pother yesterday. They didn't see how they was to manage without orderin' up more food—they felt that empty inside."

"They're two young 'uns growin' fast, and health's comin' back to both of 'em. Children like that feels like young wolves an' food's flesh an' blood to 'em," said Mrs. Sowerby. Then she smiled Dickon's own curving smile. "Eh! but they're enjoyin' theirselves for sure," she said.

She was quite right, the comfortable wonderful mother creature— and she had never been more so than when she said their "play actin' " would be their joy. Colin and Mary found it one of their most thrilling sources of entertainment. The idea of protecting themselves from suspicion had been unconsciously suggested to them first by the puzzled nurse and then by Dr. Craven himself.

"Your appetite is improving very much, Master Colin," the nurse had said one day. "You used to eat nothing, and so many things disagreed with you."

"Nothing disagrees with me now," replied Colin, and then seeing the nurse looking at him curiously he suddenly remembered that perhaps he ought not to appear too well just yet. "At least things don't so often disagree with me. It's the fresh air."

"Perhaps it is," said the nurse, still looking at him with a mystified expression. "But I must talk to Dr. Craven about it."

"How she stared at you!" said Mary when she went away. "As if she thought there must be something to find out."

"I won't have her finding out things," said Colin. "No one must begin to find out yet."

When Dr. Craven came that morning he seemed puzzled also. He asked a number of questions, to Colin's great annoyance.

"You stay out in the garden a great deal," he suggested. "Where do you go?"

Colin put on his favourite air of dignified indifference to opinion.

"I will not let any one know where I go," he answered. "I go to a place I like. Every one has orders to keep out of the way. I won't be watched and stared at. You know that!"

"You seem to be out all day, but I do not think it has done you harm—I do not think so. The nurse says that you eat much more than you have ever done before."

"Perhaps," said Colin, prompted by a sudden inspiration, "perhaps it is an unnatural appetite."

"I do not think so, as your food seems to agree with you," said Dr. Craven. "You are gaining flesh rapidly and your colour is better."

"Perhaps—perhaps I am bloated and feverish," said Colin, assuming a discouraging air of gloom. "People who are not going to live are often—different."

Dr. Craven shook his head. He was holding Colin's wrist and he pushed up his sleeve and felt his arm.

"You are not feverish," he said thoughtfully, "and such flesh as you have gained is healthy. If we can keep this up, my boy, we need not talk of dying. Your father will be very happy to hear of this remarkable improvement."

"I won't have him told!" Colin broke forth fiercely. "It will only disappoint him if I get worse again—and I may get worse this very night. I might have a raging fever. I feel as if I might be beginning to have one now. I won't have letters written to my father—I won't—I won't! You are making me angry and you know that is bad for me. I feel hot already. I hate being written about and being talked over as much as I hate being stared at!"

"Hush-h! my boy," Dr. Craven soothed him. "Nothing shall be written without your permission. You are too sensitive about things. You must not undo the good which has been done."

He said no more about writing to Mr. Craven and when he saw the nurse he privately warned her that such a possibility must not be mentioned to the patient.

"The boy is extraordinarily better," he said. "His advance seems almost abnormal. But of course he is doing now of his own free will what we could not make him do before. Still, he excites himself very easily and nothing must be said to irritate him."

Mary and Colin were much alarmed and talked together anxiously. From this time dated their plan of "play actin'."

"I may be obliged to have a tantrum," said Colin regretfully. "I don't want to have one and I'm not miserable enough now to work myself into a big one. Perhaps I couldn't have one at all. That lump doesn't come in my throat now and I keep thinking of nice things instead of horrible ones. But if they talk about writing to my father I shall have to do something."

He made up his mind to eat less, but unfortunately it was not possible to carry out this brilliant idea when he wakened each morning with an amazing appetite and the table near his sofa was set with a breakfast of home-made bread and fresh butter, snow-white eggs, raspberry jam and clotted cream. Mary always breakfasted with him and when they found themselves at the table—particularly if there were delicate slices of sizzling ham sending forth tempting odours from under a hot silver cover—they would look into each other's eyes in desperation.*

"I think we shall have to eat it all this morning, Mary," Colin always ended by saying. "We can send away some of the lunch and a great deal of the dinner."

But they never found they could send away anything, and the highly polished condition of the empty plates returned to the pantry awakened much comment.

"I do wish," Colin would say also, "I do wish the slices of ham were thicker, and one muffin each is not enough for any one."

"It's enough for a person who is going to die," answered Mary when first she heard this, "but it's not enough for a person who is going to live. I sometimes feel as if I could eat three when those nice fresh heather and gorse smells from the moor come pouring in at the open window."

The morning that Dickon—after they had been enjoying themselves in the garden for about two hours—went behind a big rose-bush and brought forth two tin pails and revealed that one was full of rich new milk with cream on the top of it, and that the other held cottage-made currant buns folded in a clean blue and white napkin, buns so carefully tucked in that they were still hot, there was a riot of surprised joyfulness. What a wonderful thing for Mrs. Sowerby to think of! What a kind, clever woman she must be! How good the buns were! And what delicious fresh milk!

"Magic is in her just as it is in Dickon," said Colin. "It makes her think of ways to do things—nice things. She is a Magic person. Tell her we are grateful, Dickon—extremely grateful."

He was given to using rather grown-up phrases at times. He enjoyed them. He liked this so much that he improved upon it.

"Tell her she has been most bounteous and our gratitude is extreme."

And then forgetting his grandeur he fell to and stuffed himself with buns and drank milk out of the pail in copious draughts in the manner of any hungry little boy who had been taking unusual exercise and breathing in moorland air and whose breakfast was more than two hours behind him.

This was the beginning of many agreeable incidents of the same kind. They actually awoke to the fact that as Mrs. Sowerby had fourteen people to provide food for she might not have enough to satisfy two extra appetites every day. So they asked her to let them send some of their shillings to buy things.

Dickon made the stimulating discovery that in the wood in the park outside the garden where Mary had first found him piping to the wild creatures there was a deep little hollow where you could build a sort of tiny oven with stones and roast potatoes and eggs in it. Roasted eggs were a previously unknown luxury and very hot potatoes with salt and fresh butter in them were fit for a woodland king—besides being deliciously satisfying. You could buy both potatoes and eggs and eat as many as you liked without feeling as if you were taking food out of the mouths of fourteen people.

Every beautiful morning the Magic was worked by the mystic circle under the plum-tree which provided a canopy of thickening green leaves after its brief blossom-time was ended. After the ceremony Colin always took his walking exercise and throughout the day he exercised his newly found power at intervals. Each day he grew stronger and could walk more steadily and cover more ground. And each day his belief in the Magic grew stronger—as well it might. He tried one experiment after another as he felt himself gaining strength and it was Dickon who showed him the best things of all.

"Yesterday," he said one morning after an absence, "I went to Thwaite for mother an' near th' Blue Cow Inn I seed Bob Haworth.* He's the strongest chap on th' moor. He's the champion wrestler an' he can jump higher than any other chap an' throw th' hammer farther. He's gone all th' way to Scotland for th' sports some years. He's knowed me ever since I was a little 'un an' he's a friendly sort an' I axed him some questions. Th' gentry calls him a athlete and I thought o' thee, Mester Colin, and I says, 'How did tha' make tha' muscles stick out that way, Bob? Did tha' do anythin' extra to make thysel' so strong?' An' he says, 'Well, yes, lad, I did. A strong man in a show that came to Thwaite once showed me how to exercise my arms an' legs an' every muscle in my body.' An' I says, 'Could a delicate chap make himself stronger with 'em, Bob?' an' he laughed an' says, 'Art tha' th' delicate chap?' an' I says, 'No, but I knows a young gentleman that's gettin' well of a long illness an' I wish I knowed some o' them tricks to tell him about.' I didn't say no names an' he didn't ask none. He's friendly same as I said, an' he stood up an' showed me good-natured like, an' I imitated what he did till I knowed it by heart."

Colin had been listening excitedly.

"Can you show me?" he cried. "Will you?"

"Aye, to be sure," Dickon answered getting up. "But he says tha' mun do 'em gentle at first an' be careful not to tire thysel'. Rest in between times an' take deep breaths an' don't overdo."

"I'll be careful," said Colin. "Show me! Show me! Dickon, you are the most Magic boy in the world!"

Dickon stood up on the grass and slowly went through a carefully practical but simple series of muscle exercises. Colin watched them with widening eyes. He could do a few while he was sitting down. Presently he did a few gently while he stood upon his already steadied feet. Mary began to do them also. Soot, who was watching the performance, became much disturbed and left his branch and hopped about restlessly because he could not do them too.

From that time the exercises were part of the day's duties as much as the Magic was. It became possible for both Colin and Mary to do more of them each time they tried, and such appetites were the results that but for the basket Dickon put down behind the bush each morning when he arrived they would have been lost. But the little oven in the hollow and Mrs. Sowerby's bounties were so satisfying that Mrs. Medlock and the nurse and Dr. Craven became mystified again. You can trifle with your breakfast and seem to disdain your dinner if you are full to the brim with roasted eggs and potatoes and richly frothed new milk and oat-cakes and buns and heather honey and clotted cream.

"They are eating next to nothing," said the nurse. "They'll die of starvation if they can't be persuaded to take some nourishment. And yet see how they look."

"Look!" exclaimed Mrs. Medlock indignantly. "Eh! I'm moithered to death with them. They're a pair of young Satans. Bursting their jackets one day and the next turning up their noses at the best meals Cook can tempt them with. Not a mouthful of that lovely young fowl and bread sauce did they set a fork into yesterday—and the poor woman fair *invented* a pudding for them—and back it's sent. She almost cried. She's afraid she'll be blamed if they starve themselves into their graves."

Dr. Craven came and looked at Colin long and carefully. He wore an extremely worried expression when the nurse talked with him and showed him the almost untouched tray of breakfast she had saved for him to look at—but it was even more worried when he sat down by Colin's sofa and examined him. He had been called to London on business and had not seen the boy for nearly two weeks. When young things begin to gain health they gain it rapidly. The waxen tinge had left Colin's skin and a warm rose showed through it; his beautiful eyes were clear and the hollows under them and in his cheeks and temples had filled out. His once dark, heavy locks had begun to look as if they sprang healthily from his forehead and were soft and warm with life. His lips were fuller and of a normal colour. In fact as an imitation of a boy who was a confirmed invalid he was a disgraceful sight. Dr. Craven held his chin in his hand and thought him over.

"I am sorry to hear that you do not eat anything," he said. "That will not do. You will lose all you have gained—and you have gained amazingly. You ate so well a short time ago."

"I told you it was an unnatural appetite," answered Colin.

Mary was sitting on her stool near by and she suddenly made a very queer sound which she tried so violently to repress that she ended by almost choking.

"What is the matter?" said Dr. Craven, turning to look at her.

Mary became quite severe in her manner.

"It was something between a sneeze and a cough," she replied with reproachful dignity, "and it got into my throat."

"But," she said afterward to Colin, "I couldn't stop myself. It just burst out because all at once I couldn't help remembering that last big potato you ate and the way your mouth stretched when you bit through that thick lovely crust with jam and clotted cream on it."

"Is there any way in which those children can get food secretly?" Dr. Craven inquired of Mrs. Medlock.

"There's no way unless they dig it out of the earth or pick it off the trees," Mrs. Medlock answered. "They stay out in the grounds all day and see no one but each other. And if they want anything different to eat from what's sent up to them they need only ask for it."

"Well," said Dr. Craven, "so long as going without food agrees with them we need not disturb ourselves. The boy is a new creature."

"So is the girl," said Mrs. Medlock. "She's begun to be downright pretty since she's filled out and lost her ugly little sour look. Her hair's grown thick and healthy looking and she's got a bright colour. The glummest, ill-natured little thing she used to be and now her and Master Colin laugh together like a pair of crazy young ones. Perhaps they're growing fat on that."

"Perhaps they are," said Dr. Craven. "Let them laugh."

CHAPTER XXV

THE CURTAIN

AND the secret garden bloomed and bloomed and every morning revealed new miracles. In the robin's nest there were Eggs and the robin's mate sat upon them, keeping them warm with her feathery little breast and careful wings. At first she was very nervous and the robin himself was indignantly watchful. Even Dickon did not go near the close-grown corner in those days, but waited until by the quiet working of some mysterious spell he seemed to have conveyed to the soul of the little pair that in the garden there was nothing which was not quite like themselves—nothing which did not understand the wonderfulness of what was happening to them—the immense, tender, terrible, heart-breaking beauty and solemnity of Eggs. If there had been one person in that garden who had not known through all his or her innermost being that if an Egg were taken away or hurt the whole world would whirl round and crash through space and come to an end—if there had been even one who did not feel it and act accordingly there could have been no happiness even in that golden springtime air. But they all knew it and felt it and the robin and his mate knew they knew it.

At first the robin watched Mary and Colin with sharp anxiety. For some mysterious reason he knew he need not watch Dickon. The first moment he set his dew-bright black eye on Dickon he knew he was not a stranger but a sort of robin without beak or feathers. He could speak robin (which is a quite distinct language not to be mistaken for any other). To speak robin to a robin is like speaking French to a Frenchman. Dickon always spoke it to the robin himself, so the queer gibberish he used when he spoke to humans did not matter in the least. The robin thought he spoke this gibberish to them because they were not intelligent enough to understand feathered speech. His movements also were robin. They never startled one by being sudden enough to seem dangerous or threatening. Any robin could understand Dickon, so his presence was not even disturbing.

But at the outset it seemed necessary to be on guard against the other two. In the first place the boy creature did not come into the garden on his legs. He was pushed in on a thing with wheels and the skins of wild animals were thrown over him. That in itself was doubtful. Then when he began to stand up and move about he did it in a queer unaccustomed way and the others seemed to have to help him. The robin used to secrete himself in a bush and watch this anxiously, his head tilted first on one side and then on the other. He thought that the slow movements might mean that he was preparing to pounce, as cats do. When cats are preparing to pounce they creep over the ground very slowly. The robin talked this over with his mate a great deal for a few days but after that he decided not to speak of the subject because her terror was so great that he was afraid it might be injurious to the eggs.

When the boy began to walk by himself and even to move more quickly it was an immense relief. But for a long time—or it seemed a long time to the robin—he was a source of some anxiety. He did not act as the other humans did. He seemed very fond of walking but he had a way of sitting or lying down for a while and then getting up in a disconcerting manner to begin again.

One day the robin remembered that when he himself had been made to learn to fly by his parents he had done much the same sort of thing. He had taken short flights of a few yards and then had been obliged to rest. So it occurred to him that this boy was learning to fly—or rather to walk. He mentioned this to his mate and when he told her that the Eggs would probably conduct themselves in the same way after they were fledged she was quite comforted and even became eagerly interested and derived great pleasure from watching the boy over the edge of her nest—though she always thought that the Eggs would be much cleverer and learn more quickly. But then she said indulgently that humans were always more clumsy and slow than Eggs and most of them never seemed really to learn to fly at all. You never met them in the air or on tree-tops.

After a while the boy began to move about as the others did, but all three of the children at times did unusual things. They would stand under the trees and move their arms and legs and heads about in a way which was neither walking nor running nor sitting down. They went through these movements at intervals every day and the robin was never able to explain to his mate what they were doing or trying to do. He could only say that he was sure that the Eggs would never flap about in such a manner; but as the boy who could speak robin so fluently was doing the thing with them, birds could be quite sure that the

actions were not of a dangerous nature. Of course neither the robin
nor his mate had ever heard of the champion wrestler, Bob Haworth,
and his exercises for making the muscle stand out like lumps. Robins
are not like human beings; their muscles are always exercised from the
first and so they develop themselves in a natural manner. If you have
to fly about to find every meal you eat, your muscles do not become
atrophied (atrophied means wasted away through want of use).

When the boy was walking and running about and digging and
weeding like the others, the nest in the corner was brooded over by
a great peace and content. Fears for the Eggs became things of the
past. Knowing that your Eggs were as safe as if they were locked in a
bank vault and the fact that you could watch so many curious things
going on made sitting a most entertaining occupation. On wet days
the Eggs' mother sometimes felt even a little dull because the children did not come into the garden.*

But even on wet days it could not be said that Mary and Colin
were dull. One morning when the rain streamed down unceasingly
and Colin was beginning to feel a little restive, as he was obliged to
remain on his sofa because it was not safe to get up and walk about,
Mary had an inspiration.

"Now that I am a real boy," Colin had said, "my legs and arms and
all my body are so full of Magic that I can't keep them still. They want
to be doing things all the time. Do you know that when I waken in the
morning, Mary, when it's quite early and the birds are just shouting
outside and everything seems just shouting for joy—even the trees
and things we can't really hear—I feel as if I must jump out of bed
and shout myself. And if I did it, just think what would happen!"

Mary giggled inordinately.

"The nurse would come running and Mrs. Medlock would come
running and they would be sure you had gone crazy and they'd send
for the doctor," she said.

Colin giggled himself. He could see how they would all look—
how horrified by his outbreak and how amazed to see him standing
upright.

"I wish my father would come home," he said. "I want to tell him
myself. I'm always thinking about it—but we couldn't go on like this
much longer. I can't stand lying still and pretending, and besides
I look too different. I wish it wasn't raining to-day."

It was then Mistress Mary had her inspiration.

"Colin," she began mysteriously, "do you know how many rooms there are in this house?"

"About a thousand, I suppose," he answered.

"There's about a hundred no one ever goes into," said Mary. "And one rainy day I went and looked into ever so many of them. No one ever knew, though Mrs. Medlock nearly found me out. I lost my way when I was coming back and I stopped at the end of your corridor. That was the second time I heard you crying."

Colin started up on his sofa.

"A hundred rooms no one goes into," he said. "It sounds almost like a secret garden. Suppose we go and look at them. You could wheel me in my chair and nobody would know where we went."

"That's what I was thinking," said Mary. "No one would dare to follow us. There are galleries where you could run. We could do our exercises. There is a little Indian room where there is a cabinet full of ivory elephants. There are all sorts of rooms."

"Ring the bell," said Colin.

When the nurse came in he gave his orders.

"I want my chair," he said. "Miss Mary and I are going to look at the part of the house which is not used. John can push me as far as the picture-gallery because there are some stairs. Then he must go away and leave us alone until I send for him again."

Rainy days lost their terrors that morning. When the footman had wheeled the chair into the picture-gallery and left the two together in obedience to orders, Colin and Mary looked at each other delighted. As soon as Mary had made sure that John was really on his way back to his own quarters below stairs, Colin got out of his chair.

"I am going to run from one end of the gallery to the other," he said, "and then I am going to jump and then we will do Bob Haworth's exercises."

And they did all these things and many others. They looked at the portraits and found the plain little girl dressed in green brocade and holding the parrot on her finger.

"All these," said Colin, "must be my relations. They lived a long time ago. That parrot one, I believe, is one of my great, great, great, great aunts. She looks rather like you, Mary—not as you look now but as you looked when you came here. Now you are a great deal fatter and better looking."

"So are you," said Mary, and they both laughed.

They went to the Indian room and amused themselves with the ivory elephants. They found the rose-coloured brocade boudoir and the hole in the cushion the mouse had left, but the mice had grown up and run away and the hole was empty. They saw more rooms and made more discoveries than Mary had made on her first pilgrimage. They found new corridors and corners and flights of steps and new old pictures they liked and weird old things they did not know the use of. It was a curiously entertaining morning and the feeling of wandering about in the same house with other people but at the same time feeling as if one were miles away from them was a fascinating thing.

"I'm glad we came," Colin said. "I never knew I lived in such a big queer old place. I like it. We will ramble about every rainy day. We shall always be finding new queer corners and things."

That morning they had found among other things such good appetites that when they returned to Colin's room it was not possible to send the luncheon away untouched.

When the nurse carried the tray down-stairs she slapped it down on the kitchen dresser so that Mrs. Loomis, the cook, could see the highly polished dishes and plates.

"Look at that!" she said. "This is a house of mystery, and those two children are the greatest mysteries in it."

"If they keep that up every day," said the strong young footman John, "there'd be small wonder that he weighs twice as much to-day as he did a month ago. I should have to give up my place in time, for fear of doing my muscles an injury."

That afternoon Mary noticed that something new had happened in Colin's room. She had noticed it the day before but had said nothing because she thought the change might have been made by chance. She said nothing to-day but she sat and looked fixedly at the picture over the mantel. She could look at it because the curtain had been drawn aside. That was the change she noticed.

"I know what you want me to tell you," said Colin, after she had stared a few minutes. "I always know when you want me to tell you something. You are wondering why the curtain is drawn back. I am going to keep it like that."

"Why?" asked Mary.

"Because it doesn't make me angry any more to see her laughing. I wakened when it was bright moonlight two nights ago and felt as if the Magic was filling the room and making everything so splendid that I couldn't lie still. I got up and looked out of the window. The room was quite light and there was a patch of moonlight on the curtain and somehow that made me go and pull the cord. She looked right down at me as if she were laughing because she was glad I was standing there. It made me like to look at her. I want to see her laughing like that all the time. I think she must have been a sort of Magic person perhaps."

"You are so like her now," said Mary, "that sometimes I think perhaps you are her ghost made into a boy."

That idea seemed to impress Colin. He thought it over and then answered her slowly.

"If I were her ghost—my father would be fond of me," he said.

"Do you want him to be fond of you?" inquired Mary.

"I used to hate it because he was not fond of me. If he grew fond of me I think I should tell him about the Magic. It might make him more cheerful."

CHAPTER XXVI

"IT'S MOTHER!"

THEIR belief in the Magic was an abiding thing. After the morning's incantations Colin sometimes gave them Magic lectures.

"I like to do it," he explained, "because when I grow up and make great scientific discoveries I shall be obliged to lecture about them, and so this is practice. I can only give short lectures now because I am very young, and, besides, Ben Weatherstaff would feel as if he was in church and he would go to sleep."

"Th' best thing about lecturin'," said Ben, "is that a chap can get up an' say aught he pleases an' no other chap can answer him back. I wouldn't be agin' lecturin' a bit mysel' sometimes."

But when Colin held forth under his tree old Ben fixed devouring eyes on him and kept them there. He looked him over with critical affection. It was not so much the lecture which interested him as the legs which looked straighter and stronger each day, the boyish head which held itself up so well, the once sharp chin and hollow cheeks which had filled and rounded out and the eyes which had begun to hold the light he remembered in another pair. Sometimes when Colin felt Ben's earnest gaze meant that he was much impressed he wondered what he was reflecting on, and once, when he had seemed quite entranced, he questioned him.

"What are you thinking about, Ben Weatherstaff?" he asked.

"I was thinkin'," answered Ben, "as I'd warrant tha's gone up three or four pound this week. I was lookin' at tha' calves an' tha' shoulders. I'd like to get thee on a pair o' scales."

"It's the Magic and—and Mrs. Sowerby's buns and milk and things," said Colin. "You see the scientific experiment has succeeded."

That morning Dickon was too late to hear the lecture. When he came he was ruddy with running and his funny face looked more twinkling than usual.* As they had a good deal of weeding to do after the rains they fell to work. They always had plenty to do after a warm deep sinking rain. The moisture which was good for the flowers was also good for the weeds, which thrust up tiny blades of grass and points of leaves which must be pulled up before their roots took too firm hold. Colin was as good at weeding as any one in these days, and he could lecture while he was doing it.

"The Magic works best when you work yourself," he said this morning. "You can feel it in your bones and muscles. I am going to read books about bones and muscles, but I am going to write a book about Magic. I am making it up now. I keep finding out things."

It was not very long after he had said this that he laid down his trowel and stood up on his feet. He had been silent for several minutes, and they had seen that he was thinking out lectures, as he often did. When he dropped his trowel and stood upright it seemed to Mary and Dickon as if a sudden strong thought had made him do it. He stretched himself out to his tallest height and he threw out his arms exultantly. Colour glowed in his face and his strange eyes widened with joyfulness. All at once he had realised something to the full.

"Mary! Dickon!" he cried. "Just look at me!"

They stopped their weeding and looked at him.

"Do you remember that first morning you brought me in here?" he demanded.

Dickon was looking at him very hard. Being an animal charmer he could see more things than most people could, and many of them were things he never talked about. He saw some of them now in this boy.

"Aye, that we do," he answered.

Mary looked hard too, but she said nothing.

"Just this minute," said Colin, "all at once I remembered it myself—when I looked at my hand digging with the trowel—and I had to stand up on my feet to see if it was real. And it *is* real! I'm *well*—I'm *well*!"

"Aye, that tha' art!" said Dickon.

"I'm well! I'm well!" said Colin again, and his face went quite red all over.

He had known it before in a way, he had hoped it and felt it and thought about it, but just at that minute something had rushed all through him—a sort of rapturous belief and realisation, and it had been so strong that he could not help calling out.

"I shall live for ever and ever and ever!" he cried grandly. "I shall find out thousands and thousands of things. I shall find out about people and creatures and everything that grows—like Dickon—and I

shall never stop making Magic. I'm well! I'm well! I feel—I feel as if I
want to shout out something—something thankful, joyful!"

Ben Weatherstaff, who had been working near a rose-bush, glanced
round at him.

"Tha' might sing th' Doxology,"* he suggested in his dryest grunt.
He had no opinion of the Doxology, and he did not make the suggestion with any particular reverence.

But Colin was of an exploring mind and he knew nothing about
the Doxology.

"What is that?" he inquired.

"Dickon can sing it for thee, I'll warrant," replied Ben Weatherstaff.

Dickon answered with his all-perceiving animal charmer's smile.

"They sing it i' church," he said. "Mother says she believes th'
skylarks sings it when they gets up i' th' mornin'."

"If she says that, it must be a nice song," Colin answered. "I've
never been in a church myself. I was always too ill. Sing it, Dickon. I
want to hear it."

Dickon was quite simple and unaffected about it. He understood
what Colin felt better than Colin did himself. He understood by a
sort of instinct so natural that he did not know it was understanding.
He pulled off his cap and looked round still smiling.

"Tha' must take off tha' cap," he said to Colin, "an' so mun tha',
Ben—an' tha' mun stand up, tha' knows."

Colin took off his cap and the sun shone on and warmed his thick
hair as he watched Dickon intently. Ben Weatherstaff scrambled up
from his knees and bared his head, too, with a sort of puzzled half-
resentful look on his old face, as if he didn't know exactly why he was
doing this remarkable thing.

Dickon stood out among the trees and rose-bushes and began to sing
in quite a simple, matter-of-fact way, and in a nice strong boy voice:—

> "Praise God from whom all blessings flow,
>   Praise Him all creatures here below,
>   Praise Him above ye Heavenly Host,
>   Praise Father, Son, and Holy Ghost.
>   Amen."

When he had finished, Ben Weatherstaff was standing quite still
with his jaws set obstinately but with a disturbed look in his eyes,
fixed on Colin. Colin's face was thoughtful and appreciative.

"It is a very nice song," he said. "I like it. Perhaps it means just what I mean when I want to shout out that I am thankful to the Magic." He stopped and thought in a puzzled way. "Perhaps they are both the same thing. How can we know the exact names of everything? Sing it again, Dickon. Let us try, Mary. I want to sing it, too. It's my song. How does it begin? 'Praise God from whom all blessings flow'?"

And they sang it again, and Mary and Colin lifted their voices as musically as they could, and Dickon's swelled quite loud and beautiful—and at the second line Ben Weatherstaff raspingly cleared his throat, and at the third he joined in with such vigour that it seemed almost savage, and when the "Amen" came to an end Mary observed that the very same thing had happened to him which had happened when he found out that Colin was not a cripple—his chin was twitching and he was staring and winking, and his leathery old cheeks were wet.

"I never seed no sense in th' Doxology afore," he said hoarsely, "but I may change my mind i' time. I should say tha'd gone up five pound this week, Mester Colin—five on 'em!"

Colin was looking across the garden at something attracting his attention, and his expression had become a startled one.

"Who is coming in here?" he said quickly. "Who is it?"

The door in the ivied wall had been pushed gently open and a woman had entered. She had come in with the last line of their song and she had stood still listening and looking at them. With the ivy behind her, the sunlight drifting through the trees and dappling her long blue cloak, and her nice fresh face smiling across the greenery she was rather like a softly coloured illustration in one of Colin's books. She had wonderful affectionate eyes which seemed to take everything in—all of them, even Ben Weatherstaff and the "creatures" and every flower that was in bloom. Unexpectedly as she had appeared, not one of them felt that she was an intruder at all. Dickon's eyes lighted like lamps.

"It's Mother—that's who it is!" he cried, and he went across the grass at a run.

Colin began to move towards her, too, and Mary went with him. They both felt their pulses beat faster.

"It's Mother!" Dickon said again when they met half-way. "I knowed tha' wanted to see her an' I told her where th' door was hid."

Colin held out his hand with a sort of flushed royal shyness but his eyes quite devoured her face.

"Even when I was ill I wanted to see you," he said, "you and Dickon and the secret garden. I'd never wanted to see any one or anything before."

The sight of his uplifted face brought about a sudden change in her own. She flushed and the corners of her mouth shook and a mist seemed to sweep over her eyes.

"Eh! dear lad!" she broke out tremulously. "Eh! dear lad!" as if she had not known she were going to say it. She did not say, "Mester Colin," but just "dear lad" quite suddenly. She might have said it to Dickon in the same way if she had seen something in his face which touched her. Colin liked it.

"Are you surprised because I am so well?" he asked.

She put her hand on his shoulder and smiled the mist out of her eyes.

"Aye, that I am!" she said; "but tha'rt so like thy mother tha' made my heart jump."

"Do you think," said Colin a little awkwardly, "that will make my father like me?"

"Aye, for sure, dear lad," she answered, and she gave his shoulder a soft quick pat. "He mun come home—he mun come home."

"Susan Sowerby," said Ben Weatherstaff, getting close to her. "Look at th' lad's legs, wilt tha'? They was like drumsticks i' stockin' two month' ago—an' I heard folk tell as they was bandy an' knock-kneed both at th' same time. Look at 'em now!"

Susan Sowerby laughed a comfortable laugh.

"They're goin' to be fine strong lad's legs in a bit," she said. "Let him go on playin', an' workin' in th' garden an' eatin' hearty an' drinkin' plenty o' good sweet milk an' there'll not be a finer pair i' Yorkshire, thank God for it."

She put both hands on Mistress Mary's shoulders and looked her little face over in a motherly fashion.

"An' thee, too!" she said. "Tha'rt grown near as hearty as our 'Lizabeth Ellen. I'll warrant tha'rt like thy mother too. Our Martha told me as Mrs. Medlock heard she was a pretty woman. Tha'lt be like a blush rose* when tha' grows up, my little lass, bless thee."

She did not mention that when Martha came home on her "day out" and described the plain sallow child she had said that she had no confidence whatever in what Mrs. Medlock had heard. "It doesn't stand to reason that a pretty woman could be th' mother o' such a fou' little lass," she had added obstinately.

Mary had not had time to pay much attention to her changing face. She had only known that she looked "different" and seemed to have a great deal more hair and that it was growing very fast. But remembering her pleasure in looking at the Mem Sahib in the past she was glad to hear that she might some day look like her.

Susan Sowerby went round their garden with them and was told the whole story of it and shown every bush and tree which had come alive. Colin walked on one side of her and Mary on the other. Each of them kept looking up at her comfortable rosy face, secretly curious about the delightful feeling she gave them—a sort of warm, supported feeling. It seemed as if she understood them as Dickon understood his "creatures." She stooped over the flowers and talked about them as if they were children. Soot followed her and once or twice cawed at her and flew upon her shoulder as if it were Dickon's. When they told her about the robin and the first flight of the young ones she laughed a motherly little mellow laugh in her throat.

"I suppose learnin' 'em to fly is like learnin' children to walk, but I'm feared I should be all in a worrit* if mine had wings instead o' legs," she said.

It was because she seemed such a wonderful woman in her nice moorland cottage way that at last she was told about the Magic.

"Do you believe in Magic?" asked Colin after he had explained about Indian fakirs. "I do hope you do."

"That I do, lad," she answered. "I never knowed it by that name but what does th' name matter? I warrant they call it a different name i' France an' a different one i' Germany. Th' same thing as set th' seeds swellin' an' th' sun shinin' made thee a well lad an' it's th' Good Thing. It isn't like us poor fools as think it matters if us is called out of our names. Th' Big Good Thing doesn't stop to worrit, bless thee. It goes on makin' worlds by th' million—worlds like us. Never thee stop believin' in th' Big Good Thing* an' knowin' th' world's full of it—an' call it what tha' likes. Tha' wert singin' to it when I come into th' garden."

"I felt so joyful," said Colin, opening his beautiful strange eyes at her. "Suddenly I felt how different I was—how strong my arms and legs were, you know—and how I could dig and stand—and I jumped up and wanted to shout out something to anything that would listen."

"Th' Magic listened when tha' sung th' Doxology. It would ha' listened to anything tha'd sung. It was th' joy that mattered. Eh! lad, lad—what's names to th' Joy Maker," and she gave his shoulders a quick soft pat again.

She had packed a basket which held a regular feast this morning, and when the hungry hour came and Dickon brought it out from its hiding place, she sat down with them under their tree and watched them devour their food, laughing and quite gloating over their appetites. She was full of fun and made them laugh at all sorts of odd things. She told them stories in broad Yorkshire and taught them new words. She laughed as if she could not help it when they told her of the increasing difficulty there was in pretending that Colin was still a fretful invalid.

"You see we can't help laughing nearly all the time when we are together," explained Colin. "And it doesn't sound ill at all. We try to choke it back but it will burst out and that sounds worse than ever."

"There's one thing that comes into my mind so often," said Mary, "and I can scarcely ever hold in when I think of it suddenly. I keep thinking suppose Colin's face should get to look like a full moon. It isn't like one yet but he gets a tiny bit fatter every day—and suppose some morning it should look like one—what should we do!"

"Bless us all, I can see tha' has a good bit o' play actin' to do," said Susan Sowerby. "But tha' won't have to keep it up much longer. Mester Craven'll come home."

"Do you think he will?" asked Colin. "Why?"

Susan Sowerby chuckled softly.

"I suppose it 'ud nigh break thy heart if he found out before tha' told him in tha' own way," she said. "Tha's laid awake nights plannin' it."

"I couldn't bear any one else to tell him," said Colin. "I think about different ways every day. I think now I just want to run into his room."

"That'd be a fine start for him," said Susan Sowerby. "I'd like to see his face, lad. I would that! He mun come back—that he mun."

One of the things they talked of was the visit they were to make to her cottage. They planned it all. They were to drive over the moor and lunch out of doors among the heather. They would see all the twelve children and Dickon's garden and would not come back until they were tired.

Susan Sowerby got up at last to return to the house and Mrs. Medlock. It was time for Colin to be wheeled back also. But before he got into his chair he stood quite close to Susan and fixed his eyes on her with a kind of bewildered adoration and he suddenly caught hold of the fold of her blue cloak and held it fast.

"You are just what I—what I wanted," he said. "I wish you were my mother—as well as Dickon's!"

All at once Susan Sowerby bent down and drew him with her warm arms close against the bosom under the blue cloak—as if he had been Dickon's brother. The quick mist swept over her eyes.

"Eh! dear lad!" she said. "Thy own mother's in this 'ere very garden, I do believe. She couldna' keep out of it. Thy father mun come back to thee—he mun!"

CHAPTER XXVII

IN THE GARDEN

In each century since the beginning of the world wonderful things have been discovered. In the last century more amazing things were found out than in any century before. In this new century hundreds of things still more astounding will be brought to light. At first people refuse to believe that a strange new thing can be done, then they begin to hope it can be done, then they see it can be done—then it is done and all the world wonders why it was not done centuries ago. One of the new things people began to find out in the last century was that thoughts—just mere thoughts—are as powerful as electric batteries—as good for one as sunlight is, or as bad for one as poison. To let a sad thought or a bad one get into your mind is as dangerous as letting a scarlet fever germ get into your body. If you let it stay there after it has got in you may never get over it as long as you live.

So long as Mistress Mary's mind was full of disagreeable thoughts about her dislikes and sour opinions of people and her determination not to be pleased by or interested in anything, she was a yellow-faced, sickly, bored and wretched child. Circumstances, however, were very kind to her, though she was not at all aware of it. They began to push her about for her own good. When her mind gradually filled itself with robins, and moorland cottages crowded with children, with queer crabbed old gardeners and common little Yorkshire house-maids, with springtime and with secret gardens coming alive day by day, and also with a moor boy and his "creatures," there was no room left for the disagreeable thoughts which affected her liver and her digestion and made her yellow and tired.

So long as Colin shut himself up in his room and thought only of his fears and weakness and his detestation of people who looked at him and reflected hourly on humps and early death, he was a hysterical, half-crazy little hypochondriac who knew nothing of the sunshine and the spring, and also did not know that he could get well and could stand upon his feet if he tried to do it. When new beautiful thoughts began to push out the old hideous ones, life began to come back to him, his blood ran healthily through his veins and strength poured into him like a flood. His scientific experiment was quite practical and simple and there was nothing weird about it at all.* Much more surprising things can happen to anyone who, when a disagreeable or discouraged thought comes into his mind, just has the sense to remember in time and push it out by putting in an agreeable, determinedly courageous one. Two things cannot be in one place.

> "Where you tend a rose, my lad,
> A thistle cannot grow."*

While the secret garden was coming alive and two children were coming alive with it, there was a man wandering about certain far away beautiful places in the Norwegian fiords, and the valleys and mountains of Switzerland, and he was a man who for ten years had kept his mind filled with dark and heart-broken thinking. He had not been courageous; he had never tried to put any other thoughts in the place of the dark ones. He had wandered by blue lakes and thought them; he had lain on mountain-sides with sheets of deep blue gentians* blooming all about him and flower breaths filling all the air and he had thought them. A terrible sorrow had fallen upon him when he had been happy and he had let his soul fill itself with blackness and had refused obstinately to allow any rift of light to pierce through. He had forgotten and deserted his home and his duties. When he travelled about, darkness so brooded over him that the sight of him was a wrong done to other people because it was as if he poisoned the air about him with gloom. Most strangers thought he must be either half mad or a man with some hidden crime on his soul. He was a tall man with a drawn face and crooked shoulders, and the name he always entered on hotel registers was "Archibald Craven, Misselthwaite Manor, Yorkshire, England."

He had travelled far and wide since the day he saw Mistress Mary in his study and told her she might have her "bit of earth." He had been in the most beautiful places in Europe, though he had remained nowhere more than a few days. He had chosen the quietest and remotest spots. He had been on the tops of mountains whose heads were in the clouds and had looked down on other mountains when the sun rose and touched them with such light as made it seem as if the world were just being born.

But the light had never seemed to touch himself until one day when he realised that for the first time in ten years a strange thing had happened.* He was in a wonderful valley in the Austrian Tyrol and he had been walking alone through such beauty as might have lifted any man's soul out of shadow. He had walked a long way and it had not lifted his. But at last he had felt tired and had thrown himself down to rest on a carpet of moss by a stream. It was a clear little stream which ran quite merrily along on its narrow way through the luscious damp greenness. Sometimes it made a sound rather like very low laughter as it bubbled over and round stones. He saw birds come and dip their heads to drink in it and then flick their wings and fly away. It seemed like a thing alive and yet its tiny voice made the stillness seem deeper. The valley was very, very still.

As he sat gazing into the clear running of the water, Archibald Craven gradually felt his mind and body both grow quiet, as quiet as the valley itself. He wondered if he were going to sleep, but he was not. He sat and gazed at the sunlit water and his eyes began to see things growing at its edge. There was one lovely mass of blue forget-me-nots growing so close to the stream that its leaves were wet and at these he found himself looking as he remembered he had looked at such things years ago. He was actually thinking tenderly how lovely it was and what wonders of blue its hundreds of little blossoms were. He did not know that just that simple thought was slowly filling his mind—filling and filling it until other things were softly pushed aside. It was as if a sweet clear spring had begun to rise in a stagnant pool and had risen and risen until at last it swept the dark water away. But of course he did not think of this himself. He only knew that the valley seemed to grow quieter and quieter as he sat and stared at the bright delicate blueness. He did not know how long he sat there or what was happening to him, but at last he moved as if he were awakening and he got up slowly and stood on the moss carpet, drawing a long, deep, soft breath and wondering at himself. Something seemed to have been unbound and released in him, very quietly.

"What is it?" he said, almost in a whisper, and he passed his hand over his forehead. "I almost feel as if—I were alive!"

I do not know enough about the wonderfulness of undiscovered things to be able to explain how this had happened to him. Neither does any one else yet. He did not understand at all himself—but he remembered this strange hour months afterwards when he was at Misselthwaite again and he found out quite by accident that on this very day Colin had cried out as he went into the secret garden:

"I am going to live for ever and ever and ever!"

The singular calmness remained with him the rest of the evening, and he slept a new reposeful sleep; but it was not with him very long. He did not know that it could be kept. By the next night he had opened the doors wide to his dark thoughts, and they had come trooping and rushing back. He left the valley and went on his wandering way again. But, strange as it seemed to him, there were minutes—sometimes half-hours—when, without his knowing why, the black burden seemed to lift itself again and he knew he was a living man and not a dead one. Slowly—slowly—for no reason that he knew of—he was "coming alive" with the garden.

As the golden summer changed into the deeper golden autumn he went to the Lake of Como.* There he found the loveliness of a dream. He spent his days upon the crystal blueness of the lake or he walked back into the soft thick verdure of the hills and tramped until he was tired so that he might sleep. But by this time he had begun to sleep better, he knew, and his dreams had ceased to be a terror to him.

"Perhaps," he thought, "my body is growing stronger."

It was growing stronger but—because of the rare peaceful hours when his thoughts were changed—his soul was slowly growing stronger, too. He began to think of Misselthwaite and wonder if he should not go home. Now and then he wondered vaguely about his boy and asked himself what he should feel when he went and stood by the carved four-posted bed again and looked down at the sharply chiselled ivory-white face while it slept and the black lashes rimmed so startlingly the close-shut eyes. He shrank from it.

One marvel of a day he had walked so far that when he returned the moon was high and full and all the world was purple shadow and silver. The stillness of lake and shore and wood was so wonderful that he did not go into the villa he lived in. He walked down to a little bowered terrace at the water's edge and sat upon a seat and breathed in all the heavenly scents of the night. He felt the strange calmness stealing over him and it grew deeper and deeper until he fell asleep.

He did not know when he fell asleep and when he began to dream; his dream was so real that he did not feel as if he were dreaming. He remembered afterward how intensely wide awake and alert he had thought he was. He thought that as he sat and breathed in the scent of the late roses and listened to the lapping of the water at his feet he heard a voice calling. It was sweet and clear and happy and far away.

It seemed very far, but he heard it as distinctly as if it had been at his very side.

"Archie! Archie! Archie!" it said, and then again, sweeter and clearer than before, "Archie! Archie!"

He thought he sprang to his feet not even startled.

It was such a real voice and it seemed so natural that he should hear it.

"Lilias!* Lilias?" he answered. "Lilias! where are you?"*

"In the garden," it came back like a sound from a golden flute. "In the garden!"

And then the dream ended. But he did not awaken. He slept soundly and sweetly all through the lovely night. When he did awake at last it was brilliant morning and a servant was standing staring at him. He was an Italian servant and was accustomed, as all the servants of the villa were, to accepting without question any strange thing his foreign master might do. No one ever knew when he would go out or come in or where he would choose to sleep or if he would roam about the garden or lie in the boat on the lake all night. The man held a salver with some letters on it and he waited quietly until Mr. Craven took them. When he had gone away Mr. Craven sat a few moments holding them in his hand and looking at the lake. His strange calm was still upon him and something more—a lightness as if the cruel thing which had been done had not happened as he thought—as if something had changed. He was remembering the dream—the real—real dream.

"In the garden!" he said, wondering at himself. "In the garden! But the door is locked and the key is buried deep."

When he glanced at the letters a few minutes later he saw that the one lying at the top of the rest was an English letter and came from Yorkshire. It was directed in a plain woman's hand but it was not a hand he knew. He opened it, scarcely thinking of the writer, but the first words attracted his attention at once.

"*Dear Sir*:

"I am Susan Sowerby that made bold to speak to you once on the moor. It was about Miss Mary I spoke. I will make bold to speak again. Please, sir, I would come home if I was you. I think you would be glad to come and—if you will excuse me, sir—I think your lady would ask you to come if she was here.

"Your obedient servant,
"SUSAN SOWERBY."

Mr. Craven read the letter twice before he put it back in its envelope. He kept thinking about the dream.

"I will go back to Misselthwaite," he said. "Yes, I'll go at once."

And he went through the garden to the villa and ordered Pitcher to prepare for his return to England.

In a few days he was in Yorkshire again, and on his long railroad journey he found himself thinking of his boy as he had never thought in all the ten years past. During those years he had only wished to forget him. Now, though he did not intend to think about him, memories of him constantly drifted into his mind. He remembered the black days when he had raved like a madman because the child was alive and the mother was dead. He had refused to see it, and when he had gone to look at it at last it had been such a weak wretched thing that every one had been sure it would die in a few days. But to the surprise of those who took care of it the days passed and it lived and then every one believed it would be a deformed and crippled creature.

He had not meant to be a bad father, but he had not felt like a father at all. He had supplied doctors and nurses and luxuries, but he had shrunk from the mere thought of the boy and had buried himself in his own misery. The first time after a year's absence he returned to Misselthwaite and the small miserable looking thing languidly and indifferently lifted to his face the great grey eyes with black lashes round them, so like and yet so horribly unlike the happy eyes he had adored, he could not bear the sight of them and turned away pale as death. After that he scarcely ever saw him except when he was asleep, and all he knew of him was that he was a confirmed invalid, with a vicious, hysterical, half-insane temper. He could only be kept from furies dangerous to himself by being given his own way in every detail.

All this was not an uplifting thing to recall, but as the train whirled him through the mountain passes and golden plains the man who was "coming alive" began to think in a new way and he thought long and steadily and deeply.

"Perhaps I have been all wrong for ten years," he said to himself. "Ten years is a long time. It may be too late to do anything—quite too late. What have I been thinking of!"

Of course this was the wrong Magic—to begin by saying "too late." Even Colin could have told him that. But he knew nothing of

Magic—either black or white. This he had yet to learn. He wondered if Susan Sowerby had taken courage and written to him only because the motherly creature had realised that the boy was much worse—was fatally ill. If he had not been under the spell of the curious calmness which had taken possession of him he would have been more wretched than ever. But the calm had brought a sort of courage and hope with it. Instead of giving way to thoughts of the worst he actually found he was trying to believe in better things.

"Could it be possible that she sees that I may be able to do him good and control him?" he thought. "I will go and see her on my way to Misselthwaite."

But when on his way across the moor he stopped the carriage at the cottage, seven or eight children who were playing about gathered in a group and bobbing seven or eight friendly and polite curtsies told him that their mother had gone to the other side of the moor early in the morning to help a woman who had a new baby. "Our Dickon," they volunteered, was over at the manor working in one of the gardens where he went several days each week.

Mr. Craven looked over the collection of sturdy little bodies and round red-cheeked faces, each one grinning in its own particular way, and he awoke to the fact that they were a healthy, likeable lot. He smiled at their friendly grins, and took a golden sovereign from his pocket and gave it to "our 'Lizabeth Ellen," who was the oldest.

"If you divide that into eight parts there will be half a crown for each of you," he said.

Then amid grins and chuckles and bobbing of curtsies he drove away, leaving ecstasy and nudging elbows and little jumps of joy behind.

The drive across the wonderfulness of the moor was a soothing thing. Why did it seem to give him a sense of home-coming which he had been sure he could never feel again—that sense of the beauty of land and sky and purple bloom of distance, and a warming of the heart at drawing nearer to the great old house which had held those of his blood for six hundred years? How he had driven away from it the last time, shuddering to think of its closed rooms and the boy lying in the four-posted bed with the brocaded hangings. Was it possible that perhaps he might find him changed a little for the better, and that he might overcome his shrinking from him? How real that dream had been—how wonderful and clear the voice which called back to him, "In the garden—In the garden!"

"I will try to find the key," he said. "I will try to open the door. I must—though I don't know why."

When he arrived at the Manor the servants who received him with the usual ceremony, noticed that he looked better, and that he did not go to the remote rooms where he usually lived attended by Pitcher. He went into the library and sent for Mrs. Medlock. She came to him somewhat excited, and curious and flustered.

"How is Master Colin, Medlock?" he inquired.

"Well, sir," Mrs. Medlock answered, "he's—he's different, in a manner of speaking."

"Worse?" he suggested.

Mrs. Medlock really was flushed.

"Well, you see, sir," she tried to explain, "neither Dr. Craven, nor the nurse, nor me can exactly make him out."

"Why is that?"

"To tell the truth, sir, Master Colin might be better and he might be changing for the worse. His appetite, sir, is past understanding—and his ways—"

"Has he become more—more peculiar?" her master asked, knitting his brows anxiously.

"That's it, sir. He's growing very peculiar—when you compare him with what he used to be. He used to eat nothing, and then suddenly he began to eat something enormous—and then he stopped again all at once and the meals were sent back just as they used to be. You never knew, sir, perhaps, that out of doors he never would let himself be taken. The things we've gone through to get him to go out in his chair would leave a body trembling like a leaf. He'd throw himself into such a state that Dr. Craven said he couldn't be responsible for forcing him. Well, sir, just without warning—not long after one of his worst tantrums, he suddenly insisted on being taken out every day by Miss Mary and Susan Sowerby's boy Dickon that could push his chair. He took a fancy to both Miss Mary and Dickon, and Dickon brought his tame animals, and, if you'll credit it, sir, out of doors he will stay from morning until night."

"How does he look?" was the next question.

"If he took his food natural, sir, you'd think he was putting on flesh—but we're afraid it may be a sort of bloat. He laughs sometimes in a queer way when he's alone with Miss Mary. He never used to laugh at all. Dr. Craven is coming to see you at once, if you'll allow him. He never was as puzzled in his life."

"Where is Master Colin now?" Mr. Craven asked.

"In the garden, sir. He's always in the garden—though not a human creature is allowed to go near for fear they'll look at him."

Mr. Craven scarcely heard her last words.

"In the garden!" he said, and after he had sent Mrs. Medlock away, he stood and repeated it again and again. "In the garden!"

He had to make an effort to bring himself back to the place he was standing in, and when he felt he was on earth again he turned and went out of the room. He took his way, as Mary had done, through the door in the shrubbery and among the laurels and the fountain beds. The fountain was playing now, and was encircled by beds of brilliant autumn flowers. He crossed the lawn and turned into the Long Walk by the ivied walls. He did not walk quickly, but slowly, and his eyes were on the path. He felt as if he were being drawn back to the place he had so long forsaken, and he did not know why. As he drew near to it his step became still more slow. He knew where the door was, even though the ivy hung thick over it—but he did not know exactly where it lay—that buried key.

So he stopped and stood still, looking about him, and almost the moment after he had paused he started and listened—asking himself if he were walking in a dream.

The ivy hung thick over the door, the key was buried under the shrubs, no human being had passed that portal for ten lonely years—and yet inside the garden there were sounds. They were the sounds of running, scuffling feet seeming to chase round and round under the trees, they were strange sounds of lowered suppressed voices—exclamations and smothered joyous cries. It seemed actually like the laughter of young things, the uncontrollable laughter of children who were trying not to be heard but who in a moment or so—as their excitement mounted—would burst forth. What in heaven's name was he dreaming of—what in heaven's name did he hear? Was he losing his reason and thinking he heard things which were not for human ears? Was it that the far clear voice had meant?

And then the moment came, the uncontrollable moment when the sounds forgot to hush themselves. The feet ran faster and faster—they were nearing the garden door—there was quick strong young breathing and a wild outbreak of laughing shouts which could not be contained—and the door in the wall was flung wide open, the sheet of ivy swinging back, and a boy burst through it at full speed and, without seeing the outsider, dashed almost into his arms.

Mr. Craven had extended them just in time to save him from falling as a result of his unseeing dash against him, and when he held him away to look at him in amazement at his being there he truly gasped for breath.

He was a tall boy and a handsome one. He was glowing with life, and his running had sent splendid colour leaping to his face. He threw the thick hair back from his forehead and lifted a pair of strange grey eyes—eyes full of boyish laughter and rimmed with black lashes like a fringe. It was the eyes which made Mr. Craven gasp for breath.

"Who—What? Who!" he stammered.

This was not what Colin had expected—this was not what he had planned. He had never thought of such a meeting. And yet to come dashing out—winning a race—perhaps it was even better. He drew himself up to his very tallest. Mary, who had been running with him and had dashed through the door too, believed that he managed to make himself look taller than he had ever looked before—inches taller.*

"Father," he said, "I'm Colin. You can't believe it. I scarcely can myself. I'm Colin."

Like Mrs. Medlock, he did not understand what his father meant when he said hurriedly:

"In the garden! In the garden!"

"Yes," hurried on Colin. "It was the garden that did it—and Mary and Dickon and the creatures—and the Magic. No one knows. We kept it to tell you when you came. I'm well; I can beat Mary in a race. I'm going to be an athlete."

He said it all so like a healthy boy—his face flushed, his words tumbling over each other in his eagerness—that Mr. Craven's soul shook with unbelieving joy.

Colin put out his hand and laid it on his father's arm.

"Aren't you glad, father?" he ended. "Aren't you glad? I'm going to live for ever and ever and ever!"

Mr. Craven put his hands on both the boy's shoulders and held him still. He knew he dared not even try to speak for a moment.

"Take me into the garden, my boy," he said at last. "And tell me all about it."

And so they led him in.

The place was a wilderness of autumn gold and purple and violet blue and flaming scarlet, and on every side were sheaves of late lilies standing together—lilies which were white or white and ruby. He remembered well when the first of them had been planted that just at this season of the year their late glories should reveal themselves. Late roses climbed and hung and clustered, and the sunshine deepening the hue of the yellowing trees made one feel that one stood in an embowered temple of gold. The newcomer stood silent just as the children had done when they came into its greyness. He looked round and round.

"I thought it would be dead," he said.

"Mary thought so at first," said Colin. "But it came alive."

Then they sat down under their tree—all but Colin, who wanted to stand while he told the story.

It was the strangest thing he had ever heard, Archibald Craven thought, as it was poured forth in headlong boy fashion. Mystery and Magic and wild creatures, the weird midnight meeting—the coming of the spring—the passion of insulted pride which had dragged the young Rajah to his feet to defy old Ben Weatherstaff to his face. The odd companionship, the play-acting, the great secret so carefully kept. The listener laughed until tears came into his eyes, and sometimes tears came into his eyes when he was not laughing. The Athlete, the Lecturer, the Scientific Discoverer was a laughable, lovable, healthy young human thing.

"Now," he said at the end of the story, "it need not be a secret any more. I dare say it will frighten them nearly into fits when they see me—but I am never going to get into the chair again. I shall walk back with you, father—to the house."

Ben Weatherstaff's duties rarely took him away from the gardens, but on this occasion he made an excuse to carry some vegetables to the kitchen and being invited into the servants' hall by Mrs. Medlock to drink a glass of beer, he was on the spot—as he had hoped to be —when the most dramatic event Misselthwaite Manor had seen during the present generation actually took place.

One of the windows looking upon the courtyard gave also a glimpse of the lawn. Mrs. Medlock, knowing Ben had come from the gardens, hoped that he might have caught sight of his master, and even by chance of his meeting with Master Colin.

"Did you see either of them, Weatherstaff?" she asked.

Ben took his beer-mug from his mouth and wiped his lips with the back of his hand.

"Aye, that I did," he answered with a shrewdly significant air.

"Both of them?" suggested Mrs. Medlock.

"Both of 'em," returned Ben Weatherstaff. "Thank ye kindly, ma'am, I could sup up another mug of it."

"Together?" said Mrs. Medlock, hastily overfilling his beer-mug in her excitement.

"Together, ma'am," and Ben gulped down half of his new mug at one gulp.

"Where was Master Colin? How did he look? What did they say to each other?"

"I didna' hear that," said Ben, "along o' only bein' on th' stepladder lookin' over th' wall. But I'll tell thee this. There's been things goin' on outside as you house people knows nowt about. An' what tha'll find out tha'll find out soon."

And it was not two minutes before he swallowed the last of his beer and waved his mug solemnly toward the window which took in through the shrubbery a piece of the lawn.

"Look there," he said, "if tha's curious. Look what's comin' across th' grass."

When Mrs. Medlock looked she threw up her hands and gave a little shriek, and every man and woman servant within hearing bolted across the servants' hall and stood looking through the window with their eyes almost starting out of their heads.

Across the lawn came the Master of Misselthwaite, and he looked as many of them had never seen him. And by his side, with his head up in the air and his eyes full of laughter, walked as strongly and steadily as any boy in Yorkshire—Master Colin!

THE END

APPENDIX

MY ROBIN

Published, New York: Stokes, 1912; London: Putnam, 1913.

THERE came to me among the letters I received last spring one which touched me very closely. It was a letter full of delightful things but the delightful thing which so reached my soul was a question. The writer had been reading "The Secret Garden" and her question was this: "Did you own the original of the robin? He could not have been a mere creature of fantasy. I feel sure you owned him." I was thrilled to the centre of my being. Here was some one who plainly had been intimate with robins—English robins. I wrote and explained as far as one could in a letter what I am now going to relate in detail.

I did not own the robin—he owned me—or perhaps we owned each other.

He was an English robin and he was a *person*—not a mere bird. An English robin differs greatly from the American one. He is much smaller and quite differently shaped. His body is daintily round and plump, his legs are delicately slender. He is a graceful little patrician with an astonishing allurement of bearing. His eye is large and dark and dewy; he wears a tight little red satin waistcoat on his full round breast and every tilt of his head, every flirt of his wing is instinct with dramatic significance. He is fascinatingly conceited—he burns with curiosity—he is determined to engage in social relations at almost any cost and his raging jealousy of attention paid to less worthy objects than himself drives him at times to efforts to charm and distract which are irresistible. An intimacy with a robin—an English robin—is a liberal education.

This particular one I knew in my rose-garden in Kent.* I feel sure he was born there and for a summer at least believed it to be the world. It was a lovesome, mystic place, shut in partly by old red brick walls against which fruit trees were trained and partly by a laurel hedge with a wood behind it. It was my habit to sit and write there under an aged writhen* tree, gray with lichen and festooned with roses. The soft silence of it—the remote aloofness—were the most perfect ever dreamed of. But let me not be led astray by the garden. I must be firm and confine myself to the Robin. The garden shall be another story.

There were so many people in this garden—people with feathers, or fur—who, because I sat so quietly, did not mind me in the least, that it was not a surprising thing when I looked up one summer morning to see a small bird hopping about the grass a yard or so away from me. The surprise was not that he was there but that he *stayed* there—or rather he continued to hop—with short reflective-looking hops and that while hopping he looked at me—not in a furtive flighty way but rather as a person might tentatively regard a very new acquaintance. The absolute truth of the matter I had reason to believe later was that he did not know I was a person. I may have been the first of my species he had seen in this rose-garden world of his and he thought I was only another kind of robin. I was too—though that was a secret of mine and nobody but myself knew it. Because of this fact I had the power of holding myself *still*—quite *still* and filling myself with softly alluring tenderness of the tenderest when any little wild thing came near me.

"What do you do to make him come to you like that?" some one asked me a month or so later. "What do you *do*?"

"I don't know what I do exactly," I said. "Except that I hold myself very still and feel like a robin."

You can only do that with a tiny wild thing by being so tender of him—of his little timidities and feelings—so adoringly anxious not to startle him or suggest by any movement the possibility of your being a creature who *could hurt*—that your very yearning to understand his tiny hopes and fears and desires makes you for the time cease to be quite a mere human thing and gives you another and more exquisite sense which speaks for you without speech.

As I sat and watched him I held myself softly still and felt just that. I did not know he was a robin. The truth was that he was too young at that time to look like one, but I did not know that either. He was plainly not a thrush, or a linnet or a sparrow or a starling or a blackbird. He was a little indeterminate-coloured bird and he had no red on his breast. And as I sat and gazed at him he gazed at me as one quite without prejudice unless it might be with the slightest tinge of favour—and hopped—and hopped—and hopped.

That was the thrill and wonder of it. No bird, however evident his acknowledgement of my harmlessness, had ever hopped and *remained*. Many had perched for a moment in the grass or on a nearby bough, had trilled or chirped or secured a scurrying gold and green beetle and flown away. But none had stayed to inquire—to reflect—even to seem—if one dared be so bold as to hope such a thing—to make mysterious, almost occult advances towards intimacy. Also I had never before heard of such a thing happening to any one howsoever bird loving. Birds are creatures who must be wooed and it must be delicate and careful wooing which allures them into friendship.

I held my soft stillness. Would he stay? Could it be that the last hop was nearer? Yes, it was. The moment was a breathless one. Dare one believe that the next was nearer still—and the next—and the next—and that the two yards of distance had become scarcely one—and that within that radius he was soberly hopping round my very feet with his quite unafraid eye full upon me. This was what was happening. It may not seem exciting but it was. That a little wild thing should come to one unasked was of a thrilling-ness touched with awe.

Without stirring a muscle I began to make low, soft, little sounds to him—very low and very caressing indeed—softer than one makes to a baby. I wanted to weave a spell—to establish mental communication—to make Magic. And as I uttered the tiny sounds he hopped nearer and nearer.

"Oh! to think that you will come as near as that!" I whispered to him. "You *know*. You know that nothing in the world would make me put out my hand or startle you in the least tiniest way. You know it because you are a real person as well as a lovely—lovely little bird thing. You know it because you are a soul."

Because of this first morning I knew—years later—that this was what Mistress Mary thought when she bent down in the Long Walk and "tried to make robin sounds."

I said it all in a whisper and I think the words must have sounded like robin sounds because he listened with interest and at last—miracle of mir-acles as it seemed to me—he actually fluttered up on to a small shrub not two yards away from my knee and sat there as one who was pleased with the topic of conversation.

I did not move of course, I sat still and waited his pleasure. Not for mines of rubies would I have lifted a finger.

I think he stayed near me altogether about half an hour. Then he disap-peared. Where or even exactly when I did not know. One moment he was hopping among some of the rose bushes and then he was gone.

This, in fact, was his little mysterious way from first to last. Through all the months of our delicious intimacy he never let me know where he lived. I knew it was in the rose-garden—but that was all. His extraordinary freedom from timorousness was something to think over. After reflecting upon him a good deal I thought I had reached an explanation. He had been born in the rose-garden and being of a home-loving nature he had declined to follow the rest of his family when they had made their first flight over the wall into the rose-walk or over the laurel hedge into the pheasant cover behind. He had stayed in the rose world and then had felt lonely. Without father or mother or sisters or brothers desolateness of spirit fell upon him. He saw a creature—I insist on believing that he thought it another order of robin—and approached to see what it would say.

Its whole bearing was confidence inspiring. It made softly alluring—if unexplainable—sounds. He felt its friendliness and affection. It was curi-ous to look at and far too large for any ordinary nest. It plainly could not fly.

But there was not a shadow of inimical sentiment in it. Instinct told him that. It admired him, it wanted him to remain near, there was a certain comfort in its caressing atmosphere. He liked it and felt less desolate. He would return to it again.

The next day summer rains kept me in the house. The next I went to the rose-garden in the morning and sat down under my tree to work. I had not been there half an hour when I felt I must lift my eyes and look. A little indeterminate-coloured bird was hopping quietly about in the grass—quite aware of me as his dew-bright eye manifested. He had come again—of intention—because we were mates.

It was the beginning of an intimacy not to be described unless one filled a small volume. From that moment we never doubted each other for one second. He knew and I knew. Each morning when I came into the rose-garden he came to call on me and discover things he wanted to know concerning robins of my size and unusual physical conformation. He did not understand but he was attracted by me. Each day I held myself still and tried to make robin sounds expressive of adoring tenderness and he came each day a little nearer. At last arrived a day when as I softly left my seat and moved about the garden he actually quietly hopped after me.

I wish I could remember exactly what length of time elapsed before I knew he was really a robin. An ornithologist would doubtless know but I do not. But one morning I was bending over a bed of Laurette Messimy roses* and I became aware that he had arrived in his usual mysterious way without warning. He was standing in the grass and when I turned my eyes upon him I only just saved myself from starting—which would have meant disaster. I saw upon his breast the first dawning of a flush of colour—more tawny than actual red at that stage—but it hinted at revelations.

"Further subterfuge is useless," I said to him. "You are betrayed. You are a robin."

And he did not attempt to deny it either then or at any future time. In less than two weeks he revealed a tight, glossy little bright red satin waist-coat and with it a certain youthful maturity such as one beholds in the wearer of a first dress suit. His movements were more brisk and certain. He began to make little flights and little sounds though for some time he made no attempt to sing. Instead of appearing suddenly in the grass at my feet, a heavenly little rush of wings would bring him to a bough over my head or a twig quite near me where he would tilt daintily, taking his silent but quite responsive part in the conversations which always took place between us. It was I who talked—telling him how I loved him—how satin red his waistcoat was—how large and bright his eyes—how delicate and elegant his slender legs. I flattered him a great deal. He adored flattery and I am sure he loved me most when I told him that it was impossible to say any-thing which *could* flatter him. It gave him confidence in my good taste.

One morning—a heavenly sunny one—I was conversing with him by the Laurette Messimys again and he was evidently much pleased with the things I said. Perhaps he liked my hat which was a large white one with a wreath of roses round its crown. I saw him look at it and I gently hinted that I had worn it in the hope that he would approve. I had broken off a handful of coral pink Laurettes and was arranging them idly when—he spread his wings in a sudden upward flight—a tiny swift flight which ended—among the roses on my hat—the very hat on my head.

Did I make myself still then? Did I stir by a single hairbreadth? Who does not know? I scarcely let myself breathe. I could not believe that such a thing of pure joy could be true.

But in a minute I realized that he at least was not afraid to move. He was perfectly at home. He hopped about the brim and examined the roses with delicate pecks. That I was under the hat apparently only gave him confidence. He knew me as well as that. He stayed until he had learned all he wished to know about garden hats and then he lightly flew away.

From that time each day drew us closer to each other. He began to perch on twigs only a few inches from my face and listen while I whispered to him—yes, he *listened* and made answer with chirps. Nothing else would describe it. As I wrote he would alight on my manuscript paper and try to read. Sometimes I thought he was a little offended because he found my handwriting so bad that he could not understand it. He would take crumbs out of my hand, he would alight on my chair or my shoulder. The instant I opened the little door in the leaf-covered garden wall I would be greeted by the darling little rush of wings and he was beside me. And he always came from nowhere and disappeared into space.

That, through the whole summer—was his rarest fascination. Perhaps he was not a real robin. Perhaps he was a fairy. Who knows? Among the many house parties staying with me he was a subject of thrilled interest. People knew of him who had not seen him and it became a custom with callers to say: "May we go into the rose-garden and see The Robin?" One of my American guests said he was uncanny and called him "The Goblin Robin." No one had ever seen a thing so curiously human—so much more than mere bird.

When I took callers to the rose-garden he was exquisitely polite. He always came when I stood under my tree and called—but he never at such times *met* me with his rush to the little door. He would perch near me and talk but there was a difference. Certain exquisite intimate charms he kept for me alone.

I wondered when he would begin to sing. One morning the sun being strong enough to pierce through the leaves of my tree I had a large Japanese tent umbrella arranged so that it shaded my table as I wrote. Suddenly I heard a robin song which sounded as if it were being trilled from some tree at a little distance from where I sat. It was so pretty that I leaned forward to see exactly where the singer perched. I made a delicious discovery. He was not on a tree at all. He was perched upon the very end of one of the bamboo ribs of my big flowery umbrella. He was my own Robin and there he sat singing to me his first tiny song—showing me that he had found out how to do it.

The effect of singing at a distance was produced by the curious fact that he was singing *with his bill closed*, his darling scarlet throat puffed out and tremulous with the captive trills.

Perhaps a robin's first song is always of this order. I do not know. I only know that this was his "earlier manner." My enraptured delight I expressed to him in my most eloquent phrases. I praised him—I flattered him. I made him believe that no robin had really ever sung before. He was much pleased and flew down on to the table to hear all about it and incite me to further effort.

In a few days he had learned to sing perfectly, not with the low distant-sounding note but with open beak and clear brilliant little roulades and trills. He grew prouder and prouder. When he saw I was busy he would tilt on a nearby bough and call me with flirtatious, provocative outbreaking of song. He knew that it was impossible for any one to resist him—any one in the world. Of course I would get up and stand beneath his tree with my face upturned and tell him that his charm, his beauty, his fascination and my love were beyond the power of words to express. He knew that would happen and revelled in it. His tiny airs and graces, his devices to attract and absorb attention was unending. He invented new ones every day and each was more enslaving than the last.

Could it be that he was guilty—when he met other robins—of boasting of his conquest of me and of my utter subjugation? I cannot believe it possible. Also I never saw other robins accost him or linger in their passage through the rose-garden to exchange civilities. And yet a very strange thing occurred on one occasion. I was sitting at my table expecting him and heard a familiar chirp. When I looked up he was atilt upon the branch of an apple tree near by. I greeted him with little whistles and twitters thinking of course that he would fly down to me for our usual conversation. But though he chirped a reply and put his head on one side engagingly he did not move from his bough.

"What is the matter with you?" I said. "Come down—come down, little brother!"

But he did not come. He only sidled and twittered and stayed where he was. This was so extraordinary that I got up and went to him. As I looked a curious doubt came upon me. He looked like Tweetie—(which had become his baptismal name) he tilted his head and flirted and twittered after the manner of Tweetie—but—could it be that he was *not* what he pretended to be? Could he be a stranger bird? That seemed out of the question as no stranger bird would have comported himself with such familiarity. No stranger surely would have come so near and addressed me with such intimate twitterings and well-known airs and graces. I was mystified beyond measure. I exerted all my powers to lure him from his branch but descend from it he would not. He listened and smiled and flirted his tail but he stayed where he was.

"Listen," I said at last. "I don't believe in you. There is a mystery here. You pretend you know me and yet you act as if you were afraid of me—just like a common bird who is made of nothing but feathers. I don't believe you are Tweetie at all. You are an Impostor!"

Believable or not, just at that moment when I stood there under the bough arguing, reproaching and beguiling by turns and puzzled beyond measure—out of the Nowhere darted a little scarlet flame of frenzy—Tweetie himself—with his feathers ruffled and on fire with fury. The robin on the branch actually *was* an Impostor and Tweetie had discovered him red-breasted if not red-handed with crime. Oh! the sight it was to behold him in his tiny Berseker rage* at his impudent rival. He flew at him, he beat him, he smacked him, he pecked him, he shrieked bad language at him, he drove him from the branch—from the tree, from one tree after another as the little traitor tried to take refuge—he drove him from the rose-garden—over the laurel hedge and into the pheasant cover in the wood. Perhaps he killed him and left him slain in the bracken. I could not see. But having beaten him once and forever he came back to me, panting—all fluffed up—and with blood thirst only just dying in his eye. He came down on to my table—out of breath as he agitatedly rearranged his untidy feathers—and indignant—almost unreconcilable because I had been such an undiscriminating and feeble-minded imbecile as to be for one moment deceived.

His righteous wrath was awful to behold. I was so frightened that I felt quite pale. With those wiles of the serpent which every noble woman finds herself forced to employ at times I endeavoured to pacify him.

"Of course I did not really believe he was You," I said tremulously. "He was your inferior in every respect. His waistcoat was not nearly so beautiful as yours. His eyes were not so soul compelling. His legs were not nearly so elegant and slender. And there was an expression about his beak which I distrusted from the first. You *heard* me tell him he was an Impostor."

He began to listen—he became calmer—he relented. He kindly ate a crumb out of my hand.

We began mutually to understand the infamy of the situation. The Impostor had been secretly watching us. He had envied us our happiness. Into his degenerate mind had stolen the darkling and criminal thought that he—Audacious Scoundrel—might impose upon me by pretending he was not merely "a robin" but "The Robin"—Tweetie himself and that he might supplant him in my affections. But he had been confounded and cast into outer darkness and again we were One.

I will not attempt to deceive. He was jealous beyond bounds. It was necessary for me to be most discreet in my demeanour towards the head gardener with whom I was obliged to consult frequently. When he came into the rose-garden for orders Tweetie at once appeared.

He followed us, hopping in the grass or from rose bush to rose bush. No word of ours escaped him. If our conversation on the enthralling subjects of fertilizers and aphides seemed in its earnest absorption to verge upon the emotional and tender he interfered at once. He commanded my attention. He perched on nearby boughs and endeavoured to distract me. He fluttered about and called me with chirps. His last resource was always to fly to the topmost twig of an apple tree and begin to sing his most brilliant song in his most thrilling tone and with an affected manner. Naturally we were obliged to listen and talk about him. Even old Barton's weather-beaten apple face would wrinkle into smiles.

"He's doin' that to make us look at him," he would say. "That's what he's doin' it for. He can't abide not to be noticed."

But it was not only his vanity which drew him to me. He loved me. The low song trilled in his little pulsating scarlet throat was mine. He sang it only to me—and he would never sing it when any one else was there to hear. When we were quite alone with only roses and bees and sunshine and silence about us, when he swung on some spray quite close to me and I stood and talked to him in whispers—then he would answer me—each time I paused—with the little "far away" sounding trills—the sweetest, most wonderful little sounds in the world. A clever person who knew more of the habits of birds than I did told me a most curious thing.

"That is his little mating song," he said. "You have inspired a hopeless passion in a robin."

Perhaps so. He thought the rose-garden was the world and it seemed to me he never went out of it during the summer months. At whatsoever hour I appeared and called him he came out of bushes but from a different point each time. In late autumn however, one afternoon I *saw* him fly to me from over a wall dividing the enclosed garden from the open ones. I thought he looked guilty and fluttered when he alighted near me. I think he did not want me to know.

"You have been making the acquaintance of a young lady robin," I said to him. "Perhaps you are already engaged to her for the next season."

He tried to persuade me that it was not true but I felt he was not entirely frank.

After that it was plain that he had discovered that the rose-garden was not *all* the world. He knew about the other side of the wall. But it did not absorb him altogether. He was seldom absent when I came and he never failed to answer my call. I talked to him often about the young lady robin but though he showed a gentlemanly reticence on the subject I knew quite well he loved me best. He loved my robin sounds, he loved my whispers, his dewy dark eyes looked into mine as if he knew we two understood strange tender things others did not.

I was only a mere tenant of the beautiful place I had had for nine years and that winter the owner sold the estate. In December I was to go to Montreux for a couple of months; in March I was to return to Maytham and close it before leaving it finally. Until I left for Switzerland I saw my robin every day. Before I went away I called him to me and told him where I was going.

He was such a little thing. Two or three months might seem a lifetime to him. He might not remember me so long. I was not a real robin. I was only a human being. I said a great many things to him—wondering if he would even be in the garden when I came back. I went away wondering.

When I returned from the world of winter sports, of mountain snows, of tobogganing and skis I felt as if I had been absent a long time. There had been snow even in Kent and the park and gardens were white. I arrived in the evening. The next morning I threw on my red frieze garden cloak and went down the flagged terrace and the Long Walk through the walled gardens to the beloved place where the rose bushes stood dark and slender and leafless among the whiteness. I went to my own tree and stood under it and called.

"Are you gone," I said in my heart; "are you gone, little Soul? Shall I never see you again?"

After the call I waited—and I had never waited before. The roses were gone and he was not in the rose-world. I called again. The call was sometimes a soft whistle as near a robin sound as I could make it—sometimes it was a chirp—sometimes it was a quick clear repetition of "Sweet! Sweet! Sweetie"—which I fancied he liked best. I made one after the other—and then—something scarlet flashed across the lawn, across the rose-walk— over the wall and he was there. He had not forgotten, it had not been too long, he alighted on the snowy brown grass at my feet.

Then I knew he was a little Soul and not only a bird and the real parting which must come in a few weeks' time loomed up before me a strange tragic thing.

I do not often allow myself to think of it. It was too final. And there was nothing to be done. I was going thousands of miles across the sea. A little warm thing of scarlet and brown feathers and pulsating trilling throat lives such a brief life. The little soul in its black dew-drop eye—one knows nothing about it. For myself I sometimes believe strange things. We two were something weirdly near to each other.

At the end I went down to the bare world of roses one soft damp day and stood under the tree and called him for the last time. He did not keep me waiting and he flew to a twig very near my face. I could not write all I said to him. I tried with all my heart to explain and he answered me—between his listenings—with the "far away" love note. I talked to him as if he knew all I knew. He put his head on one side and listened so intently that I felt that he understood. I told him that I must go away and that we should not see each other again and I told him why.

"But you must not think when I do not come back it is because I have forgotten you," I said. "Never since I was born have I loved anything as I have loved you—except my two babies. Never shall I love anything so much again so long as I am in the world. You are a little Soul and I am a little Soul and we shall love each other forever and ever. We won't say Goodbye. We have been too near to each other—nearer than human beings are. I love you and love you and love you—little Soul."

Then I went out of the rose-garden. I shall never go into it again.

NOTE ON THE DATE OF THE STORY

ALTHOUGH *The Secret Garden* is sometimes assumed to have been set around the time it was written, internal evidence suggests that Burnett was thinking of a much earlier period—perhaps as early as 1860.

Mr Roach refers to Colin: 'You'd think he was a whole Royal Family rolled into one—Prince Consort and all' (p. 147); Prince Albert, the Prince Consort, died in 1861. When Mary is waiting in the private hotel in London (p. 12), she sees buses and cabs, but no motor cars or trams: trams were first introduced in the 1860s. Mrs Medlock's bonnet would have been unfashionable by the end of the century, but quite normal in the 1860s (unless, of course, Burnett is making a critical point). The travel arrangements are revealing (pp. 17–18): presumably Mrs Medlock would have travelled first class with Mary, and would have travelled in a dining car, had they been available. The Midland Railway did not introduce dining cars until 1882–4, with electric light from 1903. The basic contents of the luncheon basket (p. 17) suggests an early version of the product compared with the rather lavish menus of the turn of the century. The story cannot be set much earlier than 1860, because Mrs Medlock wears a coloured photograph of her late husband 'who had died years ago', and photographic studios only became popular in the mid-1850s.

EXPLANATORY NOTES

5 *Mary Lennox*: Elizabeth Gaskell's *North and South* (1855) begins with the wedding of the beautiful Edith to Captain Lennox; his regiment is stationed in Corfu. Alison Lurie ('Introduction' to *The Secret Garden* (New York: Penguin, 2002), xvi) suggests that Mary's surname might derive from the name of the fine-china manufacturer Walter Scott Lenox, thus implying Mary's fragility. Lenox's company produced the first official USA State Dining Service, for President Wilson, in 1918.

Ayah: Indian nurse or lady's maid.

Mem Sahib: term of respectful address used by Indians in the colonial era towards Englishwomen in authority: Madam plus 'Sahib', meaning 'Sir'—from Urdu 'friend, companion, master'.

about nine years old: in the manuscript this is altered to 'ten years old', but the change was not adopted.

6 *hibiscus*: hibiscus flowers are part of the Hindu ritual offerings to both Kali, the powerful mother goddess, representing the fierce and protective female principle, and Ganesha, the elephant-headed Lord of Success, and destroyer of obstacles, vanity, selfishness, and pride.

gone to the hills: the British established around fifty 'hill stations' as retreats from heat and disease. Two of the most famous are Shimla in Himachal Pradesh, the 'summer capital of the Raj', and Udagamandalam (Ootacamund) in Tamil Nadu. Rudyard Kipling's *Plain Tales from the Hills* (1888) gives perhaps the most well-known account of this aspect of life in the Raj.

7 *forgotten by every one*: the manuscript adds: 'By midnight of the following day the pretty Mem Sahib & her husband had died also' (scored out).

10 *Basil who thought of it first*: Burnett subverts the 'Sleeping Beauty' motifs of Perrault and Giambattista Basile (whose *Pentamerone* was translated by Sir Richard Burton in 1893): 'Thus it hardly seems coincidental that the first boy on whom Mary so fiercely turns after he has invaded her female sanctuary should be named Basil' (U. C. Knoepflmacher, 'Repudiating "Sleeping Beauty"', in Beverly Lyon Clark and Margaret R. Higonnet (eds.), *Girls, Boys, Books, Toys: Gender in Children's Literature and Culture* (Baltimore: Johns Hopkins University Press, 1999), 11–24 at 24).

11 *"Mistress Mary . . . marigolds all in a row"*: this rhyme (with the last line as 'And so my garden grows') is first recorded in the earliest surviving book of English nursery rhymes, *Tommy Thumb's Pretty Song Book Vol. II*, published by Mary Cooper (*c.*1744). In other versions, the final line contains cuckolds, cowslips, lady bells, columbines, and muscles. There has been some speculation that it is a religious satire dating from

the sixteenth century. See Iona and Peter Opie, *The Oxford Dictionary of Nursery Rhymes* (Oxford: Clarendon Press, 1973), 301.

11 *where home is*: the manuscript reads 'where Home is'.

sent to her last year: in her survey of the relevant literature of the late nineteenth century, Judith Rowbotham found 'no example of a book for the adolescent market which advocates children staying beyond six or seven with their parents in Indian conditions. The question of survival seems to have been accepted as being too acute' (*Good Girls Make Good Wives: Guidance for Girls in Victorian Fiction* (Oxford: Blackwell, 1989), 206).

Archibald Craven: some critics have seen the name 'Craven' as indicative of a cowardly character—despite the fact that 'Archibald' means 'bold or brave'.

Misselthwaite Manor: probably derived from missel-thrush and the common Yorkshire suffix 'thwaite', meaning paddock or land cleared from forest. It may also be an echo of (one of) the two Micklethwaites in West Yorkshire, one near Haworth, the other now part of Wetherby.

12 *boarding-school*: Kipling gives a disturbing account of children sent to English boarding school from India in his bitter autobiographical story 'Baa Baa Black Sheep', in *Wee Willie Winkie* (1888).

Mrs. Medlock: critics have suggested that the housekeeper's name is indicative of her character—'meddle' and 'lock'—but it may have derived from the River Medlock, which rises near Oldham and flows into the River Irwell in Manchester, or from the east Manchester suburb of Chorlton on Medlock.

mantle: a loose sleeveless cape or cloak.

purple velvet flowers: by the 1870s bonnets were old-fashioned or for the particularly demure.

13 *black crêpe hat*: mourning for parents in the nineteenth century was for a year, during which black crêpe, and crêpe-decorated bonnets were worn.

15 *"Riquet à la Houppe"*: one of Charles Perrault's *Histoires ou Contes de Temps Passé* (1697). A French film version was released in 1908. Perrault's book also contains the story of Bluebeard, which, as John Sutherland notes (*Can Jane Eyre Be Happy?: More Puzzles in Classic Fiction* (Oxford: Oxford World's Classics, 1997), 68–70), lies behind the story of *Jane Eyre*. The Riquet story can be read either as a parable of male domination, or, as being 'about the power of love and the need to see beyond appearances, both themes of *The Secret Garden*' (Roderick McGillis, ' "Secrets" and "Sequence" in Children's Stories', in Hugh T. Keenan (ed.), *Studies in the Literary Imagination*, 18/2 (1985), 35–46 at 37).

17 *was shaking her*: depending on which part of Yorkshire Burnett was thinking of, the journey would have been either on the Great Northern Railway from King's Cross and thence onto the North Eastern Railway (NER), or on the Midland Railway from St Pancras. If it was the NER, Robin

Coulthard, Librarian and Archivist of the NER Association informs me, 'lunch baskets could be purchased in the 1890s from any NER station with a refreshment room, which means all the principal stations; the empty baskets together with crockery and cutlery could be handed in at any staffed wayside station for return. The sample menus . . . for these baskets were rather more varied and ambitious than [Burnett's] which seems quite artisan!' On the Midland system, according to Peter Witts, Information Officer, Midland Railway Society, trays of tea cost 6*d*. (in 1903); before May 1900, luncheon baskets cost 3*s*., were ordered in advance, and a boy from the refreshment room would have met the train. The baskets could contain hot or cold food. The earliest mention of luncheon baskets on the Midland is 1885. The lamps in the carriage would probably have been oil lamps: gas lamps replaced oil lamps on the NER from *c*.1888, and on the Midland in the 1890s.

Thwaite Station: the nearest station to Fryston Hall, Yorkshire, where Burnett stayed with the Earl of Crewe (Secretary of State for India 1910–11) in December 1895, would have been Burton Salmon, Ferrybridge, or Castleford on the NER. The only Thwaite on the British railway system was Thwaite Flat Junction on the Furness Railway, near Barrow.

brougham: one-horse closed carriage with two or four wheels.

outside platform: Robin Coulthard points out that 'some wayside stations did have a short length of platform fronting the road outside to facilitate loading and unloading, particularly milk churns. They could easily be manhandled straight onto the platform off the farm cart. The platform may well have also served to permit the gentry to gain easy access to their coaches—indeed this may have been their initial purpose.' Peter Witts suggests that on the Midland system some stations had a loading dock so that road carriages could be loaded onto trains.

footman: liveried manservant 'employed chiefly to attend the carriage and wait at table' (*Shorter Oxford English Dictionary*).

20 *opened the door for them*: compare Jane Eyre's arrival at Thornfield (chapter 11) which, as Ann Thwaite notes, is 'too reminiscent . . . to be coincidental' (*Waiting for the Party: The Life of Frances Hodgson Burnett, 1849–1924* (London: Secker and Warburg, 1974), 220):

> We were now, as far as I could see, on a sort of common; but there were houses scattered all over the district; I felt we were in a different region to Lowood, more populous, less picturesque, more stirring, less romantic.
>
> The roads were heavy, the night misty; my conductor let his horse walk all the way, and the hour and a half extended, I verily believe, to two hours; at last he turned in his seat and said, 'You're noan so far fro' Thornfield now.'
>
> Again I looked out: we were passing a church: I saw its low broad tower against the sky, and its bell was tolling a quarter; I saw a narrow galaxy of lights, too, on a hillside, marking a village or hamlet. About

ten minutes after, the driver got down and opened a pair of gates; we
passed through, and they clashed to behind us. We now slowly ascended
a drive, and came upon the long front of a house: candle-light gleamed
from one curtained bow-window; all the rest were dark. The car stopped
at the front door; it was opened by a maid-servant; I alighted and
went in.

'Will you walk this way, ma'am?' said the girl; and I followed her
across a square hall with high doors all round.

20 *where you'll live*: this is the opposite of the situation in chapter 6 of *Little
Lord Fauntleroy* where Cedric (who can dress himself), has a suite of
rooms to himself, in one of which 'there were shelves full of books, and on
the tables were numbers of toys—beautiful, ingenious things'.

21 *housemaid*: the middle rank of female servants in a great house. The
ranks were scullery-maid, kitchen-maid, between-maid, housemaid,
chambermaid, and parlourmaid. Lady's maids and housekeepers were
'upper' servants.

tapestry . . . embroidered on it: technically incorrect, as tapestry has images
woven into it.

Martha: the name is possibly derived from association with the biblical
story of Mary and Martha (Luke 10: 38–42); Mary sits at Jesus's feet,
while Martha works. Towards the end of Charlotte Yonge's *The Daisy
Chain* (1856, ii. 24) the injured Margaret 'was perfectly content and
happy. She knew the temptation of her character had been to be the ruler
and manager of everything, and she saw it had been well for her to have
been thus assigned the part of Mary rather than of Martha.'

salaams: a low bow (in India) with the palm of the right hand placed upon
the forehead (*Shorter Oxford English Dictionary*).

22 *blacking-brush*: for applying the black-lead polish to cast-iron grates.

out o' kindness: the manuscript originally added the words 'when Mother
died' (scored out).

23 *a man an' a brother*: 'Am I not a man and a brother' was the motto on the
emblem of a kneeling slave, produced for the Society for the Effecting of
the Abolition of the Slave Trade (1787) and which was produced as a very
popular cameo by Josiah Wedgwood. It became widely used in the USA,
and was praised by Benjamin Franklin.

25 *quite new to her*: an example of Burnett inverting a familiar scene. In
Mrs Craik's *The Little Lychetts* (1855) Eunice Lychett ('a great, ugly,
awkward girl') finds herself in the house of her benefactor:

For in Mr Linnington's household, everything was on the most homely
and frugal scale. Comforts, hitherto familiar to me as light and air,
were here unheard-of luxuries. I never shall forget Sally's look on the
first morning when I came down stairs, as I thought very early—at
half-past eight—and gently hinted that I always liked a fire to dress by,

and that Bion couldn't eat anything for breakfast but sweet biscuits and coffee.

'Coffee! Biscuits! There beant no such things heard of at Stoneyhide. And—Miss—I make so bold to say that in my young days children never had nothing nor milk or porridge. And they got up at six to eat it, too. Mr. Linnington be done his breakfast and off to th' quarry a hour sin'.'

I was dumb-foundered! not by Sally's bluntness, for she was too good-natured to be really rude; but by the prospect before me of our coming life.

sixteen shilling a week: Martha's weekly wage as housemaid would have been about 6s.; Mrs Medlock, as Housekeeper, would have earned about £1.

Dickon: in the manuscript, initially 'Dick'.

27 *buried th' key*: the manuscript added: 'She had a fall in it the day before she died' (scored out).

was not playing: T. S. Eliot's 'Burnt Norton' (1935; *Four Quartets*, 1942) shares some of these images:

> Other echoes
> Inhabit the garden. Shall we follow?
> Quick, said the bird, find them, find them,
> Round the corner. Through the first gate,
> Into our first world, shall we follow
> The deception of the thrush?
> . . . the drained pool . . .
> Go, said the bird, for the leaves were full of children,
> Hidden excitedly, containing laughter . . .

The same kind of imagery recurs in the final chapter (see p. 207).

29 *winter song*: the winter song of the robin is generally considered to be wistful or plaintive. See Appendix, 'My Robin'.

30 *forrad*: forward.

31 *head gardener*: Mrs Richmond, *In My Lady's Garden* (1908), 14, describes the starling as 'a first-rate under-gardener'.

Ben Weatherstaff: compare 'The Gardener' in Robert Louis Stevenson's *A Child's Garden of Verses* (1885):

> The gardener does not love to talk.
> He makes me keep the gravel walk;
> And when he puts his tools away,
> He locks the door and takes the key.

32 *Dang me*: possibly a slip on Burnett's part: this is American rather than Yorkshire dialect.

hide their nests from him: in the manuscript, this is followed by a deleted passage:

They feel as if he was one of 'em when he goes swingin' by on his crutches.'

"Is he lame?" said Mary.

"He broke his ankle once stepping into a rabbit hole an' it was put together wrong. An' ever since he's gone on crutches—but he doesn't mind that, doesn't Dickon."

33 *green door*: in A. A. Milne's *Winnie-the-Pooh* (1926, chapter 1), Christopher Robin 'lived behind a green door in another part of the forest'. In the O. Henry story 'The Green Door', in his collection *The Four Million* (1906), the hero, one Rudolph Steiner, brings food to a starving girl he finds behind a green door in a tenement, and starts to nurse her back to health.

37 *servants' hall*: dining room for servants.

39 *toothache all day*: compare *Jane Eyre* (chapter 11) when Jane hears a 'curious laugh; distinct, formal, mirthless':

'Mrs. Fairfax!' I called out: for I now heard her descending the garret stairs. 'Did you hear that loud laugh? Who is it?'

'Some of the servants very likely,' she answered: 'perhaps Grace Poole . . . I often hear her; she sews in one of these rooms. Sometimes Leah is with her: they are frequently noisy together.'

The laugh was repeated in its low, syllabic tone, and terminated in an odd murmur.

'Grace!' exclaimed Mrs. Fairfax.

I really did not expect any Grace to answer; for the laugh was as tragic, as preternatural a laugh as any I ever heard.

40 *moithered*: bothered, confused, bewildered (dialect).

swum out: flooded (dialect).

42 *brocade*: this motif recurs in the mouse-filled cushion, and in Colin's bedroom (pp. 90, 103, 205). Brocade is material woven with a raised pattern, and also a cloth of gold and silver made in India.

a sharp, curious look: echoes of Louisa May Alcott's *Jack and Jill* (1880, chapter 4) in Jill's sickroom:

The bare wall with its brown spiders no longer confronted her, but the colored print of a little girl dancing to the tune her father was playing on a guitar, while a stately lady, with satin dress, ruff, and powder, stood looking on, well pleased. The quaint figure, in its belaced frock, quilted petticoat, and red-heeled shoes, seemed to come tripping toward her in such a life-like way, that she almost saw the curls blow back, heard the rustle of the rich brocade, and caught the sparkle of the little maid's bright eyes.

Burnett used the same device in *In the Closed Room* (1904):

As she raised her head she found her eyes looking directly into other eyes which gazed at her from the wall. They were smiling from the face of a child in a picture. As soon as she saw them Judith drew in her breath and stood still, smiling, too, in response. The picture was that of a little girl in a floating white frock. She had a deep dimple at one corner of her mouth, her hanging hair was like burnished copper, she held up a slender hand with pointed fingers and Judith knew her. Oh! she knew her quite well. She had never felt so near any one else throughout her life.

not quite believe it true: Misselthwaite Manor may be derived from the castle in George MacDonald's *The Princess and the Goblin* (1872). In chapter 2, the Princess Irene is searching the castle:

> Up and up she ran—such a long way it seemed to her!—until she came to the top of the third flight. There she found the landing was the end of a long passage. Into this she ran. It was full of doors on each side. There were so many that she did not care to open any, but ran on to the end, where she turned into another passage, also full of doors. When she had turned twice more, and still saw doors and only doors about her, she began to get frightened. It was so silent! And all those doors must hide rooms with nobody in them!

(See Humphrey Carpenter, *Secret Gardens: The Golden Age of Children's Literature* (London: Allen and Unwin, 1995), 189.) Burnett had used a similar image in *The Shuttle* (1907, chapter 37, 'Closed Corridors'):

> To spend one's days perforce in an enormous house alone is a thing likely to play unholy tricks with a man's mind and lead it to gloomy workings. To know the existence of a hundred or so of closed doors shut on the darkness of unoccupied rooms; to be conscious of flights of unmounted stairs, of stretches of untrodden corridors, of unending walls, from which the pictured eyes of long dead men and women stare, as if seeing things which human eyes behold not—is an eerie and unwholesome thing.

43 *mahouts or palanquins*: there seems to be some confusion in Burnett's mind here: 'mahout' (Hindi) is an elephant-driver; the seats, often with curtains, are howdahs or houdas. A palanquin is a form of sedan chair, carried by humans.

48 *daffydowndillys*: daffodils (dialect).

50 *it was an old key*: the symbolic key recurs in Victorian literature, notably in George MacDonald's 'The Golden Key' (*Dealings with the Fairies*, 1867) and Lewis Carroll's *Alice's Adventures in Wonderland* (1885); nineteenth-century dramatizations of Perrault's *Bluebeard*, which centres on a key, were sometimes subtitled 'The Hazards of Female Curiosity'.

51 *took the key*: the manuscript reads 'took the key home;' ('home' then deleted).

52 *dough-cake*: cakes made from left-over bread dough as a family treat, often at the end of a day's baking (Sarah Hunt).

wild beast show . . . in York once: travelling menageries were very popular in the nineteenth century. Albert Haslam's menagerie and circus toured

Lancashire and Yorkshire; one of the biggest was James Bostock's and
George Wombwell's business which flourished from 1883 until the end of
menageries in 1932 (when it was sold to London Zoo).

53 *peddlin'*: peddlers were regulated from 1871.

54 *want me to kiss you?*: compare the conversation in *Jane Eyre* (chapter 4),
between Jane and the maid Bessie:

> 'And so you're glad to leave me?'
>   'Not at all, Bessie; indeed, just now I am rather sorry.'
>   'Just now! and rather! How coolly my little lady says it! I daresay now
> if I were to ask you for a kiss you wouldn't give it me: you'd say you'd
> *rather* not.'
>   'I'll kiss you and welcome: bend your head down.' Bessie stooped; we
> mutually embraced, and I followed her into the house quite comforted.
> That afternoon lapsed in peace and harmony; and in the evening Bessie
> told me some of her most enchanting stories, and sung me some of her
> sweetest songs.

55 *skipped red into thy cheeks*: open-air exercise for girls had been encouraged
in the USA since the 1830s. The widely influential columnist Fanny Fern
(Sara Willis Parton) wrote in a story 'The Tom Boy' in *The Play-Day
Book* ((New York: Mason, 1857), 122, 123): 'I say fly kites; play ball; drive
hoop . . . soil your hands and faces . . . do anything that's innocent, but
don't grow up with crooked backs, flat chests, sallow faces, dull eyes, and
diseased brains . . . Don't mind being called "a tom-boy" . . . and Nature
will reward you with strong straight backs, full chests, bright eyes, rosy
cheeks, and a long life.' The encouragement of exercise may also have
been based on Herbert Spencer's evolutionary arguments about female
education in *Education: Intellectual, Moral and Physical* (1860).

56 *as excited as she was*: in Mrs Molesworth's *An Enchanted Garden* (1892,
chapter 1) it is a wren who shows the way:

> Suddenly on the short green turf there appeared a tiny figure, a wren,
> so tame that she hopped fearlessly to within a very short distance of
> the little brother and sister, and then, standing still, seemed to look up
> at them with her bright eyes, her small head cocked knowingly on one
> side . . . The wren hopped on a few steps, still looking back at them. The
> children slipped off the seat and moved softly after her without speaking.
> On she went, hopping, and then fluttering just a little way above the
> ground, then hopping again, till in this way she had led them right across
> the wide stretch of lawn to some shrubberies at the far side . . . They both
> stood still and looked. Yes, there was Madam Wren on the topmost bar of
> a dilapidated wooden gate, standing between two solid posts at what had
> once been the entrance to the beautiful garden of an ancient house.

57 *inside*: the manuscript reads 'inside'—without the italics.

58 *standard roses*: roses trained to grow from a single stem.

had ever seen in her life: Burnett described the garden at Maytham, Rolvenden in Kent, that she had rented from 1898 to 1907: it 'was entered by a low, arched gateway in the wall, closed by a wooden door. The ground underneath the twisted, leaning old apple tree was cleared of all its weeds and thorns and sown with grass and then at every available place, roses were planted to climb up the ancient trunks and over the walls.'

59 *I wish it wasn't*: in Burnett's ghost story, *In the Closed Room* (1904), Judith finds the abandoned roof garden of a dead girl, whose ghost revives the garden: 'she stood among the dried, withered things and looked in tender regret at them. "I wish they were not dead," she said softly to the silence. "It would be like a garden if they were not dead."' (Quoted in Ann Thwaite, *Waiting for the Party: The Life of Frances Hodgson Burnett, 1849–1924* (London: Secker and Warburg, 1974), 182–3.)

61 *narcissusis*: narcissi (dialect).

purple flags: the common name in the USA for the purple iris.

62 *besides her A B C*: the manuscript originally added 'if she's got any sense at all.' (scored out).

63 *SOWERBY*: critics have suggested that the name is intended to suggest the fecundity of Susan Sowerby—'sower' and (less frequently) 'sow'. But it could simply be a Yorkshire-sounding name: Sowerby is a village in west Yorkshire, south of Halifax.

68 *bachelder*: bachelor (dialect).

71 *flight 'em*: frighten them.

Dickon: Dickon has been seen as a version of Hareton Earnshaw, who marries his cousin Catherine Linton in *Wuthering Heights*. They both have an affinity with the Yorkshire earth, and with animals (see Susan E. James, '*Wuthering Heights* for Children: Frances Hodgson Burnett's *The Secret Garden*', *Connotations*, 10/1 (2000/1), 59–76 at 64).

72 *Mignonette*: the mignonette has small yellowish-white flowers with reddish pollen stalks, growing on tall spikes. It is associated with health. Most of the flowers that Dickon praises are '"poor men's flowers"—old fashioned plants held the positive connotations of plenitude, variety, individuality and a kind of stability equivalent to homeliness' (Michael Waters, *The Garden in Victorian Literature* (Aldershot: Scolar, 1988), 124).

75 *MISSEL THRUSH*: in J. M. Barrie's *The Little White Bird* (1902, chapter 2), David, when the narrator first meets him, is a missel-thrush—'all children in our part of London were once birds in the Kensington Gardens'. The missel-thrush is the largest of thrushes; it is occasionally found in gardens and on open moorland, and it will defend fruit trees or growths of mistletoe to provide its winter food. Its traditional name is 'Stormcock' because it sings in bad weather.

76 *ought to be cut out*: I. Lilias Trotter, *Parables of the Cross* (1890) makes links between spirituality and gardening—in this case, pruning:

A stage of dying must come over the plant before the new leaves can grow and thrive. There must be a deliberate choice between the former growth and the new; one must give way to the other; the acorn has to come to the point where it ceases to keep its rag of former existence, and lets everything go to the fresh shoot: the twig must withdraw its sap from last year's leaf, and let it flow into this year's bud.

And before the soul can really enter upon a life of holiness, with all its blessed endless possibilities, a like choice must be made: all known sin must be deliberately given up, that the rising current may have its full play . . .

Look at our parable. If you picked off one of the dead leaves and examined the leaf-stalk through a microscope, you would find that the old channel is silted up by a barrier invisible to the naked eye. The plant has shut the door on the last year's leaf, condemning it to decay, and soon without further effort the stalk loosens, the winds of God play around it, and it falls away.

77 *nesh*: delicately (dialect).

78 *white-thorn knobstick*: in Burnett's *That Lass o' Lowrie's* (1877, chapters 19 and 29), Joan Lowrie's father carries his worldly goods tied to his knobstick, which he is prepared to use as a deadly weapon against Joan's future husband, Fergus Derrick.

79 *Canterbury bells, an' campanulas*: Canterbury Bells (*Campanula medium*); campanulas: bellflowers (from Latin: dim. bell).

84 *coloured photograph*: photographic portrait studios became popular from around 1854; they were pioneered by Adolphe Disderi.

89 *wandering on and on crying*: reminiscent of the scene in chapter 3 of *Wuthering Heights* (1847), when the narrator, Lockwood, is dreaming: 'I heard distinctly the gusty wind, and the driving of the snow . . . a most melancholy voice sobbed, "Let me in—let me in!" "Who are you?" I asked . . . "Catherine Linton," it replied, shiveringly . . . "I'm come home, I'd lost my way on the moor!"'

92 *doesn't want to see me*: in Mrs Craik's fairy tale, *The Little Lame Prince* (1875, chapter 2), the King, for more than two years after his wife's death, 'was generally too ill and too melancholy to pay much heed to' Prince Dolor, his son.

out in the fresh air: in Mrs Craik's *The Little Lychetts* (1855, chapter 7), 'The Master's' comment on Bion, the little boy spoiled by his pampered life in India, is:

he does not look strong, though I think there is nothing really the matter with him, and I'm a bit of a doctor, too. The best thing you can do is to let him have plenty of food and fresh air, and keep him merry, and make him hardy. One of my lads is delicate too, but I never do anything more than this.

98 *Hindustani*: the language of northern India, basis of both Urdu and Hindi; the word was used in colonial India to mean Urdu.

100 *RAJAH*: Indian king or prince.

102 *young nowt*: nothing, good-for-nothing (dialect).

'*rose cold*': spring or early summer hay fever: also 'rose fever'.

110 *slamp*: lie down, put down (dialect).

112 *flute*: to whistle or sing in flute-like tones (*Shorter Oxford English Dictionary*).

114 *munnot*: must not (dialect).

116 *scarce ever thrives*: the manuscript reads: 'She says us has all got to be loved an' have fresh air or us can't be healthy.'

125 *four-posted bed*: an example of Burnett parodying herself. She had used a very similar scene in *A Little Princess* (chapter 4)—except gender and method are reversed. Lottie is having a tantrum, and Miss Amelia cannot cope with her. Miss Minchin asks the angelic Sara for help:

> 'I dare say you can manage her. Go in.' And she left her.
> When Sara entered the room, Lottie was lying upon the floor, screaming and kicking her small fat legs violently . . . Sara stood by the howling, furious child for a few moments, and looked down at her without saying anything. Then she sat down flat on the floor beside her and waited. Except for Lottie's angry screams, the room was quite quiet. This was a new state of affairs for Miss Legh, who was accustomed, when she screamed, to hear other people protest, and implore and command and coax by turns. To lie and kick and shriek, and find the only person near you not seeming to mind in the least, attracted her attention . . . Having paused for a few seconds to find this out Lottie thought she must begin again, but the quiet of the room and of Sara's odd, interested face made her first howl rather half-hearted.
> 'I—haven't—any—ma-ma-ma-a!' she announced; but her voice was not so strong.
> Sara looked at her more steadily, but with a sort of understanding in her eyes.
> 'Neither have I,' she said.
> This was so unexpected that it was astounding. Lottie actually dropped her legs, gave a wriggle, and lay and stared. A new idea will stop a crying child when nothing else will.

127 *most of his fright and illness was created by himself*: Mary Baker Eddy wrote. 'Sickness is a growth of error, springing from mortal ignorance or fear. Error rehearses error. What causes disease cannot cure it. The soil of disease is mortal mind, and you have an abundant or scanty crop of disease, according to the seedlings of fear. Sin and the fear of disease must be uprooted and cast out' (*Science and Health with Key to the Scriptures*, 1875, chapter 7).

131 *graidely*: great, fine (dialect).

132 *shape*: do well, improve (dialect).

138 *bromide*: probably potassium bromide, an ionic salt used as a sedative; also a generic term for sedative.

143 _clemmin'_: hunger.

145 _otters' and badgers' and water-rats' houses_: perhaps an echo of Kenneth Grahame's _The Wind in the Willows_ (1908).

"_bedding-out plants_": plants grown in greenhouses and then transferred to beds for display.

147 _Prince Consort_: Prince Albert, the Prince Consort, died in 1861.

151 _scents and scents_: in Burnett's autobiography, _The One I Knew Best of All_ (1893, chapter 3: 'The Back Garden of Eden'), she remembered the garden of one of her childhood homes:

> But the Back Garden was full of beautiful wonders. Was it always Spring or Summer in that enchanted garden which, out of a whole world, has remained throughout a lifetime the Garden of Eden. Was the sun _always_ shining? Later and more material experience of the English climate leads me to imagine that it was not _always_ flooded and warmed with sunshine, and filled with the scent of roses and mignonette and new-mown hay and apple-blossoms and strawberries all together.

155 _Happen_: perhaps (dialect).

156 _grey film_: presumably the nictitating membrane, or third eyelid, which protects the eyes of birds and some animals.

157 _besom_: northern British dialect—difficult or unruly woman. Literally a broom made of twigs; associated with witches.

158 _almost unnatural strength_: compare Susan Coolidge's _What Katy Did_ (1872, chapter 13), when Katy, after four years, manages to stand: 'It seemed as if her will had been asleep; and now that it had waked up, the limbs recognized its orders and obeyed them.' Mary Baker Eddy (_Science and Health_, chapter 12) wrote, 'Instead of blind and calm submission to the incipient or advanced stages of disease, rise in rebellion against them. Banish the belief that you can possibly entertain a single intruding pain which cannot be ruled out by the might of Mind, and in this way you can prevent the development of pain in the body.'

160 _Magic_: Roderick McGillis in _A Little Princess: Gender and Empire_ ((Boston: Twayne, 1996), 22) notes that Burnett's use of the idea of magic 'invests her world with spirit'. In _The Secret Garden_ ' "magic" . . . clearly signifies a spiritual power . . . in _A Little Princess_ "magic" betokens a divine presence that takes care of little princesses, those who believe in good things'.

161 _You can!_: reminiscent of the scene in _Heidi_ (chapter 12: 'Something Unexpected Happens') where Clara finds she can walk, supported by Heidi and (reluctantly) by Peter:

> And Clara went on putting one foot out after another until all at once she called out, 'I can do it, Heidi! look! look! I can make proper steps!' And Heidi cried out with even greater delight, 'Can you really make steps, can you really walk? really walk by yourself? Oh, if only grandfather

were here!' and she continued gleefully to exclaim, 'You can walk now, Clara, you can walk!'

Clara still held on firmly to her supports, but with every step she felt safer on her feet, as all three became aware, and Heidi was beside herself with joy.

168 *fakirs*: a Muslim religious beggar; applied loosely to Hindu devotees and naked monks (*Shorter Oxford English Dictionary*).

169 *as strong as Dickon*: Colin is using 'affirmations' or 'affirmative prayer' which was characteristic of the 'New Thought' and the 'Self Help' movements. 'A preference for "affirmations" over arguments [became] one of the features that divided practitioners of the New Thought from those of Christian Science' (Beryl Satter, *Each Mind a Kingdom: American Women, Sexual Purity, and the New Thought Movement, 1875–1920* (Berkeley and Los Angeles: University of California Press, 1999), 71). Affirmations were developed by the French psychologist Émile Coué [de Châtaigneraie] as 'autosuggestion'.

171 *dervishes*: Sufi Muslim friars, some of whom dance or sway as part of their religious rites.

174 *champion prize-fighter*: prizefighters fought for championship belts. The Queensberry Rules for prizefighting were introduced in 1866–7; the last 'sanctioned' bare-knuckle fight was in 1889. The Lonsdale belt for boxing was introduced in 1909.

175 *rockcress*: or Wall Cress: the variety *Arabis* has dense white flowers in the spring.

176 *came to th' Manor*: in 'Surly Tim', Burnett's first really successful story (1877), Tim observes:

'I've allus thowt 'at th' Lord-a'-moighty knew what He wur doin' when he gi' th' woman t' Adam i' th' Garden o' Eden. He knowed he wur nowt but a poor chap as couldna do fur hissen; an' I suppose that's th' reason he gi' th' woman th' strength to bear trouble when it comn'.'

177 *blue cloak*: for some critics, the cloak (originally a shawl in the manuscript) has identified Mrs Sowerby with 'the Virgin Mother of Christianity'— often simultaneously with a pagan nature goddess or the corn queen. See, for example, Christine Wilkie, 'Digging up *The Secret Garden*: Noble Innocents or Little Savages?', *Children's Literature in Education*, 28/2 (1997), 73–83 at 78.

fresh milk an' bread: compare *Heidi* (chapter 12):

Then came the walking, and every day she [Clara] found it easier and was able to go a longer distance. The movement gave her such an appetite that the grandfather cut his bread and butter a little thicker each day, and was well pleased to see it disappear. He now brought out with it a large jugful of the foaming milk and filled her little bowl over and over again.

180 *in desperation*: Gillian Avery cites a similar transformation through lavish breakfasts of the 'peevish, wilting' Emily by Harriet Beecher Stowe's eponymous Pussy Willow (*Our Young Folks*, 1866–7) (*Behold the Child, American Children and their Books 1621–1922* (London: The Bodley Head, 1994), 158–9).

181 *Bob Haworth*: perhaps an echo from the Brontës' Haworth Parsonage.

187 *In the robin's nest . . . come into the garden*: this passage is similar to the anthropomorphism of Sarah Trimmer's *Fabulous Histories* (1786) (later *The History of the Robins*), a best-selling Evangelical text throughout the nineteenth century.

191 *than usual*: the manuscript adds:

> "I'm goin' to bring thee a new creature" he announced.
> "Has it fur or hair or feathers?" Colin asked It was one of their games to make guesses about "creatures"
> "Hair—an' sometimes fur i' winter"
> "Does it go on four legs or two legs?"
> "Ive seed it on four an' Ive seed it on two," answered Dickon
> "Does it sing or bark or howl?" asked Mary
> "It sings an' barks an' it howls when its crossed."
> "It can do all three," answered Dickon "Tha'd never guess in th' world."
> They made other guesses [*sic*]

193 *Doxology*: a short formula in praise of God. Burnett quotes the 'Common Doxology', written in 1674 by Thomas Ken as the final verse of the hymn 'Awake, my soul, and with the sun'.

195 *blush rose*: an old-fashioned cottage-garden delicate pink climbing or rambling rose, with pale green leaves and few thorns.

196 *worrit*: worry (dialect).

what does th' name matter? . . . Big Good Thing: see Burnett's *The Lost Prince* (1915, chapter 21):

> 'All thinking is part of the Big Thought,' said Marco slowly. 'It KNOWS—It KNOWS. And the outside part of us somehow broke the chain that linked us to It. And we are always trying to mend the chain, without knowing it. That is what our thinking is— trying to mend the chain. But we shall find out how to do it sometime. The old Buddhist told my father so—just as the sun was rising from behind a high peak of the Himalayas.'

This may also be an echo of Theosophical thought, as in H. P. Blavatsky's *The Secret Doctrine, the Synthesis of Science, Religion, and Philosophy* (1888, 'Preface' to volume 1):

> But it is perhaps desirable to state unequivocally that the teachings, however fragmentary and incomplete, contained in these volumes,

belong neither to the Hindu, the Zoroastrian, the Chaldean, nor the Egyptian religion, neither to Buddhism, Islam, Judaism nor Christianity exclusively. The Secret Doctrine is the essence of all these. Sprung from it in their origins, the various religious schemes are now made to merge back into their original element, out of which every mystery and dogma has grown, developed, and become materialised.

200 *nothing weird about it at all*: Mark Twain satirized this kind of thinking in the figure of Aunt Polly in *The Adventures of Tom Sawyer* (1876, chapter 12):

> She was a subscriber for all the 'Health' periodicals and phrenological frauds; and the solemn ignorance they were inflated with was breath to her nostrils. All the 'rot' they contained about ventilation, and how to go to bed, and how to get up, and what to eat, and what to drink, and how much exercise to take, and what frame of mind to keep one's self in, and what sort of clothing to wear, was all gospel to her, and she never observed that her health-journals of the current month customarily upset everything they had recommended the month before. She was as simple-hearted and honest as the day was long, and so she was an easy victim.

A thistle cannot grow: this seems to be the first appearance of this saying in print; it may be an original Burnett-ism, although it comes from a popular genre. For example, 'Cut a rose for your neighbour, and it will tell two buds to blossom for you' or 'Rubbish is rubbish when it lies about—compost when it's all of a heap—and food for flowers when it's dug in' from Mrs Ewing's *Mary's Meadow and Other Tales of Fields and Flowers* (1886) which includes 'The Little Gardener's Alphabet Of Proverbs'. Burnett used a similar idea in her *The Land of the Blue Flower* (1909, Part Two): 'If you put into your mind a beautiful thought it will take the place of the evil one . . . The first law of the earth's magic is this one. If you fill your mind with a beautiful thought there will be no room in it for an ugly one.'

gentians: gentians also appear at the climax of *Heidi* (chapter 23):

> Here another unexpected sight met her gaze, for there, under the trees where the long branches had left a clear space on the ground, stood a great bush of the most wonderful dark blue gentians, as fresh and shining as if they were growing on the spot. She clasped her hands, enraptured with their beauty.
>
> 'How exquisite! what a lovely sight!' she exclaimed. 'Heidi, dearest child, come here! Is it you who have prepared this pleasure for me? It is perfectly wonderful!'

strange thing had happened: this is perhaps an echo of Friedrich Froebel (1826): 'We give room and time to young plants and animals, well knowing that they will develop and grow according to the laws inherent in them . . . Why does man, wandering through gardens and fields, meadows and groves, fail to open his mind, and refuse to listen to the lesson which nature silently teaches?' (quoted in Juliet Dusinberre, *Alice to the Lighthouse: Children's Books and Radical Experiments in Art*, 2nd edn. (London: Macmillan, 1999), 10).

202 *the Lake of Como*: a favourite resort since Roman times, and on the 'Grand Tour'; it was visited, for example, by P. B. Shelley, and described by Mark Twain in *The Innocents Abroad* (1867, chapter 22).

203 *Lilias*: Scottish form of Lily or Lillian. In flower symbolism (very popular in the late Victorian/Edwardian period) the lily denotes purity and innocence. It seems unlikely that there is an echo of Lilith, Adam's first wife, depite her connection with the Garden of Eden, and her popularity with Rossetti, Browning, and MacDonald.

Lilias Trotter was a missionary in Algiers whose *Parables of the Cross* (1890) and *Parables of the Christ-Life* (1899) use metaphors of plants and flowers, with beautiful colour illustrations, to demonstrate spiritual rebirth. For example, from the beginning of *Parables of the Christ-Life*:

> Stoop down and look into that withered grass, and a whole new world of God's handiwork will come into view in the burnt-up tangle. For of all the growing things out here, the seed-vessels are among the most wonderful. Even little insignificant plants that would hardly catch your eye when in flower, develop forms of quaint beauty as the capsules ripen. And now that all is finished, they lie stored with vitality in the midst of the seeming loss around.

where are you?: compare *Jane Eyre*, chapter 35:

> I saw nothing: but I heard a voice somewhere cry—'Jane! Jane! Jane!' Nothing more.
>
> 'O God! what is it?' I gasped.
>
> I might have said, 'Where is it?' for it did not seem in the room—nor in the house—nor in the garden: it did not come out of the air—nor from under the earth—nor from overhead. I had heard it—where, or whence, forever impossible to know! And it was the voice of a human being—a known, loved, well-remembered voice—that of Edward Fairfax Rochester; and it spoke in pain and woe, wildly, eerily, urgently.
>
> 'I am coming!' I cried. 'Wait for me! Oh, I will come!' I flew to the door, and looked into the passage: it was dark. I ran out into the garden: it was void.
>
> 'Where are you?' I exclaimed.

208 *inches taller*: the climactic meeting is very similar to Herr Sesemann's meeting with Clara at the end of *Heidi* (chapter 23):

> Herr Sesemann was delighted to have come to the last steep bit of his journey, in another minute or two he would be with his little daughter, and he pleased himself with the thought of her surprise. But the company above had seen his approaching figure and recognized who it was, and they were preparing something he little expected as a surprise on their part.
>
> As he stepped on to the space in front of the hut two figures came towards him. One a tall girl with fair hair and pink cheeks, leaning on Heidi, whose dark eyes were dancing with joy. Herr Sesemann suddenly

stopped, staring at the two children, and all at once the tears started to his eyes. What memories arose in his heart! Just so had Clara's mother looked, the fair-haired girl with the delicate pink-and-white complexion. Herr Sesemann did not know if he was awake or dreaming.

'Don't you know me, papa?' called Clara to him, her face beaming with happiness. 'Am I so altered since you saw me?'

Then Herr Sesemann ran to his child and clasped her in his arms.

'Yes, you are indeed altered! How is it possible? Is it true what I see?' And the delighted father stepped back to look full at her again, and to make sure that the picture would not vanish before his eyes.

'Are you my little Clara, really my little Clara?' he kept on saying, then he clasped her in his arms again, and again put her away from him that he might look and make sure it was she who stood before him.

MY ROBIN

211 *in Kent*: Burnett's last visit to Maytham Hall, Kent, was in 1907.

writhen: twisted, contorted.

214 *Laurette Messimy roses*: pink China roses with yellow or copper tints, introduced by Guillot fils, France, 1887.

217 *Berseker rage*: possibly a mistake or variant spelling for *Berserker*. Berserkers were Norse warriors who 'fought on the battle-field with a frenzied fury known as the "berserker rage"' (*Shorter Oxford English Dictionary*).

The Oxford World's Classics Website

www.worldsclassics.co.uk

- Browse the full range of Oxford World's Classics online

- Sign up for our monthly e-alert to receive information on new titles

- Read extracts from the Introductions

- Listen to our editors and translators talk about the world's greatest literature with our Oxford World's Classics audio guides

- Join the conversation, follow us on Twitter at OWC_Oxford

- Teachers and lecturers can order inspection copies quickly and simply via our website

www.worldsclassics.co.uk

American Literature

British and Irish Literature

Children's Literature

Classics and Ancient Literature

Colonial Literature

Eastern Literature

European Literature

Gothic Literature

History

Medieval Literature

Oxford English Drama

Poetry

Philosophy

Politics

Religion

The Oxford Shakespeare

A complete list of Oxford World's Classics, including Authors in Context, Oxford English Drama, and the Oxford Shakespeare, is available in the UK from the Marketing Services Department, Oxford University Press, Great Clarendon Street, Oxford OX2 6DP, or visit the website at www.oup.com/uk/worldsclassics.

In the USA, visit www.oup.com/us/owc for a complete title list.

Oxford World's Classics are available from all good bookshops. In case of difficulty, customers in the UK should contact Oxford University Press Bookshop, 116 High Street, Oxford OX1 4BR.

	Late Victorian Gothic Tales
JANE AUSTEN	Emma
	Mansfield Park
	Persuasion
	Pride and Prejudice
	Selected Letters
	Sense and Sensibility
MRS BEETON	Book of Household Management
MARY ELIZABETH BRADDON	Lady Audley's Secret
ANNE BRONTË	The Tenant of Wildfell Hall
CHARLOTTE BRONTË	Jane Eyre
	Shirley
	Villette
EMILY BRONTË	Wuthering Heights
ROBERT BROWNING	The Major Works
JOHN CLARE	The Major Works
SAMUEL TAYLOR COLERIDGE	The Major Works
WILKIE COLLINS	The Moonstone
	No Name
	The Woman in White
CHARLES DARWIN	The Origin of Species
THOMAS DE QUINCEY	The Confessions of an English Opium-Eater
	On Murder
CHARLES DICKENS	The Adventures of Oliver Twist
	Barnaby Rudge
	Bleak House
	David Copperfield
	Great Expectations
	Nicholas Nickleby
	The Old Curiosity Shop
	Our Mutual Friend
	The Pickwick Papers

TROLLOPE IN OXFORD WORLD'S CLASSICS

ANTHONY TROLLOPE

The American Senator

An Autobiography

Barchester Towers

Can You Forgive Her?

The Claverings

Cousin Henry

The Duke's Children

The Eustace Diamonds

Framley Parsonage

He Knew He Was Right

Lady Anna

Orley Farm

Phineas Finn

Phineas Redux

The Prime Minister

Rachel Ray

The Small House at Allington

The Warden

The Way We Live Now